W9-ARO-766

WE ARE
ONLY GHOSTS

WE ARE
ONLY GHOSTS

JEFFREY L.
RICHARDS

JOHN SCOGNAMIGLIO BOOKS
KENSINGTON BOOKS
www.kensingtonbooks.com

This book is a work of fiction. Names, characters, businesses, organizations, places, events, and incidents either are the product of the author's imagination or are used fictitiously. Any resemblance to actual persons, living or dead, events, or locales is entirely coincidental.

To the extent that the image or images on the cover of this book depict a person or persons, such person or persons are merely models, and are not intended to portray any character or characters featured in the book.

KENSINGTON BOOKS are published by

Kensington Publishing Corp.
119 West 40th Street
New York, NY 10018

Copyright © 2024 by Jeffrey L. Richards

All rights reserved. No part of this book may be reproduced in any form or by any means without the prior written consent of the Publisher, excepting brief quotes used in reviews.

All Kensington titles, imprints and distributed lines are available at special quantity discounts for bulk purchases for sales promotion, premiums, fund-raising, educational or institutional use. Special book excerpts or customized printings can also be created to fit specific needs. For details, write or phone the office of the Kensington Special Sales Manager: Kensington Publishing Corp., 119 West 40th Street, New York, NY, 10018. Attn. Special Sales Department. Phone: 1-800-221-2647.

The JS and John Scognamiglio Books logo is a trademark of Kensington Publishing Corp.

Library of Congress Control Number: TK

ISBN: 978-1-4967-4281-0

First Kensington Hardcover Edition: November 2023

ISBN: 978-1-4967-4283-4 (ebook)

10 9 8 7 6 5 4 3 2 1

Printed in the United States of America

WE ARE
ONLY GHOSTS

PART I

NEW YORK CITY
1968

PART I

NEW YORK CITY
1968

1

A creature of habit, the man arrives at the same time every weekday afternoon. He selects the table on the far right at the front of the café, perhaps a vantage point of some sort. Most men have eschewed wearing hats these days, but some still honor the practice. The gentleman is one such man, a traditionalist, even beyond the fedora. When he removes his hat, he reveals immaculately groomed gray hair. While much about him presents a man in his late fifties or perhaps older, his stature speaks of a confidence from younger, fitter days. The combination draws the eye.

Once settled, the gentleman orders coffee ("Strong, and none of that weak brown water you serve the French") and a pastry ("Only if it is fresh, otherwise bring me nothing"). When he speaks, it is in impeccable, methodic, and practiced English. If you listen intently and have an ear for these details, you detect slight traces of European intonations, definitely German, possibly Austrian.

As headwaiter of Café Marie, Charles Ward has marked the man's daily arrivals since he first stepped foot in the café a little over two weeks ago. Most often, he attends the man, their interactions brief and pointed. Should one of the other waiters attend him, Charles makes a point to observe. A gentleman prone to particularities can pose a challenge.

Given his penchant for wearing hats and the fact that he is distinguished, as older men with money tend to be, and handsome, the gentleman stirs Charles. But it is more than base desire. Something about the man pricks and scratches at Charles, an irritation that can't quite be identified.

Then the woman appears.

Preparing coffee service for another table, Charles does not mark her arrival. But he, and the entirety of the café, hears clear and loud when she declares, "*Dis* place *iz* a dump."

In response to the dark disdain of the woman's voice, Charles cringes. The voice echoes through him. He stiffens, as if fingers have seized the base of his neck and throttled him. He shudders at the wave of swift memory that floods through him, an unexpected submersion into the waters of the past.

He tries to calm himself with reason. Of course, his body has misunderstood due to a trick of acoustics and distance. Otherwise, it makes no sense. Still, with rising dread, Charles knows that when he looks, he will not find a trick. He will find her.

From the service area, Charles peers out into the open room of the café. Indeed, there she sits, stout and hard, and unpleasant, as always. Even if he wants to pretend he is mistaken, he cannot. If she is anything, she is unmistakable, hunkering in Charles's memory, implacable as a marked grave. Though her back is to Charles, denial is futile, he knows it is her. How many times had he imagined stepping up behind her, one of her husband's belts wrapped in his fists, taking her by surprise?

How could he ever forget her?

He couldn't.

He can't.

He hasn't.

Charles isn't sure how long he stands at the back of the café, watching her. His hands shake with the confusion that sits deep in the core of his reality as his mind attempts to understand the moment, which has suddenly flipped and twisted itself into some unnatural contortion.

The high, bright ting of a spoon against the side of a coffee cup brings Charles back to himself, to the moment at hand. What was he doing? Ah, yes . . . Pushing aside the confusion of the woman's existence in his present-day world, Charles sets about his duties. He arranges cups and saucers on a tray, sugar and fresh cream, a silver-plated coffee urn. He makes his way to his guests, two deeply handsome Italian men, who are discussing business with much passion. At the table, Charles pours their coffees with his usual aplomb. Not a clink of porcelain, not a misplaced drop of coffee. He is a professional, after all.

Only when he has returned to the service area does another fact enter his understanding. A fact far more stunning. If the woman is her, then the gentleman can only be him.

And here, with the denial that has haunted him ever since the man entered the café two weeks ago unable to sustain itself, Charles truly falters. Something in the process of his existence breaks. An omission of a beat, a breath, a vital flow reduced to near halting causes the moment to sway and lengthen to its fullest point. Charles grips the counter, anchoring himself within the vertiginous moment.

His breath comes in shallow gasps. Panic, something he hasn't felt in a long time, spumes through his chest. How Charles hates panic, the heat and fluster, the swell and weight, the way it gums his thoughts.

Though still unsure of his equilibrium, Charles finds enough focus to walk the length of the dining room, his pace sure and measured. He ignores all about him, especially the gentleman and the woman. He knows one tick of contact with a customer can bring a request, and the moment would, once again, trap him. So, he paces forward until he exits the café through the French doors that open onto Sixty-Third Street. Outside, he pauses beyond the entrance, letting the spring air cool his flushed skin.

From his apron he retrieves a lone Viceroy cigarette, his allotment for the workday. Usually, he steps down the sidewalk to hide the act from his customers. There is nothing as distasteful as watching a waiter suck at a cigarette, then return to his station in a reek of ash and smoke. But today Charles hovers near the doorway. He nicks glances at the gentleman and his wife. From this angle, and with a sense of understanding, Charles sheds any lingering doubt as to who she is, who he is, who they are.

His hand jitters as he brings the cigarette to his lips. He pulls at the smoke and lets it sit in him, hoping perhaps that his lungs will catch fire and he'll combust right on the spot. He hazards another glance, then an outright stare. Once he knows to look for Berthold in the face of the gentleman, he is unmistakable. He is there in the Germanic set of the jaw; in the straight, narrow nose; in the steel gray of the eyes. He is there in the entirety of the gentleman.

How he has missed this fact for even a moment, let alone two weeks, is beyond him. He used to be so observant, so aware. He has softened with age and security and distance, and the realization unnerves him.

Everything around Charles remains unchanged. The brownstones that line the block remain standing. The newspaper store across the street still sells its newspapers and cigarettes and gum. A few doors down, Sal the barber stands behind a gentleman, cutting his hair and chatting, as he always does, most likely about some baseball game that happened the previous evening. At the east end of the street, steamy smoke bellows from the dry cleaners. Much to Charles's amazement, all remains as it was. Given his shocking transportation back to the past, he expected to see a world as violently transformed as he feels. But the world at large has not altered one whit. People continue to pass by, hurrying about their business. Somewhere down the street, a car horn bleats, then falls silent, as if awaiting a response that never comes.

For Charles, the moments languish in that wavering ether between past and present. The seismic shift within continues as internal tectonic plates readjust in the aftermath of this new consciousness. They move into new positions, nudging and cracking previous solidifications, creating a new—

"Charles?"

Jarred, Charles looks at Jacques, standing in the doorway of the café, his face betraying great concern. Jacques is far too free with his emotions for Charles's taste, but what can you do about the young and the French?

"Are you okay?" Jacques asks, only a trace of his Parisian accent evident. He has been working to mask it, to sound as American as possible. He is close but for the persistent liquidity of his speech, a quality so indicative of Romance languages. He can't seem to master the coarse banality of the American language, especially its slang. "*Si primitif et laid*," he says. And Charles can't help but agree.

"Yes, I am fine," Charles responds, more to himself than to Jacques. He offers a soft smile, which he knows will assuage Jacques's concerns. He stubs out the cigarette on the bottom of his shoe, then slips it into his pocket. He abhors litter, especially in front of Café Marie.

Jacques offers his own smile, sweet and charming, infectious in its lack of guile. Having been in America only a year or so, Jacques looks up to Charles. While he is young and cute, Charles knows his naivete is a calculated affectation. Jacques, he knows, is not as adolescent as he portrays himself to be. But it is a good act, one that works with the customers.

When Charles reenters the café, he makes a point to catch the gentleman's attention. With a slight challenge, Charles holds the moment and searches for mutual recognition in the gaze but finds none. After a moment of curious hesitation, the gentleman tenders a dismissive nod. The wife does not see the exchange, oblivious as always.

2

Of course, the gentleman returns the next day.

As Jacques tends to the man, he attempts a bit of dull banter ("How are you today, sir? Are you enjoying the change in weather?"). Quite the puppy at times, Jacques can be energetic to the point of annoyance. Berthold, never one for idle chitchat, then or now, shoos him away without a response.

The aborted interaction makes Charles smile.

Typically, Charles does not make himself known to his customers. At the table, he will greet them with a noninteractive "Good day." He will offer his name, should they need to call out to him for any reason (though he will ensure they will not find reason to do so). He will accept their order and bring anything they request, but with as little intrusion as possible. He imagines himself a ghost, an apparition, leaving no mark upon the men and women he serves. They have come to Cafe Marie for the coffee and the pastries, yes, but above all, they have come for the illusion of being somewhere other than New York City. But with the gentleman, with Berthold—Charles forces himself to say his name, if only to himself—Charles makes a point to catch his eye when he arrives, to ensure he is seen and known. Each day, he searches Berthold for recognition, searches for that realization that shook Charles in a mere breath of a moment, but each day he is denied, and each day the questions continue.

His next workday off, after completing the laundry, the shopping, and other household chores, Charles makes his way uptown from his apartment in the East Village. He strolls the scattered streets of Manhattan. Here and there, he lingers outside the shops he passes: a clothing store, a record shop, his favorite bookstore. At street corners, he watches people rush for no other reason than to keep pace with the energy of the people around them. He stands still, letting the crisp air agitate about him, as if time itself were slamming against his resistance.

Continuing uptown, he intentionally walks through Times Square, through the press of awed and excited tourists as they oscillate this way and that. He watches them crane their necks upward in feeble attempts to capture it all. They take snapshot pictures that will develop with blurred figures and hazy edges, and they will feel they have captured the true essence of New York City. And perhaps they have.

Meaty aromas waft from the hot dog carts that feed endless lines of rushed businessmen and cheap tourists. For a moment, the smell entices, but then the tinny, acrid smell of the steaming water infiltrates, reminding Charles of the taste of blood. With his hunger teased, he makes his way to the Automat at Forty-Second and Broadway. Charles has always liked the sleek stainless-steel environment of the Automat. Now long past its prime, it's like the future has somehow been trapped in the past.

Still, Charles enjoys standing in line, his plastic tray gliding smoothly along the stainless-steel countertop. He marvels in front of the wall of small windows that present the day's offerings: meat loaf, roast beef, chicken soup, peas and carrots, a baked chicken leg, myriad sandwiches. His head swoons with the numerous options, which, when combined, will assemble a complete meal. He drops his coins into the slot and hears the clicking release of the window. When he removes his ham and cheese sandwich, he peers inside to glimpse the inner workings of the place. He spies an older Negro woman, dressed in her bright white Automat uniform with baby blue apron, as she moves in choreographed precision to replace the empty cubby with another, at-the-ready sandwich. She catches Charles watching her. He smiles and nods. She does the same, then returns to her work. A pour of coffee from one of the whimsical dolphin-head spigots, which always brings a smile to Charles's face, completes his meal.

At the crowded counter, Charles sits elbow to elbow with the secretaries on their lunch breaks. They wear tight yet respectable skirts and florid blouses. Harsh red lipstick bleeds at the edges of the bite marks they leave in their tuna sandwiches. They chat and gossip in hushed, catty whispers about their bosses ("I swear, it's like working for an octopus. I spend most of my day swatting at his hands. But look at the scarf he gave me!") and about their love lives ("Four dates and he hasn't even tried to kiss me! Might as well be dating my sister!"). The chatter comforts in its banality.

After finishing his sandwich, Charles considers a slice of cherry pie. He likes the pies at the Automat. While he loves the fresh, delicate French pastries at Café Marie, sometimes he desires something simple and heavy with lard. Charles never feels more American than when he craves cherry pie. But he doesn't indulge. He swivels away from the counter and the office girls and exits back into the swarm of Times Square. He continues north.

To any person marking Charles's route, it would appear purposeless, without aim, like that of a man free from obligation or expectation. Which might be true, but that doesn't mean he is a man without destination.

On Sixty-Third Street Charles nears Café Marie but is on the opposite side of the street. He slows his pace and haunts the moment. He checks his watch. Despite his disciplined stroll and stop for lunch, he is early. He slips into the newsstand.

"Good afternoon, Charles," Mrs. Leifer greets. She reaches for a pack of Viceroys and places it on the counter, along with a book of matches.

"Good afternoon," Charles says in return.

Charles darts a glance toward the café. Berthold, stationed at his usual table, sips his coffee as he reads the *New York Times*. Charles wonders if Berthold looked for him as he entered, or was his absence unmarked? Every other moment or so, Berthold cuts at a piece of pastry, strudel, his favorite. Unhurried and easy, he will not be leaving for another twenty minutes if he stays true to his usual schedule, which Charles has no doubt he will. Berthold was always a regimented man.

"Not working today?" Mrs. Leifer asks, bringing Charles back to the transaction at hand.

As he is dressed in casual dungarees, a button-down shirt, and worn brown loafers, Mrs. Leifer knows the answer to her question. "Then why are you in my store on your day off?" is the true question.

"Not working today." Charles gently shoves her unasked question aside as he pays for the cigarettes.

He knows his lack of elaboration perturbs Mrs. Leifer. She likes to know the goings-on in her neighborhood, and the methodic, predictable Charles Ward stepping out of his routine goads her curiosity. He ignores her prying look and offers a "Good day" as he exits the store.

On the sidewalk, Charles stands exposed. He doesn't worry that Berthold will notice him. Dressed in civilian wear, Charles will be invisible to his customer. He's been invisible for weeks while standing right next to him; across the street he will be nothing more than a shadow of any other person in the world. Nor does Charles worry about William, the other waiter on duty, who is only ever concerned with how much gratuity he can charm from customers. Crass and obvious to Charles, he is an excellent waiter, nonetheless. No, his real worry lies with Jacques.

Something akin to an infatuation has aerated the space between them from the moment they met over a year ago. A silly and childish interest that might have waned with time and familiarity, but for an evening of too many drinks that ended up in Charles's bed. Not that Charles is such a great lover, but he knows more than some, certainly more than Jacques, especially when expressing passion, even if fabricated. The young can be so gullible and often misconstrue lust for something more intoxicating. Jacques was smitten and then some. Flattering, of course, to have a young man, one almost twenty years younger, pursuing you, especially at forty-two. So, Charles succumbed to his own desires a few more times. He believed it harmless fun, even while denying that he likes Jacques more than he should. But the age difference made matters quite improbable, he decided.

But presently, Charles concerns himself with what Jacques might think of seeing him lingering outside the café on his day off. *Are you here for me?* Jacques might wonder. *Please, be here for me.*

Charles hastens up the block and ducks into Schneiderman's Soda Shoppe a few doors down. After settling in a booth by the window, Charles signals the young waitress, who is daydreaming behind the counter. A Hunter College girl, Charles suspects, given the textbook over which she hovers. He orders a chocolate egg cream and watches her go about her task. Does she work to send herself through school, he wonders, or merely to supplement the pocket money her parents send? Is she an out-of-town student whose father doesn't understand the expense of living in Manhattan?

She delivers the egg cream. A noncommittal smile tugs at the corners of her lips before she about-faces, as if she fears any further engagement might pull her too far from her studies. She returns to her position behind the counter and pages lazily through the book.

While Charles envies her college life, he doesn't begrudge her momentary boredom, that gelatinous postadolescent state of being not a child, not an adult (as long as she is beholden to her parents and their money, despite the nickel-and-dime tips tossed on the soda shoppe counter). Perhaps he envies her life—but only for a moment, because what good does any of it do?

Charles lights a cigarette, leaving the waitress to her ennui, and returns to his present world. The past few days have brought a clutter of questions about Berthold and Frau Werden. How long have they been in New York? How long in America? Had they been here even before Charles arrived? What of the children? The most persistent questions return again and again: How does Berthold not recognize him? How did Charles not recognize him the moment he stepped foot in Café Marie? Time has changed them both, of course, but so much that it has diluted their memories of each other to nonexistent?

Charles confesses he has not thought of the Werdens in years, not outright. Of course, they ghost his life like others from his past: his parents, his sisters, Havel, Eliáš, Maude, Mrs. Perkins, various others, the human debris that litters one's past as one moves from moment to moment, from there to here. Occasionally, they flicker into memory at unexpected moments like halos in double-exposed film, irresolute blurs that cloud his thoughts, causing him to teeter on the edge between past and present. But Charles makes sure never to cross the line, never to go back there. He's never sure he'll find his way back.

But to sit and think of Berthold, Frau Werden, Marlene,

Geert, to remember that time of his life . . . No, he has not done that in years. Even now his mind resists the return, standing at the wall he's spent a lifetime building, protecting him from the memories and the debilitating emotions they summon. You can't survive if you're a jumble of emotion, vulnerable and exposed and weak. How Charles loathes weakness—in others, yes, but mostly in himself.

Lost in the tumult of his own thoughts, Charles almost misses Berthold strolling past, catching sight of him the moment before he walks out of the frame of the soda shoppe window. But Charles doesn't panic, doesn't rush. He takes the time to finish his egg cream, refraining from slurping at the sediment like some ill-bred schoolboy. When he's finished, he places a few dollars on the table and nods to the waitress on his way out.

As Charles suspected, Berthold walks as he speaks—measured, thoughtful, planned. He does not weave among the foot traffic to force time along, like so many in this city. No, with a pace born of his soldiering days, he exhibits sureness and meaning with each footfall. That ingraining does not leave you after you set the rifle down, shed the uniform, flee the country.

As Charles falls into step, impersonating Berthold's gait and cadence, he witnesses once again Obersturmführer Werden in the man's posture and focus. He can see the *Obersturmführer* bedecked in his uniform, the deep steel gray designated for special occasions: official Wehrmacht events, family holidays, or the rare visit from Reichsführer Himmler. Here Charles allows a memory to break through of how nervous and excited Berthold could be when Himmler scheduled a visit, like a child anticipating the arrival of his favorite uncle, all chatter and tremble as he readied himself. Was he desperate for acknowledgment, for recognition, for the *Reichsführer*'s approval, or was he maybe ducking disapproval, which could lead to discipline, a transfer, death? Either way, Berthold needn't have worried. Handsome and fit, exemplary in appearance and duty, he was the perfect soldier. Still, he jittered with excitement, so much so that he could not tie his tie. Charles stepped in to calm him. As they stood face-to-face, he took Berthold's fumbling hands in his and held them at his sides, their faces millimeters apart.

"Breathe, Berthold," Charles instructed.

Once Berthold had calmed his panic, Charles released his hold. With Berthold's arms hanging at his sides, Charles commenced to tie the tie, flipping and looping the satin fabric with certainty and deftness. Funnily enough, Berthold had taught Charles the ritual only months before.

"Every young man should know how to tie a tie, Charles. Didn't your father ever teach you?" Berthold had asked as he escorted Charles upstairs, a rare moment when the two of them were alone in the house after the children had departed for school and Frau Werden had gone out to run errands. Berthold had lingered before heading to the camp for the day, as he did on occasion. In his and Frau Werden's bedroom, Berthold and Charles had stood side by side in the large mirror over the dresser. Charles mimicked Berthold's movements as he watched his own in the mirror. Concentration darkened Berthold's gray eyes to the color of wet pavement.

"It's harder when you think about it. I'm so used to just doing it. I'm getting so confused," Berthold chuckled as he continued to configure the fabric over and over again, tying and untying, ensuring Charles marked each step. Charles laughed, as well, but learned each step, each flip and loop and tug and adjustment, so one day in the near future he would stand in front of Berthold and tie his tie for him before sending him off to the camp at Auschwitz to meet with Reichsführer Himmler.

And to complete the circle, in the very distant future, Charles would tie his own tie every day with quick, deft precision. He rarely stood in a mirror to do so, because Berthold was right: it was harder when you thought about it.

If his math is correct, Berthold was younger then than Charles is now, and the thought surprises Charles. How adult Berthold seemed then. How strong and big and in control, even in those unsure moments. And how unlike Charles now, at the age of forty-two.

Berthold turns onto Fifth Avenue, then meanders down the street. No, that is not correct. Berthold does not meander. He does not saunter. He does not amble or ramble or wander. Nor does he march or trek or stamp, as he might have done in his soldiering days. But while he can assess what the man is not, Charles cannot seem to define the essence of this present-day Berthold. He does not present as contrived, created, or imagined. His movements do not reek of manufacture or calculation, unlike Charles's walk and speech, his entire existence, if he's being honest. Berthold, on the other hand, is pure and unfettered—at least at this moment, while walking. Of course, Charles expects nothing less of him.

Berthold continues east as Charles shadows him. They migrate as one, step-by-step, block by block, along Lexington Avenue. The sidewalk crowds grow denser. So much so, Charles must weave here and there, skirting a pair of sharply dressed women pausing to window-shop, sidestepping a mother pushing a pram, speeding his pace to pass a trio of businessmen in no hurry to return to the office. Up ahead, Berthold's path and pace remain straight and steady and unhurried.

At one of the Lexington storefronts half a block past Seventy-Second Street, Berthold stops. Charles pauses a few doors down, lingering at a storefront for children's clothing, the style entirely frivolous and too expensive to be worn for such a short time in one's life. With furtive glances, he sees Berthold unlock the door to the shop, then enter.

Lynch's Jewelry is small and unassuming in comparison to the other more flagrant boutique shops that line the avenue. As Charles approaches the shop, his pace slows to a linger on the far edge of the windowpane, hopefully unseen. Berthold hang his hat on a hook on the back wall then turns to stand among the bright glass display cases. He surveys the landscape as if back in Auschwitz, surveying the daily goings-on of the camp. Then Berthold takes up a cloth and steps over to a case to wipe it down.

With Berthold fixated on cleaning, Charles takes advantage of the unguarded moment to inspect the shop. The display cases are uncluttered, sparse even. An arrangement of diamond rings inhabits one case. A few necklaces lounge seductively in another. One case displays a single watch. The presentation is select, verging on meager, unlike the shops in the Diamond District, with their cases bursting with heaps of diamonds, as if they are cheap prizes in a penny arcade. The result here is serene and luxurious. Charles moves away from the window before Berthold has the chance to mark him. He walks away from Lynch's Jewelry with the understanding that Berthold is Mr. Lynch, owner and proprietor. He walks away with the knowledge that this is who the Obersturmführer is now.

3

Just as Obersturmführer Berthold Werden had been in his military days, Mr. Lynch is a man of regimen and routine. In the ensuing days, Charles measures Mr. Lynch's daily life.

Mr. Lynch departs his apartment building every weekday at 7:21 a.m. By 7:30 a.m. he arrives at a café on Seventy-Sixth Street, not far from Madison. There he dines on one soft-boiled egg, sliced tomato, toast, on which he spreads the thinnest layer of marmalade, and coffee. He reads the *New York Times*, except for Wednesdays, when he reads the latest issue of *Der Spiegel*, surprising in its flagrancy. At 8:15 a.m. he pays his check. He reaches the jewelry store by 8:23 a.m., at which time he returns the jewelry to its display cases in time for Lynch's Jewelry to open at 9:00 a.m. Timing and pace do not alter no matter the weather, sun or rain.

Charles notes that the so-called Mr. Lynch does not consult his watch throughout this process, moving through the morning on timed instinct that has hardened into unalterable routine. Come 12:15 p.m., a boy from the local deli delivers a small brown sack containing lunch. Every day the same: a sandwich composed of some type of deli meat and cheese, coleslaw, and a pickle. Mid-afternoon, 2:15 p.m., to be precise, Mr. Lynch departs for Café Marie, and he arrives at 2:30 p.m. He finishes exactly at 3:15 p.m., something Charles had never noticed until then. Within forty-five minutes to the second, he sits, orders, consumes his coffee and pastry, pays, and departs. Mr. Lynch returns to the shop to complete the workday at 5:00 p.m., at which time he methodically removes the jewelry from the display cases, stores it in a back office, presumably in a safe, tallies the day's register, turns out the lights, locks the door, and heads home.

The precision of the routine, the never-faltering mechanics, fascinates Charles. Berthold Werden has created a new life in which he need not worry over the quotidian deviations that trip up other men.

With Lynch's Jewelry closed on the weekends, Charles continues to follow his quarry. On Saturday morning he trails Mr. Lynch to Grand Central. In the ticket line, Charles, heady in his daring, stands directly behind Mr. Lynch, so close that one casual glance back could undermine the subterfuge. Still, Charles breathes in Mr. Lynch, finding memories in his cologne. No, not cologne, shaving soap. Surely, he doesn't still use the same after all these years. Of course he does. Charles breathes deep, catching the familiar hints of spearmint and bitter almond.

"Antica Barbieria Colla," Berthold said, reading the Italian name to Charles, his pronunciation florid and beautiful. "I found it during my time in Italy and won't use anything else. Difficult to come by these days, so we must be sparing with it."

They stood before the mirror in the upstairs bathroom, where the light was best, the door locked against the rest of the family. Oh, the anger that had flared under Frau Werden's skin at the order that they not be disturbed.

"I am teaching Charles to shave. Look at this silliness on his face." Berthold had referenced Charles's chin and mustache hairs, sprouting in straggly, unassertive patches. "We can't have him running about like this."

Frau Werden had harrumphed her disapproval, but what could she say against her husband? Nothing, but she would take it out on Charles later, that much he knew.

"Can I come, Papa?" Geert asked, stopping his father on the stairs. "I want to learn to shave, too."

"You are too young," Berthold informed his son. "You won't have whiskers for years to come."

Berthold turned from his son. Charles watched the hurt and embarrassment rash Geert's face. Then the glare trained on Charles, as if he were the reason for the rejection. Unnerved, Charles followed Berthold up the stairs.

"First, you must prepare the soap," Berthold instructed. He dropped a fresh shaving soap into the mug. "I have sensitive skin and need a thicker lather, so I use less water."

With vigorous whisking and churning with the shaving brush, Berthold frothed the lather. The mint and alcohol stung Charles's nostrils and teared his eyes. Once prepared, Berthold turned to Charles, brush in hand. He halted.

"You should remove your shirt," Berthold advised. "The first time can be messy."

Charles complied and stood bared in the brightness of the bathroom. He crossed his arms in front of his pale, thin chest. Berthold smiled at Charles's shyness.

"Stand up straight, Charles," Berthold ordered. "You are a handsome young man."

Charles dropped his arms and straightened himself to full height, almost an inch taller than Berthold, surprising both of them.

After dipping the brush into the mug, Berthold touched it to Charles's face. He applied the lather in small swirls, explaining, "This movement makes the hair stand up so you can get a close shave."

The lather nipped and cooled at the same time, and Charles

initially gasped as the brush bristles scratched at his skin. Afterward, Berthold turned Charles to the mirror. The unfamiliar might mistake them for father and son, though closer inspection revealed the differences between them. After months in the Werden home, Charles had regained most of the weight lost in the past few years, though he was still thinner and weaker than a boy his age should be. His skin no longer held that sallow hue. His dark hair had grown back and was now an unruly mop, controlled only by a healthy dose of the *Birken Haarwasser* tonic Berthold had brought him from the camp. In contrast, Berthold was every bit a man in stature and weight and muscle and, most of all, confidence.

Berthold took up the straight razor and positioned himself behind Charles, pressing his body against Charles's. He brought the razor up to Charles's cheek and let it hover. Charles followed the movement with his eyes, careful not to make any movements.

"See how I am holding the razor, my little finger resting on this metal curve?" Berthold schooled. "This will provide the control you need. You must have control, Charles. That is key."

Berthold brought the razor closer, and Charles instinctively pulled back.

"I'm not going to hurt you, Charles," Berthold assured him, talking to Charles's reflection. His left hand, resting on Charles's naked belly, skimmed up to his chest and pulled Charles tighter to him. "Trust me."

Even though he was almost an inch taller than Berthold, Charles felt small and childish in his presence, especially when naked. His thin, pale chest, hairless and bony (he could still see and easily count his ribs, despite his weight gain), looked inferior compared to Berthold's manly body. He placed his hand on top of Berthold's. He leaned back, resting against Berthold. The blade grazed down his cheek, leaving smooth pink skin in its wake. Berthold caught Charles's eye in the mirror and raised an eyebrow, as if to say, "See, I told you."

To this day, Charles still shaves with a straight razor. He assumes Berthold does, as well, and fights the urge to touch his cheek to confirm his assumption. If nothing else, he wishes he could ask Berthold where he finds Antica Barbieria Colla in Manhattan. Charles has been unable to locate it for years.

They board the train to Scarsdale. Charles sits a few rows behind Berthold, an oddly intimate proximity after the past couple of weeks of trailing him from such a distance. When they arrive at the Scarsdale station, they ride in separate taxis to Murray Hill Road.

"Stay back, please," Charles instructs the driver as Berthold's taxi pulls into a driveway.

"Hey, buddy," the cabbie protests, "we doing something unkosher here? I don't wanna be mixed up in anything illegal."

"Nothing of the kind," Charles assures him.

"Then what're we doing here?"

Charles leans back in the seat. He rests his head so that he stares out the back window up at the tilted sky with its smattering of gray clouds. "That's a good question."

The driver waits for his instructions, but none come.

"So? What's it gonna be, buddy? You getting out or what?" The driver prods. "I don't got all day."

Charles glances up the long, circular drive leading to the house. The taxi that had carried Berthold returns without him.

"Take me back to the station," Charles directs.

The driver casts a suspicious glance into the rearview mirror, shrugs, then turns the cab around.

4

On his next weekday off, Charles makes his way back to Scarsdale alone. He has no plan beyond having the taxi drop him at the end of the driveway of the house on Murray Hill Road.

"You don't want me to take you to the house?" the driver asks.

"This is fine," Charles responds as he exits the taxi.

He surveys the quiet neighborhood. He assumes he can linger only so long before someone notices. Someone is watching. Someone is always watching strangers in upscale neighborhoods in places like Scarsdale. They will observe him lurking and loitering, and if he does not leave soon enough for their comfort, they will call the police to report a stranger in their midst.

He walks partway up the drive, to a bend where a trio of trees cluster. The thick-branched firs provide a shield but only from the homes across the street. To anyone in Berthold's house, Charles is completely visible. He scans the façade of the generic, stately, very American two-story house and its numerous windows, fifteen in all. No shadows or silhouettes appear. No movements behind drawn curtains. Charles breathes deeper. But standing yards from Berthold's home, he still doesn't understand why he has made this morning excursion to Scarsdale. Did he think he'd find Frau Werden doddering about the grounds, tending to gardeners and yard workers? Did he think she would recognize him? Then what? Invite him in to recount the old days over fresh-baked streusel and coffee? Or has she forgotten him, as her husband has, the years between there and here dulling her senses, her instincts? Or does she think him dead long ago, so she won't connect the man on her doorstep to the past?

Shaking the questions from his mind and before he loses what little nerve he retains, Charles steps to the front door. He claps the knocker against the door in three short strikes and waits, breath held full and heated. He understands he has just knocked on the door to madness.

The door opens. Frau Werden, looking as she did when she came to Café Marie and much as she did twenty-five years ago. Yes, slightly older, plus definitely fatter (she was never a petite woman), but it is still unmistakably her.

"Yas?" Frau Werden inquires of the stranger she appraises, her accent coloring the word as a guttural demand.

Charles is unable to speak. In the wake of his momentary silence, her irritation, always smoldering below the surface, flares. He has seen the look a thousand times. Her lips tighten. Her eyes squint to slits. Her neck stiffens, and her right fist, empty at present, contracts into itself.

"Young man," she snaps, "you go away now."

She starts to close the door, but Charles reaches out to stop her. "No."

Her eyes widen. Her mouth slackens to a slight gape. She retreats half a step as she pushes the door against the stranger. Charles realizes she is panicking. She may still be stout and strong—he can tell by the pressure she uses against the door—but she is no longer sure of her strength. And certainly, she is no match for a grown man at this age. He savors her fear for a moment before explaining.

"My car broke down," he announces. "I was hoping to use your phone. That is all, madam."

Her push against the door eases, though she continues to eye him. She relents. "It is here in the hall."

Charles enters Berthold's home. Once the front door has shut behind them, the foyer falls dark, and his eyes have to adjust. The forest-green paint and deep mahogany wood moldings blend into the dark of the wood flooring. The effect encases them. She directs him to the phone on a mahogany console table. In the ornate mirror over the console, Charles watches Frau Werden hovering.

"Do you know the number for the taxi?" he asks.

"It is there, in the yellow book." She points at a shelf in the console table.

Charles rings the number.

"Where am I?" he asks.

She narrows her eyes at him. "Do you not know you are in Scarsdale?"

"Yes. But the address of the house?" Charles clarifies with a smile.

Frau Werden produces a blush, which softens her, makes her seem almost girlish. She shakes her head and chuckles delicately. Delicately!

"You are at Murray Hill Road, number twenty-four," she tells him.

Once the taxi dispatcher confirms the cab, Charles moves to make his departure.

"*Danke, Fräulein,*" he says, to both of their surprise. Is he testing her? "You are very kind."

"*Du sprichst Deutsch?*" she says, looking at him differently.

"It has been many years," he confesses, "but *ja, ich spreche Deutsch.*"

Frau Werden relaxes. Unlike her husband, she has not even attempted to lose her accent. She has learned English, but that is all you will get from her, she seems to say with each German-accented utterance. "It is good to hear. Very good to hear. This town is so . . . American. Please come. Wait inside. Would you like coffee? Cake? I have cake. *Bitte.*"

"I have taken enough of your generosity," Charles begs off. The genuine eagerness of her offer unnerves him. He never speculated over the extent of their interaction beyond knocking on the door. What on earth would he speak to Frau Werden about? Her daily travails? Her husband? Her children? No, he can't. "But I thank you."

He exits before she can press. He hurries toward the street, even though the taxi is fifteen minutes away. He glances back and finds her still in the doorway, watching his retreat. She cannot hide the pall of loneliness that has overtaken her.

Back in Manhattan, back in the safety and sanity of his apartment, Charles wonders if he has stepped too close to the fire. When Frau Werden is next with her husband, will she speak of the man who came to their door? How he spoke German? As they drift through a meal of roasted chicken and blanched green beans (over which Frau Werden will spoon a sauce of melted butter and thyme), will she describe the man to her husband? Will Berthold recognize the waiter from Café Marie in her description? Will they both recognize the man and the waiter as Charles? Why does neither of them remember him?

And with this last question, his chest wrenches with a childish pain he hasn't felt in years, decades, that ugly sense of abandonment. He knows how ridiculous the reaction is, but it comes so swift and unexpectedly he cannot block it before it hits like an assassin, a sharpshooter high on a roof, rifle and scope trained directly on him, marking him for execution.

Why is he doing this to himself?

Charles should end this obsessive pursuit. He should return to his routine of work and home. No more day trips to Scarsdale. No more stalking Berthold. No more lurking in the shadows across from Lynch's Jewelry. No more dogging Berthold's stroll from home to work to Café Marie to work to home. No more. On his next day off he should address neglected household chores. He should go to the park or the movies or a museum or sit in his apartment and stare at the walls. He should return to his life as it was before this bizarre aberration occurred.

But Charles understands whether he pursues him or not, Berthold will continue to exist, in this city, in Charles's life, as an inescapable fact. He will continue to dine at Café Marie. He will continue to insist on fresh Danishes and strong European-worthy coffee. And Charles will continue to bring them to him in his prompt and professional manner and struggle to pretend he does not know this man from his past who does not recognize him.

5

Despite internal protestations, and weak in the face of dogged curiosity, Charles returns to Scarsdale on his next weekday off from Café Marie. This time he does not dawdle on his way to the Lynch home on Murray Hill Road, instructing the taxi to drop him at the doorstep. He clangs the door knocker twice with authority. A white pastry box balances on the palm of his left hand.

When the door opens, it takes only a moment for Frau Werden to recognize the man on her doorstep.

"You," she declares with masked pleasure. "Has your car broken again?" she offers as a joke. A joke!

Charles smiles. "*Nein, Fräulein.* I have come to thank you for your generosity."

Frau Werden's cheeks bloom pink, and her head tilts coquettishly. "I have not been a fräulein for many years, young man, but thank you."

She steps aside, and Charles enters.

"I am Frau Lynch, though here in America, they call me Mrs. Lynch," she states with obvious distaste.

"Well, Frau Lynch, I do thank you for your help the other day and thought you might like some fresh pastries." Charles extends the box, and Frau Lynch lifts the lid to inspect the offering.

"*Schneebälle?*"

Of course, he knows she was always partial to a *Schneeball*.

Without a word, she breaks off a small taste. Her eyes widen with approval. "These are fresh."

Charles nods. "I baked them this morning."

Her eyes narrow. Mistrust has always been her nature. "You? They are good."

"A family recipe." Charles wants to chuckle over his white lie, for it is her own recipe, one that adds marzipan to the traditional ingredients.

"And you have a *Schneeballeneisen?*" she questions. "You must, to form them so perfectly."

"Handed down from my grandmother." Another lie. He found one years ago in a small store on the Lower East Side and purchased it in a moment of nostalgia.

Frau Lynch nods approval. She hazards another taste. "We need coffee, yes?"

Charles follows Frau Lynch as far as the living room.

He halts at the entrance to the room. While he knows the sofa and chairs and mahogany coffee table and matching end tables and heavy bookcases cannot be the same from that house in Poland twenty-five years ago, they are eerily similar. She has attempted to replicate that world and has succeeded all too well. So much so, Charles can picture Berthold sitting in the leather chair, reading the evening paper after his day at the camp. There, at the end of the sofa, sits Marlene, stitching the hem of her light blue dress, which had seen better days, or maybe she reads a schoolbook or merely daydreams, as she did so often. She lifts her eyes to Charles when he enters the room with her mother's coffee or her father's brandy or an evening snack of sliced apples and cheese for Geert, who plays with his army figures, waging battles on the carpeted floor. Charles could picture the familial scene of domesticity as if he had never left that house.

"You sit," Frau Lynch instructs. "I will make the coffee."

Charles nods but does not sit, a defiance he could never attempt when he was under Frau Werden's rule in Poland. As a guest in Mrs. Lynch's house in Scarsdale, he wanders about the room, as if wandering in a shop or a museum. Tapestries of various sizes and scenes adorn the walls. There are plants in large ceramic pots, wayward vegetation that blooms about the room. At a cluttered bookcase, he lingers. Among the decorative books and the numerous figurines sit photographs in ornate pewter frames.

The most prominent is a professional portrait of Mr. and Mrs. Lynch, the kind produced in a department store. Husband and wife sit in front of a blue paper background, possibly meant to represent the sky but too flat to inspire. Berthold is handsome, of course, in his navy suit, his hair still a mix of brown and gray, his eyes bright despite the wan smile. Frau Werden looks as good as Charles has ever seen her look. She was never a pretty woman, as far as he has known her. In the picture, her hair is neat, and a touch of makeup brings color to her cheeks and lips. Her dowdy dress is a lighter, complementary blue to her husband's suit and the fake sky. The effect is very American.

On the shelf below, a photo of a handsome man stands among a flock of porcelain ducks. Charles slowly realizes the man is Geert. His hair is very blond, and his eyes are bright blue, and with his clear, smooth, fair skin, the look is quintessentially Aryan. Charles must admit the chubby, ill-tempered lad has grown into quite the attractive man. Finally, something of his father comes to the surface.

On a lower shelf sits a photo of a grown Marlene, so recognizable by her smile, unchanged from her youth. That shy, alluring sensuality, so out of place in her parents' home back in Poland, radiates from this photograph her mother has chosen to display. The shot is candid, unprofessional, taken out in nature somewhere. It is alive, unlike the portrait of the Lynches and the photo of Geert. The picture makes him happy.

Frau Lynch returns with a tray of dainty porcelain cups and a small silver urn. She sets the tray on the coffee table. Charles remains at the bookcase.

"You have children," Charles comments, nodding at the portraits.

Pouring the coffee, Frau Lynch nods. "A boy and girl. The girl is a mother herself. She lives far away. The boy still acts like a boy in many ways. Maybe if he had a wife . . . ? He lives in the city. Still, we don't see him much. 'Too busy,' he says. What is busy if you don't have a wife and children?"

Charles sees another photograph. This of the entire family, taken years before, possibly when he was in their lives. But was this after they fled? Were they the Lynches or still the Werdens? Perhaps neither, trapped in some sort of limbo between then and there and now?

"Come. Sit," Frau Lynch orders as she places his cup and saucer on the table.

Charles sits on the sofa as she plates the *Schneebälle,* first one for him and then another for herself. After pouring hew own cup of coffee, Frau Lynch joins Charles on the sofa. With each delicate tear of the pastries, powdered sugar snows down onto their plates. Frau Lynch pops a piece of pastry into her mouth and holds it there for a moment before she offers another nod of approval. Charles hates the pride flushing through him, for it reminds him of the past, of the relief he used to feel when she would toss him a rare nod or smile for some chore he had performed to her liking. He accepted this praise hungrily back then, as if a street urchin catching a tossed coin, and he accepts it now with equal starvation need.

"And what of your parents...?" Frau Lynch halts and looks at Charles with curiosity. "I don't know your name, young man."

"Excuse me?"

"I was going to say your name and realized I do not know it," she admits, flustered.

Charles sieves through the names Frau Werden used to call him back in the day. All the ugly, hateful barks of *boy* or *Judenschwein* or, most often, *Hure* as she ordered him to clean, to fetch, to leave her sight. Tamping down the flash of fresh anger rising to his throat, he works up a smile. "I apologize, Frau Lynch. I thought I had introduced myself. I am . . ."

Here Charles stumbles. Reflex urges him to say, "I am Charles Ward," as he has stated thousands of times over the past twenty years, but something stops him. Is this a moment of reclamation, this moment with Frau Werden, of all people?

He is stuck in one of those rare occasions when life overlaps. Past and present fold one over the other, a distortion in which he can emerge or reemerge, whichever he chooses. In the hesitation, he realizes he thinks of himself as Charles. He speaks as Charles.

Frau Lynch waits for his reply, plucking another pinch of pastry. She smiles a guilty smile, as if she's a child caught stealing.

"I am Charles," he tells Frau Lynch. "Charles Ward."

"Charles," Frau Lynch repeats.

He wonders if this will connect him for her with the young man from Auschwitz. The young man her husband brought into their home and forced into her life. The young man who cleaned her home during the day, served her dinner in the evening, then bedded her husband at night, while she slept.

"Charles," he states again, with a slightly taunting smile. "This is who I am."

Frau Lynch returns the smile blankly, for she has no idea who he is. "Such a good German name."

Charles nods. "Yes, it is."

She pinches another piece from her *Schneeball* and dips it in her coffee. "Tell me about you, young man," Frau Lynch orders.

Charles hesitates. "Me? There is nothing to tell."

She eyes Charles with insistence, the old Frau Werden bleeding through. Of course, he cannot refuse.

He recites the current version of his story, a vague ramble of places and times and events he has crafted. "I was born and raised in Upstate New York, the only child of German immigrants. I moved to the city to attend college but did not complete my degree. Still, I remained in the city. I presently work in a restaurant. One day I wish to open my own restaurant." He throws in this last part to show that he is not a typical stagnant American. He is someone with purpose and drive, at least in his fabrications.

"And your parents?" Frau Lynch asks. "Do you see them often?"

Charles cues the sadness. A rehearsed tilt of his head is followed by a slight hunch of his shoulders to convey an eternal melancholy. He shakes his head. "No. They have passed."

Frau Lynch clucks her tongue. "Ah, yes. Now, this is true."

Charles seizes with confusion and then panic, fear that he's been found out. "Pardon?"

"Your story is as I tell mine," Frau Lynch confesses. "A reading from a paper. This is what we do."

"We?"

"Foreigners," she declares with bitterness. "We hide here, in America. Hide who we are with stories created so the people don't ask questions. What? We should be ashamed for not being from this boring, ugly country?"

"You think my story is a lie?"

She nods but smiles, as well.

On the inside, Charles panics. Has he been caught? Has she recognized him?

She continues to pick at her pastry and sip at her coffee. Yes, she knows he has lied about his life, but he is only a fellow immigrant who wears an American mask. He returns her smile.

"I must practice my performance, I suppose," Charles concedes.

Frau Lynch nudges him with her elbow as she leans toward him. "Your secret is safe with me."

They pass the hour of his visit in a tentative yet casual comfort. Frau Lynch speaks of their time in Brazil before immigrating to America. She speaks of the small, ugly town in which they lived: "At least this Scarsdale is civilized." She speaks of the jungle: "Unbearable, hot and suffocating. I thought I would die." And of the "savages": "Practically naked, exposing their dirty brown skin with no shame at all!" She speaks of her son, Raymond Lynch, who lives in the city: "Spoiled but a good boy." She speaks of Marlene, who is still Marlene, with consternation: "Always defiant, she fell in love with one of those dirty Brazil men to spite me, I'm sure. Though he is not as savage as the others and is a business partner of Herr Lynch." She expels the details as if draining an infection of pus.

Charles offers some truths in recounting his life. How he came to America as a young man shortly after the war. How he made his way in the city by the grace of other immigrants and his own determination.

Neither admits to or speaks of their time in Poland.

6

The next day, as he enters Schneiderman's, the girl behind the counter, Norma, according to her name tag, welcomes him with a nod of recognition, then turns to make his chocolate egg cream without conversation. Charles sits in his booth.

He has become a regular, and he likes the feeling.

"You make a very good egg cream for a young woman," Charles comments when she sets the heavy glass down in front of him. The froth, a resting fluffed cloud, threatens to overflow but doesn't.

Norma shrugs. "My grandfather likes them."

"That's sweet."

"I suppose," Norma offers with another shrug.

"What are you studying?" Charles inquires.

Norma looks back at the counter, where her textbook lies open. "Art."

The singular word hangs in the air for a moment.

"From a textbook?" Charles asks. "Sounds tedious."

"To say the least," Norma confirms. "It's better when we get to go to the museum. Or even when the professor shows us slides. Reading about art is so dry. Have you been to the

Whitney? That's my favorite, besides the small galleries in the Village, of course. I like the new stuff, you know, modern. Warhol, de Kooning, Pollock. Exciting stuff. Actual ideas, rather than pretty colors and trees and Jesus. There are too many paintings of Jesus for my taste."

Quiet, adrift Norma isn't so quiet and adrift when the subject is art. Her passion vibrates off her like sound waves, pulsating at Charles. He does not know much about art and can't even pretend to understand the modern artists, but he's been to the Met a time or two. "What about Van Gogh or Picasso? They were modern in their day, yes? And Gauguin? I like his natives works."

Norma cannot shield her disappointment.

"They're interesting, I suppose, in context," Norma agrees with reluctance. "Picasso, at least, continues to explore. That's the thing, you see. So many artists get praised for something, and then they stick with it, try to re-create whatever first pleased people. They don't try to excite again in a different way. They get trapped. They grow stale."

"Van Gogh grew stale?" Charles asks.

"Sure," Norma declares. "Might be why he went crazy, you know. Stuck the way he was. Same themes. Same colors. Same brushstrokes. Same, same, same. Enough to drive anyone mad."

Charles smiles at her youth, her confident ignorance.

"Hey." Norma nods toward the window. "That man is staring at you. You know him?"

Charles is surprised to find Berthold standing outside the soda shoppe.

A moment of panic passes before Charles steadies himself. "Yes, I know him."

Berthold continues watching Charles for a moment, then nods. Charles blushes but nods in return. With a crisp about-face, Berthold continues down the sidewalk, most likely returning to the jewelry store.

"Interesting," Norma muses.

Charles watches Berthold until he is out of sight. "Very."

The next day, at Café Marie, Charles stands at Berthold's table, preparing his coffee service.

"I saw you, yes?" Berthold inquires, setting aside his newspaper. "In that ice cream shop."

"They make a very good egg cream."

Berthold nods as Charles continues the coffee preparation.

"I have not had an egg cream in years," Berthold comments and then takes up his paper again.

Charles retreats to wait on other customers.

When Berthold leaves the café, Charles stands outside smoking, blatantly, only a short way down the sidewalk. Charles can imagine the disappointment Berthold would have for him if he only knew who he was. He thinks to hide the cigarette but decides against it. As Berthold approaches, Charles offers, "Have a good day, sir."

"I am going to that shop to have an egg cream," Berthold announces.

"Very good," Charles replies calmly. But he is staggered by the man's decision to break from his routine.

Berthold loiters in proximity to Charles, who looks at him quizzically. There is a strange and rare uncertainty to Berthold's stance. He's never known Berthold to express such uncertainty. Of course, he is remembering the Berthold of twenty-five years ago. With age comes uncertainty, does it not? Charles wonders if Berthold is unsure of how to extricate himself from their unscripted interaction. A tension—nervous, confused—radiates.

"Well, I must return to the café," Charles states, allowing Berthold his exit. He takes a quick drag, then extinguishes the half-smoked cigarette on the bottom of this shoe. He slips the butt into his apron pocket. "Enjoy your egg cream."

"Join me," Berthold says in a tone that is more order than request.

Charles stops. When he turns to Berthold, he finds an anxious plea moored in the usual sternness of his eyes.

"I can step away for a moment," Charles assures himself as much as Berthold. "Let me tell the other waiter. I can meet you there."

"I will wait," Berthold states.

Hesitating to leave Berthold out on the sidewalk, as if he is a lost child, Charles hurries into the café. William is happy to work the café on his own, which means more tips for him.

"I'm just down the street," Charles assures him, should he need assistance.

Outside, Charles and Berthold stroll the short way to Schneiderman's in silence. A familiar comfort settles in Charles, which calms his breath and heartbeat.

After delivering the egg creams—chocolate for Charles, vanilla for Berthold—Norma returns to her position behind the counter.

"I am Charles," Charles tells Berthold and extends his hand across the table. The gesture feels absurd, not only in the realm of the present but also of the past.

Berthold takes the offered hand in his. The older man's skin is soft, reflecting a life in which he has performed minimal labor. It is the skin of a manager, an overseer of men who perform tasks under his direction. But the grip is firm, though not aggressive, strong but not threatening, the tempered handshake of a businessman. This is not the Berthold Charles once knew. This is a different man.

"I am Wallace Lynch," Berthold says by way of confirmation.

Charles takes a moment. He absorbs the new information. *Wallace Lynch*, he says to himself. *This is Wallace Lynch. This is who he is now.* "Wallace Lynch."

Wallace Lynch smiles. "Yes. I am Wallace Lynch."

"Pleasure to meet you, Mr. Lynch."

"A pleasure to meet you, Charles."

Wallace Lynch realizes he is still holding Charles's hand. Their respective arms hover above the white laminate tabletop. With a blush, Wallace releases the clasp. Charles relaxes his fingers, and both hands retreat.

"Charles. I have always liked that name," Wallace observes. "I had an uncle by that name."

"I was named after an uncle," Charles states with a smile.

"And your last name?"

"Ward. Charles Ward. Very generic. Don't you think?"

"Yes, but generic is good."

"And of what origin is Lynch?" Charles looks into his egg cream and stirs.

"Jewish," Wallace Lynch states with no hint of irony.

Charles knits his brow.

"No, it does not sound very Jewish," Wallace agrees. "Once, long ago, my people were Lichtzers. At some point someone altered it, as so many did when they came to America. An ancestor seeking to assimilate, I'm sure. I've thought about changing it back, but such trouble, you know, to alter one's entire identity. Still, someone's name says so much about them, don't you think?"

The recitation of the fabricated Lynch history impresses Charles. As Frau Lynch stated, the story must be told in a thoughtful, leisured pace, and Berthold has perfected the speech. Charles would believe this man if he didn't know better.

"And Ward?" Wallace Lynch inquires in turn.

"A bastardized version of some other name, I'm sure. I'm afraid I've never inquired."

Wallace nods with a hint of disappointment. "A family's history is very important, Charles. To know where one's people are from is to know who you are, the core of you. We're losing that with each new generation, especially here in America. I fear there is no sense of history here. It's all too new and modern."

"And changing all the time," Charles adds.

"And diluted by too many different people wanting to be American."

"But is that not why people came to America? To be American?"

"Yes, most do, I'm sure. Of course, most of my people came to escape persecution," Wallace Lynch declares, reaffirming his Jewish story. No faltering breath, no hesitation, no guilt. Charles is amazed by the conviction. "Not that we have not experienced our fair share here in America. At least they have not rounded us up into ghettos and camps."

The appropriated history stuns Charles, and he must fight back a snort of incredulous laughter. He takes a sip of the cooling egg cream to quell the sound.

"But now is not the time for ghost stories," Wallace Lynch decides, with a wave of his hand.

Charles welcomes the deflection.

"Have dinner with me this evening," Wallace Lynch states without prelude. Charles looks up and observes Berthold's confidence in the invitation.

"How can I refuse?" Charles asks, because he doesn't know the answer to the question. How could he refuse now that life has brought him and Berthold back together? How could he refuse as he sits here across from this man who has taken so much from him and given as much in equal turn? How could he refuse when he has no idea what is being offered, by Berthold or by God, each always conspiring to their own ends? How can he refuse? He can't.

7

Located on the Upper East Side, Michelangelo's, the restaurant where Charles meets Wallace Lynch, still possesses a fair amount of swank to its décor, though it is edging past its prime. Old Italian in style and ambiance, with dark woods and red velvets, the atmosphere bespeaks of darkness and privacy, and this explains its allure to the varied couples, of all gender and race combinations, who inhabit its tables and booths.

"Mr. Lynch has already arrived," the maître d' informs Charles, his voice intimate. "Follow me."

With steady, erect grace, he leads Charles to the back of the dining room.

Wallace rises at Charles's approach. He greets him with an outstretched hand and a controlled smile. There is a force to this handshake, a dominance, unlike earlier in the day.

"Mr. Ward," Wallace Lynch announces with exaggerated formality, speaking a touch too loud. "So glad you could join me."

Charles smiles and plays his part. "My pleasure, Mr. Lynch."

They sit. The maître d' presents Charles with his menu, then does the same to Wallace. He offers the wine list to Wallace, as well.

"Enjoy, gentlemen." The maître d' smiles upon departing with measured swiftness.

A young busboy comes over to silently fill their water glasses, then retreats with equal wordlessness.

"Do you like red wine? I never used to, but lately . . . well . . . I quite like it. But if you don't, we could have white. Or both. Whichever is fine with me."

Charles smiles. This stammering man is a stranger, but his nervous mien endears in a way the commanding Obersturmführer Berthold Werden never could. "Red would be fine."

"Good." Wallace releases a held breath, as if Charles decided something much more dire than merely the evening's wine selection. "Very good."

Charles leans in, capturing Wallace's scattered attention. "There's no need to be nervous, Mr. Lynch. Not with me, at least."

"Nervous?" Wallace questions with hyper nonchalance. "Why would I be nervous? I'm just having dinner with a friend."

Charles sits back in his chair, eyeing Wallace with a knowing smile. "Are you? Are we?"

"Yes," Wallace assures him. "Just dinner with a friend. Nothing more."

With a nod, Charles keeps his eyes trained on Wallace. "I apologize, then."

"Why ever for?"

"I believe I misunderstood your invitation," Charles confesses, though he knows he did not. Still, he sees now that Wallace Lynch requires a gentle touch. If this man didn't inhabit the body of Berthold Werden, Charles might believe him to be truly timid and scared.

How absolutely surreal this play in which he has found himself, Charles thinks.

Wallace nods at one of the waiters standing in attendance. The man, older, distinguished, refined, steps forward with a series of crisp yet smooth movements. He attends the pair with a slight tilt to his upper body, so Wallace does not have to raise his voice beyond regular speech. Wallace orders a French red, and the waiter whisks away.

"If you feel you misunderstood the invitation," Wallace queries, the innocence in his voice sounding contrived, "what did you think the invitation was for, if not dinner?"

And the cat and the mouse enter the arena, but who is which? Charles wonders.

"I suppose I sensed something more . . . interesting, shall I say?"

Wallace smiles, a breach in the levee he's pretending to hide behind. He knows the motive behind his invitation as surely as Charles does. But caution is the order of the day for a man such as Wallace Lynch, with more to lose than the headwaiter of Café Marie.

"Interesting?" Wallace seems to speculate about the options buried within the word. "Now I'm interested."

Charles laughs. "That's a start."

"You make this seem as if it should be easy," Wallace says. He glances around, possibly for the waiter bringing the wine, in need of its support.

"Well, whatever 'this' is does not need to be difficult."

As if already tired of the game, Wallace Lynch relents. "Maybe for you. You're young, a different generation, yes? For me, for men of my era . . ."

Nodding, Charles reaches across the table, Wallace watching the movement intently. Charles taps Wallace's wedding ring.

"It's what we did back then," Wallace Lynch states, as if offering a confession. "Marry young and have children, and that's that."

"People still do that."

Wallace nods. "Yes, but they don't have to, at least not so young or at all. My son is in his late thirties and is still not married. He should do so, because it might give him some focus—

but that's a different matter. However, no one looks askance at him for not being married. A different time, certainly."

Charles nods with understanding.

"You're not married," Wallace states.

"No."

"Doesn't your family wonder?" Wallace asks, returning to the subject at hand.

Charles is amazed that Berthold mentioning his family does not gut him right then and there. Merely a question asked by a man with whom he might or might not be on a date. He has never felt more cemented in his identity as Charles Ward than he does at this moment.

"I do not have any family," Charles reports. "Orphaned at a young age."

The news doesn't startle Wallace as it might someone else. But he offers a solemn nod. "I am sorry to hear that."

With a curt wave, Charles assures him, "It was long ago."

Much to Wallace's relief, the waiter returns and presents the bottle of wine for inspection. Wallace approves it with a glance. After the tasting, also approved, the waiter pours the wine with great aplomb. He would make a wonderful addition to Café Marie, Charles thinks, should he ever come looking for a position there.

"And your family?" Charles continues once the waiter has departed. "Your wife, your son . . ."

"A daughter, as well." Wallace smiles.

"And your daughter. Are you a happy family?"

Wallace considers the question. "It is a family. Same as any, I would suspect. What is that quote about families?"

"From Tolstoy? All happy families are alike?" Charles offers.

"Yes, that's the one."

"But each unhappy family is unhappy in its own way," Charles says, finishing the quote.

With a slight twinge, Wallace sips at his wine before taking a full drink.

"Were you ever in love, Mr. Lynch?"

Wallace Lynch flinches ever so slightly. Or is it Berthold who flinches? Charles isn't sure how separate or entwined the men are.

"That's quite a bold question, don't you think?" Wallace determines. "We have only just met, Charles, and I'm to confess my heart to you? You kids today are entirely to open and free. It's rather unnerving."

"I'm hardly a kid," Charles assures him. "And isn't it easier to speak freely with a stranger, someone you doesn't know enough to judge you?"

Wallace considers this rationale for a moment. "You might be right. Very well. Have I ever been in love? I suppose when we married. At least I believed I was. And in time, I came to love her as my wife, but . . ."

Shaking his head, Charles explains, "No, not with your wife. With a man. Were you ever in love with another man?"

With a quick glance about them, Wallace tenses. "I beg your pardon?"

Charles smiles at the flustering. If this is an act by Berthold, it verges on perfection.

"Come now," Charles teases. "I thought we were beyond the game."

Wallace starts to protest, but Charles stops him. "Mr. Lynch, we both know why you invited me to dinner, and we both know why I accepted," Charles continues. "I am not married, because I am not attracted to women. As you have said, it is a different time, a different generation. I had no family pressuring me, no traditions to adhere to. I've been alone for a long time, so I make my own choices. I've been lucky."

"Yes, you have," Wallace agrees, a grade of jealousy coloring his voice. "And you have been in love? With a man?"

"I believe so. Yes," Charles confesses. "Long ago there was someone."

Wallace nods but doesn't press the matter. He escapes his companion's gaze by taking a moment to butter a roll, though he does not eat it. The butter glistens in the dim light.

"There was a boy," Wallace confesses. "Well, not a boy. He was a young man."

"And you loved him?"

"Yes, very much." Pain cracks through his words. "His name was Charles, as well. I just realized you have his name."

"I do."

"And to be honest, you remind me of him. You have since I first saw you at the café weeks ago."

"Yes?" Charles feigns surprise. "In what way?"

Wallace shakes his head. He takes a gulp of wine. "A feeling."

"And what happened to your young man?"

"This was years ago, as well, during the war. We were separated. I would think he did not make it."

Charles lets the moment sit. He reflects upon that long-ago morning outside Bayreuth, Germany, the last time they saw each other before fate or happenstance brought them to this restaurant. He wonders if Mr. Lynch also recalls what happened next: how Berthold turned on his heels and returned to his family, who were waiting for him in the car. He knew Berthold cared for him. Why else let him live? But loved him? That has never occurred to Charles.

"I chose my wife and children, you see," Wallace explains. "How could I not?"

"Did he love you?"

Here there is a break to Wallace's composure with a visible slump to his shoulders. "He should not have, if he did."

Wallace finishes his wine and pours another glass. Charles notices a mild tremor to Wallace's hands.

"Why are we speaking of this, anyway?" Wallace asks with mild perturbance. "Ghosts. Always ghosts with you."

With a chuckle, Charles stands and removes his suit jacket. He places it on the back of his chair, then retakes his seat. "Every once in a while, ghosts come back to life, Berthold."

"God, I hope not," Wallace Lynch states before he suddenly understands what Charles has said. He tenses visibly, but the old German officer within offers a restrained smile at the same time. "I do not understand, Charles. Please explain."

Charles leans toward Wallace, then whispers, one word at a time, "I know who you are."

The man forces a soft chuckle, as if he is dealing with a not-bright child. "Of course. I am Wallace Lynch. I told you this earlier. Are you confused?"

Charles admires the conviction, the dedication, and the easy air of dismissal. But, then again, he would expect no less. But he senses the panic searing through Berthold at this moment of exposure. There is no turning back. The name has been uttered and cannot be taken back, a summoning as deadly as a call to Beelzebub himself.

"No, actually, it is you who is confused, Berthold," Charles states matter-of-factly. "My dear Obersturmführer Berthold Werden."

A visible jolt shocks through Berthold. His body stiffens in challenge, chest pushing forward as he breathes deep and his spine straightening. His entire being squares as his stern shoulders lift, then roll back. His head rises to face Charles with naked anger and determination. There is something practiced yet natural in the presentation. Charles is now sitting across the table from Berthold, unmasked.

"And you want what?" Berthold questions. He answers his own query in a tone of condescension toward Charles. "Money, of course."

A laugh. "I don't want money."

"Please, not revenge," Berthold chides with disdain. "How boring. Avenging whom? Parents, siblings, all the Jews of the world? Trust me, dear boy, money is much more practical."

"You haven't figured it out," Charles states with wonderment. "You don't know who I am."

"You are Charles Ward," Berthold states. "A made-up name, I'm sure."

"Yes. A made-up name," Charles states as he unbuttons, then begins to roll up his left shirtsleeve.

Berthold watches Charles's movements closely, betraying irritation at the dramatics of the display. He is a businessman, after all, so he wants to get to the business at hand.

When his sleeve rises past his forearm, Charles stretches out his arm in full supine display. Even in the ambient light of the restaurant, the scar rising from the flesh is visible. Berthold casually examines the arm, but without comprehension. Then the moment of realization finally washes over him. He emits a sharp breath, then reaches out to touch the scar, his fingers tracing the raised rectangle of flesh. Without looking up from the scar, he utters, "Charles."

PART II

BAYREUTH, GERMANY 1944

8

Berthold hands Charles the papers.

They stand beyond the car in which the rest of the Werden family waits. Frau Werden looks away from her husband and the boy, as she calls him, though he is far from a boy now. He wasn't a boy when he entered their home at seventeen. Charles glances over to see her staring in the direction opposite to them, staring into the desolate German countryside. Charles can picture her hidden face, stern and pink with anger, her lips tightened in frustration and, most of all, jealousy.

In the backseat, the son, Geert, reads a book, as if the family is on any other outing to the country. Marlene, sweet, dramatic Marlene, feigns sleep to hide her tears.

Berthold has stopped the car outside a large, austere brick house on the German side of the Sudetenland border. Beyond them the countryside, ravaged by winter, lingers under a dismal sunrise. Trees, stripped of their leaves and bark, stretch naked, long-stemmed arms into the ashen sky. Like claws, they reach upward, as if to shred the gray cloth of winter cover, in search of the hidden sun. The house is grand but is also a victim of time and the harsh German weather.

"Bayreuth is near?" Charles asks.

Berthold glances about, orienting himself, then nods to the west. "That way, about three kilometers, I would think. Maybe five?"

Charles looks in that direction but sees only more barren land. He turns back and looks at the papers.

He is still "Charles," as he has been for the past three years, but Berthold has altered his surname.

"Charles Werden."

"Yes," Berthold confirms. "This is who you are now."

Just as he becomes one of them, Charles thinks bitterly, they abandon him.

But Charles does not mention this. It will do no good. Berthold has caved to his wife's threats.

"You have made me fifteen?" Charles questions, reading the paper.

"That will give you at least two years before they must release you."

"I am too big for fifteen."

"Big for fifteen but small for twenty. It will be fine," Berthold assures him.

Charles glances at the house. "Must I?"

They both know the answer, so Charles does not expect or receive a response to this question.

"Remember all I told you."

Charles nods.

"And take care of that." Berthold nods toward Charles's left arm, the bandage peeking from the sleeve of his coat. "Change the dressing often and apply salve two or three times a day."

Berthold places his hand on Charles's cheek and lets it linger, knowing his wife is not looking. Charles smiles to assure Berthold he understands. How could he not?

Berthold nods and turns on his heels, crisp and sure, a soldier's retreat. He walks back to the car. The engine rumbles and rattles, as if the car is anxious to get back on the road and distance the family from this trivial nonsense.

Charles watches, hoping for Berthold to stop, to change his mind, to defy her, take him with them, but of course, he does not. The car pulls away. In the side mirror, Charles finds Berthold, his eyes fixed wide on the dirt road of the German countryside. Berthold doesn't look back. Only Geert does, his tongue sticking out from the back window.

9

Standing outside the orphanage, Charles considers his options. If he plays his part well, he might have safety, at least for a while. But if he doesn't . . .

He examines the papers again, reviewing the information of his new life until the details are in his bones and he can recite them without prompting doubt or suspicion. He takes up his small satchel, one of Geert's, which contains a change of clothes and a few Reichsmark Berthold slipped him when Frau Werden wasn't looking. Charles also packed the shaving razor Berthold gave him, as well as the used bar of Antica Barbieria Colla shaving soap. How he is to pass for fifteen when he is already shaving, he has no idea.

To the west lies Bayreuth, Berthold's childhood home. Charles feels an odd kinship vibrate through him, as if the town belongs to him by some odd sense of association. Beyond the orphanage, out toward the horizon, thistle grows rampant. It juts out of the hard ground, tall and thick and impenetrable. Farther east, fields of winter-dead grass cover the barren land. The expanse stretches unbroken, except a stray tree here and there, before rising into a grouping of low mountains, impossibly far away.

Charles contemplates the dirt road. They drove for hours, most of the night, and he's not sure how far he is from Oświęcim. Not that he would return there or go anywhere else in Poland. Then Charles realizes the moment is his. Up until now, his life has been subject to the will of others: his parents, the Nazis, Berthold. He could easily knock on the orphanage door, tell his woeful tale, and step inside for the next three years of his life. Or . . .

He turns toward Bayreuth.

As he enters the town, its grandeur reminds Charles of Prague, though on a smaller scale. Bayreuth's buildings imitate the intricate Baroque style that dominates Prague. A church boasts statues of trumpeting cherubs and winged angels, sentries against evil. Municipal buildings appear to be pedestals for the gods of mythology, who stare off into the distance. The feeling of the décor oppresses yet also comforts.

Charles wanders the quiet morning streets, his footfalls echoing in the spaces between the buildings. In a cobblestoned town square, he settles on the edge of a fountain, dormant for the winter, adorned by a cadre of stone warriors straddling dangerous lions and wild stallions in an act of fierce battle. Around him, Bayreuth wakes. A delivery truck trundles along the cobbled streets. A group of men trudge to work. Charles picks up the smell of fresh coffee and pastries, which spurs his hunger.

Charles counts his money, almost three hundred in Reichsmarks and Reichspfennigs. Berthold has been generous. To be honest, Charles has no idea what anything costs but assumes he can afford coffee and a buttered roll, maybe a splurge of jam, if available. Down the narrow street, a small konditorei stands open for business.

The konditorei is warm. Charles doesn't realize how cold he is until he steps into its comforting heat of the small dining room. A bell chimes above him, bringing forth a woman from the back area. Tall, thinner than she should be, likely from a lack of proper nourishment, the woman appears in her midthirties. A bright floral scarf contains the woman's brown curls, pushed back from her haggard yet gentle face. Wiping her hands on a dishrag, she walks up to the counter with a smile. But her eyes reflect the weary resignation of war.

"*Guten Morgen, gnädige Frau,*" Charles offers with a forced casualness that belies his nerves, for what if she recognizes him as a filthy Jew pig? What if she rings for *die Polizei* the moment he turns his back? Charles keeps his distance, as if his Jewishness is a rancid odor only Germans can smell.

"*Guten Morgen,*" the woman returns, her voice bright, though not exactly cheerful. "How can I help you?"

Charles hems. He realizes he has never before been in a konditorei by himself. He has never ordered a coffee or a buttered roll with or without a splurge of jam.

"I'm afraid we don't have much today," the woman apologizes, as if that is the reason for Charles's hesitation. "I do have coffee, though, better than the *Ersatzkaffee* that most of the other shops serve." She leans over the counter and offers a conspiratorial wink. "I have a connection."

"Coffee would be good, *bitte, gnädige Frau,*" Charles ventures.

"You're new here, in Bayreuth, yes?" the woman asks as she prepares Charles's coffee. She speaks with her back to him. "At least I've not seen you before. Are you visiting? We receive so few visitors these days. Oh, I'm so tired of this war."

Half turning to Charles, she smiles and throws him another wink. "Don't tell the Führer."

Charles can't help but smile. "I won't."

Setting the coffee down on the counter, she chatters on. "I

love Germany, of course. Heil Hitler and all that, but business has gotten so bad lately. I'll be lucky to have five or six customers all day. A year ago, we were overrun, couldn't keep up. That'll be four marks, which is too expensive, I know, but coffee is so hard to get these days, with or without a connection."

Charles likes the woman immediately; she makes him feel comfortable. He can't remember the last time he's had a breezy conversation. A customer and a konditorei worker chatting. Even though he knows he shouldn't, he can't help but like her. He hands her a five-mark note.

"You don't say much, do you?" the woman asks. "Don't let my treacherous talk scare you. I'm tired. I've been up for hours already, and the day's only begun."

"You don't scare me," Charles promises.

"Good." The woman holds out Charles's change of one mark, but he waves it away. She nods and tucks it into her apron. "What's your name? I am Frau Hueber."

She extends her hand over the counter. Charles takes it.

"You look more like a fräulein than a Frau."

Blushing, she takes her hand back. "You're sweet, but I'm an old married lady."

"I am Charles."

"*Hallo*, Charles," Frau Hueber chimes.

Charles smiles. "*Hallo*, Frau Hueber."

Frau Hueber nudges the mug. "Sit before your coffee gets cold. It's not good cold."

Charles selects a table by the window and sips at his coffee, which is better than the coffee that found its way to Auschwitz and then to the Werden house.

"Sorry we don't have sugar," Frau Hueber calls from the counter. "What little I get, I must use for the pastries. We do have milk, if you'd like. It's powdered but better than nothing."

Charles doesn't want her to bother. "It's fine. Thank you."

After coming from behind the counter, Frau Hueber places a

creamer of milk on the table. "I can tell you don't drink your coffee black. I have a sense about these things."

With a sheepish grin, Charles sparingly adds a drop of milk to the coffee, not even enough to change its color.

"Put in as much as you'd like. Powder I can get." Frau Hueber laughs. She sits in the chair across from him and stares brazenly. "You're a mystery, Charles. I can tell."

Charles averts his eyes. "I'm no mystery."

"But you are." Frau Hueber contradicts him. "A new face in Bayreuth, especially in the midst of war, is mysterious."

"There's nothing to tell, please," Charles begs. He tries to recall key points from the biography that Berthold created for him. The tale clusters in his head as a jumble of out-of-sequence notes. He snatches at something to offer her. "I am from Wieden."

Frau Hueber nods. "I have heard of Wieden. South, yes? And what is a young man like you doing so far from home, Charles?"

Frau Hueber walks back behind the counter. Charles watches, puzzled. She returns, carrying two plates. She places one in front of Charles and the other on her side of the table. On each plate sits a piece of pastry. "I got hold of a few apples the other day. Not the best, but good enough to make a strudel for the first time in months."

Charles reaches for his money; Frau Hueber waves him away.

"They will only go to waste with no customers, so what does it matter if they are bought or given?" She picks at the flaky golden crust of her pastry, her thin fingers peeling apart the layers. "Eat. Tell me, why are you not in Wieden?"

Charles stalls by tasting the strudel. "Butter?"

"*Ein Ersatz,*" she confesses. "But better than most substitutes."

Nodding, Charles takes another bite. He can taste the inferior products, different from those in the pastry at the Werden home. Berthold pilfered fresh ingredients from the officers' supply at Auschwitz, including real butter and milk and actual eggs. Charles could only imagine the ire of Frau Werden if she had to produce eggs from yellow powder and water. Still, the pastry is good, the apples fresher than Frau Hueber suggests, the cinnamon lending an earthy bite.

"Are you running away from home, Charles?" Frau Hueber asks with a mischievous smile. "If so, can I go with you?"

Returning her smile as best he can, he shakes his head. "No, I did not run away. Not really."

Her eyes widen. "See! Mystery!"

Goodness, but he likes this Frau Hueber, the comfort and ease of her, even with her prodding. Charles wants to entrust her with his secrets, but she is a German, and he is her enemy (or vice versa, he isn't sure which). So, he recites the story of how he ended up in Bayreuth, as crafted by Berthold.

"The Jews came at night while my family slept. Half a dozen of them, mostly men but a couple of women, as well. Maybe escaped from a nearby camp. They dragged us from our beds, my father and mother, my older brother. They tied us up. They beat my father and brother without mercy. Some of the men did things to my mother in the other room. I heard her screams. I will never forget her screams. Then they killed them all in front of me, making me watch. The men wanted to kill me, too, but the women stopped them. I do not know why."

Here Charles pushes up the sleeve of his coat and reveals his bandaged forearm. Marlene applied a fresh bandage during the car ride, but already hieroglyphics of spotting blood have seeped up to the surface, revealing a language he does not understand. Frau Hueber reaches out, as if to touch his arm, but doesn't. Her hand halts in the air, fingers glazed with the sheen of the ersatz butter from the strudel.

"They burned my flesh," he states gravely. "They marked me like the Nazis mark the Jews."

"Oh, Charles," Frau Hueber sighs.

He looks up to find tears welling in her eyes. She believes him! He feels both relieved and guilty.

"It's still bleeding," she remarks and gently unravels the wrappings. The top layer of bandage falls away, but the second layer clings to the blood that leaches from the wound. Frau Hueber fingers the gauze with gentle determination, peeling the gossamer from the muck of the wound, until she reveals the burnt flesh, ugly and raw. She gasps again.

"They used a fireplace poker," Charles declares, and his body shudders at the remembrance of the searing pain. "They said I was one of them now, *ein Jude.*"

Frau Hueber swallows hard. "We must clean this proper before it gets infected. I have ointment. I burn myself all the time. Come."

In the kitchen, pots and pans are piled in the sink, and baking sheets and serving dishes are scattered about the counters. Drifts of flour, globs of icing, and mounds of nuts and dried fruit litter the surfaces. Charles looks at Frau Hueber, who offers a shy smile.

"Baking is messy business, Charles, especially when you're on your own."

"It's only you?" Charles asks.

Frau Hueber begins cleaning and redressing Charles's wound. "And my daughter, Elsbeth. But at six she plays more than helps."

She applies salve to the wound. The coolness calms the blistered and fevered flesh. Her touch is tender as she lightly smears the salve onto his arm, ensuring not to press or anger the injury further. With fresh gauze, Frau Hueber wraps the wound and tapes the ends in place. Charles lowers his jacket sleeve.

"*Danke schön.*"

Frau Hueber waves his gratitude away. "Where do you go now?"

Charles shrugs. "I don't know. I have not thought very far ahead. I just could not stay in Wieden."

Frau Hueber regards Charles a moment, then offers a curt bob of her head. "You will stay here. Help me in the konditorei. I can't pay, but you can sleep in the storeroom as long as you like, until you know where you are going."

In the harsh, unrelenting light of the kitchen, the Frau appears even more tired. The dull gray bruising of the skin under her eyes makes her look drained and fraught.

"*Danke*, Frau Hueber. I am grateful."

She offers a hopeful smile and releases a breath Charles didn't realize she was holding. "That is good, Charles. That is very good. Do you have your papers?"

"Of course." Charles hands over the papers Berthold created for him.

"I do not care, but the soldiers in town do," she explains. "If they ask, I need to know they are in order."

She examines his papers with care and scrutiny. "Werden. I know this name."

Charles draws a cautious breath. "Yes. My father was from Bayreuth. That is why I came here."

"What was your father's name?" she inquires, not looking up from the paper.

"Werden . . ." Charles dodges before confessing, "Berthold . . . Berthold Werden."

Frau Hueber nods. "I remember his name from school. He was older, but I knew his name."

Distress seizes Charles. "My father did not speak of his family often. Are they still here? Maybe I should stay with them?"

"They left long before the war. I do not know where," she says.

Charles nods with hidden relief.

Frau Hueber has him retrieve a cot from the cellar to set up in the storeroom. "Not the most comfortable . . ."

Charles laughs. "I have slept on worse, I'm sure."

"Very good," Frau Hueber replies "Rest. Tomorrow we begin."

With that, Frau Hueber welcomes Charles to his new world.

10

At first, Charles's work at Frau Hueber's konditorei is the same as his chores in the Werden house, though without the constant threat of a beating, so he adapts in quick time. He spends his days cleaning up after Frau Hueber in the kitchen and after the customers in the dining room. He washes dishes and wipes down tables; he restocks shelves and accepts the sparse deliveries that arrive each week.

Like most Germans, Frau Hueber shops at the state-run grocery for the basic goods of daily life, but it is on the black market that she negotiates for specialty goods and ingredients. Once Charles registers with the city office, he turns over his ration booklet to Frau Hueber.

"Every little bit helps," she informs him. "The more ration cards I can use to barter, the better."

In quick time, he assists with the early morning baking. Under Frau Hueber's tutelage, he learns to prepare the pastries for the day, based on ingredients she secured the previous day. She mothers as she demonstrates handling different types of dough. Some, like with the heartier breads, require an aggressive kneading. Others, such as the light, flaky dough of the *Franzbrötchen*, need a delicate and deft hand.

"This was Herr Hueber's favorite," Frau Hueber says, reminiscing over the *Franzbrötchen*, then offers a dry chuckle. "I had to travel all the way to Hamburg to learn from his mother!"

Charles knows from the way Frau Hueber speaks his name, with measured and concentrated sureness, that her husband is dead. He does not inquire after the details. He will allow her the time to reveal her secrets as she chooses.

Elsbeth, Frau Hueber's daughter, is a cheery six-year-old with bright eyes. She reminds Charles of his sister Dussie when they were young and still in Kladno. Elsbeth scurries and skips about the konditorei, as if she knows nothing of war. Sometimes she plays waitress, taking coffee orders, bringing out pastries, and wiping down tables.

Within days she takes to calling Charles *Onkel*. Charles likes the title for he knows he will never be anyone's true uncle.

Charles prefers to keep to himself in the kitchen. He enjoys the warmth and aromas. He likes the tools used for cooking and baking, which fill the drawers and line the shelves and hang on the wall. He likes the feel of the heavy metal pans and the whisks and spoons and ladles and cookie cutters. He especially likes the copper pots that dangle from hooks in the ceiling, clanging like church bells whenever he fetches a pot to prepare *Dampfnudeln* or a saucepan to make caramel.

Most often he works in the kitchen alone, but on weekends, when not in school, Elsbeth will wander in from the dining room, her eyes glazed with boredom.

"Can I help, Onkel?" she asks with reverence, because she knows the kitchen is not a place for play.

Charles teaches her to form the *Rumkugeln*, a perfect task for tiny hands. Standing on a stool next to him, Elsbeth is meticulous, ensuring each rum ball is uniform before placing it on a serving plate. Soon she has assembled a pyramid of chocolate treats.

"What next, Onkel Charles?" She beams, eager to learn, eager to help. Elsbeth is so much like Dussie, Charles wants to cry and take her in his arms and tell her he is sorry, as he never did when Dussie was alive. When they were too busy being annoyed big brother and annoying little sister to realize anything beyond the pettiness of childhood—and then it was too late.

Squelching the tears that churn inside, he shows Elsbeth how to soak the rum balls in the chocolate bath prepared with cocoa powder, beet sugar, and shortening. In perfect mimicry, she releases them with great tenderness into the bath. One, two, three at a time slip into the smooth, liquid chocolate before she fishes them out with a slotted spoon. She lets the chocolate rain back into the bowl and places them upon a chilled baking sheet.

"I'm glad you're here, Onkel," Elsbeth states as she chases a *Rumkugel* swimming in the bowl of chocolate. "Mama likes that you're here, too."

Charles leans toward her. "I like it, too."

In the evening, Charles joins Frau Hueber and Elsbeth upstairs in their apartment for dinner. At the small kitchen table, they dine on whatever is available that day at the ration center: potatoes most often, sometimes carrots or peas or kale, a small portion of beef or bacon if they are lucky. Frau Hueber is not as good a cook as his mother was, or even as good as Frau Werden, but she treats Charles as an adult, even though she believes him to be fifteen. She discusses the war and Germany's prospects of prevailing and the consequences if it does not. She asks for his opinions and listens respectfully. At first, he looks at her as a sister; Frau Hueber brings to mind his sister Zofia and the woman she might have been one day. But soon enough, he realizes they are friends, something he never anticipated.

After two months in Bayreuth with Frau Hueber and Elsbeth, Charles has forgotten about moving on. Despite being in the midst of the enemy, Charles comes to like Bayreuth. An oversized hamlet is quaint and charming in many ways. Even in the gray of December and January, Bayreuth cannot hide its colors. While most of its buildings tend toward light sand-colored stone offset by bright reddish-orange terra-cotta roofing and forest-green awnings, here and there an apartment house will be painted buttercup yellow or sunset orange, adding whimsy and joy to the scene. Charles loves to stroll the narrow streets when he is not working, enjoying the fresh air and the freedom.

In his first weeks in Bayreuth, Charles is stopped repeatedly by the soldiers constantly patrolling the town streets. Each time it is a different set of soldiers, always in pairs. Within a month of his arrival, Charles determines he has been stopped by every soldier in Bayreuth.

"You there!" they call out. *"Komm her!"*

Charles approaches with his papers unpocketed and outstretched. He stands before them for inspection as they assess him with military scrutiny and review the thin pieces of paper. When satisfied, they wave him away as if he is a pest. During the first few inspections, he panics, his heart thundering with fear. He fidgets and shuffles. Sweat breaks the surface of his forehead and upper lip, and he wipes at his face with the sleeve of his coat.

"What is the matter with you, boy?" a soldier asks, more irritated than suspicious.

Charles swallows, but his throat is dry. "I have been ill, *mein Herr.*"

The soldier pulls back as he returns the papers to Charles. "Go home and rest."

"Drink hot tea," his partner advises.

"My mother put honey in mine," the first soldier comments. "Always helped with a sore throat. Do you have a sore throat, boy?"

Charles shakes his head. "No, *mein Herr.*"

"That is good," says the partner, "since there is no honey."

They continue their patrol, leaving Charles on the sidewalk, still shaking from panic.

Eventually, the soldiers come to know him as another resident and stop checking his papers, leaving him free to walk the cobblestoned streets as any other German. He nods to the men and women who recognize him from the konditorei or whom he passes with frequency in his wanderings. They are generous with returned nods and a friendly "Guten Tag" or a routine "Heil Hitler," which Charles returns. Soon, Charles determines ruefully that Germans are very nice, as long as you are one of them.

While he explores every street and alley and nook and cranny of the small town, Charles most often finds his way to the *Hofgarten* by the New Palace. Despite the war raging beyond its borders, Bayreuth has maintained the gardens, ensuring they remain pristine yet natural, as if touched only by the hands of God. Charles wanders the meticulous grounds, winding along the maze of paths among the flower beds, dormant in the winter, the sculpted bushes and trees along the canal, and the various statues, which appear out of nowhere, as if ghosts. But no matter the path he might take, he always ends up at the gazebo. A sense of security fills him as he sits beneath the gazebo's bright azure-blue dome. Snow-white columns—gilded at the top with brilliant gold—support the grand canopy. On occasion, when he feels most secure, happy even, he wonders about Berthold and the Werden family. He wonders where they ended up. He wonders if they were captured or if they made their escape as planned. Each time he is unsure which scenario he wishes to be true. He wonders about his own fate— what will become of him when he is discovered?—for he knows it is only a matter of time. While he likes Frau Hueber and Elsbeth, possibly loves them as he would his own family, and the life he is creating in Bayreuth, he knows he cannot stay. Every day in Bayreuth, in Germany, is a risk.

One afternoon, Charles enters the town library. Immediately, he is overwhelmed by the smell of the place, deep and earthy and comforting. After nodding to the attendant at the information desk, he wanders the aisles. With the shelves packed from top to bottom and side to side with books, his eyes have a difficult time focusing on any one title. He reaches out a hand and glides his fingers gingerly along the spines of the books, feeling the textures of the covers and the indents of the words embossed in the cardboard and leather-like wrappings. Charles can't remember the last time he was in a library, at school, before the war, most likely. He has not read a book in years.

Returning to the attendant at the front of the library, a stern yet disinterested woman, Charles requests an atlas.

"The maps of Germany are in the geography section, aisle twenty-seven."

"*Danke, meine Dame.* And the maps of the world? They are there, as well?"

The woman lifts her head from her work to peer at Charles over the rims of her glasses. Her eyes narrow with scrutiny until she finally nods. "*Ja*, they are there."

The attendant's glare follows him to aisle twenty-seven, where Charles selects the one world atlas to be found. Hiding at a table in the back, he opens the dense tome and sees the full scope of the earth, truly, for the first time in his life. It spreads across two pages. He finds Czechoslovakia, then Kladno and Terezín. He finds Poland and Oświęcim. He finds Germany and Bayreuth. Stunned, he realizes he has lived a very small life: in a small town, a small ghetto, a small cellar, all within a modest three-thousand-kilometer radius.

Charles sits back in his chair, overwhelmed by it all.

From an imaginary perch above the earth, he sees himself as the crumb he is. He is indistinguishable from any other: the attendant at the information desk, Frau Hueber and Elsbeth, Berthold and the Werden family. Indistinguishable from his family, dead and buried in their graves in Poland.

The thought of the immense world immobilizes him. In the

atlas, he surveys his options. Everywhere looks so close yet far away. Bayreuth is not that far from the Czechoslovakian border, with Kladno some two hundred kilometers to the east. But he cannot go back home. Not that he thinks of Kladno as his home any longer. If he considers the idea of home, he imagines the Werden house, but he won't go back there, no matter if the Russians have arrived or not. To the northeast of Kladno sits Terezín. He thinks of Eliáš and wishes he could be with him again, even if it means going back to the ghetto. But you can enter the lion's cage only so many times before your luck runs out.

He moves his finger out of Czechoslovakia and to the west. He knows the Germans are in France and Belgium and Luxembourg. He believes they are in the Netherlands, as well, and up into Denmark. What of Britain? The Germans have not conquered England, yet. But would Britain take him in as a German? "But I am only a 'paper' German," he will tell them, one that exists only because of fabricated documents. But what other kind of German is there? We are all only what our papers say we are.

With no other choice, he decides, he will risk it. Surveying the map, the various routes, he determines he will need to find his way to the port in Antwerp and from there . . . he isn't sure, but it's a start.

Returning to the konditorei, he advises himself not to tell Frau Hueber of his plans. He doesn't want to add more concerns to her already heavy load. So, he will continue to wake at his usual time every morning to start the pastries and prepare the café. He will continue to join Frau Hueber and Elsbeth for dinner in their apartment at the end of the workday. He will still wander the streets of Bayreuth. He will nod to those he passes or will exchange pleasantries. He will accept the few Reichsmarks and Reichspfennigs Frau Hueber offers for his work. He will continue to add them to the monies Berthold gave him. But eventually, one morning Frau Hueber will come downstairs to start her day and will find him gone. She will find the kitchen cold and quiet. His place in the storeroom will be tidy and empty, as if he had never been there. Panic will grasp at her chest, but she will not allow it to take hold. She will need to start the ovens and the coffee and get the doughs ready. She will need to prepare powdered eggs for Elsbeth and herself for breakfast and prepare the dining room in time for opening. She may miss him and wonder where he is, but only for a short while, because he will not have been the first. Happens all the time during war, doesn't it? People disappearing?

11

Each night, as he readies the pots and pans, Charles considers the next day his last in Bayreuth. The following morning, he will leave, he tells himself. But each morning he wakes with the weight of the day's responsibilities and the dogmatic call of routine, which edge him out of bed and into the kitchen.

I'll just get the pastries started, he thinks, *so Frau Hueber is not so overwhelmed when she finds me gone.*

But soon enough he is lost in his work, and Frau Hueber is greeting him with a comforting "Guten Morgen, Charles. Hast du gut geschlafen?"

He sighs and tells her, "*Ja.* I slept well. And you?" And the day proceeds as the day before and the day before that.

One evening, after clearing the dinner plates and sending Elsbeth off to bed, Frau Hueber produces a bottle of wine.

"I splurged," she admits with guilt as she presents the bottle to Charles. "We've earned a little treat, don't you think?"

"I'll get the glasses."

Charles enjoys the deep red body of the wine, which hints at berries and spice. Pepper, he thinks.

"Have you had wine before, Charles?" Frau Hueber asks as she swirls the wine in her breakfast juice glass.

"Once, a long time ago." Charles recalls an evening in Kladno with his mother and Havel. It feels like it was decades ago, though it must be no more than three years. "This is much better."

"It is good, I must admit."

More silence, comfortable and friendly, as they settle deeper in their seats. As Charles watches, Frau Hueber appears lost as she fingers the rim of her glass.

"Is everything okay, Frau Hueber?" Charles inquires, bringing her back to their evening. It is, of course, an inane question to ask anyone in a country at war.

With a quick shake of her head, she smiles. "I drifted."

"You're tired, I'm sure."

She shrugs.

Another moment of silence passes.

"I lied, Charles," Frau Hueber confesses. "I didn't splurge on the wine. I've had this bottle for two years."

Charles waits for further explanation, but Frau Hueber lets her finger continue to trace the rim of the glass. She watches, as if falling under a hypnotist's spell. He wants to say her finger skates the edge as if a figure skater gliding over pure ice, but her hands are too rough, too raw, far from delicate from too much work day in and day out.

"Today is my anniversary," Frau Hueber discloses, a shadowed smile playing at her lips. "Herr Hueber and I married nine years ago today."

Unsure how to respond, Charles allows Frau Hueber her moment to remember, maybe to grieve that she is celebrating with Charles and not her husband. A gloom seeps up to the surface of the moment. Frau Hueber pales, her skin graying, as she grapples with her emotions.

"He was to come home a little over two years ago." She

speaks in that monotone voice people find within themselves when they report distressing facts, strained of all emotion. "A quick weekend, mind you, not permanent. We hadn't seen each other since right after Elsbeth was born. I bought the wine for his return."

Another pause in the reporting as she takes a sip.

"He died in Africa," she reports with a good hint of incredulity. "Can you imagine? This man who was born and raised in Bayreuth dying in some place called Tunisia. Amazing."

Nodding, Charles could only say, "I've never heard of Tunisia."

"I had to look it up on the map," Frau Hueber admits. "It's in the northern part of Africa, on the coast across from Italy. Why our troops were there, I have no idea. What does Hitler need with Africa? Or Italy? Or France? None of it makes sense. I don't understand war, Charles. Not at all."

And Charles wants to school her as Berthold taught him, explain to her that war is never about people but always about land. But he knows that won't explain why Herr Hueber died. The land was never going to be his, so why should he be the one who died for it?

Tears slip down Frau Hueber's cheek, and she wipes at them with irritation. "I'm sorry, Charles. This was to be a relaxing evening."

She takes up her glass and offers a silent toast. While she cheers to the life and death of Herr Hueber, Charles offers a quick prayer for his parents and sisters. Then he and Frau Hueber spend the rest of the evening, as long as the bottle continues to hold wine, in quiet peace.

12

In the end, Charles never makes the decision to leave Bayreuth.

With early April comes the slow release of winter. The sky clears to blues brighter than Charles remembers at any time in his life. The vibrant greens of the grasses and trees radiate with perfection. The ecstatic yellows and reds and lilacs and whites of the flowers burst from the corpse of winter, bathing Bayreuth in a phantasmagoria of color and fragrance. And Charles decides to accept it all. It is not a conscious decision. He does not state it aloud, not even to himself. The only evidence is that he stops actively thinking that the next day will be his last in Bayreuth.

He is content with the decision. He breathes fully, as if coming up to the surface after a deep dive in a bottomless ocean. His greetings to fellow Germans when strolling about the town are more genuine. Though others might not notice the change, Charles feels the difference. His chest does not tighten as they approach. His nerves don't jangle out of fear an inconsequential exchange will reveal his true identity. Instead, he greets each passerby with a sincere "Guten Tag." He stops and engages in full conversations, no matter how banal, chatting about the weather, about how lovely the flowers are. He discusses the latest movie at the movie house (usually German propaganda) and gossips about so-and-so flirting with that shopgirl or so-and-so who got too drunk at the biergarten the other night.

"You're quite chipper these days, Charles," Frau Hueber remarks one afternoon. "It is good to see."

With a blush, Charles smiles. "I am enjoying the weather."

It is early afternoon, not quite time for the after-lunch customers, those who eat their meager meals at home, then splurge for a sweet treat at the konditorei, so the place is empty. Charles and Frau Hueber sit by the window, a shared piece of stollen, buttered and panfried the way Herr Hueber liked it, between them. They don't chat, merely sit with each other. Theirs is a comfortable silence between friends.

A droning commences, like the sound of a bee close to the ear. Frau Hueber cocks her head toward the street.

"You hear it, too?" Charles asks, setting down his fork.

They step out onto the sidewalk. Up and down the street, their neighbors exit their businesses and homes, as well. All eyes lift to the blue sky.

"*Was ist das?*" Herr Kraenzel inquires of them, standing in the doorway of his dry goods store two doors down.

"We are not sure, Herr Kraenzel," Frau Hueber admits. "Charles?"

From down the street a man screams incoherently and waves his arms.

"Who is that?" Herr Kraenzel asks, squinting his eyes.

Someone else, closer to them, translates, saying everyone must go back inside. To find safety.

"Safety?" Herr Kraenzel asks Frau Hueber and Charles. "Safety from what?"

In answer, a plane roars and swoops low overhead. Herr Kraenzel and Frau Hueber and Charles and the others who line the sidewalk instinctively duck as the plane's shadow dives at them before soaring past. Another plane follows, equally as low. Then two more thunder past in rapid succession.

"They're not ours," Charles observes as he seizes Frau Hueber by the arm and pulls her into the konditorei.

In the distance, the first bombs fall. The earth shudders. The floor vibrates, and walls and windows tremble. Dishes and coffee cups rattle on shelves. Charles's bones rattle in his body. More bombs hit, still in the distance—but for how long?

"Elsbeth!" Frau Hueber screams.

The desperation in her eyes reminds Charles of his mother on that long-ago morning in the fields of Oświęcim, Poland. Charles has always thought his mother panicked for herself, but now, looking into the eyes of Frau Hueber, who wants only to get to her daughter to protect her from the bombs falling on their small town, he realizes his mother panicked because she realized she could not save her daughters.

"Hurry!" Charles orders as they rush out.

In the street, the attack shakes and shatters throughout Bayreuth. Charles, leading Frau Hueber, hugs the sides of buildings as they skirt down alleyways and side streets. They scurry as if they are the singularly hunted rather than part of a mass target. As they near the school, other terrified people converge in response to the attack.

Usually, those retrieving their children linger outside and await the students' exit, but today protocol be damned as parents run into the building without pause. Frau Hueber calls out to Elsbeth as she, too, rushes into the school. The first inside return with sons and daughters in tow. Children scramble and trip to keep up as adults hurry them away. Schoolbooks and papers, pencils and *Ölkreiden* fall out of clumsily closed satchels; a couple of disparate, wayward shoes are discarded in the flight. A small bright green coat lies trampled on the ground.

Frau Hueber returns, Elsbeth skittering behind her. Charles scoops Elsbeth into his arms and holds the child to his chest, as he would have Dussie if he could have saved her that day. They return to the konditorei as the bombing continues, getting closer, louder as three airplanes become four, then five. "Americans," someone rushing by declares. The planes roar in and out of view overhead. One or two fire machine guns, which rat-tat-tat, just like in the movies. Bullets rip through the air with screaming precision.

Back in the konditorei, the floor is strewn with broken dishware and glasses. Charles ushers Frau Hueber and Elsbeth down into the rarely used cellar. Among the boxes of supplies and tables and chairs in need of repair, they clear spaces in which to sit. They huddle by trunks of Herr Hueber's belongings, which Frau Hueber has not found the strength to rummage through since his death. Once settled, they hear the planes and guns and bombs continue their onslaught. Elsbeth bites at her lips. She has not yet experienced war in her town, despite the hundreds of soldiers who tread the streets with guns and rifles. For her, the treading of their boots is a sound of comfort. Today Charles realizes, she understands something Jewish children learned long ago: there is no safety in this world.

In time, the planes leave the sky, like clouds after a storm. Bayreuth emerges to survey the damage and count the wounded and the dead. The cleanup begins. Citizens band together to clear fallen stones and bricks from the sidewalks and streets so traffic can resume. In houses throughout the town, survivors sweep up picture glass and shattered ceramics and damaged furniture. They load the debris, along with any memories attached to it, into garbage pails and place them out on the street for collection.

Before they can finish the full task of righting the town, the Americans return in a few days' time. Once again, they drop bombs and spray bullets, terrorizing the town and creating choruses of agonizing screams that echo through the streets, almost as loud as the bombs.

After the second attack, the residents of Bayreuth tidy their homes once more. They sweep the floors and right the pictures and reposition the knickknacks that survived. They dust the dining tables and end tables. They shake the plaster and debris from the linens, from coats and scarves, which they rehang after righting fallen coatracks.

Then the Americans return. Word spreads: Bayreuth will fall. Radio bulletins report on the carnage. Charles and Frau Hueber learn that the planes destroyed thousands of buildings and homes. Hundreds upon hundreds of Germans are dead. Despite the pain and fear of American occupation, there is a collective sense of relief that at least the bombing and destruction will stop.

Frau Hueber and Charles and Elsbeth clean up the konditorei for the third time in less than two weeks. Frau Hueber clears the shelves of intact dishware to wipe surfaces. Elsbeth is assigned the task of sweeping. Charles concentrates on making sure the kitchen is operational, should the Americans allow them to reopen for business.

After entering the kitchen with an armful of dishes, Frau Hueber sets them in the sink without a word. She runs water over the dishes.

"The bombing has been bad," Charles tells her. "But we have been luckier than most."

She stands at the sink, saying nothing, watching the tub fill. She adds a frugal amount of soap.

"The Americans will be fair, I suspect," Charles continues. But how can he comfort her when her livelihood lies at the edge of ruin?

She shrugs. "They might, yes. But, Charles . . ."

Charles waits.

Frau Hueber shuts off the water and turns to him. "You need to leave before the Americans come."

Confused, Charles starts to speak, but Frau Hueber halts him.

"I know you are Jewish."

Panic flares through him. He wants to protest but does not have the energy. He merely asks, "How?"

"Your coloring, your features. I suspected early on. And your story was . . . too convenient. Did you burn yourself?"

"It's a long story," Charles sighs.

"I think we have time."

So, he recounts the real story for her. He starts in Czechoslovakia with the invasion of the Nazis and finishes with stepping tentatively into her konditorei some five years later. She says nothing, her thoughts hidden and impenetrable through an uncharacteristic austere stare. He is not scared that she might turn him in. For what does it matter to the Germans of Bayreuth if he is Jewish now that the Americans have come?

After a moment, Frau Hueber takes his hand. "You are a lucky boy, Charles."

He weighs her assessment but does not respond. Instead, he accepts the warmth of her hand.

"But I don't know how long your luck will last," she cautions. "I don't know what the Americans will do. They might imprison us. They might kill us. Who knows?"

"Then let's leave. Before they come," Charles begs. "You and me and Elsbeth."

She pats his hand before drawing hers back.

"This is our home," Frau Hueber states. "I don't want to leave Bayreuth. But you must."

He confesses his previous plans to leave, and she scolds him. "Well, I am glad you did not leave without saying goodbye. I would have never forgiven you, Charles. Nor would Elsbeth."

The next morning, they have breakfast in the apartment upstairs, the gloom of the uncertain future lurking about like a lost ghost. They speak of the cleanup still to be done, in the shop and in the city. They talk of the weather. They make no mention of the Americans or Charles's departure.

Once the table has been cleared and the dishes have been washed and put away, Charles casually states that he plans to take a stroll for fresh air, now that the dust and dirt of the town's destruction have resettled.

"That is fine." Frau Hueber nods, knowing the unspoken truth. "A stroll would be nice."

They hug, a grateful, familial embrace. He kisses Elsbeth on her forehead and tells her goodbye.

"See you later, Onkel," Elsbeth says as she sits down with her coloring book.

Downstairs, standing at the door of the konditorei, his satchel slung over his shoulder, Charles chokes back tears. As he prepares to step outside for yet another journey to another unknown place, his shoulders slump. The satchel slips downward, but he straightens it, then opens the door, triggering the bell to chime.

Upstairs, Frau Hueber pretends not to hear it.

13

Days pass as Charles treks closer to the German border. At night, he shelters in unoccupied barns or sheds. If unable to find substantial shelter, he hides behind bushes. Once or twice, he boldly requests a ride with a passing farmer. But, for the most part, he avoids all vehicles and people. He hears no news about what is happening in the country. Has Germany fallen? Is the war over? Is the world free again?

In Frankfurt he steals away on a train headed to Cologne. He disappears in the dark of a storage car, tucking himself behind a wall of cargo crates. He drifts off but is only on the surface of sleep, alert to any signals of danger. After arriving in Cologne, he lingers in the train station, blending into the crowds and hiding in plain sight.

Come morning, Charles boards the train to Brussels. He does not stow away in the cargo hold for the short two-hundred-kilometer trip. Instead, he sits in the passenger car with the others, at least until the train conductor enters with a request to see tickets. Then he casually moves to the next car. He plays this game of hide-and-seek until the train enters the station, where he disembarks among the other passengers.

In Belgium he takes to the roads again, feeling less safe than he had in Germany now that he is, at least on paper, a German in a foreign land. He does not risk accepting rides from passing cars or trucks. Even though the distance to Antwerp is no more than fifty kilometers, he walks for the majority of the day, his pace slow and cautious but steady, then harbors for the night outside of town.

As he enters Antwerp the next morning, Charles feels a shift in the atmosphere. The air becomes thick and moist and salty to the taste. He's never been in a seaside town, and each breath brings the tang of seawater. He watches the people on the streets. They look like any other people he's seen in Czechoslovakia and Poland and Germany. Eavesdropping on conversations of passersby, he is surprised how similar their language sounds to German. Though he can't understand everything, a word here and there jumps out at him. The similarity comforts him. He migrates toward the wharf, guided by the ever-thickening air.

The docks teem with crowds and activity, overwhelming in its energy and noise. Charles attempts to survey the area, his eyes dodging the people, men mostly, hurrying this way and that. Most of the activity centers down below, at the docks, so Charles lingers on the upper level, where locals out for morning strolls stop to watch the melee, as if watching a theatrical play. Shops and offices rim the perimeter of the walkway.

In one of the office windows, Charles sees a sign in German that reads TICKETS FOR PASSAGE. Once inside the office, Charles approaches the ticket booth where a man, young but older than Charles, works but then Charles hesitates from speaking, unsure how he, a German, at least on paper, will be received here.

"Yes?" the man asks, though he does not look up from his work.

After a cough to clear his throat and to urge himself

on, Charles almost croaks when he speaks. "Do you speak German?"

Unfazed, the man nods. "Of course."

While relieved by the man's blasé response, Charles remains alert for any shift in the situation. "I would like passage to England, please."

"No passenger ships today. The Channel's active."

"Active?"

At this, the man looks up from his work, trains his solid brown eyes on Charles, with a queer expression. "With warships."

Blushing over his stupidity, Charles offers a shy smile of apology.

"How old are you, boy?" The man leans forward, closer to the glass, to get the full picture of Charles.

"Twenty, sir," Charles states, hoping he doesn't request his papers. "I have always looked younger."

The man nods. "Well, the next passage to England should depart in two days, if it can. The ticket will run you twenty-one francs."

After pulling out his money, Charles lays it out on the counter. "How much is that in Reichsmark?"

"No Reichsmark, only francs."

A knot tangles in Charles's stomach. "But all I have are Reichsmark." "Worthless here in Belgium now."

The attendant returns to his work. Charles lingers helplessly at the window, not sure what to do, where to go. This latest turn of events immobilizes him with confusion and fear. After a moment, the man sighs. He jots something down on a slip of paper, which he passes to Charles.

"Try your luck at the docks. This ship sometimes allows passage in exchange for work."

Docked at pier ninety, the *Keurvorst van Vrijheid* is a small freighter, at least in comparison to the others, some of which block out the skyline. Still, the *Keurvorst van Vrijheid* towers in front of Charles. Men, as strong and intimidating as the ship itself, load cargo of crates and trunks and sacks. Some of the men stack handcarts four and five crates tall and glide their way up the walkway. Others hoist heavy sacks as easily as if lifting a small child onto their shoulders to watch a passing parade. Their thick muscles bulge with the strain of the work, though their faces remain carefree, content.

On the edge of the work, a shorter man barks at the men in a language Charles does not understand. In between his barks, he scans and flips through and makes marks on a stack of papers on a clipboard.

Charles determines he must be the captain, or someone kind of manager at least, overseeing the loading of the ship. As he approaches the man, Charles trembles, as he did long ago, when his mother sent him to the steel mill in search of work. Once again, he feels like that naïve, thin fifteen-year-old.

"Excuse me, sir," Charles tenders in German.

The man does not acknowledge Charles, keeping his eyes trained on his men and the work. Charles stands near the man, taking in his strength and his musky scent, which competes with the salty air. Charles has never been in the presence of such a man, not even at the steel mill, a man so strong and sure, despite being smaller than the men he commands. But Charles must leave this country no matter what, so he tries again.

"Sir?"

The man tilts his head slightly, as if hearing the drone of a passing gnat, then turns his gaze onto Charles. His taut skin, as tan as any hide of overworked leather, makes the whites of his eyes stark and clear. He seems to know why this boy stands before him. He aims a squinted eye toward Charles. "Too small," he determines dismissively and turns back to his men.

Charles clears his throat, the salt in the air causing a dry swallow. "I was told there was work . . . in exchange for passage."

The man laughs a quick snort of a laugh. "And I'm going to kill that bastard at the ticket office if he sends me any more children. Too small, I said."

"I'm not a child, sir," Charles stammers. "I'm older than I look."

"I don't care about your age, boy!" the man barks. White spittle foams in the corners of his mouth. "See that cargo? I need men who can haul. Not boys!"

Even though his chest seizes with panic, Charles realizes the man does not frighten him. If Charles could endure Frau Werden, he can endure this man, so he stands his ground.

"I can do other things, sir."

Eying Charles again, the man offers a slight sneer. "I'm sure you can, boy."

"I can clean, sweep, mop, cook, anything you want."

"Every day another boy comes begging to travel to America. Let me tell you, it's not so great over there."

"America?" Charles questions. "Do you not sail to England?"

"England? America? What's the difference?" the captain asks. "Too many people and filth wherever you go. Better off staying here."

Confused, Charles takes a step back. He looks at the row of gigantic tankers and steamers and the dozens of tugboats that linger nearby. He watches the throng of stevedores in their well-choreographed ballet. Back and forth, they glide and grunt at each other and make jokes. They exchange playful and not-so-playful jabs at shoulders and chests, a band of brothers versed in their secret language, same as the men at the steel factory in Kladno years ago. But while such men make him nervous, they don't scare him anymore.

Does one of these other ships sail to England? he wonders. He'd have to inquire at each. Go through the same inquisition as he is now enduring with this man.

"Giving up that quick, are you?" The man snorts another laugh.

"No," Charles replies. "I don't quit."

"Good, because once you're out on the ocean, there isn't any quitting, unless you die." The man stares Charles in the eye. "You going to die?"

"No, sir!" Charles barks with confidence.

"We'll see," he chuckles. "Go on board and see Johann. He'll know what to do with you."

"Thank you, sir." Charles offers a quick salute.

The man waves him away. "Just don't fucking die. Or do. Doesn't matter to me. Fish have to eat, too, I guess."

Charles doesn't know much of England and knows even less of America. But all he needs is a ship to get him out of Europe, away from Germany and Germans, so he hurries on board before the man has a chance to change his mind. He darts past the crew and stevedores and their cargo. Once he is on board, the gentle rocking of the docked ship unnerves him. With his arms outstretched to steady him, he navigates the narrow passageways.

Within minutes, he is lost in the labyrinth of passageways, though he didn't truly have a path when he boarded. He asks one of the less surly-looking men, "Johann?"

The man directs him to a storeroom on a lower deck. There Charles finds a young man overseeing the loading of the ship's supplies. Not as weather hardened as the other men on the ship, Johann still intimidates with his certain confidence as he directs men bigger and stronger than himself as they deliver various cargo. He finds Charles lingering in the background of the activity.

"I guess you're my help this passage," Johann states to Charles. One glance takes Charles's measure from tip to toe; then Johann nods. "You'll do, I suspect."

Johann puts Charles to work in the supply room next to the galley. With little ceremony save a formal exchange of names, he hands Charles a list and instructs him to ensure the delivery of all the supplies.

"I'll show you your quarters later," Johann states. "We're already behind, so get to work."

After Johann departs, off to some other area of the ship, Charles allows a moment of panic before setting to work. It's all moving so fast, he's had no time to think. What will he do in America? Where will he go? How will he survive? They are the same questions he asked himself about England, but at least he had an idea of London, if only a vague map in his head. America is a complete mystery. They are the enemy, at least according to Berthold and the citizens of Bayreuth and the newsreels he's seen at the movie houses. But Charles is used to living among the enemy.

But none of that matters if he doesn't get there, he tells himself. He takes a breath and focuses on the task at hand.

Charles counts sacks of potatoes, bushels of cabbages, cans of beans, and bags upon bags of rice. He checks off the cleaning supplies (lye, soap, mops, brooms, buckets, sponges, and scrub brushes). He quickly works his way down the list. Once all is accounted for, he shelves all the items.

When Johann returns to check on his new assistant, he is impressed. "Still much to be done, but it looks like you'll keep up."

Johann is Danish, young, not much older than Charles. Spending most of his time belowdecks, he is not weatherworn like most of the other men on the ship. He exudes a sense of maturity and wisdom and confidence, which contrasts with the comportment of the crew of toughs."

"They're generally a good lot," Johann advises Charles when he asks about the men, "but best to stay clear."

Johann sends Charles to the galley. As Charles peels potatoes, the engines roar to life in the bowels of the ship. Charles stops peeling, letting the growling vibrations seep into his bones. He knows this rumbling feeling from his time in the steel factory, so he waits as his body remembers.

When the tanker moves out to sea, Charles's stomach clenches as the ship tilts and rocks. He clutches the counter to stable himself.

Johann enters the galley and sees the young man's grimace. "You'll get used to it soon enough," he says firmly but gently. "Or you won't. Either way, no turning back now."

"I'll be fine," Charles responds but continues to hold the counter. "I think."

Johann laughs, but it's not mean. He's a man who understands. "We'll prepare a meat and potato stew," Johann says, keeping to the schedule. "I keep it simple but hearty."

He directs Charles to a ship recipe. While it presents rather bland on paper, Charles doesn't deviate for fear of reprisal. As the stew cooks, Charles and Johann prepare for the meal service. They load stacks of white ceramic bowls onto a cart, as well as spoons and napkins and serving utensils. Following Johann, Charles wheels the cart down to the crew's mess hall. The large room is lined with wooden tables secured to the floor. There are twenty tables in all with each able to seat eight people.

"You'll serve from here," Johann tells Charles, pointing to a table at the front of the room.

"Me?" Charles asks as he surveys the room, imagining it full of the crew members, all burley and loud and raucous.

"You'll be fine," Johann assures Charles. "I'll be here."

Charles prepares pitchers of water and places them on the

WE ARE ONLY GHOSTS 91

serving table along with glassware. He slices numerous loaves of bread that will accompany the stew, stacking the slices on serving platters which he places by the water pitchers.

"The men will help themselves to the water and bread," Johann advises Charles. "You need only to plate up the stew."

Once the stew is finished, Charles brings the large pot to the mess hall. Johann sounds a signal throughout the ship's speakers, alerting the men that the meal is ready. Within minutes, the hall is crowded with men as they jockey their way through the serving line. They jostle and cajole each other but few of them mark Charles's presence, merely accepting their bowls of stew as they make their way down the table to the bread, the cutlery, and the water. The process moves quickly and smoothly. Johann assists here and there but for much of the event stands off to the side, letting Charles handle the food and the men.

After the last man has finished his second portion and left the hall, Charles proceeds to clean the hall. He clears the dishes and glasses and cutlery and brings them to the galley to be washed. He picks up the discarded napkins and pieces of bread that have fallen to the floor. He wipes down the tables and sweeps the floor.

Once he has washed all the dishes and pots and pans and the galley itself, Charles eats his portion of the stew, set aside earlier. He devours the meat and vegetables and sops up the gravy slices of bread. When he's finished, he's full and exhausted.

"Very good, Charles," Johann says when he returns to survey the work. "Very good, indeed. But we have another meal today, so no rest for us. Trust me, you don't want to see these men hungry."

Johann offers a smile, but Charles feels he's not entirely joking.

That evening in his quarters, a tiny cabin with a bed and not much else, Charles collapses from a fatigue he has never experienced. He thinks back to the chaos of the preceding days and weeks: the bombings, his escape, and now a voyage to America, of all places.

A knock on the door startles him. Johann enters and stands in the doorway for a moment, looking at Charles on his bed.

"You need to keep this door locked," Johann warns. "Some of the men . . . don't know how to behave, if you know what I mean."

Charles nods. He knows what Johann means.

"Stay close to me and you'll be fine," Johann assures him.

Johann's dark blond hair frames his soft features, pale skin, and piercing blue eyes. Charles is uneasy from his glances but also finds he likes the attention.

Charles asks about America.

"It is not my favorite place, but it's a good place to start over or disappear, whichever your aim," Johann says with a reassuring grin. "I know a woman who lets rooms. You will be fine."

The next day Johann gives Charles a German to English dictionary and teaches him a bit of English while they work in the galley. He also pays Charles wages in American dollars, even though the original deal was passage only.

"You cannot go to a new country without money," Johann warns.

"You are too kind, Johann," Charles says, because he understands the money comes from Johann's own pockets, yet he asks for nothing in return.

On the third day of the voyage, after the crew has been fed their lunch and the galley cleaned and prepped for dinner, Charles sneaks out of his cabin. The passageways are quiet as he threads through the maze. He makes his way upward to the deck.

The ocean wind, cold and damp, assails him as he steps outside. But Charles doesn't feel its assault, so stunned is he by the sight of the ocean. The vastness overwhelms. Cautiously, he steps to the railing to soothe a bout of nausea.

"You shouldn't be out here." Johann steps up beside Charles.

"It's amazing."

"I know," Johann agrees. "It's why I do this."

They stand at the railing, both gazing out. Johann with an understanding borne of experience, borne of a hundred oceanic crossings, and borne of the certainty that he will reach the other side, as he always has. While Charles gazes out through the eyes of a child, his naivete as wide as the ocean upon which they sail. He possesses no certainty, not for the moment or the future.

Three days later, the ship docks at one of the ports in Brooklyn. As the crew disembarks, the local stevedores hurry forward, some speaking Dutch, some German, while others converse in English. Still others speak languages Charles doesn't know. It is an unintelligible melee, as confusing as Babel itself.

Charles steps off the gangway and onto the dock. The energy of the Brooklyn seaport, greater than that in Antwerp, rushes at him. He stands still, soaking it in, trying to understand it, but he can't. It is so strange, so unnatural as it rubs against him. The energy of hundreds of people swirling about like an ill-formed cyclone, erratic and dangerous.

"You'll get used to it," Johann promises.

Charles isn't so sure.

Johann walks Charles inland to the street, to the stop for the bus bound for Manhattan.

"You'll be fine," Johann assures him again as Charles boards the bus. "It'll take time, but you'll be fine."

Charles offers a grateful yet unsure smile. When the bus doors close and Johann turns to leave, Charles feels, yet again, abandoned to the world.

14

As the bus crests the midpoint of the Williamsburg Bridge, the city of Manhattan comes into full view. A fortress of gray buildings reaches toward the equally gray sky. Charles scans the jagged skyline, which stretches in either direction beyond his field of vision.

In the city proper, the buildings become an infinite backdrop, broken only by the hordes of people crowding the sidewalks, moving quick and sure, a unified mass. The bus lumbers down the crowded street alongside cars and taxis and trucks competing for road space. When the driver pulls to the curb, people disembark, and then others clamor on, a practiced act of urban choreography. Once the door closes, the bus trudges back into traffic. Car horns bleat in protest, but the bus driver does not shy away or acquiesce to their complaints. After the fourth or fifth stop, Charles is so disoriented he has no idea where they are. The map in his mind that Johann drew for him has blurred to scribbles. Panic crowds his chest.

At one of the stops, the driver leans toward Charles and taps his leg. "This is you, Mac."

Charles stares at him without blinking. The driver taps the piece of paper in Charles's hand, on which Johann has written the address of the place for let.

"Here," the driver states again and points outside.

"Oh!" Charles exclaims. He leaps from his seat and hurries off the bus. On the sidewalk he turns and offers an excited "*Danke!*" Then, remembering not to be German, he renders a less enthusiastic but well-stated "Thank you," but the bus has already pulled away.

In the swarm of foot traffic, Charles braces himself against the men and women rushing about him. While it appears they do not see him, they swarm around him with a fluidity that unnerves yet impresses.

Charles glances at the address on the paper. He suddenly doesn't understand the words, though Johann recited them numerous times and made him parrot the sounds, and the slight panic he felt on the bus ignites like a fire being fed gasoline. Heat sears through his chest and neck and face. Johann instructed him to walk east once the bus dropped him at his stop, but he has no idea which direction is east. At the intersection the street signs tell him he is at the corner of Allen Street and Grand Street. He looks at the paper to see if the words match, but they don't. He scans the streets again, looking helpless.

"You lost there, buddy?"

Charles turns to see a man in a small newspaper booth. He doesn't understand what the short, old, gruff-looking man has said, but there is a welcoming tone to his voice. Charles approaches the booth and hands him the paper. The man reads the address.

"You're close, my boy, very close," he says, his Irish brogue lilting and trilling with great beauty. Charles wonders if all Americans speak this way. If so, he'll never master the accent. "Go down Grand here and take a left. You're very close."

Charles looks puzzled.

"Ah," the man tells Charles. "New to the country, are you? I was once, too, my boy. Come."

The man steps out of the small hutch and walks Charles to the street corner. He faces Charles east and points. "You go that way, laddie, to Orchard Street." Here he points at the street name on the paper. "Then you hook a left," he says, and he hooks his thumb left. "Got it?"

Nodding, Charles mimics the man's gestures. He points straight down Grand Street, then points at the street name on the paper and hooks his thumb left.

"There you go, my boy!" The man cheers and claps Charles on the back.

"Thank you," Charles offers, still unsure.

The man laughs. "See! You'll be fine! Just fine!"

With a quick wave to the man, Charles crosses the roadway and heads east on Grand Street.

Immersed in the horde of pedestrians, Charles is pushed along by their pace. Any attempt to move out of the rush meets with resistance, a barrier of movement, so he quickens his pace to match their energy.

At the corner of Grand and Orchard, he hooks a left, as instructed. While still busy, with people hurrying about their morning, Orchard Street is not as overwhelming as Grand Street, and he is able to slow his pace, thankful for the comparative quiet, though his nerves do not calm down. Even with all the turmoil he's experienced in the past five or six years, he's never felt so lost, so alone, so scared. But he can do nothing but continue forward.

Perkins's Boardinghouse juts out from the row of tenement houses lining the street as if refusing, by sheer tenacity, to be overshadowed by the newer apartment houses that have come after it. Its determination makes Charles smile as he mounts the stone stairs of its stoop. He rings the bell next to the name "Perkins" on the panel.

Frau Perkins is as nice as Johann said she would be. She is older and small, yet sturdy, definitely of German stock. Charles informs her he has arrived in America that very morning and has been sent to her by Johann.

"Oh, dear boy!" she exclaims in German. "Come! Come!"

Charles follows Mrs. Perkins—"Don't call me Frau Perkins here . . . It's Mrs. in America"—into the dim foyer of the building. At the end of the short hallway, past the staircase, they enter a living area. Much like Mrs. Perkins, the space is small and cheery and bright. Mrs. Perkins leads Charles through the "setting parlor," then the dining room, with its large table and mismatched chairs, and into the kitchen, where she stations him at the small table.

"Now, what do I have to eat?" she inquires of herself as she peers inside her refrigerator. "I know you're hungry, coming off the sea. You smell of the ocean, like my husband used to. Mr. Perkins, God rest, lived and died on the sea. Now, don't be shy, boy. Speak up. I got some beef from last night. That'll make a hearty sandwich, for sure. You like beef, of course. Everybody likes beef. I like it rare, so that'll have to do."

With the plate of beef, she moves to the counter. From a bread box she retrieves a half loaf of bread and begins carving off thick slices.

"How old are you, *Junge*? Can't be more than sixteen by the looks of you. Where is your mama? Your daddy? Why are you in America all by yourself at such an age? Though I've seen younger than you, to be sure."

She doesn't turn to face Charles as she interrogates, diligent in her preparations. She slathers the bread slices with a thick brown mustard. She mounds the bread with a generous helping of beef. She cuts some onion slices, pungent to the eye even from a distance, and adds them to the sandwich.

"My parents died," Charles relays, his lack of emotion surprising him. "I am alone now."

Mrs. Perkins halts her movements and her shoulders slump, but only for a moment, as she takes a breath. She turns to face him. "Well, you're in my home now."

She places the sandwich in front of Charles, then pours a glass of milk. She sits with him while he eats. "Now, you'll need to get a job. Have you worked much? How old are you?"

No longer needing to lie about his age, despite what his papers might state, Charles declares, "I am twenty."

"Goodness, I never would have guessed," Mrs. Perkins confesses and assesses him once again. "You're a small one. But don't worry. You'll fatten up. Everyone does in America! Look at me! I was as skinny as you when I first came!"

After he finishes his sandwich, Mrs. Perkins shows him the space for let. The basement apartment is one of three single rooms walled off from each other by nothing more than thin panelboard. The space comes with a narrow bed no wider than a cot, a wooden chair, and a two-drawer chest.

"Plenty for your purposes, yes," Mrs. Perkins states. For cooking, she points out a hot plate and cautions him, only half in jest, "Don't burn the place down."

He shares a bathroom—sink and toilet only—with the other occupants of the basement. He has shared less with more.

"First order of business for you, young man, is to learn English," Mrs. Perkins declares. "Of course, I know a man. He is good and cheap. You will start this afternoon. No time to waste in America."

Mrs. Perkins leaves Charles to his room, his own room, his first since Dussie was born. He doesn't count the cellar in the Werden house or the storeroom at Frau Hueber's. Neither was truly his. He unpacks his knapsack, places his meager possessions in the chest of drawers: three ill-fitting shirts, long since outgrown; two pair of pants; his shaving supplies; and not much else. He sits on his bed, misshapen with lumps but soft enough. He does not have a window, but that is fine. If he wants fresh air, he can step outside. He is free to do that now without worry. There are no soldiers on the streets of America who will stop him and ask for his papers. It's an odd feeling, this sense of unrestrained freedom. He's not sure if it feels good or not. It almost feels like a trap.

As promised, Mrs. Perkins introduces Charles to Mr. Leon, an English instructor, that afternoon. They sit in Mrs. Perkins's kitchen as she prepares coffee.

"Mr. Leon has helped a lot of immigrants, Charles," Mrs. Perkins crows with a sense of pride. Mr. Leon, a quiet man in comparison to Mrs. Perkins, blushes. "He's a very good teacher."

"I only guide," Mr. Leon demurs. "It is up to the pupil to do the work."

"Charles will do the work, yes?" Mrs. Perkins assures Mr. Leon and warns Charles at the same time.

Charles nods and replies in English, "Yes."

"See! He's learning already!" Mrs. Perkins squawks. "He will do well here!"

For his first few weeks in America, Charles does no more than meet Mr. Leon and study every day. While the English language, its complex nuances, does not come easy, he picks it up quicker than most, Mr. Leon insists.

In the meantime, Mrs. Perkins knows another man who can help Charles get his papers in order, to guarantee a job. She does not tell Charles the man's name.

"Better that way," Mrs. Perkins asserts

They meet at night in an abandoned warehouse on the Lower East Side, not far from the wharf. The air holds the smell of the East River, heavy and moist, much like in Antwerp but not as fresh. Inside the warehouse, Charles pauses and waits for his eyes to adjust to the immediate darkness. In the distance, beyond the dark, a light hangs in the air, as faint as a ghost.

The shadow of a man steps into the weak glow of the light.

"Come," he calls.

Charles makes his way toward the man. The scrape and shuffle of his footsteps echo in the damp silence.

As he nears, the man holds out his hand. "Papers."

Of course, Charles hands them over without question, as trained as any monkey in the circus.

The man is not what Charles expected. Most men on the black market possess a shade to their eyes, their being; they are someone vague and lightly drawn, undefined beyond a radiation of greed and deviousness. But this man, plain and ordinary and unthreatening, you might easily pass by on the streets and never notice.

He examines Charles's papers. "So, what do you want?"

"To be American."

"Who doesn't, kid? You got a name in mind? Bob or Joe or Mike? Who do you want to be?"

Charles considers for a moment. "I can stay Charles, yes?"

The man shrugs. "Sure. Maybe go by Chuck. Gotta change the last name, though. Werden is too foreign."

The man places a briefcase on the tabletop and removes a stack of papers, some pens, a stamp of some sort, and a small booklet. He prepares the new papers. Charles stands at the ready, in case he needs to volunteer more information. The man works methodically, slowly. Within the hour Charles is holding his new passport and birth certificate.

Charles reads the forged documents. "Charles Ward?"

"Yes," the man says. "This is who you are now."

Charles nods. "I am Charles Ward."

"Listen, kid. Keep your nose clean. If anyone investigates

that Social Security number, they'll find you dead and buried in California. Got it?"

Confused by the request, Charles Ward assures the man that he has a handkerchief to keep his nose clean. Wondering why the man laughs long and hard, Charles leaves the warehouse and steps into yet another new life.

15

Charles's meager funds dwindle quickly. With rent to Mrs. Perkins, payment for lessons from Mr. Leon, the purchase of food, and the expenses for a new identity, Charles Ward is broke by the end of his second month in America.

Mrs. Perkins sends him to a grocery shop for work.

"I know everyone there is to know in this neighborhood, my boy," Mrs. Perkins crows. "And almost all owe me something. It's the American way!"

The next day Charles starts work as a stock boy. The pay is not so much, but it is better than the nothing in his pockets. So, he cheerfully stocks shelves and bags groceries and unloads delivery boxes six days a week. The owner, Mr. Feuerstein, is an Austrian Jew who came to America well before Hitler came to power. When Charles first saw Mr. Feuerstein, he thought he would be gruff, off-putting, but when he spoke, it was calm and gentle, the voice of a man who has found comfort in his life.

Mrs. Perkins assures Charles that Mr. Feuerstein views him not as a German but merely as another worker. Still, Charles tells Mr. Feuerstein that he is not German but rather Czech. And he is Jewish, too.

Sitting behind his somewhat messy desk in the small office in the back of the store, which also doubles as an extra storage room, Mr. Feuerstein nods. "Thank you for telling me, Charles. But a word of advice, don't be Jewish."

Confused, Charles doesn't respond.

"I am not ashamed, and you should not be, either," Mr. Feuerstein clarifies. "But the pendulum is always swinging, Charles, and rarely in our favor. Be American, yes, but maybe not Jewish, if you don't have to be."

Charles nods. It is not the first time he has been told to adapt in order to survive, so he will heed Mr. Feuerstein's advice.

At Mrs. Perkins's apartment building, Charles keeps to himself but encounters the other residents on occasion.

In the mornings, as he heads out to work, Charles meets up with Sam, who has occupied the last room in the basement for years. Sam works the docks. A brusque man in his forties, Sam is hardened and beaten by a life of laboring work, every moment etched into his dark, ruddy face framed by a shock of tousled black hair. He grunts as he strikes out each morning in the opposite direction from Charles.

"He's a big old pussycat," Mrs. Perkins assures Charles. "Pays his rent and never causes trouble, which is how it should be."

On the main floor, along with Mrs. Perkins, lives Miss Miller, a teacher at one of the elementary schools on the West Side of Manhattan. When not tucked in her room, Miss Miller steals about the place, a delicate, innocuous presence. Around the house, they call her "the spinster." At least, Mrs. Perkins does.

"Spends most of her time reading in her room," Mrs. Perkins gossips. "Never married and most likely never will. She's not a homely girl, but the poor thing is all alone in the world. Seems a shame to live one's life and not have something to show for it, like a husband and children."

Charles speaks to Miss Miller whenever he comes upon her. He makes a point to smile and offer a "Good day." Miss Miller responds in kind, never anything further. Still, Charles likes her. He likes her stealth, the way she appears in rooms without notice. She inhabits space as if a mere wisp of smoke. She wears long dresses, causing her to appear to glide across the floor—an ethereal presence haunting Mrs. Perkins's apartment house. He's not entirely sure she is not a ghost.

On the second floor lives Kessler. Charles is never sure if that is his first or last name. Not much older than Charles, Kessler works as a low-level clerk in a shipping office. He resembles a weaselly-looking boy, though he is an adult. Every workday he wears the same clerk's uniform: brown twill pants, white collared shirt, brown tie, and brown vest. Charles never speaks to Kessler, and Kessler never speaks to Charles. They nod if they encounter each other in the entry-way or the communal living room, but that is all. Charles knows not why, nor does he concern himself with the reason. Kessler noticeably bathes once a week, the same day he launders his uniform.

"It's fine in the winter months," Mrs. Perkins concedes. "But in the summer, he can get stout."

Then there is Maude Allen.

"I'm going to be a great actress, so remember my name," Maude says breathily the first time they meet. He encounters her in the foyer one afternoon, as he enters the house. She stands midway up the staircase, as if preparing to make a grand entrance. She gives him a moment to commit her name to memory.

"Maude Allen," Charles recites.

"That's me," Maude crows. "And who might you be?"

"Charles. I am Charles Ward."

"What a perfectly ordinary name," Maude offers with a lighthearted laugh. "I myself used to be Clara Applebee. How dreadful is that? A spinster name if I ever heard one. Though I loathe saying such a thing with Miss Miller skulking about. You've met Miss Miller, yes?"

Charles nods.

"Poor old thing, don't you think?" Maude laments. "I'm sure Mrs. Perkins has given you the dope on all us poor souls, the gossipy old bird. Do you think she prefers women? Miss Miller, that is, not Mrs. Perkins. Oh, don't look so ghastly! Some women do, you know. Well, you'll find out soon enough in this city. Where are you from? Not New York, I can tell!"

Maude tosses her head back and laughs artificially, filling the stairway with a ringing gaiety.

"I've been here only a few months in New York, but a few months can feel like years, I will tell you that, Charles. Hmmm . . . Charles. I like it. Perhaps not so ordinary, after all."

Charles doesn't respond, not that he could have interrupted her monologue, anyway. By the time he takes in her stream of words, translates it into German (surprised he doesn't instinctively convert it to Czech first), then formulates a response, Maude has hurried on to the next subject. Which is fine with him, because Maude is fun to watch talk. Charles can imagine her in the movies. She fashions her hair in the look of the day: medium length and curled to frame her oval face. Her makeup might be too heavy for daytime but still looks fresh and bright. Especially her red lips, which pucker and pout as she speaks. Her teeth are a bright white against the red of the lips. Charles fancies her a Kewpie doll come to life.

She is off to an acting class, she announces, and invites Charles along. The invitation is impetuous yet genuine. Charles suspects most of Maude's actions are impetuous yet genuine.

"Afterward, I can show you the city. Have you seen it yet?

Not this ratty area, which I loathe. Have you seen the Empire State Building? Central Park? Broadway? Oh, you must see Broadway, Charles!" And here she becomes breathless. "It is the most beautiful place in the world!"

Her passion rises to beatific, and Charles fears she might swoon. But it dissipates, and she descends the rest of the staircase, slowly and elegantly. Her fingers caress the banister with each measured step.

Out on the streets, Maude weaves her way uptown on foot, with Charles lagging a pace behind.

"I prefer to walk. Be among the people, absorb their essence so I can use it in my acting," Maude exults with affected refinement. Charles suspects the decision to walk has as much to do with saving the five cents for the bus, which is fine with him.

Turning onto Broadway, they come upon hundreds of people gliding down the street.

"Don't fight it, Charles," Maude calls out gaily over the din of the herd. "Move with them."

Maude finds a breach in the crowd and spears through, agile and quick. Charles rushes to her side. He asks if there is something special happening today.

"Why? Because of all the people?" Maude laughs. "Oh, dear, no. It's always like this! Simply fabulous, isn't it?"

Charles isn't so sure. How does one live in a crowd like this, with never a moment to oneself? New York reminds him too much of the ghettos of Czechoslovakia.

The farther north they travel, the thicker the crowds swell, and Charles, intimidated, feels his pace falter. Maude clutches at his arm, pulling him through the crowd.

"Mustn't stop, Charles! That's the most important rule of the city!"

Maude's acting class meets in a small, repurposed apartment in Midtown. Charles and Maude arrive hot and sweaty from the brisk walk, and she leads them to the back of the room, away from the others. Maude pats at her moistened flesh with a handkerchief. Seven or eight young men and women mill about and chat and glance at the new arrival. Maude offers a slight wave.

"They're so intrigued by you, Charles," Maude says, her voice low and dramatic. "How wonderful."

The living room of the apartment is filled with cheap wooden folding chairs, which form five short rows. Maude has Charles sit in the last row.

"I'll let the teacher know you're accompanying me this one time. He won't mind. He likes cute boys," she states with a wink. If she was hoping to shock Charles, he has to admit she has, not so much with her statement but her nonchalant attitude. She approaches an older gentleman, handsome, in his fifties, with longish gray hair combed back away from his face. He sits off to the side of the activity, reading a newspaper. As Maude whispers to him, she nods toward Charles. The teacher follows her glance, offers a nod to Charles.

"Professor Tork says it's fine," Maude reports when she returns to Charles. "I'm going to go say hi to the gang. Are you okay here?"

Charles assures her he is fine. He's enjoying the new experience, weary of his meager American life of working and sleeping and learning English.

The other students cluster in groups. Some chat and gossip; others recite lines, annoyed when they have to refer to the pages clutched in their hands. Charles loves that Maude immediately becomes the center of each group that she enters, her infectious light enchanting each person in an instant. Frivolous kisses are offered in the form of light pecks on the cheek, coupled with quick hugs.

"All right, my charges," Professor Tork declares as he steps before the room. "Let us begin."

The students settle in the first two rows. Professor Tork's suit, which might have seen better days, is nonetheless stylish and adds to his attraction, Charles notices. He has a generous smile, which he trains on his pupils and then directs to Charles for the briefest of moments. He nods to Maude, who stands.

"Professor Tork, fellow actors, I'd like to introduce my new friend who is joining us today. Charles." Maude sweeps her hand toward her companion. A smattering of applause welcomes him.

"Very pleased to have you with us, Charles," Professor Tork proclaims with genuine sentiment. "I trust you will join the exercises."

Charles blushes and nods.

"Well, then," Professor Tork says, moving on, "everyone stand, please."

Professor Tork ushers the class through a series of vocal and physical drills. He eyes Charles to spur him to participate. They sing vowels, which stretches their mouths and jaws and lungs and vocal cords. They stretch their bodies, their limbs. Professor Tork instructs them to reach for the ceiling and has them flap their arms like the wings of butterflies. The class does this with great gravity, not the least bit embarrassed. Charles follows along as best he can, but feels he must look silly and childish, so he doesn't sing as loudly or reach as high as the others. Still, Professor Tork singles out his attempts. "Very good, Charles."

After the warm-up exercises, Charles elects to sit in back as the students perform prepared scenes. Maude is first, joined by one of the boys. She is quite good, Charles thinks. Simple and real, not hammy or overdramatic, as he suspected she might be from their encounter in the foyer of Mrs. Perkins's house. Other students perform their scenes, but none are as good as Maude. They all know it.

"You're very good," Charles tells Maude after the class. They walk north toward Central Park.

"Thank you." Maude accepts the compliment with delicate grace. "I enjoy it, you know. That's why I do it. What do you enjoy, Charles?"

Charles pauses. All he's done for the past six years is survive, and there's no talent in that. "I don't know."

"There must be something. Everyone loves something."

But what if Charles doesn't love anything? He thinks hard and offers that he likes to cook.

"See, there's something!" Maude beams as if she has switched on a light for Charles.

Charles laughs in agreement. He does like to cook, to bake; at least he enjoyed it at Frau Hueber's konditorei in Bayreuth.

Maude takes Charles past the theaters of Broadway. She declares that one day, she will be on the "big" stages of New York City, though Charles isn't sure what that means. The buildings are beautiful, even if they lack the intricacy and minute details most European architects favored. But if he blots out the surrounding scene, he can imagine being in Kladno or Prague or Bayreuth, and a pain surges through him, a pain of loss and loneliness that immobilizes him.

He wonders what his family would think of New York. He knows his father would hate it. He hated Prague: "Too many people and buildings for my taste." So, New York City would overwhelm him beyond bearing. His mother? She might enjoy the city for moments at a time, but she would miss being in a house of her own, miss having a yard in which she could keep an eye on her children. She would not want to live on top of others and have them live on top of her. Dussie would love it. Her energy would fit into the vibrant, excitable city. And Zofia? She would like the freedom the girls have here in New

York City. The way they dress and flounce about in scandalous skirts and dresses. She would like Maude.

"Come on, Charles!" Maude calls from down the block, surprised to find him still standing in front of the Booth Theatre. "There is so much still to see!"

With reluctance, Charles leaves the thoughts of his family and hurries to catch up.

16

Only a month later, Maude is cast in her first show.

"It was only a matter of time," Maude informs Charles, with the first hint of superciliousness he's heard from her. But she is quick to demur, saying, "It's a small, little production of a thing, but . . . it's a start."

Opening night and the theater, a converted movie house on the Lower East Side, passed its prime some time ago, is charged with excitement as Charles takes his seat. The modest theater crowd seems like a gathering of family and friends of the cast. He recognizes Maude's friends from the acting class and Professor Tork, who offers a warm nod to Charles. A further scan of the audience finds Miss Miller sitting alone. She acknowledges Charles with a wisp of a smile.

The lights dim, and the crowd hushes. The curtain rises, revealing Maude sitting on a settee, working at a piece of needlepoint. Light applause echoes among her friends, but she is absorbed in her stage work, a play of thought and emotion worrying her brow. A gentleman arrives onstage. Maude does not acknowledge him beyond a small pause in her finger work.

The gentleman is handsome and tall, and his fingers anxiously fidget with a pocket watch attached to his vest by a silver chain. He takes a shallow breath.

"Please, Abigail," he pleads.

Maude, or Abigail as she is then, lets a smile play about her lips, but only for the audience. She leaves the gentleman waiting as she extends the moment. Then, unable to contain herself any longer, she turns to him and her face flushes.

"Of course, Harold. Of course I'll marry you!"

The play is little more than a mediocre drawing room comedy, but Maude is luminous in the role of Abigail. She acts with verve and subtle comedic flare, all with hints of a darkness that ultimately reveals itself. While her coactors present their characters as caricatures, Maude inhabits Abigail thoroughly. By the end of the play, Charles decides that Maude is too good for the play and the theater.

Backstage afterward, Charles finds it easy to compliment Maude. "You were magnificent," he gushes, jockeying for space among a crush of friends and acquaintances and strangers all seeking to bask in her glow.

"Do you think so?" Maude asks, though the query rings hollow. She fully knows how wonderful she was. "Oh, Charles! It's only the beginning, isn't it?"

The cast, as a small group of invited friends and family, including Charles, gather at a pub not far from the theater, with Maude the toast of the party. She takes it all in humble stride. When called upon to make a speech, she declares, "I cannot rest on this one evening, this one performance. I must strive to be better the next time and the time after that."

"She *was* wonderful," Professor Tork announces as he appears at Charles's side.

"You must be proud," Charles offers.

The professor nods. "She is a natural."

Professor Tork hands Charles the glass of champagne he's

been holding, then flags down a waiter moving among the crowd with a tray of pre-filled glasses of champagne. The professor and Charles find a booth sufficiently apart from the jubilant crowd.

"And you?" Professor Tork inquires. "I had hoped you might return to our class."

"I'm no actor." Charles blushes at the thought of being on-stage, so exposed.

"Ah, but we are all actors." Professor Tork offers a generous smile that lights his eyes. "Acting, my dear Charles, is as natural to us as breathing, though most people don't realize it. We are both acting right now."

Charles shakes his head. "You are?"

"Of course!" the professor exclaims. "I'm sitting here before you, acting the role of an acting teacher."

"But you *are* an acting teacher, aren't you?"

He laughs. "Yes, I am. At least that's how I make my living. Don't get me wrong, I enjoy teaching, but that is not who I am. It is my profession, and I must act when I perform that profession. I become Professor Tork when I stand in front of a class. When I'm alone, however, or with family and friends, I am Larry. When I am Lawrence, I am acting again—because that is not who I am, either. Do you understand?"

Charles ponders the idea. He thinks about all the roles he himself has played in his life so far.

Of course, Charles Ward is his name now, a name given him by a stranger in a warehouse, though he is not Charles Ward. He speaks English because that is what Charles Ward does as an American. Charles Ward stocks shelves in a grocery store and makes deliveries because that is his job. Before that, he was Charles Werden, a German baker in a German town in Germany. When he was merely Charles, he was a prisoner and a *Hure* in the Werden home. He cooked and cleaned and kept himself small and willing and alive.

For a brief time, he was a number, nothing more. Not a man, not even human. At some point, though the memory has grown faint, he was Karel Benakov: a Jew in Terezín, a factory worker in Kladno, a son and brother. And as each of these characters, he performed the roles as required.

But who is he when no one is looking?

"So, what we do onstage is what we do in our lives, though a bit more exaggerated," Professor Tork went on, warming to the subject. "Writers write characters, put them into situations, and the actors act out those situations as if they were those characters. It's very simple. Same with life. The gods or fate, what have you, create situations for us, and we are forced to create new characters to deal with the new situations. But I fear we may be entering a more philosophical area here. I blame the champagne."

Professor Tork offers a charming smile that sits on the brink of being tipsy. Charles averts his gaze from the professor's eyes to his hands. The fingers are long, masculine, thick, nicely shaped, and manicured thoughtfully. They are the hands of a man who does not do manual labor, might never have.

"The crux of what I'm saying, Charles," the professor concludes, "is that once you know the character, either onstage or in life, you begin to think and feel like him. The rest is easy. Good actors don't think too much."

After taking a final sip from his champagne flute, Professor Tork states that he would like to help Charles. "I see in you something of myself when I first came to this city."

"I don't think I want to be an actor," Charles says nervously.

Professor Tork chuckles. "No. Of course not. But I know people. People who can help."

Charles wonders what Tork wants from him for this pledge of support. Of course, he will pay the price, if he has to, but still he wonders. He's entered into these arrangements with eyes shut too many times, but not anymore.

But the professor requests nothing in return. Charles isn't sure he trusts this one-sided transaction, but decides not to resist. That's not what the character of Charles Ward would do. So, within a week, thanks to Tork's machinations, Charles stands in front of William Budd, who sits on the board of trustees of the New York Public Library.

Mr. Budd makes a call.

"I've got a young man here . . . ," Mr. Budd states, and within the span of a four-minute phone conversation, Charles Ward has a new job at the library.

"Low level and menial," Mr. Budd confesses, "but it's a start. That's all a man needs, right?"

17

The work at the New York Public Library is quiet, occasionally dull, and perfect.

Charles spends his days on the third floor, in the Berg Collection division, under the strict supervision of Mrs. Ayers, one of the manuscript librarians. Unqualified to present the rare offerings of the collection to the members of the public requesting them, Charles retrieves the artifacts from the archives room and replaces them, but only after three weeks' training on how to properly handle the artifacts. With the reverence of a priest presenting the body of Christ, Charles brings the requested item, resting with the weight of its history on the flat palms of his gloved hands, to the reading room. There he places it on the table in front of the scholar, usually conducting archival research on a particular author, with Mrs. Ayers standing sentry. Once the artifact is situated, Charles steps back into the shadow of Mrs. Ayers, who assists the patron with a breadth of knowledge of each artifact that stuns Charles. If the item is very old, very rare, such as something from the collection of papers of Nathaniel Hawthorne or the notebooks of Thackeray, Mrs.

Ayers will turn the pages as the scholar sits idle, hunching forward, frustrated at the thwarted interaction. Charles notices that Mrs. Ayers holds her breath as she leans over to turn the page with her gingerly touch.

When the scholar has finished reviewing the work—many scribble notes for whatever project has brought them to the library—Charles returns the artifact to the archives room, to its proper place.

"Everything on course, Mr. Ward?" Mrs. Ayers questions upon his return to the reading room, as if she were the captain of the SS *New York Public Library*.

"Yes, Mrs. Ayers."

And with a curt nod, she continues her work.

Such is life in the library: quiet and on course. Charles likes it very much.

But soon the quiet and solitude follow him home. With his life in America settled into a comfortable routine, Charles finds himself lonely for more.

After her minor success in her theatrical debut, Maude wins another role in a better play and a larger, more prominent theater which keeps her busy most days and evenings. Another role follows and then another, as her acting career starts to flourish and soon she "simply must move uptown to be in the thick of it".

"Of course we'll stay in touch, Charles!" Maude exclaims during her goodbye in the foyer of Perkins's Boardinghouse. But her exit from the boardinghouse was her exit from his life, as well, and Charles knew as much at the time, even if she didn't.

So, Charles spends his evenings and weekends alone in his small cubicle of a room at the boardinghouse. He might linger about after dinner while Mrs. Perkins cleans up, and even assist her, much to her protestations, in order to hear her chatter about the day or gossip about the neighbors, but he is the only one in the house to do so. The communal areas of the house are not very communal at all, with the other inhabitants hurrying back to their rooms directly after dinner, not to be seen again until the next day. Some evenings he might stroll the streets of the neighborhood, to vary the days and distract from the boredom. And, on occasion, he will splurge his meager earnings on a movie show. And it is there, in the dark of a movie house in the Bowery, that he has his first encounter with another man in America.

One Sunday afternoon, Charles sits in a showing of *The Dolly Sisters*, some silly musical with Betty Grable and June Haver. Partway through the movie, a man takes the seat next to him. As the man nestles into the seat, he brushes his arm against Charles's. A moment later, the man's knee bumps against Charles's knee, and this is followed by a whispered "Pardon." Then, without further contact or warning, the man places his hand on Charles's leg, high, near his crotch. For Charles, the moment freezes with confusion and concern before understanding pushes everything aside, revealing the need, the desire to be touched. Since Berthold, he has been intent only on survival and hasn't even for a moment thought about sex or love or simply being with someone else.

So, Charles doesn't push the hand away. He faces the screen, where Betty Grable and June Haver vamp a song, though Charles doesn't know which actress is which, and lets the man's hand roam about, then fumble with the buttons of his trousers. He should stop him. Surely, they will be seen or caught, but then the man takes Charles's cock out of his pants and leans over and takes it in his mouth. Charles closes his eyes. He blocks out the movie and the people around him. He blocks out the library and his lonely life at Mrs. Perkins's. He blocks out everything but the feeling. It does not take long for Charles to finish, his body shuddering with no more passion than a sigh, ever quiet in his release, born of his time in the Werden house.

The man departs as stealthily as he arrived.

Then there are other men, brief encounters in the dark of the movie theater, in the bushes of Central Park, in alleys late in the evening. Quick physical releases, sometimes mutual, sometimes not, that stave off the loneliness for the brief amount of time they are happening. But the feeling of not being alone never lingers longer than the smell of the sex.

Once or twice, the men attempt to linger afterward, to chat ever so blithely as they tuck their cocks back into their trousers. Usually, they start with "What's your name?" which always strikes Charles as comical and embarrassing. To have been so intimate without the first notion of who the other is in the world. But is that not their lot in life, he wonders, the lot of the *warme Brüder*, as they are called in German, who must hide in the shadows, in the dark movie theaters, in the bushes, and sometimes in the cellars of their own homes? And after he tells them his name, what more will they want to know about him? Which story would he tell them? And then what would they do together beyond the bushes or the movie house? No, it's all too much to fathom, all that unknown.

It was easy with someone like Maude, who wanted to speak only about herself and her life, rarely venturing into the details of Charles's existence. But not everyone is as self-focused as Maude. Most others are curious about the lives of the people they encounter. Charles is. After a tryst with a man, he can't help but wonder about his life, who he is out there in the real world, beyond these isolated moments. He encounters quite a few men with wedding rings—they are the most voracious, like Berthold was, at least in the beginning—and Charles thinks about their wives, their children, their parents, their coworkers and friends, who know nothing about what this man does on the occasions when he is not to be found.

"You're late dear," the wife will say when he comes in the house. "I've already fed and bathed the children."

"I'm sorry," he will profess. "I had . . . a late call at the office/ a flat tire/ the need to touch and be touched by another man . . ."

What kind of life is that? Charles has enough lies to keep straight; he doesn't need any more.

No, it is best this way, Charles tells himself time and time again.

But on occasion, a man will spark imaginings of more than a quick, fleeting moment. Thoughts of capturing what he'd had with Eliáš so long ago. But, in the end, the barriers, the protective walls prove as impenetrable as the dark gray stone walls of Terezín, where he left Eliáš.

Trent Waltham frequents the New York Public Library daily. Older than Charles by at least twenty years, Mr. Waltham exudes the sureness of a man with money and power, reminiscent of Berthold, at least in countenance. Dashing in a movie star way, with dark, wavy hair and languid brown eyes, he dresses in what Charles has heard described as natty, trendy, and stylish.

Charles knows Mr. Waltham watches him as he lingers on the periphery of his interactions with Mrs. Avery, none too subtle with his leering. At first, the attention unnerves Charles (and prompts Mrs. Ayers to warn Charles of "the likes of men like Mr. Waltham"). She also explains that Mr. Waltham is a man of leisure. When Charles asks Mrs. Ayers the meaning of this phrase, he learns it means that Mr. Waltham is rich, as he suspected.

"He does not need to work," Mrs. Ayers continues, an envious edge to her voice. "He spends his days as he pleases, with no care of money. He fancies himself a writer, but he's been coming here for years and has yet to produce even one published work."

After months of surreptitious voyeurism, his glances periodically returned, Mr. Waltham speaks to Charles.

"Have you read Dickens?" he inquires in a rare moment when Mrs. Ayers has left them alone as she oversees another researcher's request. Charles has been allowed to turn the pages of some legal notices contained in the Charles Dickens collection.

"No. Not yet," Charles responds, his throat dry from nervousness over being permitted to touch such a priceless artifact.

"You must," Mr. Waltham decrees. "He is the most amazing writer. I'm working on a biography."

From there a conversation begins, mostly about Dickens, but about other writers, as well. In time, they carry the conversation beyond the rooms of the library into restaurants for a lunch here and there, much to Mrs. Ayers's disapproving gaze, though she has no recourse to control her employee's personal time.

They dine in restaurants that leave Charles in awe and fear of their grandeur. He fidgets in his chair and hems with timidity when spoken to by the waiter.

"You must act like you belong, Charles," Mr. Waltham instructs. "These people who work here have no idea if you work in a library or own the entirety of New York City. They take their cues from you. If you act scared, they will treat you poorly. If you act confident, they will treat you as such. It's all perception."

During their lunches, they continue to discuss books and literature. At least Mr. Waltham does. Charles has little to add to the conversations, but that does not seem to bother his companion, who is content to hear himself pontificate on this author or that one. Mr. Waltham is another Maude, someone merely looking for an audience, be it a full theater or a young, uneducated man who works at the New York Public Library.

After their first dinner together, Mr. Waltham brings Charles to his home, a four-story brownstone on the edge of Central Park. The wealth astounds Charles. He has never seen such finery, not even in the movies. As he trails Mr. Waltham, Charles gawks at the artworks, the furniture, the luxurious fabrics, and the knickknacks made of porcelain and gold. The home feels like a museum, curated and untouchable.

Mr. Waltham leads Charles directly to the bedroom. With no ceremony, he kisses Charles hard. He paws at Charles's body, not unlike the men Charles finds in the parks and alleyways, quick and desperate, afraid of getting caught. The sex is aggressive and ugly. Once naked, shirt off and pants down, Charles is turned and pushed onto the bed. He braces himself because he has been through this before. While the entry is not as violent as he previously experienced, the fuck is not enjoyable. There is no tenderness, no care. Charles closes his eyes against the assault. It will be over soon, he can tell. Like so many of the men he has encountered lately, Mr. Waltham is all business, with only one goal in mind.

Afterward, Charles does not linger, not that he is asked to do so.

"The driver can take you home," Mr. Waltham states once Charles has tidied himself. Mr. Waltham slips on a silk robe and stands by the bedroom door. "I've rung down while you were in the bathroom. He is waiting for you at the bottom of the stairs."

The coldness confuses Charles, but he does not dwell in the moment.

"Thank you, Mr. Waltham." Charles nods. "Will I see you at the library tomorrow?"

Mr. Waltham is flustered briefly, then shakes his head. "No, I have read all I care to read there."

Unsure what to say, Charles hesitates.

"The driver is waiting," Mr. Waltham says to spur Charles into action.

Charles offers another nod as he leaves.

In the car headed home, Charles wonders what he did wrong

to cause Mr. Waltham to turn in such a way. He mulls over the evening and then the entirety of their interactions, from the library to that evening's encounter. He cannot pinpoint a moment, an event. Then he realizes that he does not care. The chasm between the man of leisure and the immigrant library clerk was always going to be too expansive for either of them to traverse. Better to understand that before one of them falls in. He stares out the window at the city, the people out and about, bustling even at that hour. He will never understand where they are always going in such a hurry.

Almost a year would pass before Charles would attempt anything more than a sordid tryst with a stranger.

Sitting in a café in Greenwich Village, Charles overhears a man speaking Czech to the waiter. He can't help eavesdropping, surprised at how the language he hasn't spoken in years comes back to him, full and clear. After the waiter leaves, Charles, contrary to his usual behavior, reaches out and taps the man on the arm. *"Jste ech?"*

Jiří Dobrý is not much older than Charles. Though he is thin, there is a solid Eastern European countenance about him. His green eyes pierce when they look at you, as if he is searching for a stronghold. His jawline is strong and set, even when he smiles. Charles invites him to his table. As they trade life stories, Jiří tells Charles he spent time in Auschwitz. What were the odds, they wonder aloud, of finding another like themselves in such a crowded city?

Jiří spent two years in the camp. While he does not speak of that time, his body tells the story: the dull bluish-gray tattoo that ghosts on the flesh of his forearm, scars that are etched on his skin, a limp that speaks of a broken bone never set, so it healed incorrectly, a smile that reveals a missing tooth, one that rotted from lack of hygiene.

Before Auschwitz, Jiří was a schoolteacher in Prague.

"I liked being around the children." He lights up as he remembers. "Especially the younger ones. They are the most eager to learn, always asking questions. I was very good with them."

But in America, he is not a teacher. He has pursued teaching opportunities in the city, but they say he must have an American degree. He found work as a deliveryman for the *New York Times*.

"Will you go back to school?" Charles asks.

"I am fine at the newspaper." Jiří's says but his voice is heavy with sadness and anger and his shoulders slump with the resignation of his fate here in America.

The pall of Auschwitz hovers over them like a cloud. It shadows them as they meet for lunch and Charles finds Jiří staring off into space, eyes dark and still. It is there when they sit in a movie theater and Charles reaches for Jiří's hand, which jerks away with panic. It is there when Charles sleeps over at Jiří's small basement apartment and their sex is tender but desperate. Jiří kisses deep, with a hunger Charles has never experienced. He pulls Charles inside him, his legs wrapped around Charles's waist, and he clings to Charles with such force, Charles fears his rib cage will collapse. Afterward, as Jiří sleeps, Charles stares at the tattoo on Jiří's arm. He lays his scarred arm next to Jiří's. He tries to remember his number but can't. Later, he startles awake to Jiří's nightmarish screams.

The pall of Jiří's two years spent in Auschwitz, though Charles believes he never left, collides with the pall of Charles's guilt over not enduring more. Their relationship lasts no more than a couple of months.

The only other person of note to Charles was a Spaniard with dark hair, dark skin, and a certain earthy smell that was not unpleasant. It was that rare tryst that moved from a salacious encounter in Central Park to a stroll through the streets of New York.

At eighteen, Edgardo Ramos is younger than Charles. A congenial young man, the son of a diplomat, he is free and open and daring in his youth and privilege.

"Walk with me?" he asks after their encounter, which had them both entirely too undressed for any sort of hasty getaway should they be interrupted by anyone other than a like-minded gent.

The day is warm and pleasant, late spring, as they approach Sixty-Eighth Street.

"Have you ever been to Café Marie?" Edgardo asks.

"I do not know the place," Charles confesses.

"Ah! But you must!" Edgardo exclaims in that wonderfully ecstatic way Western Europeans have. "I will bring you there *ahora!*"

Situated on a tree-lined street, among the opulent town houses of the Upper East Side and not far from the upscale boutiques of Madison Avenue, Café Marie exists to conjure memories of Paris, of the bistros found far from the conventional environs of l'avenue des Champs-Élysées. For Edgardo, the place recalls the cafés in Barcelona. Small, intimate, and cramped, the place offers décor that will be frozen in time for years: mostly French, with hints of other European countries. With a macédoine of chairs and tables, banquettes and throw pillows, Café Marie brings to mind a weary prostitute painted past her prime but still peddling her wares, much to her chagrin.

An advertisement on the wall opposite the entrance portrays a laughing Marie Antoinette tossing her head back, exposing her scandalous neck. Her powder-white wig towers tall and precarious yet without fear of crumbling as she proclaims her infamous edict "Let them eat cake!"

"Isn't she divine?" Edgardo says, prodding.

In the spring and summer, and often well into the fall, the bistro's tables spill out onto the sidewalk. The regulars long to be where they can isolate and pretend ill-waged wars, failing dictators, and righteous coups didn't force them to this foreign land.

That Café Marie caters to the well-heeled émigrés of New York City is more than apparent. To the ruffian immigrants of the city who come in search of sanctuary in which to plot their next move, Café Marie says, *Take your whispers of revolutions and rebellions and talk of political coups to the cafés and bars of the Lower East Side and the Bowery, where they belong, for your utopian ideals will not survive here!*

The coffees at Café Marie have been imported from their mothers' lands, if those lands had the good fortune to fall under British rule: Africa, Sri Lanka, the isles of the Caribbean, India. And some that have not: France, of course, and Italy and Spain. All paired deliciously with a bounty of pastries. Classic French delicacies dominate, as they should, but tea cakes from England and baklava from Greece and *capuchinos* from Cuba, also figure prominently. And, of course, there is cake, lots and lots of cake.

Cigarette smoke clouds the air, distorting time and place. The men of Café Marie speak of business and war and the business of war, of their wives and mistresses — all with the banality of discussing the weather. The women chat of their fashions and their men with equal triviality. Couples, rarely consisting of husband and wife, discuss the financial angles of their romantic arrangements.

The waitstaff, too, have come from foreign shores, as displaced as their customers. Men and boys who have fled in search of something beyond their accursed lots in life. Anything more interesting than the ennui of living dull, insignificant lives. Still others have come in search of nothing, driven by a wanderlust that will forever deny them rest or happiness. They will call Café Marie home for weeks, months and, every so often, years.

Almost immediately, Café Marie reminds Charles of Bay-reuth and Frau Hueber's konditorei: the aroma of the coffee, the sweet scent of pastries. Then there is the amalgam of languages that intoxicate the air like the clouds in an opium den, a dense potage of French and Italian and Spanish and . . . Was that German?

Charles returns to Café Marie time and again, if only to be ensconced rightfully among fellow émigrés. Soon enough, he meets Madame Harriet, owner and proprietress. While American, she has spent much time abroad with her husband, Monsieur Randall.

"You have an air about you, Charles," she coos, for she coos everything she says. "An air that freshens and I want that here at Café Marie."

She will not take no for an answer once she learns he has worked as a pastry chef. She makes him a generous offer.

Much to Mrs. Ayers's disappointment, Charles states his intention to depart the library. She is most annoyed at having to train another young man. After some time at Café Marie, as his income increases, Charles moves out of the basement of the boardinghouse on Orchard Street.

"I do hate when my children leave me," Mrs. Perkins cries. "But I am happy for you, Charles."

He will miss Mrs. Perkins and her cooking and her chatter, but the house has not been the same since Maude departed, and it has never been his home. It pains him to think of Maude out there in the same city yet vanished from his life. But how many people have come and gone in his life, never to be seen again? Too many and still he is so young.

Charles finds a small apartment situated a few floors above a book and music store on East Seventh Street. It is another neighborhood of immigrants, Ukrainians, for the most part, but also Czechs. He likes hearing his old language again, even though he pretends not to understand when someone speaks to him in Czech.

"Do you not speak English?" he asks. "You should in America."

Over time, Charles fashions a quiet life that suits him. A life he lives unsettled and unchanged some twenty years before his past returns in the form of Berthold.

PART III

NEW YORK CITY
1968

18

In the days after revealing himself to Berthold, Charles calls in ill to the café, something he has never done before at Café Marie. For five days, he isolates. He knows he should turn Berthold over to the authorities, send him back to Germany to stand trial for his crimes, as others have. Barely a year ago, Nazi hunter Simon Wiesenthal found SS-Hauptsturmführer Franz Stangl in Brazil, and they extradited him to West Germany. When Charles watched the news footage of Stangl being loaded onto the plane in São Paulo, shackled at the wrists and ankles to hobble him, he watched from a distance, a man far removed from the events of World War II, a man far removed from the events of his own life, a man who wondered if it even mattered anymore. *What was done was done*, Charles thought as he watched the news. The almost one million people they accused Stangl of killing were dead. Stangl lived his life in plain sight, never even changing his name, for over twenty years. And by the time of his capture, he was probably closer to death with or without being captured, so hadn't he already won the game? Hadn't all the ones who'd escaped prosecution won, including Berthold Werden?

Charles should be angry. He should be seething with rage over the likes of Stangl and Berthold, over all the Nazis, free or not. He should be in a rage for all the lives they took, including his own. He should, but all he feels is numb, which he thought would feel like being empty, hollow, drained. But he now understands that numbness has its own weight, its own pressure and gravity, as if he is a bag filled with cement, slowly solidifying into the shape of him. He isn't sure when this numbness filled him, but now that he understands the feeling, he knows it has been his way for years. One more survival tactic.

That night at the restaurant quickly took on a tone of surrealism. After the revelation, Charles and Berthold sat silent as the restaurant's waitstaff bustled about them. A waiter stepped forward to recite the evening's specials. Neither Charles nor Berthold heard him, and the waiter stepped away as unacknowledged as he had been upon arrival. Berthold stared at Charles. Charles couldn't remember if he'd ever seen Berthold so vulnerable. The exposure frightened Charles for some reason.

"How have you been, Charles?" Berthold finally broke through the silence.

The banality of the question made Charles laugh. Not a chuckle or a snigger, but a bursting guffaw, which startled Berthold and the diners in their immediate vicinity.

"I've been fine, Berthold," Charles stated through his laughter. "How about you?"

Berthold glared at Charles with an odd gleam of fatherly disappointment. Charles shook his head and rose from the table.

"I can't, Berthold," Charles confessed and walked out of the restaurant.

When Charles finally returns after a full workweek's absence, Jacques fawns over him. He offers to perform Charles's preparation duties. He offers to take his first table. He offers to take all his tables.

"I am quite well now, Jacques," Charles assures the doting boy.

"I'm so happy to hear that." Jacques beams. "I called you many times, but you never answered. I worried."

"Ah, that was you." Charles can't disregard the jolt of disappointment that shakes him. At the same time, he chastises himself for thinking Berthold would go so far as to seek out his phone number and call him. Then he chastises himself for wanting, for needing Berthold to go so far as to seek out his phone number and call him. And Charles feels that long-ago pang of hurt and confusion ring anew. That need to know that it all meant something. God, how he hates the incessant need to know that this world, this life has some sort of meaning. The need and the search can drive a man mad.

Charles steps outside for a cigarette. The afternoon crowd will wander in soon, and he must shove aside his own anguish. As usual, he stands away from the café. Not for the first time, he contemplates quitting smoking. The act disgusts him, makes him feel weak. He abhors the stains that discolor his index and middle fingers on his right hand. They glare at him, as permanent as any tattoo or scar, and he has enough of those already.

As he extinguishes and pockets the butt, Charles finds Berthold standing outside the café. Berthold looks hesitant, peering inside with worry and expectation. Charles watches. For a moment he imagines Berthold in shackles, like Stangl. He's surprised that the image doesn't comfort as he thought it should.

"Hello, Mr. Lynch," Charles offers as he approaches.

Berthold turns with a start but at once looks relieved. "Charles, you're back."

"Mr. Lynch. Is that what I am to call you?"

"That is who I am now."

"Is it?" Charles places his hand on Berthold's cheek. The man's eyes widen in panic, but they don't widen with a perceived threat but out of fear of such a public display between two men, and his mouth moves in voiceless protest. Charles holds Berthold's head so they are face-to-face.

"I will call you Wallace Lynch, if you wish," Charles says. "But that is not who you are. You are Berthold. You will always be Berthold."

Berthold steps back, away from Charles's touch.

As they enter the café, Jacques stands at a table, preparing to pour coffee for a young couple who chat with each other, oblivious to Jacques's presence, as it should be. "We are only ghosts, after all," Charles is fond of saying to the other waiters, especially the new ones. Jacques glances up from the table and Charles watches his eyes cloud over with confusion at the odd proximity of Charles to Wallace, waiter and customer. Jacques scowls and such a sign of emotional weakness unnerves Charles.

"You are working today?" Berthold asks.

"Of course," he says, as if the previous five days of absence never occurred.

"Then I should like some strong coffee," Berthold states, just shy about of his usual demanding tone, but a wink hides in the sternness, an acknowledgment of the putting on of the mask. "Are the pastries fresh? I have a desire for a blueberry Danish, but only if it is fresh. Do not bring it if it is not fresh."

Charles can't help but smile. "Of course, Mr. Lynch."

Jacques follows Charles to the service area.

"Charles?" Jacques asks with pointed concern. "What were you speaking about with that horrid man? I wish he wouldn't come in here at all."

"He's not so horrid," Charles responds. "Just curt."

"Curt? What is this?"

"It means he is abrupt. *'Brusque' en français.*"

"*Mais oui! Il est très* curt!" Jacques exclaims, relishing speaking French again, if only for a moment.

"He is German, so not out of character," Charles explains.

Charles brings Berthold his coffee service and blueberry Danish, which is fresh, of course.

"You can come by this evening?" Berthold asks under his breath. "We should speak, Charles. *Bitte*."

And it is this *bitte*, a word never before uttered to him by Berthold, that causes Charles's body to tremble. He falters mid-pour, spilling a single drop of coffee onto the saucer. But Berthold does not scold—that was Frau Werden's role—merely dabs at the spill with the corner of his napkin.

"Yes," Charles answers without further hesitation, "I will come."

The doorman nods with recognition as Charles approaches the apartment building. He saw Charles many times haunting the sidewalks as he stalked Berthold.

"Good evening, sir," he offers, his voice wary. "How may I help you?"

"I am here to meet with one of your tenants. Mr. Lynch."

"Ah, yes. The clerk will announce your arrival."

In the elevator Charles experiences a nervousness he hasn't felt in years, the feeling of being unsure of his next move. He hates the feeling. He hates being unsure.

"I wasn't certain you would come," Berthold confesses when he opens the door.

Charles is surprised Berthold would confess such a thing. He enters the apartment, closes the door behind him, and stands in front of his host. Berthold steps slightly closer.

"And now that I am here?" Charles asks.

"I am curious why."

Berthold steps over to a bar cart. He pours two scotches. With his back to Charles, he drinks most of one and refills the glass. Turning, he hands Charles his drink.

"I am equally as curious, I'm sure," Charles admits.

"Tell me, Charles," Berthold says, leading him deeper into the apartment, "why did you wait to reveal yourself?"

Charles follows Berthold into the living room. The apartment is well appointed but sparse, unlike the Lynch home in

Scarsdale. The look is modern and sterile, as if the apartment is for show rather than for living. Charles assumes the place came with the décor.

Neither he nor Berthold sits, both hovering, unnerved, alert.

"Actually, I didn't recognize you until you came in with Frau Werden. Very careless, I know. But you didn't recognize me at all. Have I changed that much?"

"You are a man now, Charles," Berthold states with what sounds like a sense of astonishment. "And to be honest, I never imagined you to be here, so I didn't connect you to . . . then."

Charles nods. "Possibly that's why I didn't recognize you, either. But Frau Werden. She has not changed at all. Though I suppose she is Mrs. Lynch now, which doesn't fit her at all."

"No, it doesn't."

"And her Christian name?"

"Doris," Berthold reports. "Doris Lynch."

Charles laughs. "She does look like a Doris."

"It was her nanny's name. As was Lichtzers."

"Her nanny was Jewish," Charles states with a certainty that Berthold confirms with a nod. "Interesting. Wallace and Doris Lynch. A nice Jewish couple."

"They are," Berthold assures Charles. "He plays his part more so than she does."

"Of that I am certain." Charles doesn't mask his disdain. "And their children?"

"Marlene would not change her name. You know how stubborn she could be. She became Marlene Lynch. She is in Brazil. Married. We don't hear from her as much as we would like."

"Brazil?" Charles asks with feigned surprise, as if he had not already heard all this from Frau Werden.

"That's where we ended up." Berthold sounds wistful. "Many of us did."

"Nazis?"

"Germans."

"And the boy?" Charles continues.

"Here in New York. Though we don't see him much, either."

"Still the *schmendrick*?"

Berthold laughs. "He is in finance and does well enough. As I said before, he has not married yet. He is very American. Which is good, I suppose."

"You don't sound like the proud father."

"No. I have failed as a father, Charles," Berthold declares with finality, as if the realization has at that moment fallen upon him. "Possibly, I have failed as a man."

"There is no doubt," Charles states plainly, without anger or indictment. "But most men do. Men who have done far less than you."

Berthold slumps under the weight of Charles's rebuke.

Charles steps in front of Berthold. He waits until he looks up. His eyes sheen with pain, guilt, shame, but only a sheen, a slight veil, blurs the indifference underneath. "Tell me, Berthold . . ."

"Why did I kill them?"

"Why did you leave me?"

And the question startles them both with its childishness and long-seeded pain.

"Charles." Berthold's voice softens, becomes delicate, reminiscent of those long-ago nights. "You know I couldn't—"

"No!" Charles barks. "You could have! You owed me that much!"

Charles steps back a pace as Berthold rises and they stand face-to-face. Berthold touches Charles's cheek, as he did that day in the German countryside, on the outskirts of Bayreuth, his palm warm against Charles's skin. Charles waits for the feeble, familiar excuses to be repeated. As if they haven't coursed through his memory a million times since that day.

But Berthold doesn't speak. He leans forward and kisses

Charles on the lips, timid and unsure. The act surprises Charles, but his lips remain tight against Berthold's. His entire body remains tight, resistant, even as the familiarity rushes through body.

"Is that your idea of an apology?" Charles questions, but not as harshly as he intended.

The moment jolts between them. Charles hates the need that courses through him, the need and the desire, not just to be touched and kissed in general, but to be touched and kissed by Berthold. He hates that he's never felt this way with anyone else, not with any of the strangers he's encountered or any of the men he's dated or even with Jacques. And he hates that these emotions make him feel like that desperate young man he was back in Oświęcim. Not the young man who did what he needed to do to survive, but the young man who fell in love with Berthold, despite all he did. The young man who has woken from his yearslong sleep to stand here in this room with Berthold once again. The young man who leans forward and accepts Berthold back into him.

Sex between the two men is different some twenty-five years removed from each other. While the familiarity remains, their bodies have changed, their needs have changed, their reasons for connecting have changed. Berthold's touch is hesitant as he explores Charles. He does not force or dominate or rush, as he did when a younger man trapped by war and family. He does not shy away from kissing, his lips tender, not as hard or as hungry as they once were. He does not shy away from holding Charles, embracing him, as if seeking to absorb him. He does not rush past these intimacies in order to bury his cock inside Charles. In fact, he does not fuck Charles at all. And he makes sure Charles finishes, something he never did in the past.

As for Charles, he accepts it all, the kiss, the touch, the care, but as he did back in the day, as he's done with every encounter he's ever had with a man, he remains on alert.

"I wish I had taken you with me, Charles," Berthold confesses.

Charles's head lies on Berthold's chest. At sixty, Berthold is not as muscular as he once was. The tone of his body is weaker—he's not fragile, as a modicum of strength remains— but in many ways, this is a new man.

"Actually, I wish I had taken only you and left them all behind to face the Russians. If I'd been a stronger man . . ."

Charles tightens his hold for a quick moment. "You never would have forgiven yourself."

"You'd be surprised how much I can forgive myself, Charles," Berthold states with an evenhanded self-confidence, which Charles envies.

19

Curiosity urges Charles to seek out Raymond Lynch, to complete the family portrait of the Werdens in America.

Even in a city as dense as New York City, Raymond is not difficult to find. According to the phone book, the only Raymond Lynch listed in the borough of Manhattan lives in the Murray Hill section of the city, on East Thirty-Seventh Street, between Lexington and Third Avenues. Charles stations himself on the sidewalk across from the apartment building. With a cup of coffee and a pack of cigarettes, he waits among the sparse early morning foot traffic. Men in smart black suits head out early, some to subways and others to town cars. Sanitation trucks rumble loudly down the street, the men riding on the back jumping down periodically to hoist, toss, and return the garbage cans with practiced choreography. A loose herd of hippies straggles by, reeking of sweat and marijuana, as they hum unknown tunes. One approaches to "bum some smokes," and Charles shakes his head firmly, sending him on his way with a mumbled "That's cool, man." Delivery trucks double-park, creating traffic snarls of impatient cars and yellow taxis. Jabbing bleats of car horns cry out into the hazy morning, to no avail.

When Raymond Lynch steps out into the morning, Charles halts at the sight of him.

Of course, Charles knew from the photo at the Lynch home that this man would be nothing like Geert Werden, the squat and rotund miniature of his mother. Geert's walk, wide and lumbering to accommodate his thick thighs, brought a flush to his apple-round cheeks during a mere stroll. But between then and now, fat, clumsy Geert morphed into tall, trim and, even though Charles loathes to admit it, handsome Raymond Lynch.

This man's stance is steady and sure as he turns his face upward toward the sun and lets it cast its ray down upon him, as if it was awaiting his arrival. His sturdy features and blond hair, darker than in childhood, are so like his father's at that age that they startle Charles. Then Raymond strikes off down the street with the arrogant gait of a typical American man who still hasn't shed his boyhood skin and so has to pretend he is a man. He barrels down the sidewalk with the overconfident expectation that all will make way for him.

"There you are, Geert," Charles remarks under his breath.

Charles hastens to cross the street to fall in line behind Raymond. Since the son does not possess the father's measured gait, Charles must hurry to keep pace. Raymond darts about the sidewalk, sidestepping others as if playing some sort of tangled game of chicken. At Lexington Avenue, he flags a taxi. Charles does the same, then instructs his driver to "follow that cab." Unlike the Scarsdale taxi drivers, New York City cabbies have no qualms about engaging in pursuit, nefarious or otherwise.

Heading downtown, they stop and start along Lexington before making their way over to Broadway. There the traffic flows with more freedom but still at a sluggish pace. In the Financial District, Raymond's taxi stops in front of the American Express Building.

Charles exists the taxi and quickly blends into the crowd of businessmen and secretaries that streams into the expansive lobby. At the row of elevators, Raymond crowds into the next available. As Charles approaches, the doors close. He watches as the elevator ascends, each floor ticked off by a light and a bell. He has no idea on which floor Raymond exits.

While Raymond Lynch might not have inherited his father's stature and stride, he does possess a hint of his regimented way of life. Every weekday, he exits his apartment building at 7:45 a.m., as punctual as his father was in his day. At Lexington Avenue, he hails a taxi down to the American Express Building. After entering the building, he works until half past noon, at which time he eats lunch across the street at the Wall Street Luncheonette. There he sits at the counter, always choosing the last seat on the right side. He orders a BLT with French fries. (Definitely not kosher, Charles notes with a smirk.) On occasion, a coworker might join him. They sit side by side and speak in low business voices.

Come the end of the workday, Raymond Lynch is not so regimented. His departure from the office can vary from six thirty to nine in the evening (perhaps later, but Charles waits no later than nine). After work, Raymond heads deeper into the Financial District to Pearl Street and Fraunces Tavern.

Raymond never dines, preferring to linger in the bar area. With its décor of dark heavy woods and brass trimmings, Fraunces Tavern wears its history and nostalgia well. Coworkers join him. Still in their suits, they loosen their ties and the top button of their dress shirts. The women who join the group, released from the shallow waters of the steno pool, dress in smart, tight skirts and blousy tops. Their makeup has been reapplied more boldly for the evening. They have released their hairstyles in a rain of bobby pins and hair-spray dust. They toss their heads back in exaggerated arcs when they laugh, exposing long, thin necks, like subservient prey.

The men, Raymond included, perform their own rituals. Bravado dominates their show. They land playful punches on each other's shoulders or chests. They offer ribbings and gibes that often border on derision, designed to chip away at each other's manliness.

From a booth in the corner, Charles watches the macho preening. At times, Raymond can be a boorish character, the former Geert stepping forward to offer a condescending sneer to one of his colleagues, which recalls the arrogance and superiority he displayed toward Charles as a child.

At work the day after he first follows Raymond Lynch downtown to the Financial District, Charles finds himself distracted, preoccupied. Customers must wave their hands to capture his attention, which wanders off as he thinks about Raymond or Berthold or even Frau Werden. One gentleman clangs his spoon against his cup, which is simply mortifying at Café Marie.

Jacques corners him in the service area. "Charles, are you okay?" His face is a muddle of concern and confusion and tenderness. "Are you ill again? I can cover for you. I don't mind."

Charles shakes his head. "I am fine, Jacques. I have not been sleeping well."

Jacques nods but is not calmed. He places a hand on Charles's shoulder. The act is fatherly and comforting even when enacted by a man twenty years younger.

"I could come over this evening," Jacques offers. "Bring wine. We have not had an evening in quite some time."

Charles considers the idea. Jacques would be a nice distraction from his distractions. He could dive into a bottle of good French red wine and then dive into this beautiful French boy and think of nothing but his lithe, firm body. How his dark olive skin contrasts to Charles's pale white flesh. He likes

Jacques's flat stomach, likes watching it rise and fall with each breath. He likes the warmth that emanates from Jacques's body as he lies on top of him like a heating blanket.

But Charles knows the evening would be only a momentary diversion for him. For Jacques, it would be another brick added to the weight of need and infatuation and will pull him further down into the depths, toward a love that can't be, not at this time, at least.

"No," Charles tells Jacques, dashing his expectant smile. "Another time? Soon?"

"Yes, another time," Jacques sighs, then returns to the dining room to hide his disappointment.

Each afternoon Charles waits upon Berthold. On the surface, they remain professional, but they find ways of connecting. A mutual reaching for the sugar spoon causes their hands to graze one another. Berthold might adjust himself in his chair, brushing and pressing his leg up against Charles's leg. Berthold lingers imperceptibly as he places his payment into Charles's hand. Silly teenage tricks that are nonetheless gratifying in a fleeting way.

A few evenings a week they meet at Berthold's apartment. Charles derives comfort in the familiarity of being with Berthold, both sexually and emotionally, someone with whom he has a shared past. But he is curious about the sense of the unfamiliar, as well. Neither man is who he once was, so the dynamics have shifted. Berthold attempts to revert to the Obersturmführer of old, the one in control, the one with all the power, especially in bed, but Charles has not been that seventeen-year-old boy for twenty-five years, and there is no returning to him. He is bigger than he used to be. He is stronger than he used to be. But, above all, he is no longer cowed by the need to survive at all costs.

When Berthold attempts to turn Charles over onto his stomach to fuck him, Charles does not acquiesce.

"I don't do that anymore, Berthold," Charles says. "I have not done that for years."

"I don't understand," Berthold confesses, his brow furrowed with confusion, exposing the wrinkles around his eyes.

"What don't you understand? I don't like it. I never liked it. I prefer to be on top."

"Oh," Berthold says, his body and his cock losing their solidity.

One evening Charles asks about Geert.

At first, Charles felt guilty about sneaking behind Berthold's back to spy on his son, not to mention the times he's been to his home in Scarsdale, having pastries with his wife. But the thrill of the intrigue overcame the guilt soon enough, and he can't deny the feeling that something has been set in motion here, though he has no idea what.

Do you see him? No? Why not? That's a shame. I know how much Frau Werden doted over him. She must be heartbroken.

"America has changed him," Berthold laments. "He thinks only of money and material pleasure. As I said, he is not married. More so, he does not even think of marrying or having children. He does not stand for anything, save the American dollar. I wish he were more like you, Charles."

The statement makes Charles laugh, for what does he stand for in this life? Survival, yes, but beyond that, he has no idea.

20

New York City on American holidays—Memorial Day, Labor Day, and the like—is a city of streets so empty the scene verges on the apocalyptic. City dwellers head to the beaches of Long Island and New Jersey; some go as far as Connecticut and Massachusetts. And those left behind enjoy the spoils. Taxis appear at the slightest rise of a hand. Shops and grocery store shelves are well stocked, and their aisles are empty of customers and mercifully navigable. Restaurants beg for customers with special pricing and prix fixe menus.

The weekend of July Fourth, Café Marie is particularly quiet. Charles leaves early, entrusting the café to Jacques. With Berthold in Scarsdale, he dreads spending the evening alone, so makes his way to Fraunces Tavern.

With the Financial District closed for the holiday, Charles assumes Raymond is among those who have deserted the city. He pictures him on the beaches of East Hampton, the guest of a wealthy friend whose parents own a home out there. Raymond would wear swimming trunks of the latest style, short and colorful, loose, not vulgar, paired with a complementary button-down, short-sleeve shirt and Top-Siders. Very present-able, ever the businessman, even at the seaside. He would have a cocktail in one hand, a cigarette in the other, and a story on his lips. Charles likes the imagined scene and is both disap-pointed and jarred to find Raymond sitting alone at the bar at Fraunces Tavern. Though Raymond does not look up at his ar-rival, Charles ducks into the restaurant area to avoid detection.

The dining room sits empty. Two waiters stand at the host stand, staring into the abyss of the empty room, which will mean empty pockets come closing time. An uninviting scene, to say the least. Despite sure exposure, Charles retreats to the more welcoming bar, with its more than a handful of patrons.

The bartender, with his smooth, sure movements when he prepares Manhattans and Negronis and martini after martini after martini, finishes polishing the glass he's drying, then turns to Charles. He nods in recognition, then pours a glass of Oban over two cubes of ice.

"Tab?" he asks as he places the drink in front of Charles.

Before Charles can speak, Raymond replies from a few stools down, "Put it on mine, Jack."

Jack nods and returns to drying his glasses. Charles tamps down the emotion that threatens to twist his features. He knows the offered drink is not a sexual overture. He has watched Raymond interact with women in his group. He has seen how he looks at them, how he finds ways to touch their bare arms or their trim waists. The desperate lechery unnerves Charles. He assumes Raymond must be lonely without the noise and energy of his pals, so he has reached out to a fellow drinker, a companion in isolation during the holiday weekend. But something in this rationale doesn't sit right inside him.

Charles takes a moment, staring at the drink in front of him. The weak amber of the liquor settles around the ice cubes. With a breath, Charles turns to face Raymond. He tips his drink to-ward him and nods his thanks.

Raymond nods in return and approaches Charles.

"Shall we take a booth?" Raymond inquires but does not wait for an answer. He walks toward the row of booths.

Charles settles across from Raymond.

"This is the booth you like, yes?" Raymond asks, then laughs at Charles's attempt at surprise. "I know you've been following me."

Charles starts to balk, but Raymond stops him.

"Please, Charles. Remember my father raised me."

Charles relinquishes all pretenses of innocence and nods ruefully. "Berthold was ever the diligent commander."

"Berthold," Raymond says, as if tasting the name Charles has just uttered. "Have you hunted him down, as well? No, I suspect he hunted you down. Of course."

"Neither," Charles states. "It was a fluke."

Raymond laughs with derision. "Nothing is a fluke when my father is involved, Charles. If you didn't find him, be sure he found you."

Charles doesn't respond, though the statement heats through him, singes the certainty that his and Berthold's reunion was happenstance or even fated. He regards Raymond for a moment, then takes a sip of his scotch. Raymond's gruff mien suddenly changes, and he sighs in some gesture of kindness.

"I never hated you, Charles," he insists. "No, that's not true. I did hate you, but not because you were a Jew. What did I care about Jews? Nothing. I was a child. I didn't give a fuck. Still don't. No, I hated you because he liked you more."

Charles laughs.

"I know what really happened now," Raymond continues. "But all I knew back then was my father liked some dirty Jew boy more than his own son."

Finishing his drink, Raymond flags the bartender. "Two more, Jack."

They sit in silence until Jack has delivered the next round.

Raymond takes another healthy sip. Charles watches, waiting for Raymond to return to the conversation. To expose more wounds. Out of curiosity, he lets Raymond lead them. Has this man waved his hands in surrender? Has he laid down his weapons? Would a soldier's son ever do such a thing without an ulterior plan? Were they ever truly at war with each other?

"I've met a few guys like him," Raymond continues, shaking his head to indicate the shock still remains. "There's a guy in the office, married with kids and all, but he's queer. It's sad, really. I'm sorry he can't be who he wants to be, you know? Still, he shouldn't betray his family like that."

"When did you recognize me?" Charles asks. He has to admit he's shaken by his carelessness. First, not recognizing Berthold, then allowing Raymond to get the upper hand. He's become too complacent in his life.

Raymond offers a smirk that recalls the thirteen-year-old brat from long ago. He's gloating that he's unnerved Charles. But then he shrugs. "I noticed you following me pretty quick, I think. You're not very good at going unnoticed, you know."

Charles doesn't respond.

"At first, I thought you were someone looking for my father. A Nazi hunter or something. I've told him it's only a matter of time before someone comes for him. Won't be soon enough, if you ask me. Figured you were waiting for me to lead you to him. So, I let you follow me around."

Charles looks at Raymond and sees a maturity that he never expected to emerge from the snide little Geert.

"From the moment I noticed you, I felt I knew you," Raymond muses, swirling the ice in his glass. "Something about you was so familiar. It was frustrating because I couldn't figure it out for the longest time. Then one night you were sitting here, in this very booth, staring off into space. Then it hit me. You used to have the same look when you were in the backyard, staring out toward the camp."

Charles finds it incredible that Geert noticed him in those vulnerable moments and that the image actually stayed with him. So unlike Geert to consider someone outside himself. But then again, what did Charles know of Geert back then beyond their designated roles in the home of Obersturmführer Berthold Werden?

"I assume you've seen my father."

"I have," Charles allows. "Surprisingly, he didn't recognize me as quickly as you. I had to tell him who I was."

"Don't let his act fool you," Raymond warns. "He knew who you were the moment he saw you. Trust me, Wallace Lynch is as sharp and just as much of a cold bastard as Berthold Werden ever was. Maybe more so."

Charles pushes at the protests rising within him, the instinctual need to defend Berthold. He pushes at this need because he hates its existence. That he, of all people, would be the one to protect Berthold, especially against his own son.

"And your mother?" Charles inquires.

Raymond lets loose a bitter laugh before he spits, "That worthless bitch?"

The vehemence shocks Charles.

"Have you seen her yet?"

"No," Charles lies.

Raymond leans in and, lowering his voice, says, "You should, Charles. You should go see her. She's old now. Old and weak."

"What happened, Geert?" Charles asks. He understands the anger toward Berthold, but why his mother? "You used to be her favorite, her *kleiner Knödel.*"

"God, my German is so bad now," Raymond confesses. "Haven't spoken it in years. What is that again?"

"Little dumpling. You were her little dumpling, Geert."

Raymond nods. "No one calls me that anymore."

"Not anyone's little dumpling?" Charles chides.

"No," he laughs. "No one calls me Geert. I've been Raymond Lynch longer than I was ever Geert Werden. I don't think of him anymore. It's hard to explain to someone who hasn't experienced it."

Charles eyes Raymond. "You know Charles is not my real name, right?"

"Really?" Raymond exclaims with astonishment.

"Your father renamed me the day he took me from the camp. I've been Charles ever since. Thirty years now."

Charles waits for the barrage of questions about his past before coming to the Werden home. But none come, as Raymond is as self-centered as Geert ever was, is interested only in the past that includes him.

"He changed my name when we went to Brazil," Raymond explains. "God-awful place Brazil. If you ever have a chance to go, don't."

He gave a drunken laugh.

"Did he tell you he bought a diamond mine? A fucking diamond mine, for Pete's sake. I mean, who does that? Herr Berthold Werden, that's who. Nazi soldier one day, Brazilian diamond miner the next. It's a crazy fucking world, Charles."

"That it is," Charles agrees.

Raymond leans forward again. "I bet you're wondering if there was another you."

Charles shakes his head in confusion. "Another me?"

"You know, another young man in the cellar. Another special boy."

Charles laughs painfully. "No, I hadn't even thought about that."

Sitting back, Raymond looks surprised. "No? I thought you'd wonder."

"I guess I assumed there would be. I wasn't the first, so why would I be the last?"

Raymond nods. "Well, you're wrong on both accounts."

A breath snags on something in Charles's chest. "What do you mean?"

"There wasn't one before or after you." Raymond offers a sly smile. "At least none that I ever saw. Maybe he had someone hidden away somewhere, but I don't think so. Once we were in Brazil, if he wasn't at work, he was at home. And when he was home, he was right there where we could see him. No sneaking away like he did with you."

Charles considers the revelation. Raymond has to be mistaken. Berthold had to have found others as he had found Charles. Some other young man, or someone trapped in a marriage like him, or a business associate, with whom he could commiserate and fuck.

But then again, as Raymond Lynch says, it is a crazy fucking world.

21

A few days later Charles returns to Fraunces Tavern.

Jack the bartender nods upon his entry and reaches for the bottle of Oban. With his drink in hand, Charles sits in his booth. Raymond steps out of his circle and joins Charles.

"I was hoping you'd come back," Raymond says as he slips into the booth.

"You were?"

"Yeah," Raymond exclaims. "I enjoyed our conversation. Didn't you? I mean, I thought you were dead, and here you are. Hell, we all thought you were dead."

"You spoke about me?"

"Marlene did. You know she had a crush on you. Another reason I hated you. Everyone liked you better."

"Except your mother."

"Well, she had her reasons, didn't she?"

Charles winces but can't help but agree.

Raymond drains his drink, then signals Jack behind the bar for another.

"Is everything okay, Raymond?"

Raymond offers a dismissive smile. "Sure. I just . . . I was hoping you'd come back, because I have something for you."

From his jacket pocket, Raymond removes a white letter-sized envelope. He holds it for a moment, as if unsure, before placing it on the table. His fingers seem ready to snatch it back at a moment's notice.

"Raymond?"

With a nervous smile, Raymond slides the envelope across to Charles.

Inside are photographs. Berthold, younger, back when Charles first knew him, dressed in his military uniforms. Some with other soldiers and officers, all in their proper SS attire. Charles fans them out, seven photographs in all, on the table before him.

"They've been marked on the back," Raymond explains as he flips them over one at a time, like a casino dealer flipping the cards of a winning hand. The backs reveal names, dates, and locations penned in a meticulous hand.

Also included are documents from Auschwitz. Order forms bearing Berthold's signature, authorizing shipments for supplies. There are letters from Rudolf Höss addressed to Berthold. Some discuss menial daily operational details, while others alert Berthold to an upcoming visit to the camp. And there are letters and memoranda from Berthold to key Hitler operatives, such as Glücks and Eichmann.

"Where did you get these?"

"I found them in our home in Brazil. Why Mother didn't destroy them, I have no idea."

Charles scans the letters while awaiting further explanation from Raymond.

"You know, if these ever fell into the wrong hands . . ." Raymond offers a grim smile and raised eyebrows.

Examining the photos again, Charles peers at the clear eyes of the younger Berthold, his intense stare, the straight-backed stance, the set jaw. The same man through and through.

"They could easily match his current handwriting now to the older signatures," Raymond suggests.

Charles looks at Raymond.

"You think yours was the only life he destroyed?" Raymond asks. His anger shades his words, even though he doesn't raise his voice. "Living in hiding all those years . . . You have no idea, Charles. And he lives his life like he always has. As if none of it, all those people never mattered."

"It didn't bother you then," Charles snipes, remembering the petty boy who enjoyed tormenting him, as long as his mother was standing by his side.

"I didn't know," Raymond says, his words excusing him so casually that Charles can't hide a derisive laugh. "No, it's true. It's not like he talked about his job at the dinner table. I knew he worked in the camp, but I didn't know about the killing. I knew Jews were held there, but I thought it was just a prison. What did I fucking know at that age?"

Charles examines Raymond and finds Geert still exists, especially in the angry clench of his jaw and the narrowed eyes. The same look he had as a child whenever he was mad at Charles for some imagined misdeed. Could he be telling the truth? Was he that ignorant of the world in which he lived? Geert never struck Charles as a naïve boy, no matter how immature.

"And Marlene?" Charles asks.

"Who knows what she knew when?" Raymond shrugs, his anger dissipating. "She knew before me. She hated Father so much, remember? Could barely be in the same room with him. When we were in Brazil, she told me what really happened in Auschwitz and Buchenwald and Dachau and Treblinka and Bergen-Belsen. And the others. I don't even know how many camps there were."

"Tens of thousands, actually," Charles says.

Raymond drops back in his seat, as if slapped by this new knowledge. "You know, if the other Nazis knew what Father was doing down in the cellar with you, they would have locked him up, too. They locked up homosexuals, Charles. Killed 'em like the Jews and the gypsies and the retarded. Fucked up."

He drains his glass, then leans forward over the spread of photo and documents. "Don't you want him to pay, Charles? Don't you ever wonder about your life if the Nazis had never come to power? God, I do all the time." No. Charles has always fought traveling the road to "what if," knowing it leads only to misery and anger. To walk that road would be a march into quicksand. He'd sink in the imaginings of his family still alive, still in Czechoslovakia, still in Kladno, still in their small home, with the Poldi Steel Factory looming in the background. Charles (though he wouldn't be Charles, would he?) would work at the factory, like his father. Most likely he would marry a nice girl from town, for that is what would be expected (just as Wallace Lynch said). He and his wife might have children or might not. And he would sneak about with other men, haunting the darkened movie theaters or the public parks as he's done here in New York, but he doesn't dwell on those imaginings. Zofia would marry and, most likely, move to Prague, free of the small life of Kladno, which she hated so. She would have children, but no more than two. She and her family would come to Kladno for weekends and holidays. And Dussie? She might marry, as well, but would stay in Kladno. Or she might live with their parents and care for them in old age. Charles isn't sure. She was so young, it's hard to imagine her any other way. And here he is, mired in the quicksand.

"Think about it, Charles," Raymond says. "Just get these into the right hands, and they'll do the rest. Then he'll pay for what he's done to you, to your family, to all of us."

"Why me?"

Here Raymond falters, and Charles glimpses Geert in the cowered posture. "I . . . I can't. I can't be the one. I hate him, but he's still my father."

Raymond gathers the photos and documents and slips them back into the envelope. He leaves the packet on the table.

"Why haven't you turned him in, Charles?" Raymond counters. "The moment you realized who he was, why didn't you call the authorities?"

Charles doesn't respond. He's avoided the question for weeks, and now, as it buzzes around him like a mosquito seeking blood, he avoids it still, despite Raymond speaking it out loud.

"Just think about it, Charles. Keep these. I have copies."

Raymond looks into Charles's eyes for a moment before scooting out of the booth to return to his group of friends.

Raymond stops short. "I almost forgot," he says as he pulls a photo from his shirt pocket. He hands it to Charles.

Charles examines the picture, taken during the Werdens' time in Poland. Marlene and her mother play badminton in the backyard during one of the summer garden parties the Werdens threw on occasion. Marlene wears a charming sundress. Frau Werden wears a knee-length skirt, unsuited for backyard play. Frau Werden's expression is determined as her racquet hits the shuttlecock. Surrounding the play, guests are sharply dressed as they drink cocktails or a fruit punch. It's a lovely moment if one doesn't know that some ten kilometers away, Jews are being exterminated by the thousands each day.

Charles slides the photo toward Raymond. "This one won't work for your purposes."

Raymond laughs. "Don't you see?" He points out two figures in the background. "There."

Charles doesn't understand. One of the figures is Berthold, but the other . . .

"That's you."

Charles picks up the photo for closer examination.

"It's the only one I found."

"Are you sure that's me?"

"Of course, Charles," Raymond assures him. "How could I forget you?"

Charles looks at the photo again, at the young man, at himself. He's not as thin as he remembers himself being back then. He must have been at the Werdens for a year by then. His hair has grown back. He is smiling. He looks like he is enjoying the party, though he is sure he was working, catering to the guests. Still, he looks happy, and he can't remember ever being happy during that time.

"I don't have any pictures of me younger."

"Well, now you do," Raymond says by way of goodbye and rejoins his group, leaving Charles to stare at the only proof of his past existence.

PART IV

OŚWIĘCIM, POLAND 1942

22

On the day of deportation, Karel Benakov loads his father, slightly more than a skeleton, onto the empty train car. He places him on the floor against the back wall. Outside, Karel's mother pleads with the SS guards and the Czech gendarmes.

"He is ill. He needs a cot, a chair. Please."

"He doesn't need a chair," a young SS guard says as he roughly lifts her into the train. "He needs a coffin."

The three-kilometer march from Terezín to the station in Bohušovice has worn them all out. Karel carried his father most of the way, with Zofia helping as best she could. As thin as he is, Alexej Benakov is still a hulk of a man. But without the strength to stand on his own, his gangling limbs and weakened spine proved heavy weights for Karel.

With his father settled, Karel rushes back as a guard hoists Dussie into the train car. She tries to shrug off the guard's manhandling even as she struggles to climb aboard. Zofia is last. A young woman of twenty, she refuses help from the guards, but they grab at her roughly, lingering on her breasts and backside as they laugh and push and pull at her. Dussie, still young at thirteen, rushes to the doorway and yells at them to leave her alone.

After yanking Dussie back, Karel shoves her at their mother. He grabs Zofia outstretched hand and pulls her into the car as the guards laugh.

"Too small, anyway," a guard says as Zofia rushes into her mother's arms.

The Benakov family huddles in back as the train car fills with other transportees. Some cry and plead, while others kick and scream, all to no end. The guards shove in more and more people. The butts of their rifles prod and club and force until the car can fit no more. The press of bodies suffocates. Feet step on feet. Elbows jab into stomachs and backs. The wooden slats of the car creak with the pressure. Satisfied, the guards force the doors to close. Padlocks clank into place. And the waiting begins as the other train cars fill with more prisoners from Terezín and other camps and towns in the area. Hours later, the train roars to life, then rattles and groans as they head eastward.

23

If driving direct from the station in Bohušovice to Oświęcim, the trip should take no more than six hours. But overladen, the train creaks and lumbers, making torturous and slow progress, the weight of the human cargo bleeding every moment from each of the five hundred kilometers of the journey, which takes almost two days to complete.

Karel tries to keep track of the hours that pass, but the autumn-tinted clouds that blanket the sky give way to one exhaustive twilight, blurring time. During the rare moments when the sun forces its way through, he catches sight of a small town, a stretch of farmland, and once a group of children waving gleefully at the train.

Shortly after dusk, the train comes to a slow, painful stop. The growl of the locomotive dies to a silence so devoid of life that it startles. Beams of light from flashlights carve at the darkness as guards stroll alongside the train cars. They speak in conversational hushes, their words indecipherable.

"What do they say?" someone asks, the whisper urgent. "Why have we stopped?"

"Hush," says another. "I am trying to hear."

But no explanations come. Every once in a while, a beam of light will punch through the slats of the train car, illuminating a jumble of panic-stricken faces.

Without the breeze created by the movement of the train, the air in the car stagnates. The sour stench of shit and piss and sweat mixes with the odor of vomit and unwashed flesh. Each breath curdles Karel's stomach. At one point, Dussie begins gagging, but there is nothing left in her stomach. Karel guides her to the slatted openings of the car for a breath of air.

Once the movements outside cease, no one speaks, not to family, friend, or God. There are no voiced speculations of what awaits them—for they all know. And Karel realizes, beyond the shit and piss and sweat and puke, the most putrid stench is the resignation that permeates the air.

As train occupants doze that night, Karel remains awake, just in case. He listens to the breathing of his family until the light of the coming dawn appears outside the train car. Shortly thereafter, the train engine grouses back to life, as do the prisoners, their fear resurfacing in an instant. The journey continues.

At some point, the air outside thickens, becoming heavy and acrid. With each breath, a bitter taste films Karel's lips and teeth and tongue and throat. Through the slats, he sees the landscape mutate to a world of mud and what looks like dirty snow. Karel suspects they are close to their destination.

The train pulls to a stop. A dark gray fog of smoke hovers under the sky.

The occupants, still and quiet, wait for an eternity.

"Where are we?" someone asks.

No one responds.

Soft cries break through but are quickly stifled, lest they draw the guards' action.

In the distance, orders are shouted. Something bangs against the side of the train, sending angry reverberations snaking along the trail of cars, like a spasm traveling the vertebrae of a spine. With each shout, each bark, each bang, prisoners scream and cry. A gunshot here and there stills the voices but only for a minute. Then the moans and wails start again.

Karel gathers his mother and sisters about his father and instructs, "Do as they say. Do not provoke them."

The door to their car jerks open with a gasp from the prisoners as daylight bursts at them like flames. Cold air blasts into the car, stunning the flesh and seizing the breath.

"Out!"

"Move!"

"*Schnell!*"

From the back of the car, Karel cannot see what is happening. He pulls his family closer, and they listen to the voices yell and shout and scream and beg, so much begging. As the car is evacuated, the prisoners herded and pulled and thrown out, the crushing pressure abates. After many hours in one position, they once again can move their limbs. Cramps seize Karel's muscles, but he ignores them and rouses his father. "Papa, you must stand."

"Karel, he cannot," his mother says. "He is too weak."

"He must. They'll shoot him on the spot."

His blunt words shock his mother, but he has no time to indulge her useless naivete, not now. From the way they were transported to the way the guards bark and order and lash out with their batons and rifle butts, Karel knows they are no longer in a place like Terezín; the quicker they understand their new reality, the better their chances.

Karel places his shoulder under his father's and directs Zofia to his other side. "We will tell them he is tired from the trip."

They wait at the back of the car as it continues to empty. Too soon they are the only ones left, except for the corpses of those lucky enough to have died during the trip. Dussie stares at the dead, her lower lip quivering. Karel places his hand on her cheek and directs her gaze away from the sight.

"Keep your eyes forward and pay attention. Do as they say, and you will be fine."

"Get out! *Schnell*!" a guard yells as he bangs his club on the floor of the train car.

Karel moves forward, and the others take his lead; at seventeen, he is the man of the family. Karel hands his father off to his mother, then jumps down. He reaches up to take his father, but a club cracks against his back, buckling him. His mother screams, but Zofia hushes her.

Holding on to the train, Karel feels the pain sear through his lower back and buttocks. The guard yanks Karel back out of the way.

"Move along," the guard instructs, his club poised for another blow.

Karel does not retreat. "He needs help."

The guard looks up at Alexej, who is leaning on his daughter, head lolling as if in a hazy summer doze. "He is dead. Leave him."

Another soldier approaches. "What is the problem here?" Seeing Alexej, he asks, "Is he dead? Leave him."

"*Nein*!" Karel's mother cries, one of the few German words she knows.

"Quiet!" The second guard commands.

"He is only tired," Karel assures the guards in German. "Ill from the train ride. That is all."

"Bring him down." The first guard instructs.

Zofia and her mother start to lower Alexej, but the second guard, impatient with this bothersome scene spectacle, yanks Alexej down like a rag doll from a shelf. Karel snatches his father about the waist, breaking his fall, and props him against the train car. He slaps at Alexej's face with his leather-gloved palm.

"Stop, *bitte*," Karel's mother pleads wearily.

Alexej does not react to the slap. His head slumps on Karel's shoulder.

The guard then shoves a gloved finger at Karel's father's eye and pushes the lid up to expose the glassy eye underneath. "Dead. Leave him."

"*Nein*," Karel begs. "See."

Karel seizes the guard's wrist, surprising him, and holds it against his father's mouth so he can feel his breath. The guard jerks his arm free as the other guard cracks the butt of his gun on Karel's cheek. The pain blinds his vision, turning it a brilliant white.

His mother screams again.

"Not dead," Karel repeats.

"What's the issue here?" Yet another soldier approaches the scene. This one, handsome and sure, wears a different uniform, one adorned with badges and ribbons and medals. The other soldiers snap to attention at his approach. Karel looks up, his cheek bleeding and throbbing. He meets the new soldier's steely gray eyes. Karel flushes when their eyes connect. Desire, inappropriate for the moment, heats his skin. He holds the officer's returned stare.

"No issue, Obersturmführer Werden." The original soldier clicks his heels with a sharp crack. "Another dead Jew."

"He is not dead!" Karel bites back.

The second soldier raises his gun, ready to strike. Karel braces for the blow, but the Obersturmführer holds up his hand, halting the soldier with a clipped "*Warten.*"

The Obersturmführer steps up to regard Karel for a moment before turning his attention to Alexej. "He's not looking well, *Junge*. True, not dead . . . but still."

"He will be better soon, Obersturmführer. *Bitte*," Karel pleads, still holding the Obersturmführer's eyes.

"Your German is good."

"I know Germany will prevail. Soon the entire world will know. Heil Hitler." Karel clicks his heels.

The Obersturmführer chuckles, a strange sound amid the cries and suffering of the rail yard. "Smart too."

"*Danke*, Obersturmführer Werden."

"Ah, and you pay attention."

Karel nods and hazards a smile of his own.

"Tell me, are you a lucky young man?" the Obersturmführer asks.

Confused by the question, Karel does not respond.

"You come to Poland, to our camp as a guest, and ask us to spare your father. He is your father, yes? I can see the resemblance. Here and here." The Obersturmführer runs his leather-clad hand along Karel's cheek and jawline. "So, I ask you again, are you a lucky young man?"

Karel leans toward the Obersturmführer and demurs. "I am as lucky as you allow me to be, Obersturmführer."

The Obersturmführer regards Karel again, oblivious to the guards and Karel's family, who are watching and waiting. Karel holds his breath and feels he might pass out from anticipation. Is he wrong in thinking the Obersturmführer might desire him? Is he reading him so incorrectly? Is he wrong to wonder what it might feel like to kiss this man who holds his father's life in his hands? Finally, the Obersturmführer smiles.

"Well, I would say you are lucky, for I am feeling generous. How about that?" The Obersturmführer laughs. "Yes, most generous. Today your father lives. I'm not sure about tomorrow, but today . . ."

"But, Obersturmführer . . . !" the second soldier starts to protest, but the Obersturmführer waves him off.

"What is one more day?"

The soldier relents and says nothing more.

"On your way, then, before I change my mind."

"*Danke*, Obersturmführer," Karel whispers, his voice still weak with fear.

Zofia rushes in to scoop up her father once again.

"*Danke*," Karel's mother offers with exaggerated sincerity, and Karel pulls her away before she irritates the Obersturmführer. Karel guesses he is not a man who accepts falsities, especially from people he would as soon see dead.

They hurry to the left, toward the lines that lead to the camp. Karel looks to the right, at the line of other prisoners, which snakes off into the dark. And Karel suspects they are headed toward death.

"*Warten!*" The Obersturmführer's voice halts the family a few paces into their escape. Karel alone turns to face him. "You, young man. Come here."

Dussie takes Karel's place, holding up her father. Her stance is precarious, and Karel fears they will all collapse like a heap of scarecrows. The slight provocation would be the opportunity the soldiers seek to shoot Alexej—maybe all of them. But he cannot refuse the Obersturmführer. He steps over as the two guards hover behind them, vigilant and eager for any excuse.

The Obersturmführer regards Karel for a moment. Karel moves a step closer.

"What is your name?" the Obersturmführer asks, his voice quieter than before.

Karel hesitates.

"Give the Obersturmführer your papers, Jew," one of the soldiers standing behind the Obersturmführer, Karel is not sure which, instructs.

Karel hands over his papers.

The Obersturmführer scans them and hands them back. Without a word, he waves Karel away, back to his family and his fate. The two guards move on to usher more stragglers out of the train cars. Only the Obersturmführer remains.

Karel braves a glance back. He decides the desire lies not

only within him. But what can be done when all around them men and women and children are being marked for life or death, including him and his family? Even from the distance the intensity of the Obersturmführer's eyes does not waver. He takes a step forward but then stops. With a quick nod to Karel, he turns in the other direction.

24

As the tattoo needle digs into the flesh of his left forearm, Karel holds his breath. In isolated blocks the number appears like a manifested ghost, then dulls instantly as his skin drinks in the black ink. A moment later, blood seeps to the surface, blurring his new identification.

After the induction process, Karel and Alexej are herded with the rest of the new prisoners to the men's camp.

"You two, in there!" a guard shouts and jabs the butt of his rifle into the small of Karel's back, causing him and Alexej to stumble out of the line. The guard laughs as Karel scrambles to keep Alexej from falling.

"You want me to get rid of that for you?" the guard taunts.

Karel doesn't respond, hurrying Alexej into the barracks and out of sight. They step into a room filled with row upon row of wooden shelves stacked four deep, a room that looks more like a storage room than a place to live. Adjusting to the light, Karel squirrels his father into an open space and tucks him tight against the wall. He climbs in next to him.

The other prisoners, some so thin and frail Karel doesn't

know if they are real or lingering apparitions, cast vague stares in their direction. Karel glares back, defiance setting his jaw. Most are too frail to be of any threat, but Karel does not want trouble.

In the dim light, Karel wipes at the tattoo, and his palm comes away with smears of ink and blood. He looks at his number. This is who he is now. He compares his tattoo to his father's — one number off. He assumes his mother and sisters are in the same sequential line, and so they are all linked not only by blood but now also by ink. He glances at the other prisoners. If the Nazis' numbering system proceeds sequentially, everyone in the camp, past, present, and future, is connected, members of a newly created tribe.

His father groans in delirium which then devolves into a hacking cough.

Someone yells, possibly in French, a language Karel does not understand, but the message is clearly in protest of the noise his father makes. Karel hushes his father, pulling him to his body, cradling his freshly shaved head to his chest to muffle the noise. He suspects his father will not survive the night. The transport to the camp and the brutal induction process have been too much for his weak body. In the depths of his mind, he wonders why his father even continues to survive.

"We'll be fine, Papa," Karel whispers. "You'll be fine. We'll all be fine, no matter what happens."

Come the dawn, Alexej still lives. Another prisoner, a fellow Czech, barely alive himself, helps Karel carry his father out for morning roll call. Together they hold the body up to look as alive as possible as the guards offer a hollow recitation of numbers.

"He won't last much longer," the man says as they return Alexej to the barracks.

Karel does not respond, unwilling to betray his father out

loud. He tucks his father back onto the wooden shelf, hiding him in the shadows. Karel then accompanies the Czech man to the breadline.

The first thing you understand in Auschwitz is that food is scarce to nonexistent. They give you only enough to keep you teetering on the brink of life for as long as you are useful, until at some point, usually in the dark of night, you cross that thin line to teetering on the brink of death. Of course, there is a black market for food and medicine. But given his father's tenuous health, Karel knows he does not have the time to search it out, let alone secure medicine to sustain his father's life. And then what does he have to barter? His body? He has a feeling that is not as valuable in Auschwitz as it was in Terezín.

After receiving a small ration, Karel joins the Czech man on his work detail, digging a hole.

"A grave," the man explains, "for the bones that don't burn."

After evening roll call, Karel brings what he can to his father, half a slice of molding bread. But his father cannot eat. Karel, his hunger a constant ache, eats the bread himself. Again, he accepts that his father will not survive the night. But something inside Alexej Benakov compels him to stay alive.

Karel and the other prisoner (still nameless, and Karel never asks) carry Alexej out for roll call and then return him to the barracks before heading to their daily labor of hollowing out the earth. Occasionally, a prisoner working with them will get a bullet in the head for some unknown reason and will fall into the hole.

"Keep working," the Czech man whispers, "or you could be next."

Every evening and every morning, Karel begs his father to eat at least a bite of bread, but he refuses. Once he raises his hand to block Karel from bringing a piece of bread to his mouth and pushes it toward Karel.

"You," he tells Karel, then turns his head away.

Karel understands that if the illness doesn't get his father, starvation will, and on their fifth night in the camp, one of the two threats pins Alexej Benakov down and talks some sense into him. Karel wakes in the morning to find his father cold and still. Karel should cry for his father, beg his forgiveness, but all he can think is, *Good. This is good, Papa.*

When the head count comes up short by one, the guards inspect the barracks. Karel looks away as his father's body is heaved out of the building like so much rubbish. The body hits the winter-wet ground with a thud. The guards instruct two prisoners to drag the corpse away. Each takes one of Alexej's arms and drags him toward the crematorium, his heels leaving rutted tracks in the mud, as if a trail for all others to follow.

After his day's work, Karel lingers by the fence that separates the men from the women, hoping to catch sight of his mother or Zofia. He assumes Dussie is in the children's barracks. A few times guards order him away from the fence, and Karel retreats, only to return again. More than a week passes before he sees Zofia emerging from a workhouse. She carries a basket of uniforms, stripped from those sent to their deaths, now clean for new arrivals. She heads to the clotheslines.

"Zofia," Karel calls in a stage whisper, but Zofia doesn't acknowledge him.

He watches as she systematically hangs the clothing, bending slowly and straightening back up with equal slowness, as if each movement pains her. He calls out to her again and again.

After the fourth call, Zofia looks at him. Her eyes show dark purple half-moons ringing the undersides. Her sunken eyes and cheeks startle Karel. Only two weeks in Auschwitz and already she looks defeated.

"Go away before they see you," Zofia says, continuing her work.

"Mama? Is she all right?"

"She's working inside. Now go."

"Papa died," Karel reports. The words escape bluntly, but she does not flinch.

"Good for him," Zofia remarks, but the statement is not cruel but heavy with envy.

"Tell Mama."

Zofia continues her work without further acknowledgment.

"You there!" Karel turns to find the Obersturmführer from the day of their arrival, the handsome one with the steely gray eyes, the one that aroused Karel's interest then and does again now, despite himself.

"Get away from that fence before you kill yourself." With a pointed gesture, he commands Karel to approach.

"Jawohl, Obersturmführer," Karel says, his voice low, more casual than it should be when speaking to a guard, let alone a commandant. His body, on the other hand, rises to attention, to meet the Obersturmführer in stature, as best he can.

The officer examines Karel with curiosity. "You're the young man from the other day, yes? With the sick father?"

Karel nods. *"Ja, mein Herr."*

"And how is he, your father? Better?" the Obersturmführer inquires with what sounds like genuine interest. But Karel knows better.

"Nein, Obersturmführer. He died."

The Obersturmführer makes a rapid-fire tsk-tsk sound. "That is too bad."

Karel does not respond.

The Obersturmführer sizes up Karel from toe to head. He places a leather-gloved index finger under Karel's chin, then tilts Karel's face up. The Obersturmführer's eyes grow dark and intense as they did the day of Karel's arrival.

Karel allows the examination, taking the moment to examine

the Obersturmführer in return. He cannot mistake the cloud of his eyes, which reminds him of Kozel back in Terezín. Karel meets the Obersturmführer's gaze. He has been appraised before in this way, and he knows when the decision will be favorable. Finally, the Obersturmführer lets his hand fall away.

"Come with me," the Obersturmführer says, his command sounding more like a cordial invitation.

25

The Obersturmführer does not live at the camp, though there is a home for him there. Instead, he lives in a quaint house well beyond the shadow of the camp, as if he is any other Oświęcim resident. When Karel follows the Obersturmführer into the home, the quiet overwhelms him. How long has it been since Karel has experienced silence, a moment free of the constant chatter of people, the cries of sadness and pain, free of the hacking coughs of the sick and dying, the bark of guards' commands or the crack of gunfire?

In the entryway Karel tries to calm the tremors of his body, his uneven breath, his quaking heart. From somewhere in the house, the kitchen most likely, the smells of that morning's breakfast linger. Eggs, sausage, coffee, aromas from another life, which assault him now. His stomach seizes with hunger.

But the Obersturmführer does not break his pace as he heads up the stairs. Karel follows him into the bathroom.

"Bathe."

"Sir?"

"Bathe," the Obersturmführer orders again. "Wash your-self."

The Obersturmführer leaves but does not close the door. Karel hesitates a moment, wary of a trap being set. He decides he doesn't care. He is out of the camp and will make the most of the time, no matter how long he's afforded. He runs the water to fill the tub. After removing his clothes, so filthy he is reluctant to leave them on the clean floor, he enters the water. He has made it too hot. He hisses in discomfort as he eases in. His skin pinks on contact. When his body adjusts, he lies back against the porcelain. He has not had a true bath in almost a year. At Terezín, he had nothing more than a splash of water in the morning—sometimes only a wipe with a wet rag already used by dozens before him. At Auschwitz he has had nothing since the hosing during the initial delousing process. So, Karel lingers in the soak of hot water and frothing soap.

At some point, the Obersturmführer reappears but stays by the door. He watches openly as Karel soaps his body, washing away the dirt and grime and smell of the past year. Afterward, Karel sits while the dirty tub water drains away. The Obersturmführer hands him a towel, extending his arm, as if reluctant to move nearer to Karel's nakedness. But his gaze does not turn away.

"Danke, mein Herr."

The Obersturmführer exits the bathroom. He leaves Karel to privately swaddle himself in the towel. Its coarse fibers scratch at his skin, but it still comforts with its luxury. When the Obersturmführer returns, he places clothing atop the commode.

"They are my son's. He is younger, but you are small. They will do." He leaves again.

Once dry, Karel dresses. The shirt swims about his shrunken, starved torso. Even on the last hole, the belt barely holds up the pants. But the clothes will do. Anything is better than the striped pajamas from the camp.

For the first time in months, Karel looks at himself in a mirror. He recoils at the reflection of the gaunt person that greets him. The flesh is pale and sallow. With his index finger, he traces the dark blurs under his eyes. The skin wrinkles over the bones before shrinking back into place. He follows the outline of his skull, much too visible under his flesh. He touches his prominent cheekbones and jawline. He pets his shorn head, the hairs prickling at his palms.

From the doorway, the Obersturmführer clears his throat. When Karel looks at him in the mirror's reflection, the man commands, "Come."

Downstairs, they pass through the living room (dense with heavy furniture and knickknacks but comfortable in its hominess) and then through the kitchen (austere, tidy). They stop at a door at the far end of the kitchen. The Obersturmführer opens the door and nods for Karel to enter. With brief hesitation, Karel steps over the threshold. The smell of dark brown earth rises up. He glances back to the Obersturmführer.

"The light is on the left."

With a tug on the cord, a light comes to life down below. Karel feels the Obersturmführer's hand press at his back, urging him to descend. Karel leans back against the pressure, then leads the way down into the cellar. In the center of the room, a lone lightbulb hangs bravely, casting the cellar in a buttery glow.

Wooden shelves, not unlike the ones upon which Karel sleeps in the camp, line three of the walls, but these house sundry goods rather than half-dead Jews. Cans of vegetables and bags of rice and beans fill the middle shelf. Cleaning supplies occupy the bottom. The top shelf stores suitcases and boxes. Other boxes and crates sit on the floor, alongside yard tools.

Karel turns to Herr Werden, who is standing a pace or two from him, and awaits fresh orders.

"You can make a pallet there," the Obersturmführer says, indicating a small open area against a cluster of crates.

"A pallet, *mein Herr*?" Karel asks. Creating a pallet for such a brief encounter seems a fruitless ceremony.

"Yes, a pallet. Where you will sleep," the Obersturmführer says, irritation audible in his words. "Did you think you would lodge upstairs? Share a room with my son? A pallet is more than you deserve."

"I am sorry, *mein Herr*. Am I not going back to the camp?"

"Not if you do as you're told."

"And what am I to do?" Karel asks, still unsure of the situation.

"You will do chores for Frau Werden, cleaning, repairing, what have you." The Obersturmführer speaks to Karel as he might a day worker instead of a Jew stolen away from Auschwitz. "You will do everything she tells you, or I *will* take you back, directly to the firing squad. You understand?"

"*Ja*, Herr Werden."

"Good."

They stand in the quiet of the cellar. Only their breathing fills the stuffy room. Karel can hear the light fixture buzzing from an erratic current. He steps toward the Obersturmführer with a newly minted confidence.

"And for you, Herr Werden?" Karel asks. "What shall I do for you?"

The Obersturmführer smiles at the understanding in Karel's eyes. But neither moves. Karel waits for the Obersturmführer to tell him what he wants. He is the one in control here, but as the moment stretches, Karel wonders if he understands this. The tension grows and swells between them, and the anticipation has Karel erect, his cock aching. He shifts his stance to release the pressure, which spurs the Obersturmführer to action. He reaches out and places his hand on Karel's cheek. His hand is hot yet tender, and Karel leans into the touch. He does not break contact with the Obersturmführer's eyes, intense in their need. The Obersturmführer's hand caresses Karel's face and roams down to his neck, where the strong fingers wrap around Karel and then tighten, not to the point of strangulation, but the possibility is there. Karel is no match for him, and they both know it. With his hand on Karel's shoulder, the Obersturmführer directs him to his knees, though he meets no resistance.

The Obersturmführer is as hard as Karel, who wastes no time in releasing the cock from its constraints within the Obersturmführer's uniform. He doesn't fumble with the belt or buttons. He doesn't let the pants drop on their own, but lowers them to the floor with care. The Obersturmführer's erection pushes at the thin fabric of his boxer shorts. Karel has a fleeting thought of pretending inexperience. Maybe the Obersturmführer thinks he is inexperienced, and that's why he selected him. But he can't contain his desire for the man, and he pulls the shorts down to fully release the man's cock. It is as strong and insistent as the man himself. When he wraps his fingers around its thickness, it is hot and eager. The Obersturmführer gasps as Karel takes him into his mouth.

"*Ja, Jude*," the Obersturmführer breathes and grabs the back of Karel's head, holding him in place. "Slow."

Karel slows down, as instructed, but still the Obersturmführer cannot hold himself back. The release is quick and intense.

With a rag, Karel cleans the Obersturmführer's penis. The Obersturmführer redresses. He does not speak, though he does not avoid Karel, their eyes continually catching. He departs without a word or an instruction.

Unsure what to do next, Karel begins clearing the area in which he will sleep. He sweeps the entire floor, not only his sleeping area. He straightens the crates and boxes, moving them about to create more space. As he rearranges the cleaning supplies, he hears footsteps on the stairs. Assuming the Obersturmführer has returned, Karel moves forward to meet him.

Suddenly, a startled cry rings out. A woman stands at the foot of the stairs. They lock eyes before she grabs a can from a shelf and throws it at him. The heavy metal slams against his hip bone, causing a striking pain.

"*Der Dieb*!" she screams and readies another tin.

"*Nein*! I am not a thief!" Karel assures her.

"Get out!"

Holding his hands up in protest, Karel calls for the Obersturmführer. The next can misses him by mere inches. Karel darts behind one of the crates.

Obersturmführer Werden appears at the top of the stairs. "What is this?"

"A Jew thief!" the woman screams, her arm cocked as she holds another metal can. "Escaped from the camp! Kill him, Berthold! Kill him!"

Obersturmführer Werden laughs as he descends the stairs. He removes the can from the woman's fist. "Lena, he is not a thief. I have brought him here to help you."

The woman eyes Karel and then her husband, both with incredulity. Her body does not relax. "I don't need help from a Jew."

Obersturmführer Werden hushes her. "Lena, stop. He will help around the house. Chop the wood."

"He's not even big enough to cut bread," she says with nasty disdain.

"He will tend the yard. Less work for you."

"Berthold, no."

He hushes her again. "If we don't like him, we will send him back, okay?"

Frau Lena Werden narrows her eyes at her husband, who touches her on her upper arm. She relaxes briefly. However, when she turns her gaze back on Karel, her eyes blaze with hatred.

"Get him out of your son's clothes," she orders before she

stomps back up the steps, colliding with a young girl about the same age as Karel. Exasperated, Frau Werden pushes the girl, jostling her back up the stairs. "Come, Marlene."

"She'll be fine," Obersturmführer Werden says with a smile. Then, to Karel's surprise, he pulls him close and kisses Karel's neck. "I will come to you tonight."

The Obersturmführer turns to head up the stairs but stops. He pivots back to Karel. "What is your name?"

Karel pauses before telling him. "I am Karel Benakov."

The Obersturmführer blanches with disgust, distorting his handsome features. "Czech, yes?"

"Yes, *mein Herr*."

The Obersturmführer returns to Karel. He looks at Karel a moment, conducting a lingering review.

"Charles," he says with finality. "Yes, from now on you will be . . . Charles." The Obersturmführer places a hand on Karel's shoulder, as if knighting him. "A good German name."

"Charles," Karel repeats, nodding. "And I can stay here?"

"You will stay here as long as I want you to stay."

"*Danke*, Herr Werden." Karel nods as the Obersturmführer departs, leaving him to settle into his new home and his new name.

26

The next evening Frau Werden allows Charles to clear the dinner table and wash the dishes. She orders him about, roughly telling him where to store this and that. She chides him when he doesn't execute a task as efficiently as she likes. A few times, she lashes out with the back of her hand, making contact with his cheek or the back of his head, her wedding ring cracking against his face or skull. With each blow, she yells, "*Schneller*, pig!"

Each insult prompts a snicker from the son. As the Obersturmführer said, Geert is bigger than Charles, not in height but in weight. He is fat all over. And though not many years younger than Charles, he still acts the child, clinging to his mother's apron strings and currying her favor.

When Frau Werden sends Charles outside to fetch wood for the evening fire, he lingers at the woodpile, the first moment of calm since the Obersturmführer took him from the camp the previous day. He thinks of his mother and Zofia and Dussie in the camp, with no idea he isn't there on the other side of the fence. For the first time in a long time, Charles recites a quick

prayer, the one his mother taught him as a child, the one he recited every night before bed. It feels ridiculous, with its childish
plea for peaceful dreams, but it also asks God to watch over his
family, so he breathes the appeal out into the dark night.

In the living room Obersturmführer Werden does not acknowledge Charles's entrance beyond a disinterested glance up
from the newspaper when he enters to build the fire. As Frau
Werden leads him upstairs to the master bedroom to start the
fire there, she pushes at him with her fist. "You are too slow,
Schwein."

After he completes the chores for the evening, Charles returns to the cellar with his night's dinner. It is a feast of boiled
potatoes, boiled cabbage, and two slices of bread, a bounty he
hasn't had since Kladno. The food bloats him because of his
shrunken stomach, but he does not waste any; he cannot.

Afterward, he lies on the pallet with a thin blanket, hating
the thought of how luxurious he feels on a cellar floor of dirt.
When he falls asleep, he sleeps deeply and completely and
dreamlessly. Until at some point in the night, he is shaken until
his eyes flutter open to see a shadow hovering. Charles panics,
pulling away.

"It is only me," the Obersturmführer says.

"*Mein Herr*, is everything okay?" Charles asks, confused.
"Are you sending me back?"

The Obersturmführer laughs. "No." He kisses Charles's
cheek. "You are too beautiful to send away."

He pulls his pajama bottoms down, revealing his already
hard cock. Charles takes him in his mouth, as he did earlier that
day. Though no less excited and intense, the Obersturmführer
is not as quick this time, even with his family asleep upstairs.
He takes his time. He caresses Charles's face and head as he
sucks the commandant. Then, to Charles's surprise, he lays
Charles back on the pallet. He unbuttons Charles's shirt, exposing his thin chest and stomach. The Obersturmführer ca-

resses Charles's flesh, pale in the dim light that filters into the cellar from outside. At the waistband, the Obersturmführer tugs his pants down. Charles lifts his hips, letting the Obersturmführer undress him fully. Before Charles can anticipate what is to come next, the Obersturmführer leans over and takes Charles's cock into his mouth. Charles assumed the Obersturmführer would insist the sex be a one-sided affair, and with amazement, he watches the Nazi commander please his cock an experienced mouth.

After a few moments, he turns Charles onto his stomach. The Obersturmführer is bigger than the other men he's taken, and Charles can't help but cry out. The Obersturmführer clamps his palm over Charles's mouth. He hushes him, his lips gently nestled in Charles's ear.

"It'll be all right," he says as he pushes into Charles. When his fingers aren't enough to muffle the pained cries, he feeds Charles a handful of blanket. Charles endures the pain until the Obersturmführer finishes. The Obersturmführer hands Charles the rag from earlier that day. When he wipes himself clean, the rag comes away streaked with blood.

"It will get easier with time," the Obersturmführer insists before leaving.

He is correct; taking the Obersturmführer gets easier with time. But not much else in the Werden house does. Frau Werden grows to despise the young Jew more as the days wear on and makes no efforts to hide her anger and disgust. Charles realizes the first time she calls him *Hure* that she knows full well why her husband has brought him into their home.

"You, *Hure*, scrub the floors!" She hands Charles a bucket and a brush hardly larger than a toothbrush.

"You, *Hure*, pluck the chicken for dinner!" She shoves the dead bird, freshly strangled, into his hands. "You miss one feather and back you go!"

She begins carrying a riding crop to bestow quick, painful

swipes. Even with the forewarning swish as the crop cuts through the air, Charles is never fast enough to duck the assaults. Welts and cuts spring up all over his body. At night, her husband kisses them and soothes them with balm. Still, he never orders his wife to stop, never snatches the crop out of her hand. He doesn't even look up from his newspaper or put down his drink. Charles understands this is the trade-off.

Geert enjoys watching the punishment inflicted upon Charles. He laughs and claps his fat hands, as if watching a play. Like his mother, he is cruel and ugly and makes no pretense about his hatred. One evening, he sits on a tree stump, watching as Charles chops wood.

"You're a *Hure*," Geert says, mimicking his mother while he swings his fat, pale legs. His shoes scrape at the grassless ground beneath. The recitation is singsong and childish (Charles doesn't believe Geert even knows what a *Hure* is), and irritation rises in Charles's throat. He struggles to ignore the boy, swinging at the log in front of him, splitting it down the middle with a clean, swift slash. His strength and muscles grow with each passing day.

"A dirty, filthy *Hure*," Geert sings.

"Geert, leave him alone," the Obersturmführer tells his son. "Go play with your toys."

Geert flushes under his father's rebuke and stomps back into the house, muttering under his breath.

Then there is Marlene, the shy, quiet daughter, who has a bigger heart. She flinches with each slap of the riding crop.

"Mother! Stop!" Marlene cries out the first time she witnesses her mother's cruelty. "You are no better than they are!"

Her mother is stunned at the outburst. The riding crop halts in mid-swing for a moment, her brutality interrupted.

"Marlene, do not speak to your mother in that tone," Herr Werden says evenly.

Marlene huffs. "She's being barbaric."

"You have to teach them," Frau Werden tells her daughter, as if Charles were a school lesson and not a human being. "They're animals, so you have to speak to them in their language, or they will never learn."

And the riding crop swishes up and back down so quickly that neither Charles nor Marlene has time to flinch before it slices at Charles's upper arm.

Younger than Charles by a year, Marlene Werden reminds Charles of Zofia, though she is not as pretty. Marlene is merely plain. No matter how she styles her hair or applies the little makeup her mother allows, she cannot rise above the blandness of her generic Germanic features. Her mother worsens matters, insisting that she wear flat brown dresses, reverent and drab. On the weekends Marlene pulls her brown hair back with a colorful scarf, which only accentuates her blandness. Still, she flounces about as if she were Aschenputtel awaiting her prince.

Charles knows he makes Marlene nervous, maybe even fearful. She never speaks to him directly or lets herself be alone with him. If she enters a room in which Charles cleans, she reels back like startled prey and leaves.

About six months after his arrival, a shift occurs. One day, when Marlene returns home from school, she comes upon Charles in the backyard, working in the small vegetable garden. "Though the soil's too full of dead Jews to grow anything useful," Frau Werden laments.

Marlene stops to watch Charles for a moment. Charles does not acknowledge her but can feel her lingering.

"Your hair is growing back," she says.

Charles runs his fingers through the strands, which have grown to half of what they were before he arrived at the camp.

Then Frau Werden calls for her to come inside. "*Schnell!*" Because everything is "*schnell*" with Frau Werden.

From that day onward, Marlene treats Charles with ever

greater kindness. At first, Marlene offers other pleasantries, which Charles accepts with skepticism, wondering what game she might be playing. But soon he realizes Marlene is not malicious, as her mother and brother are. Her exchanges become ever more pleasant. And he is astonished to find a friend among his enemies.

Besides the Obersturmführer, of course, who is both enemy and friend, lover and controller. The mix of emotions bewilders Charles on a daily basis. One moment he hates the Obersturmführer, the Nazi, the reason Charles and his family and all the other Jews in Europe sit on the brink of death at all times; and the next he can't fight the desire to be touched by him, to feel him on top of him, feel his breath as he nuzzles and whispers onto Charles's neck. Each emotion is as strong as the other, with neither dominating nor erasing the other.

Charles quickly learns the signals to anticipate the Obersturmführer's nighttime visits. A wordless energy transpires between them during dinner. As the family eats, Charles stands in the corner of the dining room, awaiting Frau Werden's orders to fetch this or that. She will raise her voice to demand he clear a dish or wipe Geert's chin.

"And anything for you, Herr Werden?" Charles asks toward the end of dinner.

If the Obersturmführer tells him no, that is that. But if he responds, "Not now. Maybe later," Charles knows to lie awake and await his arrival.

As he fights the demands of sleep, Charles sometimes hears the growl of a train bound for Auschwitz. He listens as the locomotive screams and screeches to a stop, his body remembering that night he and his family were the arriving passengers. If he holds his breath, he can make out the barking commands of the guards as they order the new arrivals out of the train. Every once in a while, gunfire cracks through the night.

Before they have sex, their ritual has Herr Werden tending to Charles's fresh wounds.

"Thank you, Herr Werden."

"Call me Berthold. Down here, you call me Berthold."

"Berthold," Charles repeats, lying back on the pallet while Berthold smooths the thick balm on his skin, the same balm he will use to fuck him later.

27

How many months have passed in the Werden household, Charles is not sure. Ten at least, and Christmas is upon them.

Marlene tells Charles the Werdens celebrate with a grand feast. "Officers from the camp come and bring their snooty wives. All of them dreadful bores."

Preparations consume the weeks leading up to the affair. Frau Werden tests recipe after recipe to ensure they will achieve excellence. If not perfect, she throws the food she has prepared in the garbage.

"*Was ist das?*" she asks as Charles watches her with a platter of duck poised over the garbage pail. "I should give this to you? You are not satisfied with what we give you, Jew?"

She dumps the duck into the trash, her gaze trained on Charles. "Touch this and I will send you back, you hear?"

"*Ja*, Frau Werden," Charles assures her and, not for the first time, wonders if returning to the camp would be worse. Which is better? Certain death or the constant threat of it?

The day of the dinner, Berthold brings home four young women from the camp to assist Frau Werden with the preparation of the meal. In the kitchen, their shorn heads bowed in deference and fear, they stand for inspection. Frau Werden, riding crop in hand, paces the line. She places the crop under the first girl's chin and lifts her head upward, revealing eyes big with fear. She does the same down the line. A bruise blooms on one's neck. Another has a harsh scratch on her cheek. Dirt and grime are caked behind ears and in the folds of necks and under their fingernails. She places the riding crop at their sides to lift arms. Charles is surprised at the muscle tone. They must be new to the camp. She places the crop between the legs of one of the girls and uses it to raise her dress. She does not wear undergarments. Frau Werden clucks her tongue.

"*Huren,*" she says to her husband with gnarled disgust. "This is what you bring me? Dirty, filthy whores to serve your commander, Berthold? What am I to do with these things?"

Berthold steps up to Frau Werden, his face close to hers. He seethes. "I don't care what you do with them, Lena. Use them. Don't use them. Send them back. Kill them here in the kitchen and serve them for dinner. I don't care. Just do your job."

After Berthold marches out of the kitchen, Charles smells the anger fuming from Frau Werden, a hot musk that reminds him of the dark earth after it's been dug out to create a grave. The women stand as still as soldiers, knowing enough not to react. Frau Werden slaps the riding crop against her leg and then slashes it across the chest of the nearest prisoner. The woman yelps.

"Get these out of my sight," Frau Werden yells at Charles. "Take them out back and hose them down. I can't stand the smell!"

Charles marches the women into the severe cold of the morning. Their threadbare frocks offer no protection. The women shiver but do not whimper or complain. Charles glances at the house, ensuring Frau Werden is not watching. But she is too busy preparing for the evening's dinner.

He steps close to the women.

"*Je n kdo z vás eška?*" he whispers.

"Yes." One of the women raises her hand, as if in school. "I am Czech. My name is Aneta."

"Excellent!" Charles brightens. "At the camp, have you heard of Růžena Benaková or Zofia Benaková? They are my mother and sister. *Prosím*! Any information you might have . . ."

The woman can't be more than twenty-five, though the hollowness of her eyes, her sallow skin, age her almost double that. Her face slackens, and she shakes her head. "No, I don't think so, but I have been here only a few weeks."

She watches Charles with worry, as if he might punish her for not giving him the answer he desires.

Charles nods. "It is okay. Thank you."

He steps back to face them all. He warns them (in Czech and then in German) not to cry out when the cold water hits them. "Frau Werden is easily provoked, trust me."

The women lift their dresses to reveal their bodies, which are already showing signs of malnutrition: concave stomachs, skin stretching from hip bone to hip bone and nestling in the grooves between their pathetic ribs, breasts hanging flat against their chests. Bruises of various colors—red, black, blue, yellow—have bloomed like ugly flowers about their pallid skin. The tattoos on their left arms brand each of them. They toss their dresses aside and stand naked without shame—for what is the use of shame anymore? The freezing water sprays their skin, dislodging dirt that has accumulated in numerous areas. They lift their breasts and their arms. They clean their sex. As they turn their backs, Charles notices Geert in the doorway, his fat face leering.

"Shoo!" Charles hisses and sprays him through the screen.

Geert squeals and screams for his mother. "Charles sprayed me!"

Frau Werden grabs Geert by the ear, then tugs him away. "Don't look at those disgusting whores!"

Once dry, the women dress in clean frocks from the camp.

Charles brings them back into the house to commence work in the kitchen. They peel and shear and chop and mince and stir and strain while Frau Werden clomps about, overseeing their work. She sends Charles to set the table.

As he does, Marlene sneaks in from the family room.

"Can I help?"

Charles glances at the door to the kitchen. "It is best I work alone. She's in a mood."

"Isn't she always?" Marlene quips, making Charles smile.

Still, Marlene hovers as he places the silverware in its proper places beside the good dinnerware Frau Werden had him bring up from the cellar and clean.

Charles feels Marlene glance at him.

"What is it, Marlene?" he asks more harshly than intended, but he wishes she would leave him to his duties.

"I saw those poor women in the yard. So horrible to be out in the cold like that!"

"I only did as she told me."

"I'm not blaming you, Charles!" she assures him. "It's Mother. It's always Mother. I don't understand how she can be so cruel."

Charles doesn't respond.

"Charles?" Marlene moves to his side of the table, leans toward him. "Do you find those women attractive?"

Charles halts his work. He sets the silverware on the table and takes a breath before looking at Marlene. He places his hand upon hers, and she instinctively pulls away, but he holds her hand firm. He fixes her with a stern gaze.

"No, Marlene," Charles assures her. "I found them sad."

Marlene relaxes and affects a concerned look. "Yes, they are sad, aren't they? The poor girls. I saw Geert leering at them. He's such a little pig. You're not like that, Charles. I don't care that you're a Jew. You're nicer than most German boys."

Charles allows a smile and a blush, then returns to setting the table. Marlene continues to trail him. When he has placed the last fork and knife and spoon, he takes up the tray of glassware. He places a white wineglass and a red wineglass to the right of each place setting.

"Marlene!" Frau Werden barks after entering the dining room, startling both Marlene and Charles. "Get away from him. How many times must I tell you?"

"I wasn't bothering him!" Marlene protests. "I was helping."

Charles shakes his head. "*Nein*, Frau Werden . . ."

"If you can't do your work, boy, I'll send you back with those disgusting *Huren*."

"I can do my work, Frau Werden. Believe me."

"Good." Frau Werden is quickly placated, too busy to follow through with any threats she might blurt out. "We have much more to do. Marlene, go get ready. You look a mess."

Frau Werden waits until Marlene leaves the dining room to survey the table setting. She straightens a fork here, a napkin there to let Charles know his work will never meet her standards, then returns to the kitchen.

Finished with the setting of the table, Charles steps back to review his work. All is set to Frau Werden's specifications, but the presentation is lacking. Charles heads outside, passing Berthold in the living room, dressed in his fine gray uniform. Of course, Berthold intentionally ignores his presence. Charles returns with an armful of evergreen branches, which he arranges down the center of the dining table. He adorns the branches with red ribbons pilfered from the Christmas tree, along with a few ornaments. He nestles wine bottles among the prickly branches. His mother created a similar arrangement once for a Hanukkah dinner, placing the children's presents among the boughs.

He is down in the cellar, dressing for the evening in the black pants and white shirt Berthold brought from the camp, when he hears Frau Werden's angered cry.

"*Was ist das*? Charles!"

After darting up the stairs and into the kitchen, Charles finds the women from the camp cowering at the wrath of the Frau. But her ire is not focused on them, so Charles tells them to get back to work.

In the dining room Frau Werden stares at the table, arms crossed tightly over her bosom. Her face is colored a deep red, as if she is on the brink of suffocation, and Charles thinks she might choke to death on her own anger. If only.

"*Ja*, Frau Werden?" Charles stands inside the doorway.

Her right arm waves at the table. "I did not tell you to do this!"

"I wanted to surprise you. It is something my mother—"

"Your mother? This is not a Jew house!"

The commotion brings Berthold in from the living room and Marlene and Geert scurrying downstairs.

"What is it now, Lena?" Berthold looks about, trying to determine the reason for her outburst.

"The table, Berthold! Look at it!"

With an irritated sigh, he does as instructed. "It looks fine."

"Fine? He has scattered these filthy branches all about!"

"It looks pretty," Marlene says. "Look at the ornaments and the wine bottles!"

"Shut up, Marlene," Frau Werden hisses.

Geert snickers, and his mother shoots him a glare that stifles him, as well.

After stepping forward, Berthold touches one of the branches. He twists one of the wine bottles, so the label faces outward. Frau Werden watches his movements but dares not speak. Charles waits, knowing whatever verdict Berthold offers, Frau Werden will mete out her punishment when the time comes.

Berthold nods his head. "It is fine."

"But—" Frau Werden begins, but Berthold silences her with a stern look.

"It is fine, Lena," he repeats. "The guests will be arriving shortly. Is everything else ready?"

Her bravado crushed but her anger still enflamed, Frau Werden merely nods.

"Good." Berthold retreats back into the living room.

Frau Werden sends the children back to their rooms to finish getting ready and says she will call them when it is time to come down for a formal introduction to guests. "Not a moment sooner!"

She and Charles stand alone in the dining room. She does not look at him, cannot. Her right fist curls at her side, as if yearning for her riding crop.

"I will deal with you later," she promises and leaves the room.

The guests arrive, five couples in all. The men, each with the same rank as Berthold or higher, wear their dress uniforms of crisp gray adorned with numerous medals and ribbons. As they stand together, the casual power is striking. The wives reveal stylish dresses as they shed their fur coats. Berthold mans the bar cart, mixing a special cocktail created for the evening. Charles slips through the group with a tray of the drinks. The guests drink liberally as they chat about the war and life in Poland and their children, but most of all about how they miss Germany.

"And where are your lovely children?" Frau Schäfer inquires.

Frau Werden calls for Marlene and Geert to join the gathering. The children are presented like *Schnickschnack* won at a festival. They offer reverent greetings of *"Guten Abend"* to the guests, then remain quiet, as previously instructed by Frau Werden.

"They're lovely," Frau Schäfer exclaims.

Frau Werden demurs. *"Danke."*

Charles spends his time moving between the guests and the

kitchen. The women from the camp plate the meals for the guests, following Frau Werden's strict instructions. Charles ensures all is presented to her specifications. He finds himself reviewing the women's work with a critical eye. When one of them leaves finger smudges on a plate, he feels the heat of irritation flush his cheeks. Such carelessness is so unnecessary.

He serves each course himself.

"I do not want to see those *Huren*," Frau Werden warned.

The dinner is a success. The guests rave over the food and the wine and the desserts—and especially the decorations.

"How clever, Lena," Frau Fischer says about the table display. "I must try this!"

Frau Werden blushes. "*Danke*. I thought it festive."

Marlene stifles a snicker.

Charles stands in a corner of the dining room, should anyone require another pour of wine, another helping of goose or potato dumplings or creamed sauerkraut. He smiles at the praise for his display, and even more at Frau Werden taking the credit. He knows he will feel the sting of the riding crop for taking the initiative, but this moment of triumph will salve the wounds better than the balm wielded by Berthold's gentle hand.

Later that night, Charles lies in bed, awaiting Berthold. He fights to stay awake, exhausted from the work, which dragged well into the night as he and the women from the camp cleaned up. Frau Werden monitored, yawning and ordering them to work faster with a weak slap of her riding crop across the tabletop. A few times she nodded off, her heavy head lulling front to back before she awakened with a startled grunt.

When they finished their work, a guard transported the women back to the camp. They did not look back as the jeep sped off into the darkness.

Charles closed and locked the kitchen door. Frau Werden stood at the far entryway, her hand on the light switch. She nodded to Charles, her usual rancor absent, before dousing the light. In the dark, he listened to her weary footsteps climb the stairs.

Later, footsteps on the cellar stairs cause Charles to stir. Candlelight glides down the staircase. It is tentative in its approach as it spills into the darkness. Charles sits up in bed. He pulls the thin covers, useless during the winter months, over his naked body. He is about to call out to Berthold, to greet him, when a small voice whispers through the cellar.

"Charles?" It is Marlene.

Panic rouses Charles from bed. He pulls on his trousers and the shirt he wore that evening. In bare feet he meets Marlene at the bottom of the stairs.

"What are you doing?" Charles halts Marlene with a not-so-gentle grasp of her upper arm. "You can't be down here."

Marlene offers a coy smile as her eyes glint with daring and . . . desire?

Charles swallows a gasp. "You must go, Marlene. Please."

Charles turns her back toward the stairs, but she shakes loose.

"Everyone is sleeping, Charles."

Charles steps in front of Marlene, blocking her from entering the cellar proper. "Your mother sleeps light, I know."

"She does not, Charles! My mother sleeps as heavily as a cow." Marlene laughs at her audacity, and Charles smells the wine from dinner still on her breath. It was her first time tasting wine. Frau Werden relented due to the celebration. Charles takes her by the arm again. She giggles. "My mother *is* a cow!"

"Well, that cow will send me back to the camp if she finds you down here. Do you want that, Marlene? Do you want to send me to my death?"

"Yes, is that what you want, Marlene?" Berthold asks from the top of the stairs.

Though his voice carries no more weight than his usual

speaking voice, the calm startles Marlene. She whirls out of Charles's grasp to face her father as he descends the stairs.

"Papa! I was only . . . ," Marlene stammers.

"Go up to your room before I bring your mother down here," Berthold says. Charles detects a whiff of amusement in his delivery.

"Please don't hurt him. He did not know I was coming."

Berthold kisses her forehead and sends her on her way. He waits until the cellar door is closed to turn back to the Charles.

"Berthold, I didn't . . ."

"I know," Berthold says, his fingers on Charles's lips, a sly smile animating his face. "She is moonstruck. Silly girl. I have seen the way she looks at you."

"No, you are mistaken."

The palm of his hand warms against Charles's cheek. "My poor boy, you have no idea how beautiful you are. But so much the better."

Berthold kisses Charles on the forehead the same as he bestowed on Marlene, the gentle kiss of a father—though his own father never kissed him in such a way. Then, with his hand at the back of his head, Berthold yanks Charles's head back so they are face-to-face. "If you ever touch her, I will take you to the wall myself. You understand?"

Not waiting for a response, Berthold throws Charles onto the mattress and begins to untie his robe.

28

Whether Berthold has become gentler or Charles has grown accustomed to him, Charles begins to look forward to Berthold's visits. Especially when Berthold begins to linger after sex, lying next to Charles in what appears to be a thoughtful silence.

At first, Charles finds Berthold's prolonged presence awkward, as he is unsure of his expectations. So, he lies as silent as Berthold until, in time, the silence becomes comfortable. On occasion, Berthold allows himself to doze. His heavy, rhythmic breathing borders on snoring but rarely crosses over. In those moments, Charles remains awake, envying how sound Berthold sleeps—unlike Charles, who is always on guard.

Berthold grows more comfortable with Charles. Every once in a while, he snuggles against Charles like a husband. The intimacy worries Charles. Every extra minute Berthold lingers increases their odds of being caught. But he accepts it, anticipates it. As Berthold slumbers, Charles keeps an eye cast toward the small window at the other end of the cellar. And with the first appearance of the coming dawn, Charles touches Berthold on the chest and whispers his name, nothing startling, only enough to rouse. Confused for a moment, Berthold searches for his place in the waking world.

"It is morning, Berthold."

And Berthold nods and smiles like a child. It is this slumbering moment between sleep and wake when Berthold is someone other than father, husband, Obersturmführer. He is naked and pure, without guise, and vulnerable enough for Charles to glimpse him freely. Charles likes to touch him during that moment. Berthold stretches, waking his limbs. The muscles in his naked back and arms flex and swell and tense. Charles fetches Berthold's pajama tops and bottoms and robe, then hands them over one item at a time. He watches the man dress, watches him brazenly, enjoying the sight of Berthold's member, now flaccid, swaying thickly between his muscled legs as he dresses. Charles wants to touch him, touch his body, but knows there is not enough time. Once dressed, Berthold is the husband and father again. He leaves without a word, returning to his bed before his wife can find him missing.

But surely, Charles thinks, the ever-vigilant Frau Werden knows of her husband's late-night desertions. How could she not? While a sound sleeper—she sleeps as heavily as a cow, as Marlene says—even she must wake in the middle of the night for a glass of water or to use the toilet. What of that first night she found her husband's side of the bed empty? How long did she wait for his return before going in search of him to ensure all was all right? As she wandered the house, looking for him, did she grow confused and worried when she found the living room empty? Did she make her way to the den, to his office, into the dining room and kitchen? Did she stand at the back door and draw the curtain to peer out into the dark? Maybe her husband was wandering in the night, wrestling with some bureaucratic burden from the camp that day? Did she look for the faint glow of a cigarette flaring like a lightning bug in the summer heat? Did she open the back door and whisper his name into the dark without a returned response?

Was it then that she turned to the cellar? Did she convince herself there was no reason for her husband to be down there in the middle of the night? Did she press herself against the cold wood of the door and listen for his voice, the sounds of him? Whatever she might have heard, Charles is confident she did not open the door, not even a crack, before returning to their empty bed. But did she return with a new realization, a bruising awareness that her life had changed forever?

Charles suspects Frau Werden knows exactly why her husband brought him into their home. Every time she strikes out at him, she proves it. Every time she hisses, "You clumsy, filthy *Hure!*" He knows the word was not chosen carelessly. The riding crop was selected intentionally. As much as he hates her, especially as she lashes him with the riding crop, Charles can't help but feel sorry for her. She is as much a captive of her husband as Charles is. He laughs bitterly to realize how much they have in common.

With spring and summer come longer days. Charles finds time to steal moments during his outside evening chores. He gazes into the distance, toward the camp, watching the clouds of smoke rise like the gray breath of the foul earth itself.

Are his mother and sisters still alive? Do they look for him in the men's yard, among the thinning men, who start to blend one into the other as they turn into skeletons? Maybe he died in the squalor of his bunk like Alexej? Or was shot in the head for some perceived infraction that peeved the wrong guard?

"Berthold," Charles says in the softness of one of their moments together after sex, as he and Berthold are lying naked and beaded with sweat in the musty cellar. "I wonder . . ."

Berthold waits. Charles adjusts his body nervously and resettles himself to try again.

"I wonder if you could find out about my family?"

Berthold's hold tightens for a brief moment; then he pulls away to look at Charles.

"I have never asked for anything from you before," Charles reminds him, and Berthold's stare softens, for he knows this is true. "I only want word. Please, Berthold."

Berthold sighs. "I will see."

Several days pass before Berthold returns to the cellar. He startles Charles awake in the middle of the night, the darkness lingering in that queer suspension of time when you have no idea in which direction time is moving.

"They are alive," Berthold declares simply. And before Charles can wake fully, Berthold retreats up the stairs.

After the solitude resettles, Charles lies in the dark with the comforting thought of his mother and sisters still being alive. He tries to picture them as he knew them, but he can't hold on to any of the images that come to him. Most likely, Dussie has changed the most, being the youngest. Would she have grown? Not without proper nourishment. She most likely is thin and pale and sickly. He remembers his last sight of Zofia, already looking defeated after only two weeks in the camp. He can't even begin to imagine how she has deteriorated after more than a year. And his mother . . . What of her former self still survives? That's when Charles begins to cry, something he hasn't done since before the war, when he was still a child. He cries for Dussie, Zofia, and his mother. He cries for himself.

29

The next time Frau Werden leaves the house on her errands, Charles sets his plan in motion. He watches her car pull out of the drive and recede into the distance. Moments later, Charles exits the house, as well, the first time since his arrival. Though he attempts to affect nonchalance, so as not to arouse suspicion in the neighborhood, he cannot control the energy pulsing through him.

He hoped he could get to the camp quickly, but from the Werden home in Harmęże, it takes him almost an hour to reach the perimeter of the camp. If Frau Werden returns to find him gone, he knows without a doubt that will be the end of him. But he can't turn back.

The absence of buildings and woods surrounding the camp, razed long ago to make the area visible, leaves Charles exposed. He loiters as far back as he can. He hunkers behind a clump of bushes, their green leafy branches providing modest cover amid the flat landscape.

Charles tries to orient himself by the vague map of the camp l ghosting in his memory. During his short time there, he covered very little ground, going from the registration building when they first arrived (the process entirely too frantic and terrifying for him to remember anything of the geography of the place) to the barracks to the food line and then to the area beyond the yard, where he worked with the others, digging graves. Now he's not sure where any of those landmarks lie.

In the camp, a cluster of ghosts walks into view, shuffling in a collective dream. Charles watches the men wander about at the insistence of a guard, who orders them here and there and back again, seemingly without purpose. Charles wonders if the Czech man who helped him carry his father out to roll call shuffles among these ghosts. He can't help but hope the man is dead, no longer suffering.

Scanning the desolate landscape between him and the camp, Charles considers ducking behind one of the tree stumps. But even if he kept himself low and small, the movement would draw attention and he and his secretive mission would be exposed. So instead, and against sanity, he stands up to his full height and steps into the clearing. Despite his jangling nerves and pounding heart, he strolls toward the camp. He knows his presence in the late morning sun will be quickly noticed; still he keeps a steady pace, maintaining a demeanor of indifference as much as possible.

He hasn't covered much ground before a command rings out. "You there! Halt!"

A guard at the fence, his rifle trained on his target, waves Charles over. "What is your business here?"

As Charles draws near, he realizes the guard is not a big man. He is barely a man at all, no older than Charles, if that. His hair, dark blond and greasy, straggles out from under his helmet. His eyes, though light, are hard like his voice and the steel of his rifle.

"I am . . ." Charles falters. The glare of the gun in his face unsettles his thoughts. But he quickly finds his words. "I am on an errand."

"An errand?" The guard regards him with deep suspicion. "For who?"

There is only one name he can offer. "Obersturmführer . . ."

"Obersturmführer who? Speak!"

"Werden," Charles finishes. "I work for Obersturmführer Werden."

The guard appraises Charles and the veracity of his alibi. The guard laughs gently and lowers his rifle. "Why did you not say so straightaway? One more moment and I would have shot you."

"I got lost."

"Obersturmführer Werden's office is around the front."

"*Danke.*" Charles hastens toward the front of the camp.

Once out of sight of the guard, he turns back the way he came, heads back home. He hurries to the point of running.

Approaching the house, Charles is relieved to learn Frau Werden has not returned. But he is behind on his chores, so he will incur a beating. It's been a long time since she's been able to justify a good thrashing, and she will relish the fresh opportunity.

That night, Berthold comes to Charles with a particular excitement in his attentions. He is more passionate and aggressive than usual. But Charles has long since learned how to take the man without pain, even on the occasions when his lust gets the better of him. Obersturmführer Werden has taught Charles well.

"So, I had a visitor today," Berthold says after he has finished and they lie in bed. His hand strokes Charles from his shoulder down to his arm and back again, languid and dreamy, as if they rest along the bank of a summer river rather than in a dark cellar in a house in Harmęże, Poland, on the outskirts of a concentration camp in Auschwitz.

Charles assumes Reichsführer Himmler made one of his surprise inspections. His visits always excite Berthold.

"I didn't see him, though." Berthold's voice is quieter than usual, almost secretive. "The guard at the west gate informed me that someone who works for me came on an errand."

Charles's body tightens. He imagines he hears the rushing of Berthold's blood through his pumping heart. He freezes. Berthold's hand continues to caress Charles's arm, never losing its rhythm or tenderness.

"Now, the only one who works for me would be you, correct?" His voice sounds naïve, but the naivete is feigned.

Charles tenses further.

"But I told myself, Charles would not be at the west gate, as I did not request him to run an errand. And my wife would do no such thing. That we both know. So, what do I make of this? Did the guard make up such a story? Unlikely. I can conclude only that it was you, Charles. Yes?"

Charles presses his face into the skin of Berthold's chest. He repositions his arms to rise, but Berthold palms Charles's back to keep him in place, a possessive gesture. "Berthold . . ."

"Hush," Berthold coos. "I understand."

Charles lifts his head in disbelief to look at Berthold. The man's face remains calm, kind.

Berthold nods. "Come with me to the camp this week. I will let you see them."

And Charles pushes himself up so quickly that Berthold is unable to maintain his grasp on him. "*Ja?*"

Berthold smiles. "*Ja.*"

"Oh, Berthold! Thank you!" Charles exclaims and throws his arms around Berthold.

30

On the appointed day, Charles rises before dawn to start his chores because he cannot sleep with the excitement buzzing through him. He makes breakfast, which will anger Frau Werden, but he does not care, not today.

"What is the meaning of this?" Frau Werden asks as she enters the kitchen and sees the table set for the family.

Charles does not respond, awaiting her rebuke, for he is sure it will come.

With a scowl, she steps over to the table and takes a taste of the eggs. Her eyes widen in surprise. "They are good."

"I've been watching you."

She snorts dismissively, but he sees a glimmer of pride in her petty face. "And the coffee?"

"Strong, like you and the Obersturmführer like. With four tablespoons of sugar added to the grounds, of course." He pours her a cup and hands it to her.

After a tentative sip, followed by a healthier draw, Frau Werden nods her approval. "The Obersturmführer will be pleased."

Later that morning, Charles sits in Berthold's office at the camp. Upon their arrival, Berthold instructed one of the soldiers in the office to have Charles's mother and Zofia brought from the women's barracks and Dussie brought over from the children's ward.

"It will take a few moments to locate them, Charles. Relax."

But it takes all Charles's concentration to sit quietly, let alone relax. His body fidgets, his legs bouncing, as he bites at his lips.

"You're very handsome today," Berthold says quietly.

Today he wears another set of clothes from one of the prisoners, brought home by Berthold. He has paired his white shirt with a tie that has a slight jazziness to its pattern, most likely from some young Jewish man who fancied himself a Beau Brummell.

"Soon. You'll see them soon. And they will see how handsome you have become during your time with me."

The phone rings. Berthold lifts the receiver, listens, then nods.

He turns to Charles. "It is time."

Charles follows Berthold out of the office and into the camp. He hoped they would bring his mother and sisters to the office building, get them out of the main part of the camp, if only for a few moments. Outside, Berthold climbs behind the wheel of a waiting jeep and gestures Charles to the passenger side.

The sun shines bright, though not warm. They drive past the barracks where his father died and the yard in which Berthold selected Charles. They barrel through the camp, Berthold tapping the horn in sharp bleats to scatter prisoners.

They approach the women's barracks but do not stop.

"Where are we going?" Charles asks, raising his voice above the roar of the vehicle's engine and the rush of the wind.

Berthold doesn't answer. They drive out of the camp proper and cross a set of railroad tracks and then another. They drive past another camp, which Charles never knew existed.

"Birkenau," Berthold advises. "None of our concern today."

In the distance appears a small reddish house, a cottage really, its quaintness out of place against the sheared landscape. Berthold stops near the house, at which stands a guard. Charles notices the place has no windows. No, it had windows at one point, but now they have been bricked up.

Exiting the jeep, Berthold motions for Charles to stay in the vehicle. He speaks to the guard a moment before he beckons Charles with a quick wave.

Charles shakes his head.

"Charles, come!" Berthold calls, his voice as high and brilliant as the sun.

Legs unsteady, Charles crosses the few yards to Berthold and the guard and the building. The grassless ground has been baked hard by the summer sun.

Charles searches Berthold's eyes for some understanding, but they reveal nothing. "Don't do this, Berthold," Charles whines.

From a sharp, quick jab of the guard's rifle into his back, Charles slams against the building. "Address him as Obersturmführer Werden, Jew!"

"Careful there," Berthold scolds the guard.

Righting himself, the pain pulsing through his lower back, Charles sees a small peep door, at eye level, in the larger door of the house.

"Open the window, Charles," Berthold instructs.

Charles hesitates long enough for the guard to jab him again.

"You wanted to see them," Berthold says evenly, without emotion. "Go ahead. See them."

With hesitation, Charles opens the door, revealing the window. Through the grime of the glass, smudged with fingerprints, he sees a small hollowed-out room, walled floor to ceiling with cement. There stand his mother and sisters, naked and trembling, clinging to one another.

Charles sickens and turns to Berthold. "Please . . ."

Berthold allows himself a cruel smile. "You should have trusted me, Charles. Now look what you've done."

"No, Berthold," Charles pleads.

He returns to the window, looks at his mother and sisters, pale and gaunt and ugly in their nakedness. His mother's breasts droop, and her stomach has collapsed in on itself. Charles forces his eyes to go no farther. Zofia looks even more sickly. Grayish-green circles the undersides of her dead eyes like smeared paint. Her cheeks have sunk so much her lips pull away from her browned teeth. But she stands straight and tall, some deep-seated dignity inhabiting her. Then there is Dussie, smaller than Charles remembers, a child again, as if time has dragged her backward.

Charles slaps at the glass. "Mama!"

His mother and sisters look up at the sound of his voice. It takes them a moment to recognize the face at the windowpane. Then they scream out and rush at the door, yelling his name and begging for help.

Karel, for he is Karel again in that moment, turns to Berthold. "I'm sorry. I won't be bad anymore. I promise!"

In two short goose steps, Berthold steps over to Karel and slaps his face hard with his open palm. The power and surprise of the strike send Karel falling first against the door and then to the ground. The pain, white and bright as the noon day sun, sears through his face and neck. Berthold stands over Karel, his expression unreadable, but still Karel (and Charles) realizes something about Berthold that he had ignored until then.

"Get up," Berthold orders. His voice is not hard or stern, merely commanding.

When Karel doesn't move quickly enough, Berthold shakes his head in disappointment. He nods to the guard, who steps forward and yanks Karel up by his armpits.

"Make him watch," Berthold orders.

Karel struggles against the guard's hold, uselessly. As if he were a rag doll, the guard hoists Karel to the window. Karel's mother and sisters continue to clamor, begging Karel for help.

"Gas them!" Berthold calls out into the morning, to someone unseen.

"No," Karel says, though the word comes out as a strangled whisper.

Dussie is first to hear the hiss. She clutches at her mother, then at Zofia, ordering them to clamp their hands over their mouths. Their eyes are wide with realization and fear and understanding, so much understanding.

Karel screams, twisting his body in the stolid grip of the guard. "Stop! Please!"

But Berthold does not say a word.

Karel doesn't know how many minutes it takes for the gas to overcome his mother and sisters. They don't stagger about like actors do in the movies, almost comically. They merely slump and crumple one by one into a naked heap of skin and bones. Foam froths from Zofia's mouth, drips onto the cement floor. In the brutal embrace of the guard, Karel watches until there is no more movement from them.

"They're dead," the guard calls out to Berthold. "Can I put him down now?"

"Fine."

Once on solid ground, Karel crumples, as well. Tears come, hard and painful. Berthold kneels beside him.

"You have seen your family, Charles. Now there is no need to sneak away from me again." He strokes Karel's hair. "Come. I must get back to work."

And Charles, for he is once again Charles, rises from the doorstep of the small home that now contains the dead bodies of his family, and follows Berthold to the jeep.

"What is to be done with them?" Charles asks as Berthold starts the engine.

"Incinerated, of course," Berthold says, as if Charles has

asked the silliest of questions. Berthold puts the jeep in reverse and backs away from the house.

As the jeep once again barrels through the morning, reversing course for Berthold to bring Charles home, Charles watches the blur of the countryside but sees only his mother and sisters gagging on the gas, panicking and begging and clinging to one another, as if they each thought the others could save them somehow. Charles has no idea how he will ever see them any other way now, as they are forever locked in his mind locked in the throes of death. Did they ever smile before, laugh, dance? Did he actually watch Dussie run through the field behind their house as she chased a terrified rabbit, her voice ringing out with delight and glee, for she wanted the bunny to let her pet it, or is his mind making up stories and images? Did his mother used to read to him and Dussie at night before bed and then kiss them each good night before slipping out of the room, leaving the door ajar so she could hear if Dussie cried out in her sleep during the night? And Zofia. Was she ever beautiful, or was she always a proud heap of naked bone and skin?

Berthold places his hand on Charles's thigh, startling Charles back to the moment. Charles looks at Berthold's fingers, strong and sure, as they squeeze the meat of Charles's leg. The act is intimate, comforting in its way. Berthold says something that's lost in the roar and rush of the wind, blown into the Polish countryside like so much ash. Charles isn't sure how to respond or even if he should. There's a bit of a smile about Berthold. Not blatant or outright, but a lightness hovers about him like a glow. And for the first time since meeting Berthold the day Karel and his family arrived at Auschwitz, Charles thinks about killing him.

At the Werden house, Charles follows Berthold into the kitchen. Berthold continues on into the living room.

Charles anticipated getting straight to work on his morning chores, knowing he was already far behind schedule, but the morning dishes have been cleared and washed and put away. The breakfast table has been cleaned, as well, a vase of flowers, freshly picked from the outside garden, standing brightly in the center. The floor appears to have been swept and mopped. Confusion as to what do to holds him in place at the door, which is where Frau Werden finds him when she enters.

"I have done your morning chores," Frau Werden states with no hint of anger or disappointment. Her voice, still matter of fact but quieter, more delicate, does not sound like hers. "The rest can wait until tomorrow. You go downstairs and rest."

Charles cannot look at Frau Werden. Already something within him has cracked, a chink in a dam threatening to collapse the entire delicate structure.

"*Danke*, Frau Werden," Charles manages, the words strangled and wet.

Downstairs in the cellar, Charles sits on his bed. The images of his mother and sisters struggling to breathe as they suck up the gas in that little red farmhouse play over and over in his mind. He does not try to stop the images. To honor them, he lets them continue in their loop. He knows with certainty that it will be their eyes that will haunt him for the rest of his life. The panic and fear and terror. Later, he will add blame and guilt to the mixture, but that first day he does not yet blame himself. No, this was Berthold.

Killing Berthold would be easy, Charles tells himself. While cleaning up after dinner, he can slip a steak knife into his pants. Frau Werden no longer watches him with such an eagle eye as when he first arrived. She has trained him confidently and now only performs a perfunctory inspection of his work before sending him to bed and shutting off the kitchen light, so she will not notice one missing knife. He will keep the knife under his pillow until Berthold comes to him. He will do it when Berthold is fucking him face-to-face. Maybe one of the nights when Berthold wants only to fuck him, his need insistent and unrestrained, barely a kiss to be shared between them, Charles merely something into which Berthold can put his cock.

Those nights are not as frequent as they used to be. Most times now, Berthold holds Charles, touches him all over, kisses him passionately and deeply, and says his name over and over and stares into his eyes while he buries himself inside Charles, taking his time. Those nights, Charles can't help but cling to Berthold, to return his kisses with equal passion, equal depth, to wrap himself around him when he enters, easy and gentle, to stare into Berthold's eyes, each locking the other in place. If it is one of those nights, Charles might not be able to kill Berthold. Berthold will be too present, will take note of Charles's every move.

But on a night when Charles is no more than an object, he will wait until Berthold is deep inside him, eyes shut to isolate the feelings, the sensations coursing through him from his cock outward. Charles will slip his hand under the pillow; will grab the knife handle as surely as he grabs Berthold's cock, with a firm, possessive grip; and, with practiced precision (for he will practice beforehand), will swiftly pull the knife out from its hiding place and then will bury it deep into Berthold's neck. Berthold's eyes will open with surprise and confusion. He will not know what has happened for a moment and will look at Charles with wonder.

Blood will seep out around the blade of the knife and will drool down Berthold's neck, which will spasm around the blade, the intrusion. Blood will drip down onto Charles, onto his naked chest and face. Charles knows the knife will be holding back the blood, like a finger plugging a hole in a dike. He knows the moment he pulls the knife out, the blood will gush out of Berthold with a force Charles can't even imagine. Where he learned this, he doesn't know, but it is knowledge he has.

Maybe he'll leave the knife in place as he bucks Berthold off him. Berthold will fall onto the bed, onto his back. His sense of

survival will kick in then, now that the moment has been dis-
pelled. He will flounder and struggle, like a flipped turtle trying
to understand how his world changed in such a brief moment.
Berthold's hands will find the handle of the knife sticking out
of his neck, and because it's a foreign object inside him, instinctively, he'll yank it out. Charles might warn him with a no, because even then he will still care about Berthold, still love him
in that strange way that he does, but Berthold won't be paying
attention to anything but the knife. And then the blood will
spurt and spray out of Berthold like an untamed spout. Will
Charles have stepped far enough away, or will the blood splat-
ter him, his still naked flesh, his chest and stomach, his face?

Berthold will cover the hole with his hands, though it will be
a useless act. The blood will flow with each beat of his heart,
flow through him as it always does, but now it will escape
through this breach in the system. And it will escape at an
alarming rate. After the initial surge of panicked energy, that
instinctive will to fight to live, Berthold will grow weaker with
each heartbeat, and Charles will stand there watching him fade.
Berthold will look at Charles, first with expectation that
Charles will help him, and after a few moments understanding
will dawn, and Berthold's expression will turn to confusion.
His eyes will ask, *Why?* Will he make the connection, or has he
deluded himself so thoroughly that he doesn't understand that
killing Charles's family was wrong and was not just three more
Jews to add to the heap?

Once Berthold is dead, what does Charles do? Should he not
kill the rest of the family? Frau Werden, certainly. Geert, probably, if he's sleeping and Charles doesn't have to see his face,
his eyes. Marlene? No, he doesn't think he could kill Marlene.
Maybe she'll come with him. And an interesting pair they
would make, she running away with the young man who killed
her family, and he running away with the daughter of the man
who killed his. Ridiculous.

And Charles falls back on his bed from exhaustion and resignation. He knows he won't kill Berthold, no matter how much he deserves it. Charles is not a killer. He is not like them. He is not like Berthold.

And maybe his mother and sisters are better off now. They looked so beaten standing in the enclosed room of the little farmhouse, so thin and ugly from all they'd been through and all that they were going to go through. Maybe, in some unintended way, Berthold committed a merciful act. Maybe he saved them from the even worse fate of living, of wasting away to nothingness while still existing. Maybe now they were beautiful again, their smiles bright, their bellies full. Maybe now they were with his father again. And Charles can't help but feel a pang of jealousy. Why does he still exist? Why must he continue in this world alone? Maybe instead of killing Berthold, he should take the knife to his own veins. Then he can be done with all this and be with his family, as well.

No. He can no more take his own life than take Berthold's. He will continue. He must get to the other side of this, because that has always been the goal.

If only one of us survives . . .

And Charles knows that Berthold is his best way to survive.

31

For Charles, the end of the war begins months before the Soviet army makes its way to Poland to liberate Auschwitz. In the weeks leading up to the first of the Soviet successes, Charles notices a shift within Berthold. At the dinner table and afterward in the den each evening, he appears preoccupied and distant. Frau Werden inquires after his mood, but he waves her away with a terse "Work, none of your concern." Frau Werden sulks under the exclusion.

At night, in the cellar, Berthold does not come for sex but for confidence. With Charles, he can be candid, open, and truthful. With Charles, he does not need to be husband, father, or commander; he is merely Berthold, man and human. The cellar becomes his haven, his sanctuary, his confessional; and Charles, the keeper of his secrets. But his confessions are timid at first, as he confides that "things are not going well" for the Germans. He lets the vague statement hang in the air.

Even though Berthold forbids the use of the radio, Charles listens to the news when Frau Werden is out on errands. Once Charles hears that the French resistance has revolted against the

Nazis and, with the help of the Americans, has retaken Paris, he understands Berthold's edict for radio silence.

Berthold sighs with resolution. "It's not good, Charles. They're fighting back and winning. It's only a matter of time. Just today I learned that Generalfeldmarschall Rommel has turned against us. Even plotted to kill Hitler. Hitler! Can you believe it? And he's not the only one."

"No?"

"There's dissent. They're wondering what it's all been for."

"And you, Berthold?" Charles inquires. "Do you wonder?"

"War is always about land, Charles," Berthold instructs, as if a professor at university. "There might be other agendas mixed in . . ."

"Like killing Jews?"

"Among others, but make no mistake, it's always about land. It's about power and wealth, and land equals power and wealth in this world. It always has."

"Land? So much death over dirt?"

"It's not as simple as that, but yes. Then they get greedy," Berthold continues. "That's always the downfall. We got what we wanted . . ."

"Austria?"

"And the Sudetenland. But then he kept taking. They never stop when they're ahead. Such arrogance."

"What happens now?"

"We keep fighting," Berthold says, but the statement lacks conviction. "Though it does not look good. The Soviets took Riga a couple of weeks ago. Then we lost against the Americans in Aachen. A big loss."

"Where is Aachen?"

"Germany. *Das Vaterland*! Our land taken from *us*!"

Then what? Charles wonders. What happens to him? His family is dead. Doesn't he have an aunt somewhere? Charles isn't sure. He doesn't even know her name. Odds are she was sent to some camp and is dead, as well. Should he return to

Czechoslovakia, to Terezín, to Eliáš? Of course, Eliáš will survive; he will find his way out the other side.

"Do not worry, Charles. Germany will prevail," Berthold recites, sounding like a propaganda newsreel.

The weeks to follow prove Berthold wrong. The Allied forces continue their march across Europe. They liberate towns in Italy and France and Byelorussia and Ukraine, and many others along the way, and seal the fates of the Axis nations. The radio informs Charles of every triumph, every collapse.

The exterminations at Auschwitz cease in November, when the Soviets begin their march through Poland.

"We are to destroy all evidence of the exterminations," Berthold says, telling Charles of the latest instructions from the Reich. "We're to dismantle the crematoriums and gas chambers, the mass graves. Complete rubbish!"

"Rubbish?" Charles asks.

"Hitler acts like a god, marching across Europe, exterminating all in his way, and now that we are in danger of defeat, he runs away like some scared child who has thrown a rock through the church window. He is not the leader we thought he was. He is a weak little man! Such a coward!"

"If you are not exterminating the prisoners," Charles asks, "what will you do with them?"

Berthold shrugs. "They starve, I suppose. They must die so they cannot tell their stories."

A few days later, Berthold returns home in the middle of the day.

"Berthold?" Frau Werden's voice is nervous, for his presence can mean only that something is not right.

Charles, in the living room, dusting the bookshelf, listens as Berthold orders his wife to pack the car.

Frau Werden freezes at the demand.

"*Schnell*, woman! Who knows how much time we have. We must get ahead of them!"

Frau Werden sends Geert and Marlene to their rooms to

pack one bag each. She orders Charles to pack her and Berthold's clothing as she throws together food for the trip. Within two hours she has everything collected in suitcases and satchels and a few boxes. She instructs Charles to stow it all in the trunk of the car or tie it to the roof.

Frau Werden sends her children to their rooms to sleep, so they will be alert for the escape. Her anxiety is so foreign, so real, that Marlene and Geert obey without question.

"We're ready, Berthold." Frau Werden tells her husband as she enters the office where he is burning documents in the fireplace.

"Good. We leave this evening," Berthold advises.

"And this one?" Frau Werden gestures toward Charles. "We leave him at the camp, yes?"

"No," Berthold says with an insistence that infuriates his wife.

"No?" Frau Werden swings her riding crop against her leg, and the slap makes her husband wince. "What? Are we to set him free? You're a fool if you think he won't turn on you, Berthold."

Berthold does not respond.

"You don't purpose to take him with us, do you?" Frau Werden questions. "No, Berthold! That I will not allow!"

Berthold steps up to his wife, his stride calm but firm and sure. He towers over her. "You won't *allow*? My dear wife, you will allow whatever I tell you. Charles comes with us."

To both Berthold's and Charles's surprise, Frau Werden stands her ground, staring up at her husband's face in defiance. But Charles sees humiliation in her eyes. "You risk our lives . . . for him?" She spits out the last word.

"I am not risking any such thing, Lena," Berthold says, softening in the face of her panic. He reaches out, causing her to flinch, before he gently cups her cheek. "You know I have a plan."

32

Frau Werden watches as Charles follows Berthold into the den, anger seething under her flushed skin. After instructing her to dispose of a box of documents, Berthold closes the door to her.

"Please don't kill me," Charles pleads, surprised by the conviction inside him, the true desire to stay alive.

Berthold turns. Pain twists his brow. "What? I would never, Charles."

He takes Charles into his arms, embracing him, despite the fact that his wife waits in the next room. After placing a quick kiss upon Charles's forehead, Berthold turns toward the glow in the fireplace, alive with whatever documents he fed it earlier. Ashes float like black snow on the breath of the flames. Taking up one of the pokers, he pushes at the smoldering logs and debris. Soon his prods become angered stabbings. He lays down the poker, leaving its tip in the fire, but he continues to stare into the flames.

"Did I ever tell you about where I'm from?" Berthold asks, both hands braced on the mantel.

"Germany?"

"Yes, Germany, but the town of Bayreuth, a small town about one hundred kilometers north of Nuremburg. Famous for its Wagner festival. Do you know Wagner?"

"Is he a *Reichsführer*, like Himmler?"

"Ha!" Berthold laughs. "No, he was a composer of operas. A favorite of many in the Reich, especially Hitler. Not to my liking, I must admit. Too dark, too dramatic. Me, I prefer Mozart. More whimsical. Anyway, Wagner lived in Bayreuth for some years before his death. The town built a concert hall to perform his operas, and each year they hold a festival. It is a lovely town."

"Why do you tell me this, Berthold?" Charles asks, more concerned with his present fate than Berthold's past.

"There is a house there, out in the countryside, in which orphans live."

"Orphans?"

"Yes, orphans, like you. Well, they would never accept a Jew, of course. Only Germans."

"Then . . . ?"

Berthold once again takes up the poker. Its tip seems to pulsate with a fierce orange from its time in the flames. He turns to Charles. "We make you German."

Charles startles awake and is disoriented for a moment, before he realizes where he is.

"Berthold?"

"I am here." Berthold comes into view, standing above Charles.

Lifting his arm to see what Berthold has done, Charles finds a hastily wrapped bandage. Blood has seeped to the surface of the bandage in patterns of ugly blossoms on the surface of the gauze. Angry pain hovers in his arm, extending beyond the wound to the entire length of his limb. He still feels light-headed, his brain suspended between confusion and under-standing. But he forces himself to sit up. "Am I German now?"

"The tattoo is gone, yes."

Charles pulls at the ends of the bandage.

"Leave it," Berthold warns. "It needs to heal."

Charles's arm drops to his lap.

"You are well enough to go?" Berthold asks.

"I think so."

"We must depart soon. On the way, I will tell you the story of who you are now."

PART V

NEW YORK CITY
1968

PART V

NEW YORK CITY
1968

33

Charles is lost in the past, where he's been since Raymond left him with the photo from his youth. In the back of the café, Jacques finds him in a daydream, when he should be preparing service for a table of French women taking a break from a shopping spree. But Charles has forgotten them.

"Charles," Jacques says quietly, so as not to distress him. When Charles doesn't respond, he touches his arm. "Are you okay?"

Jarred back to the present, Charles offers a languorous smile. They are close enough for Charles to feel the heat of Jacques's breath, which is earthy from the espresso he drinks throughout the day. He touches Jacques's face, his flesh, his solidness to ground himself.

"I . . . I'm fine," Charles stammers. "I got lost for a moment."

Jacques lingers. Moments pass before he lets his hand fall away. "You give me worry, Charles."

"No, I am fine, Jacques. I am."

But he sees that Jacques does not believe him, and he's glad someone cares for him. It has been a long time.

Jacques sees the photograph that has distracted Charles. He looks at the people with curiosity but not much more.

Charles points to the figure in the background.

"That is me."

Jacques attempts to reconcile the young man in the photo with the man before him. Jacques looks again at the small patch of black-and-white grains that form Charles's past, leaning over the table on which the photo rests. His hands knot together behind his back. He catches his breath, as if he's examining an ancient artifact, delicate and vulnerable in the toxic atmosphere of the present.

"That is the gentleman." Jacques points at Berthold. "The one who comes every afternoon. The curt one you talk to sometimes."

"Yes, that is him," Charles confirms.

Jacques nods as if he understands, but, of course, he does not. He looks at Charles as if he is meeting a new man, a man who he now knows existed prior to his entry into his life. It will take time for Jacques to connect the young man in the photo with Charles, his coworker, his friend, his sometime lover. But the connection between Charles and the gentleman will forever be a mystery, no matter how many scenarios Jacques might concoct.

That afternoon, when Berthold enters the café, Charles greets him as usual but adds a knowing nod, which Berthold returns as he doffs his hat.

"Good day, Charles."

"Mr. Lynch," Charles replies. He knows Jacques lingers in the back, watching their interaction with a fresh yet still clouded understanding. "The usual?"

Berthold questions the coldness of the headwaiter with a narrowing of his eyes. His hand moves across the table in an attempt to touch Charles as he hovers, but he stops before making contact.

Charles peers at the customer, looking for the monster Raymond wants him to turn over to the authorities. He looks for the monster who murdered his family and indirectly murdered thousands more. And he realizes he has never before looked for that man, that monster, not in the present and not in the past. He realizes he has never thought of Berthold as anyone other than the man who rescued him from Auschwitz and, in a convoluted way, loved him. Yes, he is the man who killed his mother and sisters, but only because Charles put them in jeopardy with his carelessness. But he is also the man who defied his wife and gave Charles a chance at survival after the war. The man who now looks at him with worry and concern and care. The Nazi, the soldier, the monster, Charles can't see him, at least not on the surface. Even the darkness that used to shade his eyes, his voice, his very existence is buried under years of pretending to be someone else. This Wallace Lynch has fully convinced himself that Obersturmführer Werden never existed, so far removed is the American jeweler from the Nazi soldier.

But Charles knows in his heart that jeweler and soldier are still one. Somewhere in the psyche of this man, in his bones, in the marrow of his being, the soldier breathes and lives, no matter how deep the jeweler has dug the soldier's grave.

Now Raymond wants to exhume the corpse. Reanimate it, parade it in front of the courts and the public like Frankenstein's monster. And the jeweler, the imposter, this Wallace Lynch, who lives his quiet life between New York City and Scarsdale, between his wife and now his former male lover, what becomes of him? Does he die? If so, who has murdered him? Charles, Raymond, or the jeweler himself? Or did the jeweler ever exist? Did the officer ever exist? Charles suddenly realizes he has no idea who this man is, who he ever was.

"Charles?" Berthold says to jar Charles back to the moment.

And now he dares to touch Charles, lightly on the back of

his hand. After beginning with a nudge, the finger lingers but then draws an invisible line down the back of Charles's hand and then across the terrain of his knuckles and back again. Charles turns his hand supine, and Berthold nestles his hand upon the offered bed. When he looks at Berthold, he finds concern in his eyes, but is he concerned for Charles or himself?

Charles removes the photograph from his apron. He places it before Berthold.

"What is this?" Berthold asks, his haughty demeanor resurging. It takes him a moment to recognize his wife and daughter, the guests, the glimpse of the soldier's past. "Where did you get this?"

"Geert."

"You've seen him?" Berthold looks up at Charles. He is visibly shaken by the implications of the photo and the implications of Charles interacting with Geert.

Charles sits at the table, an act of transgression at Café Marie, grounds for immediate dismissal. But today he doesn't care.

"Yes. This was taken in nineteen forty-three, the summer Frau Werden threw that garden party, remember?"

Jacques emerges from the service area and in tentative steps approaches Berthold's table. The timidity irritates Charles anew. He tells him to bring Mr. Lynch his coffee and pastry.

"Charles?" Berthold remains shaken.

"He has others, pictures of you in your uniforms. He has documents and letters."

Panic seizes Berthold. Something Charles doesn't think he's ever seen, not even in those final days before they fled Poland.

Berthold stares at the photo. His fingers appear old as they tremble at the edge of the picture. He starts to speak, but Jacques arrives with his coffee service. They wait as Jacques pours the coffee, his performance slow and measured, despite the tension of the moment. He places the piece of fresh rhubarb strudel in front of Berthold.

"Will there be anything else, sir?"

Berthold waves him away, but Jacques doesn't scurry, as he usually does after one of Berthold's curt dismissals. He turns to Charles with a raised eyebrow.

"That will be all, Jacques. Thank you."

With a dejected look, Jacques turns and hurries back to the service area.

Berthold pushes the plated pastry away.

"Geert wants me to turn you in, Berthold."

"How long have you been speaking with him?"

"Awhile," Charles confesses. "I've spoken to Frau Werden, too."

His world suddenly imploding, Berthold shakes his head. "How could you? I . . . Charles, I thought . . ."

"What, Berthold? Did you think you were in control?"

Berthold's laugh startles Charles with its guttural harshness.

"Oh, God! I never had control over this. How could I, Charles? Too many survived. I've always known someone would find me out, turn me over. But Geert? I shouldn't be surprised, the little *Scheißkopf*, but still."

"He says you ruined his life."

"Don't be a fool, Charles. I ruined his life because I cut him off. I made him get a job. He wanted to spend his time playing about the city like some prince. I suppose he thinks if he can get me out of the way, the money will be his."

Charles's mind eddies, as he is unsure who, father or son, is being more truthful. But what do any of them, including him, understand of the truth anymore?

"You need to talk to Geert." Charles is done playing middleman. He stands, then slips the photo back into his apron. Berthold's hand on his arm stops him from leaving.

"Charles . . ."

Charles hears the unasked question and feels the desperation in the grasp.

"Am I going to turn you in?" Charles says, stating the question. "What good would it do? It would not bring my mother and sisters back, would it?"

Berthold flinches at the mention of that long-ago act of killing Charles's family.

Charles considers the possibility of turning Berthold in but knows he can't. Berthold is the only past Charles has left, the only tie connecting him to Germany and Poland and, by extension, Czechoslovakia. Berthold is the last person who knew him before he became Charles. Without Berthold . . . every tether to his past would be cut, and Charles would lose that part of himself forever, would be left with some apparition of a life. When you're the only witness left to your life, how long before the doubt creeps in that it and you ever existed?

Charles returns to the back of the café, from where Jacques has been watching.

"I am back, Jacques," Charles says as he begins to tidy up the back area.

Jacques nods, but his concern and confusion remain.

34

Jacques informs Charles he has a phone call.

"It is the German," Jacques all but spits.

Charles sighs. He has grown weary of Jacques's jealousies. Since the revelation of Charles's shared past with Berthold, Jacques has been ever more petulant and possessive.

Charles answers the phone.

"Charles! You have to come!" Berthold says, his voice heavy with panic.

"What is it?" Charles asks with measured calm. He has not heard from or seen Berthold in days, not since he informed him about Geert's plans. In the meantime, Charles has found a bit of his old life again, returning to his previous existence of work and home, no deviations to Berthold's apartment or to Fraunces Tavern or to Scarsdale. The return has been good.

"Something has happened," Berthold confesses.

"I must leave for a bit, Jacques," Charles says tersely. Berthold has told him nothing save he needs him. And he knows Jacques will be none too pleased that he is running off at the beckon of "the German." "I have called Thomas. He is on his way."

Still Jacques pouts. His thick lips jut out even more than usual, and Charles has an urge to lunge forward and bite them, but he doesn't. Perhaps once this mess is behind him, maybe if he opens himself up to it, there could be something more with Jacques, something beyond the physical. If that is still a possibility. But God, he must look like such a fool to Jacques.

At Geert's apartment building, Charles exits the elevator on the sixth floor and heads down the hall to apartment 6G, as Berthold instructed. The door jerks open before he has a chance to knock. Berthold hurries him into the apartment.

Of course, Charles knew from the address that Geert's apartment would be expensive and spacious. Still, he didn't expect the décor to be so attractive. In truth, he expected the apartment to look like that of a thirteen-year-old Geert rather than the thirty-seven-year-old Raymond Lynch. The furniture is sleek and low and stylish, all of it placed perfectly, as if replicated from a magazine layout or a store showroom.

They don't linger. Berthold guides Charles to the bedroom, also modern and stylish in its furnishings. A low platform bed with Scandinavian lines, sharp and severe, dominates the space with a matching dresser and night tables. Tasteful modern art hangs on the light gray walls, adding calculated moments of color and drama. The rest of the room is neat and tidy, except for the dead body on the floor.

To be honest, the body doesn't surprise Charles. When Berthold told him something happened at Raymond's apartment, Charles knew the "something" didn't bode well for Raymond. Did he expect him to be dead? He's not sure he allowed the thought, but he now knows it was there, hovering in the back of his mind, looking for a way into his understanding.

From underneath the body, a Rorschach blotch of blood stains the carpet, and continues to grow.

"Berthold . . . ?" Charles starts, but he is distracted by the acrid smell of blood, so much blood, his question evaporates. Charles looks down again. Raymond looks so lost, so forlorn.

"I don't know why you had to look for him, Charles," Berthold scolds, his voice tight with disappointment.

Charles sees the gun in Berthold's hand, hanging at his side, his grip still tight. Charles recognizes the Walther P38 with the dark wooden handle. How many times did he watch Berthold clean the pistol in the evening, after dinner? Frau Werden would order Marlene and Geert out of the den for fear the pistol might go off by accident. How she hated her husband's guns. She demanded he keep them out of sight, though Berthold never did. They needed to be at the ready, he said.

"I keep it at the jewelry store," Berthold says, "just in case."

"It is still in good shape, like new," Charles says with amazement. "You always took such care with your guns and rifles."

"You have to, Charles, or they will not work properly when you need them, and then what good are they?"

Charles can't disagree.

"Have you called the police, Berthold?" Charles asks, though he knows the answer already.

"Don't be ridiculous, Charles," Berthold scolds. "Think. We have to get rid of the body, clean up this mess."

"We? This has nothing to do with me, Berthold," Charles asserts, though he can't deny the flash of guilt that shocks through him. He shouldn't have warned Berthold about Raymond, about the documents and photos. If only . . . "I'm going back to work, Berthold. This is yours to deal with."

Charles turns to leave, but Berthold grabs his arm, stopping him. The grip is fierce with determination.

"No, Charles," Berthold rages, though his voice stays as tight as his grip. "We need to take care of this. I need you, Charles."

Before Charles can respond, Berthold pulls him off balance,

and Charles falls against his chest in an awkward embrace. Berthold wraps his arms around Charles. The gun in his right hand presses against Charles's back. They stand face-to-face. Berthold's eyes are steady as they lock onto Charles.

"Don't disappoint me like Geert did, Charles," Berthold states. "I couldn't bear it."

35

As Charles struggles through the subsequent days, his movements and speech sound stilted, robotic, as if each action and reaction have been over-rehearsed. Jacques watches him, afraid to demand details since the day Charles left the café after the call from Berthold. Ever since that day, Jacques has sulked around the café, his distrust and disappointment baldly etched on his face. It pains Charles that he introduced such a gentle, open soul to the realities of what men can do to other men. But such is life.

"What happened, Berthold?" Charles asked as they stood over Raymond's body.

A darkness settled over Berthold. "I came to see him about the documents you told me about. He said he didn't know what I was talking about. He said you must have lied."

"I didn't—"

Berthold stopped Charles, holding up his hand, the one that still held the gun. "I know, Charles. I know you didn't lie."

"And you shot him."

"It was an accident," Berthold professed.

Charles nodded. "Of course it was, Berthold. You would never . . ."

But neither one believed this, because why bring the gun in the first place?

So, the headwaiter using a fake name and Social Security number and the escaped Nazi officer standing over the dead body of his son, whom he shot, plotted out a plan.

Every day Charles waits for news about Raymond Lynch's murder. He watches the news in the morning, before work, and in the evening, when he returns home. At Café Marie, he slips into the kitchen to eavesdrop on the radio playing in the background. Across the street in Mrs. Leifer's shop, he buys the newspaper every morning.

"Looking for anything in particular, Charles?" Mrs. Leifer inquires on the third day he comes in for both the *New York Post* and the *Daily News*.

Charles squelches panic even as he realizes Mrs. Leifer doesn't know anything. No one knows anything, except for him and Berthold.

He smiles for Mrs. Leifer like a good robot. "Just slow at the café."

Berthold maintains his routine, coming to the café every afternoon. They remain congenial to one another.

"Good day, Mr. Lynch."

"Good day, Charles."

"The usual?"

"Yes, please."

In whispered conversations, Charles learns Raymond Lynch's colleagues at work have reported him missing. The police have spoken with Berthold. "I told them the truth. Raymond and I do not speak very often and see each other even less." They spoke with Mrs. Lynch, who cried through the entire interrogation. They talked to Raymond's colleagues, especially those who joined him in drinking after work. One or more told of a man whom Raymond chatted with at Fraunces Tavern on more than a few occasions.

"Is that you, Charles?" Berthold asks, stirring a dash of sugar into his coffee.

"Yes."

"Will they be able to find you?"

"I don't know."

Charles bites at the flesh on the side of his left thumb, an old habit from childhood recently resurfaced. He can taste the drawn blood but cannot feel the pain.

36

Less than four weeks later Raymond Lynch's body is found in the marshes of Upper Manhattan, at the point where the Spuyten Duyvil Creek bleeds into the Harlem River, not far from where Berthold and Charles discarded it. After a month of exposure to the elements (cool nights, warm afternoons, all spent in the water), the corpse is unrecognizable as Raymond Lynch or Geert Werden or anyone else. Its waterlogged flesh falls in clumps from its skeleton upon the lightest touch. The man who finds the body, an older black man out for an afternoon of fishing, vomits at the sight.

The autopsy reveals that despite the gun wound in his chest, Raymond Lynch died from drowning.

"But . . . ?" Charles stammers when Berthold informs him of the cause of death. "He was dead at the apartment. There was so much blood."

They sit in a booth at Schneiderman's before Charles's shift at Café Marie.

"I suppose he wasn't," Berthold states, his voice stoic and practical, much like the news anchors Charles has been watching lately, who have a sense of removal from the subject matter of which they speak.

How Charles is supposed to go to work now with this revelation, he has no idea. His heart races, maybe trying to outrun his thoughts, the realization that he has moved from accomplice to murderer in one short sentence.

"They believe he knew his attacker," Berthold continues.

Charles barks a derisive laugh, wondering if he will faint. The sun outside brightens to a blinding white. The moment passes.

"We have to be calm, Charles," Berthold instructs, ever calculated, now as much as in his Obersturmführer days.

"We."

"They have no reason to suspect me. And they have no idea you exist. Well, they know someone of your description exists."

"Where are the documents, Berthold?" Charles wonders all of a sudden. "Where are the photos?"

Berthold looks confused, but Charles knows he is not.

"The ones your son was going to blackmail you with."

"Ah, yes, those." Berthold nods. "They are safe."

"Which means you are safe."

"I suppose."

Charles nods with understanding as he sips at his egg cream, melted to thin and watery.

37

Only a small group attends Raymond Lynch's funeral at Ferncliff Cemetery in Hartsdale, less than a five-mile drive from the Lynch home.

Of course, Wallace and Doris Lynch come to bury their only son. Raymond Lynch's coworkers attend, as well. Charles, lingering in the distance, out of sight, recognizes several from Fraunces Tavern. The men dress in business suits, while the women wear black dresses or dark-colored skirts and drab blouses. With the reticence of youth, they approach the grieving parents to offer condolences. It is obvious they are unaccustomed to such somber events. The interactions are awkward. Frau Werden's cries increase with each comforting exchange, until she is on the verge of wailing. Berthold stands firm beside her but offers little support to his wife. Charles scowls. She needs someone to hold her, to absorb her grief like a sponge, yet there is no one. And he wishes he could go to her, not to Frau Werden, but to the mother who has lost her child in such a horrible way.

A family arrives. The mother and father exit the car, then escort three girls ranging in age from mid-teens to five or six. It takes Charles a moment to recognize Marlene as the mother. And he flushes with unexpected warmth. She takes the youngest child's hand in hers, then instructs her other two daughters to hold their father's hand before she leads them all forward with a regality reminiscent of her father. Still, Charles can see the softness he remembers so well, mixed with the rectitude of a woman who knows herself and her place in the world.

Marlene and her husband, the detested Brazilian savage, dark and handsome, have created three beautiful children, whose olive skin and dark hair stand in stark contrast as they approach their grandparents, their *Großeltern*. Berthold and Frau Werden receive them with a strained welcome. Marlene disregards her mother's stiffness and takes her in her arms. Frau Werden resists at first, but she cannot deny her remaining child. She pulls her daughter to her as her tears and cries return. As the women cling to one another, the son-in-law approaches the father-in-law. He offers his hand, which Berthold accepts. Then the grandfather greets the grandchildren, shaking each of their hands, as if they are meeting at a three-martini lunch.

Still maintaining their charade, the Lynches hold a Jewish funeral for their son. A rabbi recites a short, simple eulogy for a man he clearly did not know. Most likely, the parents do not attend their local synagogue, as good Jews should. Still, the rabbi does his best to comfort. He asks the family to participate in the burial, as is custom. Berthold heaps a ceremonial shovelful of dirt into the grave. The clods of earth thud onto the wooden casket, sending an ugly, deep, resonant echo into the morning.

After the service, the coworkers and friends scurry away. The rabbi gathers his few belongings into his satchel and, after the exchange of payment, departs, as well. The Lynches and their remaining child and her family stand about the open grave for a few moments before they, too, depart.

Charles does not follow them to the home in Scarsdale, where they will shed their Jewish masks. They will not sit Shiva for their departed loved one. They will not cover their mirrors with black cloth. They will not sit on wooden boxes or low stools or on the ground to humble themselves before their sorrow. They will not tear fabric from their clothing. They will not perform any of the rituals the Jews have devised in reverence to their grief and mourning. No, Berthold and Lena Werden will sit in the dining room with their returned daughter and her too-dark husband and equally dark children. Marlene will brew coffee and plate a pastry baked that morning. Possibly Frau Werden will help, to keep herself busy and distracted. They all will agree nothing soothes grief like fresh homemade crumb cake.

38

Marlene enters Café Marie.

Stunned, Charles stands in the service area, watching as she hovers at the door, maybe waiting to be seated. Jacques, finishing with another table, instructs her to sit wherever she'd like.

Either out of proximity or intuition, Marlene selects her father's table.

"Should I wait on her?" Jacques asks, appearing at Charles's side.

"No," Charles says. "I will."

Charles takes a moment. Of course, he remembers the younger, plain Marlene, but someone more self-assured has taken over and brought her beauty to the surface.

He strolls over to her table.

"Oh, Charles!" Marlene swoons as she stands to greet him. "It's really you!"

She throws her arms around him, her embrace full and warm in its genuine affection. Charles tears up. A realization stuns him: she is the closest he will ever come to reuniting with family.

"Marlene."

"I can't believe you survived," Marlene whispers in German. Of course, she does not speak English like her parents and her brother, but he would have it no other way. Her breathless whisper reminds him of the way she talked to him back in their days together, with that sense of secrecy and conspiracy. "I'm so happy to see you."

When they break the embrace, he notices she is crying.

"God, I feel like I buried one brother and found my other."

"Always the dramatic one," Charles teases gently.

"Stop." Marlene blushes.

"I'm sorry about Geert," Charles offers, and his apology can't help but be genuine.

Marlene catches her breath. "I can't believe it. Geert? Why? If anyone in this family was going to be murdered, I would have thought it would be Father."

Charles nods in agreement.

"Come, sit," Charles says, guiding her back to the table. "What would you like? Coffee? Pastry?"

"Must you?" Marlene questions. "It's too much like—"

Charles stops her. "It is my job, Marlene, but now you have to pay me." He laughs, as much at the joke as at how absurd it is that he can make light of his past.

Still, he detects that old fire in her eyes, that fire to protect him.

"Fine. We can go somewhere else."

Waiting for him in the service area, Jacques scowls.

"Who is that, Charles?" Jacques demands, his voice stern with accusation.

Taken aback, Charles says resentfully but briefly that she is an old friend.

"The German's daughter, yes?"

"Yes."

Jacques scowls anew.

"Stop your pouting," Charles coos. He kisses Jacques on his pursed lips, surprising him. "Though you are adorable when you do so."

Jacques refuses to be swayed by Charles's charm as best his scowl softens despite himself.

"I don't understand, Charles," Jacques confesses. He looks tired, as if puzzling over Charles's life has exhausted him physically.

"She was good to me," Charles explains. "She was not like them. She cared."

Jacques glances over at Marlene.

"She's pretty," Jacques says. But Charles knows she is so much more than that.

At a bistro down the street, Charles and Marlene share a bottle of wine. Marlene tilts her wineglass this way and that, watching the intense red of the wine coat the sides before sliding back to the bottom.

"You look the same," Charles says. He ignores the little lines that feather out from her smiling eyes and lips. But that wonderful sense of youth still flutters about her.

She blushes red.

"Well, you look completely different. I don't think I would have recognized you if I passed you on the street."

"I'm not the boy I used to be."

"I hate what happened," she says.

Which part? Charles wonders, but he doesn't want to open that sarcophagus right now, so redirects the conversation: "What is it like seeing your parents again?".

"Interesting," Marlene offers with a wry smile. "This is the first time I've seen them since they left Brazil. They don't understand why I stay away. Not that they want me bringing my half-breeds into their house. Little savages, mother calls them. But if you ask me, *they're* the savages, especially Father. How he's lived with himself all these years, I have no idea." She tilts the glass and drains half the wine, staining her lips a gentle red. Charles refills her glass. He refrains from sharing the explanation Berthold offered for why he did what he did during the war. He can tell Marlene does not want to hear the propaganda of being a "good soldier." At any rate, he's not the one to make her father's case.

"Geert never forgave them," Charles states, though he knows he must tread the raw terrain of her brother with care.

She shakes her head. "That is my fault, I'm afraid."

An arched eyebrow begs her to continue.

"He was such a pest, you know," she says, with a wry smile prompted by a moment of nostalgia. "After fleeing Poland, he became so petulant in Brazil. God, he was such a child, even though he was old enough to understand what was happening. We weren't there but a week when he started whining about going home. Nothing Father or Mother said would make him stop. It was so annoying. So, one night I stole into his room and explained why we couldn't return. Told him all the things the Germans had done, all the things Father had done. Told him what happened at Auschwitz. I told him what Father did to you at night . . ."

Charles starts to protest, but she shakes her head.

"I figured it out . . . eventually. All the time he spent with you in the cellar. How he looked at you when he thought no one was watching."

Charles feels drained, as if every secret has been syphoned from his life. That is, except the last one. The death of Geert.

"God, I hated him for what he'd done to you! Then, later, when I was in Brazil, I realized the truth. I recalled the way you spoke about him. So, I began to understand that you loved him, too. I felt so stupid, Charles." Here she laughs ruefully. "How I threw myself at you that night! Remember? I could have died when I realized how silly I'd been."

"You weren't." Charles reaches across the table and takes

her hand. "You were young. We were both young. We were in a strange world . . ."

"To say the least." She laughs again, still embarrassed. "Anyway, Geert did not take the truth well. He began questioning Father about the war. He became mean to Mother, even more than I'd ever been! I wish I'd never told him, but . . . we can't change the past, can we?"

"Geert would have found out somehow. He would question the name change, the move to Brazil, the war . . ."

Marlene shrugs. "I'm sure. But in his own time, when he was more mature, able to understand it all better. I shouldn't have hurt him."

They sip their wine in silence as the restaurant around them hums.

"When do you go back?"

"In a couple of days. I don't like America," Marlene says. "It's so ugly."

"New York is not America."

"I suppose. I wish I'd brought the girls to meet you."

"But how to explain me?"

"You would be their *Onkel*," Marlene states matter-of-factly, as if she's considered the scenario a thousand times. "Onkel Charles."

Charles smiles. He would like that, being someone's uncle again.

39

Reports of Raymond Lynch's murder have faded from the evening news and the newspapers. Last Charles heard, the police had no leads. The trail is cool, if not entirely cold.

So, he's surprised when Jacques calls him at his apartment.

"Don't come to work today," Jacques whispers. "Detectives have asked about you."

At Lynch's Jewelry, Charles finds Berthold assisting a well-appointed woman, older, wrapped in a luscious brown mink that glistens softly in the overhead light of the store. Berthold shows the unimpressed woman a tennis bracelet, which he drapes over his suited arm. Charles waits at the window until Berthold looks up. He does not falter in his presentation even as Charles enters the store.

The air inside chills Charles's flushed skin.

"Good day, sir," Berthold greets. "I'll be with you shortly."

As Berthold returns to fussing over his customer, Charles wanders about the displays, as if shopping undecidedly for a present. He takes in the necklaces and bracelets and rings.

"I don't know," the woman says, her voice edging on boredom.

"Of course, you must love the piece," Berthold agrees. "Maybe take a moment alone with it."

He leaves the woman to meditate on the purchase and joins Charles by the watch cases.

"Charles . . ." Berthold keeps his voice low between the two of them.

"May I see this one?" Charles asks about a watch that has caught his eye.

Berthold stammers. "Excuse me?"

"This watch. May I see it outside the case? It's very nice."

Another moment of confusion erupts before Berthold's countenance alters. Charles watches as he becomes Wallace Lynch, jeweler. He unlocks the display case.

"Ah, yes," Wallace Lynch says, as much for Charles as for himself and the woman still contemplating her bracelet. "Rolex is quite popular, as you might know, because of the James Bond films. But this one was designed with airline pilots in mind. See, it is capable of telling the time in two different time zones. Isn't that ingenious?"

Charles leans over for a closer look. "Though only useful if you know where you're going."

"Very true. Let's try it on. I think it would look very handsome on you."

Wallace Lynch removes the watch from the case. He lays it on his open palm for a moment, tilting it this way and that to catch the light. Charles presents his wrist, and Wallace Lynch straps the watch in place.

"Yes," Wallace Lynch says, "very handsome, indeed."

Charles admires the watch. Its stainless-steel links shine with brilliance. The black face highlights the cream color of the hands. The bezel insert is a daring combination of red and blue.

"To be honest, this is an older model," Wallace Lynch confides. "Rolex has recently changed the design, but it's not to my liking. I prefer the classic look."

Charles lets his arm swing down to his side, feeling the weight of the watch, which is substantial.

The woman left to admire the tennis bracelet moves toward the door.

"Thank you for your time," Wallace Lynch calls out as she exits.

Wallace turns back to Charles, who has stepped over to a full-length mirror to admire the watch as someone outside himself.

Charles speaks to Berthold but continues to look in the mirror. "Why did you call them?"

"Don't be naive, Charles."

"You're right. But they would never have connected you or me."

"Possibly. But they weren't going to stop. They would continue to investigate. I couldn't have them endlessly snooping around my life. You know that."

"But still . . ."

"I'm sorry, Charles. What was I to do?" Berthold pleads, but a hollowness colors the sentiment.

"Save yourself. That's all any of us can do."

"Exactly," Berthold says, sounding like a proud parent.

"Well, good luck with that, Berthold." Charles says as he heads toward the exit.

"Charles, the watch."

"I think I'll keep it," Charles says, looking down at the watch, admiring it for it is a rather handsome watch. "It's the least you owe me, Berthold. If you like, tell the police I robbed you as well as murdered your son. What does it matter, anyway?"

Charles steps out of Lynch's Jewelry and into the late morning brimming with sun.

PART VI

TEREZÍN, CZECHOSLOVAKIA 1941

40

The year the Prague Gestapo sends his father to the camp in Terezín, Karel Benakov turns fifteen. By this time, Germany has occupied Czechoslovakia for two years.

They select Alexej Benakov because of his skill and strength. He will be one of the men of the *Aufbaukommando*. They will rebuild the former garrison in Terezín, reconstruct its barracks, its streets and, most of all, its walls. The Germans seek to return the garrison to its former glory. "For the Jews," they say, "a settlement of their own, for their protection and comfort."

Of course, few Jews believe the propaganda. But by then, what could they do?

On the designated day of departure, Alexej does not let the family go with him to Prague. (He calls it his "departure," even though they all know the correct word is "deportation.") At dawn, they—Karel, his mother, and his sisters—stand in the slow light of the coming morning. They watch Alexej climb aboard the flatbed truck that has come to take him away, then settle next to his fellow transportees. He is one of more than half a dozen, all bleary-eyed with sleep and nerves. The driver starts forward. With a tight, nonchalant wave, Alexej heads off to Terezín. His family watches him vanish into the shadowy morning.

Eight months later, when the rest of the Benakovs are sent to Terezín, Alexej will be a thin replica of himself. The once formidable steelworker (so tall, so sturdy that many joked he must be made of steel, too) will stand with uncertainty as he holds on to the rough-hewn wooden post of the bed to keep himself upright.

"Alexej? What have they done to you?" Růžena asks, her voice wet with tears.

Karel and his sisters stand with their mother and father in the overcrowded barracks. The air hangs heavily, putrid with the reek of unwashed clothes and unwashed bodies. Here and there pitiful groans rise from the squalor, a constant mewling that unnerves Karel.

Alexej smiles gamely as his wife reaches out to him with hesitation. Husband and wife stand before one another, nervous as teenagers alone for the first time. Then Alexej extends his thin hand out to his wife and presses her cheek.

"I will be fine," Alexej assures his wife. "I need only rest. Now let me see what they have done to you."

Růžena shyly dips her freshly shorn head as she steps into her husband's embrace. As they hold each other, Karel turns away. His father was never an affectionate man, and the sight of him clinging to his wife with obvious need embarrasses Karel. Once in his embrace, Růžena dispenses with any shame or shyness, crying and kissing her husband with desperate sadness. Then Alexej holds his wife at arm's length and looks at her with intent.

"It suits you," he says of her new hairstyle. "Now I can see those beautiful eyes."

As his mother demurs and blushes, Karel sees a hint of the young girl who captured the eye and heart of Alexej Benakov, the strongest boy in Kladno. He can see how handsome they might have been as they strolled the streets of Kladno on their way to dinner or the cinema or a dance. How enviable they must have been.

Now they cling to each other in the Terezín ghetto, the envy of no one.

And their children stand dazed from the events of the day, which began with their predawn arrival at the Prague train station. After an interminable wait, moving from point to point as instructed, they were loaded onto the bus to Bohušovice, along with hordes of other deportees. With the bus packed beyond capacity, the ride was short but arduous. Then there was the unexpected march to Terezín, three kilometers in total. Laden with their belongings, they moved slowly and unsteadily. Once they reached Terezín, the processing procedure separated them into lines of males and females. They gave their names and handed over their papers. They were ushered into vast empty rooms and ordered to strip. Workers shaved their heads and pushed them on with barking commands. They endured the delousing process: antiseptic powder that burned their flesh and the hosing down with cold water. In another room, workers covered them with delousing powder.

When Alexej turns to his children, Zofia is the first to step forward. Her approach is timid, as she is confused about the weakness in her father.

"You are so much like your mother," Alexej tells his oldest, who has somehow crossed the line into womanhood in the short time he's been away.

"Thank you, Papa." Zofia, never one to accept compliments well, blushes as she backs away.

Dussie springs forward. She throws herself into his arms and cries on his shoulder as he teeters backward.

"Aw, lentil," Alexej coos. "I have missed you so much."

Dussie climbs about her father as if climbing a beanstalk,

something she has done since she was first able to walk. But Alexej can barely endure her exuberance now.

"That's enough, Dussie," Růžena cautions, but Alexej is the one most reluctant to break the embrace.

Karel stands before his father.

"You have kept them safe."

"I did what I could, Papa."

"He has been strong, Alexej," Růžena says, moving to her son's side. "He has worked in the factory and kept food on the table."

"I worked with Havel," Karel says, though the mention of Havel's name pains him. If this is where the Nazis sent Karel and his family, people who did not resist, then Havel must be worse off, if not already dead.

"Havel was always a good man," Alexej declares.

"He was," Růžena says, her voice soft with sadness.

They stand in silence, father and son. Karel straightens, pushing his shoulders back. Still, no matter how much Terezín has beaten him, Alexej stands taller and stronger.

41

Not long after the Germans send Alexej Benakov to Terezín, Růžena sends her son to the Poldi Steel Factory.

"But what about school?" Karel pleads.

"School is no use to us now," his mother says, no longer speaking to a child. "We need money. We need food. I can only do so much."

Since the occupation, his mother has been bringing in laundry from neighbors, washing and mending their clothes. Alexej, proud as any Czechoslovakian man, did not approve. To have his wife working, as if he could not provide for their family, struck at the core of his manhood. Though he did not balk when there was extra money for vodka and tobacco. Then the Nazis reduced the pay of all the Jews working in the factory. Suddenly, Alexej was grateful for his wife's efforts. But even on the best of days, the work was sporadic. Days, sometimes weeks, went by without a single blanket to wash, a skirt to hem. As the occupation lingered, the months turning into years, Jewish hate became the order of the day. That was when even the paltry work ceased. People whom the Benakovs counted as friends before the occupation didn't want a Jew touching their clothes. Most importantly, they did not want their money going to a Jew. Růžena wondered how long they had hated Jews, hated them.

"*Feh!*" she spat at the kitchen floor. "May we live long enough to bury them all!"

So, with her husband deported and her meager work no longer coming in, Růžena Benaková orders Karel to seek work at the factory. Karel does as instructed. After placing his satchel of schoolbooks on the kitchen counter, he leaves the house, the screen door clapping shut with resounding finality behind him.

Of course, Karel has made the trek to the factory many times over the years, since the small forest in back is a favorite play area for the boys of Kladno. Karel and his friends played hunters stalking wild animals, using short branches as rifles. Or they fashioned sticks into slingshots and loaded them with dirt clods and rocks. Other times they climbed the trees or built forts and hid out until dusk.

But Karel has not been that young in years. So, the walk feels longer, each step labored from uncertainty and fear.

Outside the factory, he can hear the growl from the machinery. Its vibrations seep up from the ground into Karel's flesh and bones. As a child, he and his friends imagined the factory's rumble as the growling snore of a sleeping dragon. The memory returns, and Karel half expects snorts of fire to burst forth from the building. The closer he steps to the building, the greater it looms, ever more threatening.

Workers stream into the belly of the beast. Some of the men, friends of his father, recognize Karel. They look at him curiously. Most who enter are older, like his father. One or two might be eighteen or nineteen, but they, too, are strong and tall, more men than boys. Karel sees none as young as his fifteen years and, most assuredly, none as small as he. What could his mother be thinking? They'll never let him work in a place like this, among men and machines.

Karel turns to leave, to run back home, to be with his school-books and friends, where he belongs.

In his blind escape, he collides with Mr. Černý.

"Slow down there, young man." Mr. Černý steadies them both.

"Sorry, Mr. Černý."

"Karel? What are you doing here?" Mr. Černý asks with a ready smile. "You should be in school, no?"

Karel reddens. "Mama sent me."

Almost immediately, understanding dawns in Mr. Černý's clear blue eyes. Of course, as a senior supervisor at the factory, he knows Alexej Benakov is gone, chosen among his men for deportation to Terezín. Does he also know that the Benakov family has no money? Does he know they eat nothing but beans and potatoes, even at breakfast? Karel lingers on the brink of tears but holds fast to the instructions from his mother.

"I am here for work, Mr. Černý." He attempts to deepen his voice, but still it trembles.

Mr. Černý nods. "Yes."

Karel straightens himself to appear taller and to look Mr. Černý in the eyes.

Mr. Černý smiles at the boy, who used to visit the Černý home when he was much younger to play with his son, Bořek. "Come."

As they head toward the factory, the snarling of the machinery within increases. Karel's heartbeat speeds up with each mounting roar. Inside, Karel follows Mr. Černý through the lobby and down a hallway until they stand at the entrance to the factory floor. It spreads before him, larger than he ever imagined, as if he is standing at the beginning of an endless landscape.

Mr. Černý, oblivious to Karel's stunned gaping, has not stopped. Karel hurries to catch up. As he walks through the machinery, Mr. Černý nods to the workers, who return his greetings. Some look at Karel through narrowed eyes, questioning the presence of this boy in their world.

The second floor of the factory houses rows of glass-enclosed offices. Some sit empty, but in others, men dressed in suits like Mr. Černý preside behind desks. They read documents or talk on phones or meet with other men in suits. A few glance as Mr. Černý and Karel pass. At the end of the hall, they come to an office with a wooden door.

"Wait here." Mr. Černý disappears into the office.

Through the door, Karel hears Mr. Černý say something in German. Another voice responds in a hard, short burst of words. The door opens, and Mr. Černý beckons Karel forward.

The office is immense, bigger than the living room and the kitchen of the Benakov home together. Dark, heavy furniture attempts to fill the vastness, with little success. A large, overstuffed leather couch with matching chairs dominates the entry area. A round conference table with six chairs floats somewhere in the middle of the room. The far side of the room houses an imposing wooden desk, the front of which is intricately carved with a scene depicting soldiers on horseback waging some sort of war. Behind the desk sits a jowly man as large and heavy as the furnishings. His slicked-back gray hair glistens as the man examines Karel through wire-rimmed glasses.

"Come forward, boy!" the man barks in German.

"This is Herr Buettner," Mr. Černý explains as he nudges Karel forward.

Herr Buettner continues to glare. "You want a job."

Karel does not understand, so he does not respond.

"He does not speak?" Herr Buettner questions Mr. Černý, his bushy eyebrows arching like the backs of angry cats.

"*Ja, Herr Buettner, ich spreche,*" Karel stammers, using the small amount of German he has acquired since the occupation.

Herr Buettner nods in approval. The cat backs relax.

"I am learning," Karel says.

Herr Buettner stares at Karel, reappraising him. "You are a Jew."

Karel touches the yellow star on his jacket lapel.

"His father was sent to Terezín, Herr Buettner," Mr. Černý states. "Part of the *Aufbaukommando*."

Herr Buettner nods. His large head almost falls forward from sheer weight, but he rights it again.

"Well, then"—Herr Buettner waves a fat hand of dismissal—"find him something that is proper for a Jew."

"*Danke*, Herr Buettner," Karel exclaims, grateful for the dismissal. With a slight bow, Karel clicks his heels, as he has seen the soldiers do on the streets of Kladno. Herr Buettner chuckles and waves them away more insistently.

"You did well in there. Very well," Mr. Černý says when they are back in the hallway. "But now . . . what to do with you?"

Downstairs, Mr. Černý scans the factory floor, then Karel, as if trying to figure out a finished puzzle with one extra piece. His eyes light on something, and he nods.

"Come," Mr. Černý beckons.

Mr. Černý places Karel into the hands of a man manning the desk at the head of the row of machinery. "Find him something to do. Herr Buettner's orders."

The man starts to protest, but Mr. Černý strides away without another word. The man glares at Karel with open frustration. He rises, becoming tall and thin, as if a giraffe reaching full height. Without a word, he lifts Karel's arms, then feels the meat and bones of his torso. He shakes his head.

"What am I to do with this?" the man asks no one in particular.

Karel withers sheepishly under the glare of inspection, knowing he does not measure up.

"You speak Czech, yes?" the man asks.

"Yes," Karel answers but isn't sure if the man hears him over the roaring machines. He repeats his answer. "I speak Czech."

"Still, you're of no use to me on the floor, as little as you are. What's your name?"

"I am Karel," he replies. "I am Alexej Benakov's son," he adds.

His father's name causes a flash of respect in the man's eyes. He nods. "I am Danek. I knew your father."

Karel winces at the use of the past tense, as if his father is dead, not merely sixty kilometers north of them.

"You're too small to do this work," Danek repeats, but this time his voice is less harsh. "Anyway, Imrich does that now. So, what to do with you?"

As Mr. Černý did before, Danek scans the factory floor. Karel sees men standing in front of their machines, heads bowed as they work. Black oil and dust grime their skin until worker and machine threaten to become one.

In futility, Danek turns back to Karel. "You don't belong here. They should put you in the offices, out of harm." Something lights up in Danek's eyes. "Yes! Come!"

Karel snakes through the labyrinth of the factory floor. They come to a small enclosure constructed of wood and chicken wire, no more than six meters by four meters. Inside, a small man sits at a small desk. He is aged, his body hunched, as if he is straining under an unseen weight.

"Havel?" Danek calls.

The man, Havel, does not hear Danek call to him, his face peering closely at a piece of paper, a long, thin finger, crooked and knobbed, following the lines. Danek steps fully into the small room, capturing Havel's attention. Looking up, the man is indeed old, though his eyes are alert.

"Danek? I am working. You should be, too." The man pulls at a chain strung from his lapel, which produces a watch. He flips it open briefly, snaps it shut, and tucks it back into its hiding place, all in one swift motion. He glances at Karel, hovering behind Danek, trying to keep himself unseen. But Danek is too thin to obscure even a small fifteen-year-old boy.

Danek grabs Karel by the shoulder and pushes him forward. "Herr Buettner said to find him a job."

The old man pulls glasses down from atop his head and eyes Karel. "And what am I to do with this?"

"He is Alexej's son."

Havel nods. This means something to him, as it did to Mr. Černý and Danek and even Herr Buettner.

Danek nods in return and leaves.

Havel sighs. "Come here, boy."

Karel doesn't move immediately, still unsettled by the flurry of being shuffled from man to man to man. Havel nods to reassure him he means him no ill will. Karel steps forward and raises his arms for inspection.

Havel views Karel queerly and then shakes his head.

"I don't care about your strength, boy. I don't lift anything heavier than this pencil." Havel laughs. "I am Havel. I keep the books here. Alexej's son, eh?"

Karel nods.

Havel peers at Karel. "Yes, I see him there in your profile."

Karel's eyes widen. "*Opravdu?* I look like Papa?"

"You have his strong nose. Alexej is a good man." Havel sits back in his chair, and the wood creaks. "I suppose we could use an errand boy around here. I am getting too old to keep running up and down those stairs."

"I can do that, sir!"

"Good. But for now, you sit." Havel points to a stack of books on the floor.

As Karel moves to the designated area, Havel stops him.

"First, take that off." Havel points at Karel's coat, specifically the gold felt star stitched to his lapel.

Karel considers the star, already such a part of his life. He remembers the day his mother affixed the crude badges to each of their coats. She pricked her finger in her trembling anger, and droplets of blood stained the gold fabric.

"Why must we wear them, Mama?" Dussie asked as she petted the felt star.

"Because this is who we are now. This is who they say we are. Nothing more than *Juden*, no longer people."

"When you are out on the floor, you wear it," Havel tutors. "But in here we are not Jews. We are Havel and . . . What is your name, boy?"

"I am Karel."

"Yes, Karel, never forget that."

Karel removes his coat and hangs it on the peg on the back of the door, next to Havel's coat, which also bears a gold star.

42

As an official employee at the Poldi Steel Factory, Karel works with Havel, running errands throughout the factory. He delivers the workers' time cards to Herr Auttenberg. He fetches items for Mr. Černý, who always inquires after Karel's day, asks after his family. Every so often he delivers documents to Herr Buettner, which he does with brisk efficiency to shorten the time in the man's presence.

After a few weeks, Karel grows to like the factory. The machines no longer growl but hum instead, a constant in the background. And it does not take long for the other workers to accept Karel. They greet him when he walks the factory floor. They ask if he's heard from his father. They tease gently and call him "Little Havel."

"Men! Get back to work. Malý Havel is coming!" someone will call out, and the others will laugh and salute.

Havel is Karel's favorite by far. At lunch, they cease all work. They share butter sandwiches or boiled potatoes from home. While they eat, Havel instructs Karel on how to survive the occupation and the war.

"This is happening not only in Czechoslovakia"—Havel slices his potato as if carving steak—"but throughout Europe."

Havel confides in Karel that he spends his evenings as part of the resistance. He speaks low, even though the constant rumble of the machines provides cover.

"We do not meet to moan and groan over our fate. We create plans to destroy Hitler and defeat all the Nazis."

"I want to join," Karel finally says.

Havel shakes his head. "This is dangerous work, Karel. You have your mother and sisters, who rely on you. I have no one, so it does not matter."

"But . . ."

"Promise me, Karel. You will stay out of the resistance. Promise me you will survive. That is the strongest resistance there is."

Nibbling the crust of his sandwich, Karel nods. "I will do my best, Havel, but . . . how?"

"Adaptation, son." Havel's eyes take on a fire. "You have to adapt to the changing world, or it will cut you down. Change is inevitable, Karel. Even if the Germans hadn't come to Kladno, some other crisis would have. God challenges us to make us stronger as a people. If you adapt to it, you will survive. Look at you right now!"

Karel's stares in confusion.

"You are adapting by getting this job. It's not easy, but you are surviving and helping your whole family survive."

"And you are adapting, too?"

"Of course. Until you, I was the only Jew left in this factory. I keep my head down. I do my work. Czech Jews don't realize we are at war. In Germany they have been persecuting Jews for almost a decade, putting them in camps. You don't hear much about this, but it's happening. The Germans will do the same here. No time to be naive. You must be a man now."

Karel likes that Havel speaks to him as an equal, a Czech trying to save a fellow Czech.

"We are living in their world now. This is no longer Czecho-slovakia, so we must adapt."

Havel pulls a German grammar book from his desk drawer.

"First, you learn their language," Havel continues. "Under-stand what they say, so they cannot trap you. Your German is good, but it needs to be better."

Karel's lessons begin that day. He studies the grammar book each day at lunch and after dinner. He learns quickly. Havel tells him of the events occurring in Germany, the persecution of Jews, about Kristallnacht.

"You have heard of Kristallnacht? Of course you have not."

"What is this Kristallnacht, Havel?"

Havel recounts the "Night of Broken Glass," the pogrom carried out by the *Sturmabteilung* and the *Schutzstaffel*, Hitler's elite forces of soldiers, and the Hitler Youth, in retalia-tion for the killing of a German official in Paris by a Jewish man. The German official was only an underling, of no true im-portance to the Reich, but the Nazis used the assassination to their advantage, used it as an excuse to send the SA and SS sol-diers into the streets of Germany to destroy Jewish businesses and homes and synagogues. They dragged Jews from their homes and beat them, men and women, young and old. They killed some and sent many to internment camps.

"This happened almost three years ago," Havel says, his voice rising in anger. "In Germany, in Austria, even here in the Sudetenland! And still you have not heard of this. Every Jew should know about Kristallnacht. That is what the resistance is about, to educate Jews and to fight back. It is only a matter of time, Karel, before we are all sent to the camps. Now they pre-pare Terezín for us."

Karel suggests that Havel come home for dinner. "You must speak to Mama about this."

"I don't want to burden," Havel begs. "She has enough to concern herself."

"Come, Havel," Karel insists. "There is plenty."

Havel knows there is not plenty in the Benakov house or in any Jewish home in Kladno. But Karel is relentless.

That evening, Havel greets a flustered Mrs. Benakov. With a flourish, he removes his hat and bows, bringing a smile to Karel's mother's face. "I apologize for the intrusion, madam. Karel is very persistent."

Růžena Benaková recovers with a welcoming smile of her own. "We are happy to have the company. Dussie, take Mr. Novak's coat and set a place at the table."

"My, aren't you a beautiful young lady?" Havel coos, and Dussie blushes bright before skittering away to hang his coat. Havel chuckles.

Karel has never seen Havel so gentle. At the factory he is all business, either doing his work or teaching Karel the ways of the world.

"And this is my eldest, Zofia," Růžena says, her hands on Zofia's shoulders, as if on the shoulders of the ghost of her younger self.

"As beautiful as the next." Havel bows again.

Zofia, usually stern and pouty ("She's at that age," his mother says) offers a genuine smile.

"Such a handsome family."

And it is Karel's mother's turn to blush.

"Please, Mr. Novak, make yourself comfortable. I have a bit of wine. I insist."

"If you insist."

Karel pours.

Růžena instructs her son to pour for himself and Zofia, explaining this is a special occasion.

While the women prepare dinner, Karel sits at the kitchen table with Havel. Karel fingers the stem of the fragile but elegant wineglass, handed down from his mother's mother.

"How long have you been at the factory, Mr. Novak?" Růžena inquires.

"Many years," Havel replies and then falls silent. Karel can tell he is counting. He's seen the look many times. "Almost forty years now, goodness. And I wasn't so young when I started."

Růžena smiles. "You knew my husband, then?"

"Ah, yes!" Havel says. "Alexej is a fine man, a fine worker. So well liked at the factory. And now we have his fine son with us."

Havel claps Karel on the back.

"The spitting image of his father, yes?" Karel's mother crows.

"Rather he is his own man," Havel replies.

She looks at Karel, shaking her head. "He is still a child."

"None of us are children in this new Czechoslovakia," Havel says.

Dinner consists of the usual potatoes, skinned and boiled; carrots, gleaming with the thinnest glaze of butter; and a sliver of corned beef. Where his mother purchased the beef, Karel does not know. It isn't much, but it is tender. If cut into sparing bites and chewed slowly, it seems heartier than it is.

Havel praises the meal, which brings another blush to Růžena's cheeks, even as she apologizes for its meager size, then says the potatoes could have used more salt, the beef more pepper, the carrots more butter.

"But one does what one can these days." She smiles.

Dussie helps clear the table, always eager to play mother. Zofia excuses herself to visit girlfriends, which she does most evenings.

"These youngsters," Havel says as Zofia hurries out, "always somewhere to go. So independent, no? In my day . . ." He waves the thought away without finishing.

"Mr. Novak, I apologize, but I do not have any dessert. But please, you'll stay for coffee?"

"How could I refuse?"

Růžena sends Karel and Havel to the living room as she prepares the coffee. Havel sits on the couch, stock-still, as if afraid to wrinkle the fabric or displace the pillows. Karel plops into his father's chair, which has become his during his father's absence.

"Did you enjoy dinner?" Karel asks to make conversation, as the man of the house should.

"Of course," Havel assures him. "And your mother is lovely, yes?"

Karel mulls over the comment. It has been some time since he has seen his mother dressed in anything other than a housedress. Months since her hair was done properly at the shop in town. But on this night, even worn as she is from months without a husband, from working and worrying day and night, she seems rejuvenated.

Růžena enters and pours the coffees. Havel gazes at her as a father might watch his grown daughter, with pride in his eyes. She hands the first cup to Havel, who takes it with a gentle "*Děkuji*" and balances the delicate cup and saucer on his bony knee.

His mother offers the second cup to Karel.

First wine and now coffee, it is a special night indeed. His mother sits in the smaller chair across from Havel, sipping at her cup.

"This is nice," Havel says. "It has been too long since I have had such a lovely evening."

"A little sweet would have been nice," Růžena frets.

They sip their coffees without talk, though the silence is not uncomfortable. Karel has not seen his mother so relaxed since before his father was deported, and he is glad he brought Havel to their home.

43

Havel returns to the Benakov home often for dinner and occasionally for lunch on Sundays. Somehow, Karel's mother secures extra provisions when he comes, surprising Karel. On occasion, Havel is the one to secure the provisions, smuggling black market beef for the family dinner. Havel becomes such a regular guest for Shabbat meals that he is given the honor of reciting the blessings of the wine and challah.

Růžena Benaková clearly enjoys Havel's company, Karel notices. They chat in the living room long after the children go to bed, though Karel lies awake listening to their voices. His mother is different around Havel than with her husband. She speaks freely to Havel and offers her thoughts and opinions. Karel's father could make her nervous, though Karel never noticed this until he departed. Havel has brought out this other side of his mother, lighter, surer of herself. She is not just his mother, but a woman.

Karel hears the lilt in Havel's voice when Havel says her name: "Thank you for the coffee, Růžena." "Růžena, you keep a lovely home." "How are you this evening, Růžena?" It is sweet and endearing and makes Karel smile.

Soon enough, Havel stops his protestations about invitations to evenings at the Benakov home. He is alone in the world, his wife of thirty-odd years having passed years before.

"And no children?" Růžena inquires.

"God never blessed us in that way," Havel says in the steady voice of a man who has reconciled himself to this holy slight. "But He blessed us in many other ways. We had a good life, my Anuška and I."

Růžena smiles, and Havel returns a smile in kind, but it cannot mask the sorrow stamped on his face.

At work, Havel becomes even warmer to his assistant, as they are no longer merely coworkers. Karel continues to learn from Havel about why and how to exist in the world of gold felt stars. When they secret themselves away in their little office, Havel teaches Karel about the Nazis and their movement as they advance through Czechoslovakia and continue to march across the rest of Europe.

"Karel, you must get your mother to leave," Havel begs one day. "I know people who can get you over the border. You must convince her. I have tried but . . ."

"Papa."

Havel nods.

That evening, after he and Dussie have been sent to bed, Karel steals back out to the living room, where his mother awaits Zofia's return from a night with her girlfriends. At the threshold of the living room, Karel watches his mother dozing on the couch.

"Mama?" he whispers.

"What are you doing up? Are you all right?"

"I . . . I wanted to talk to you." He enters the living room and sits on the couch across from his mother.

"It's late, *m j mali ký.*"

The childhood endearment makes Karel smile, even though he is far from her "little one" anymore.

"Mama, we have to leave."

His mother tightens her jaw at his plea.

"Havel says—"

"I know what Havel says." Her matter-of-fact tone stops him. She straightens her back and then rubs her eyes. "I know."

Karel waits.

"I'm not sure he's right."

"I know you don't want to leave Papa. I don't, either, but . . . he can join us when he's done, when they finish . . ."

Karel attempts to sound like Havel, strong and sure, like a man. His mother stares at him, emotionless, drained. He can think of nothing else to say, though all day he rehearsed the argument in his head. When he realizes she isn't going to respond, he stands.

"Get back to bed. You have work in the morning."

"Yes, Mama."

Still, Karel doesn't leave right away. He lingers between her and the doorway, like a ghost trapped between worlds.

44

A few days later, Karel arrives to work in the morning as usual. All is by habit. He clocks in. He walks the factory floor. He nods to the men leaving from the night shift and to the men arriving for the day.

But when he enters Havel's and his office, he finds it empty.

In all the months he has worked at the factory, Havel's office has never been empty upon his arrival. Karel stands motionless, confused by the stillness of the office. After a moment, he sits at the desk, which is as it was when he and Havel left the evening before, and waits. Certainly, Havel is only running late. But after a half hour has passed, he ventures out onto the factory floor.

"Have you seen Havel this morning?" Karel asks Danek.

"He is in his office, yes? He is always in his office."

Karel asks Anděl and Janek. Neither has seen Havel. Nor has anyone else on the floor. Upstairs, Karel stops at Herr Auttenberg's office and inquires.

"Maybe he is ill," Herr Auttenberg says. "You should do his work. You are able, yes?"

Yes, Karel has learned all there is to the job, but it is Havel's job, not his.

"Still, the work must be done," Herr Auttenberg states.

Karel returns to the empty office and starts the workday. He is "Little Havel," after all.

At the end of the day and on his way home, Karel goes to Havel's house. The place sits dark in the coming twilight. He raises his fist to knock.

"They took him."

Upon turning, Karel faces a woman who has stepped out onto the next-door stoop. She watches Karel, her gaze intent but not wary. She can see Karel is not a threat.

"Excuse me?"

"Last night," she continues. "They came for him. A lot of noise. Woke me from a sound sleep."

She is an older woman, small in the way she stoops, cloaked in a thin housedress. It hangs loose about the neckline, exposing her splotched flesh. Moles and skin tags and freckles are mapped on her skin like constellations, hovering above the planets of her breasts, which push at the fabric of her dress. Her eyes are soft as she watches Karel process her information.

Karel knows better than to ask the woman who has taken Havel in the middle of the night, nor does he want to hear it spoken aloud. He nods and offers a quiet "*D kuji.*"

He turns to leave.

"Don't try to find him," the woman warns. "Don't ask questions, or you might be next, okay?"

Karel retreats from Havel's house to bring home the information.

His mother cries. After collapsing onto the couch, she holds her face in her hands. Her shoulders jerk with each sob.

"Oh, Karel!" his mother laments, "I should have listened. Now, without him . . ."

While Havel is not the first to be taken by the Nazis, his arrest suggests a finality to their own plight.

Karel returns to the factory the next day to shoulder Havel's work, as he did the day before. It is his work from then on . . . until he and his mother and his sisters are sent to Terezín some two months later.

For Karel and his family, the deportation to Terezín comes, as it has for others, without warning or ceremony. A notice on the front door of their home for the family to report to the Jüdische Kultusgemeinde in Prague in three days. A quiet resolution drapes over the Benakov house with this inevitable order. Theirs is not the only house in Kladno with a notice on the door. And in three days, they trek to the meeting point, where they, along with the other deportees, board the waiting bus. They nod to neighbors and acquaintances as they gather, but no one speaks. The transport to Prague is eerily quiet.

At the Jüdische Kultusgemeinde in Prague, the Benakovs hand over their papers for inspection. A stamp sends them to the next station in the process. There they show the stamp just received, which brings another stamp and a notation of some sort, and these send them to yet another check-in point. There they receive their final stamps and are sent to another bus, which transports them to the Prague train station. The process is succinct and refined and civilized. The Benakovs do not grouse or protest. None of the deportees grouse or protest. All make their way through the processing lines, handing over their papers when requested and continuing forward. What would be the point of stepping out of line now?

45

In Terezín all the able-bodied must work. The day after their arrival, Růžena, Zofia, and Karel are sent to receive their assignments. Though separated by gender into two lines, they stand in file in the same room.

Zofia is the first to reach the head of the line, and she stands before the committee of three women relegated to the task of assigning work to female prisoners. Always fidgeting under unwanted scrutiny, Zofia shifts from foot to foot. She twists her hands into a knobbed tangle.

"Stand still, girl," one of the women barks.

Růžena, standing next in line, places her hands on Zofia's shoulders.

"She is sturdy looking when she stands still," another woman on the committee remarks.

"Laundry?" another asks of her committee members.

"She is too pretty for anything else," the first woman says, and they all agree, sending Zofia on her way.

On the basis that she looks trustworthy, the committee sends Růžena to the kitchen, a coveted place to work in the camp. She spends her days peeling rotten potatoes and tearing at wilted cabbages for the watery soups served to the prisoners. Every day ends for her with cuts from rusted knives and burns from the stove. But it is good work.

Zofia does not adapt well. Never one for work, she complains of the aches and bruises acquired from a day's hard labor.

Růžena shakes her head. "I have spoiled you. Give it time. Your body will learn."

On good days, when he has strength, Alexej works in one of the gardens. There the prisoners tend to the vegetables that will be sent to the Nazi soldiers at the battlefront. A sympathetic supervisor puts Alexej on the watering detail, the least strenuous task. If he finds a rare moment when the guards are not watching, Alexej will sneak a potato or carrot into his trousers.

"Everyone does it, Růžena," he assures his wife when she balks at his recklessness. "Better the Nazis should get everything we work for?"

Joined by other children not yet of work age, Dussie spends her days in school. The teachers pace the students through rigorous studies and, if weather permits, athletics. They encourage the children to work on art projects, to draw and paint and write and, if inclined, to play musical instruments. Karel likes when the family gathers in the evening in the dining hall or the courtyard and their mother asks them to recount their days. If he closes his eyes and listens to Dussie describe her day at school, it feels as if they never left Kladno.

As for Karel, when the work committee learns of his experience at a steelworks factory, they send him to the metal shop.

"I tried to tell them I worked in the office, not with the machines," Karel tells his father, "but they didn't care."

"Don't worry," Alexej says. "The machines will not hurt you unless you let them. Watch what the other workers do. You will be fine. I know this."

On his first day, Karel, with conviction and assurance, steps up to a machine that fabricates tire spokes for SS motorcycles. With intent, he listens to the instructions from the worker sent to train him.

Alone with the machine, which hums and buzzes even at rest, Karel breathes. He reproduces the movements of the trainer. From the pile of freshly smelted metal rods, cut to the exact measurement, he retrieves one length. He places it in the grip of the machine and pushes the button. The rod spins as a blade glides into position to cut precise threads into the metal. Once this process is complete, Karel pushes another button to release the rod. He flips the rod to perform the same process on the opposite end. Metal filings and dust fly and fleck at Karel, covering his clothes and skin. With the threads cut into both ends, Karel stops the machine and places the rod in a bin. At some point someone will retrieve the accumulating pile of finished rods.

Once he has the movements down, the work is not scary or even difficult, only dull. Still, it earns him more rations and more freedom to move about the ghetto.

Soon enough, Karel settles into his twelve- to fourteen-hour shifts at the metal shop. He settles, as best he can, in the men's barracks, where he sleeps on a straw pallet on the floor next to Alexej in his bunk. It is comfortable enough, though rats skulk about and sometimes skitter over him during the night. Such is ghetto life.

In the beginning, the prisoners are not allocated much space in Terezín. They have only the barracks for housing and a few other buildings, which are used as the workshops. While the model camp is designed to house no more than seven thousand, the Nazis deport triple that number of prisoners to Terezín within months of its opening. And more come every day. Individual space does not exist. The barracks are especially overcrowded, given the restrictions on movement within the camp and the sheer number of prisoners. Thousands upon thousands spend their days inside limited spaces. Bodies emit all manner of odors, which befoul the air. Karel cherishes the few moments it takes to walk from the men's barracks to the workshop, when he can breathe clean air or at least not completely filthy air.

On the third day of Passover, the prisoners are allowed the day off from the workhouses—at least those that work at jobs that are not vital. The prisoners take the opportunity to get out of their quarters. Růžena and Dussie come from the women's barracks to join Alexej and Karel. Dussie rushes to her father once she sees him.

With his father in the care of his mother and sister, Karel sets off to explore the camp for the first time since his arrival. As he makes his way through the narrow thoroughfares, the hordes of prisoners amaze him. They crowd the grounds in front of the barracks. Older folks sit in clusters and bemoan their plight. Their complaints fill the air with a low nasal buzz.

Mothers tend their young, as if they are at the neighborhood park back home. While some of the children hover near the brink of malnutrition, their play is weak and listless, the scenes are sweet and heartening

Some men knot together in conspiratorial packs that look ominous. As Karel passes, their conversations stop. Are they planning a revolt, an assassination, a coup? Or are they discussing exchanges of illegal goods: tobacco, liquor, toothpaste, soap? In any case, Karel steers clear.

Gathering away from their parents and other adults, teenagers segregate themselves by gender but remain within close proximity of each other. The girls whisper and giggle and steal furtive glances at the boys, as if at a school dance, not in a prison ghetto. It is sweet and normal, and Karel smiles when he catches sight of Zofia in the mix. The boys pretend insouciance, but their posturing and returned glances reveal them to be as transparent as the thin wisps of smoke from their cigarettes.

At the border, a barricade separates Terezín the camp from Terezín the town. The handful of gendarmes posted at the barricade watch Karel's approach with concern. They exchange nervous glances. One of the men swings his rifle around from his back to the cradle of his arm.

"Stop there," one of the other men orders. He is a middle-aged man, silly looking in his recycled uniform, which balloons about his body and makes him appear like a little boy playing dress-up. "Where are you going?"

Karel halts, confused by the question. "Nowhere," he responds, for where else could he go?

The guard nods. "Good."

Standing at the barricade, Karel sees a portion of the residential world of the town, and it appears like any other Czechoslovakian town: small, quiet, and quaint, despite being a garrison town. A woman far down the street steps out of a house and walks in the opposite direction from the camp. Is she on a daily errand, or is she rushing to keep a doctor's appointment or to meet friends?

Karel watches the woman until she is out of sight. He turns back toward the camp, where he will return to his encased world, the small glimpse of freedom leaving a bitter taste in his mouth.

46

People die in the camp every day, tens upon tens upon tens from each barracks. With so many people packed into so little space, disease runs rampant, passing from one to another to another to another, like in a child's game of tag.

Diseased rats maraud the camp, so bold they stop and stare at you, as if you were the invader in their world, and maybe they're right. Everyone has lice within days of arrival, no matter how often the camp conducts delousing.

Due to the rats and the lice and the lack of food and cleanliness, pneumonia, tuberculosis, and dysentery thrive. Whichever you get begins with a cough. Every moment of the day someone somewhere in Terezín is coughing. Bodies convulse, attempting to expel whatever has taken up residence inside them.

And the bodies pile up, mostly the young and the old, those who come to Terezín already frail and weak. But healthy, strong men, like Alexej Benakov, fall ill, as well.

Workers remove the bodies from the barracks, and you watch with a convoluted mix of sorrow and anger and jealousy and relief, a soggy paste of emotions.

With so many dying daily, you would think there would be more space, but with each corpse comes another three, five, twelve live bodies to replace it.

Then one day the barricades come down and the whole of the town of Terezín opens to the prisoners. No one knows where the Nazis have sent the civilian inhabitants of Terezín, nor do they care. Their removal means more space for the prisoners, and that is all that matters.

Only after another delousing process, which includes another shearing of their hair, are they allowed into the town proper. Along with the other prisoners, Karel migrates toward the deserted streets of the old town. As a dazed mass, they test the truth of this sudden freedom. They proceed, unsure and afraid, all except Jakob Edelstein, Terezín's *Judenältester*, rotund and nebbish-looking, who steps onto a chair so all can see and hear him.

"The town is ours!" Jakob sings out in triumph, as if they have won something more than merely a widening of their encampment.

Still, uncertainty lingers. At least until a brash young mother with two toddlers sets off with purpose to find a space of her own. Others follow in a burst of ugly aggression to stake their claims to homes. The gendarmes do their best to control the chaos, but soon they step aside out of fear of being trampled. The SS guards stationed on the perimeter of the land rush do not interfere, though they hold their guns at the ready.

Karel stays back, watching the others infiltrate the vacant apartment buildings and shops and homes.

Whether out of distrust or fear or exhaustion, Alexej refuses to leave the barracks.

"Come, Alexej. The barracks are filthy," Růžena pleads. "You must be where it is cleaner, so you can get better."

Alexej, foolishly stubborn at times, shakes his head. "Here is fine. Let the others leave, and then it will be better here."

Helplessly, Růžena counsels her son. "You must look after him, Karel. You must be the father now."

In the days after the town opens, Karel strolls the streets in the evening, after the workday. He marvels at how his fellow internees have adapted to the town. Some promenade leisurely after dinner. Others chat or play cards in small groups or watch the goings-on from the windows of their apartments. The older folks still bemoan their fate but less so than before. Here and there, the rare sound of laughter rises through the streets of Terezín; sounds and emotions buzz in the air like flies on a corpse.

One evening in Brunnen Park, Karel comes upon some kids playing ball, their voices high and excited. Their game requires a broom handle and a rubber ball. None of the kids, all boys, wear gloves, so you hear the slap of the hard red ball when it hits their palms.

One of the boys notices Karel and makes his way over. Stopping a couple of feet away, he brazenly takes the time to size up Karel.

"New?" The boy, with his angular cheekbones, defined jawline, mischievous brown eyes, and strong frame, despite signs of malnutrition, appears older than Karel by at least two years. Karel knows he will be outright handsome when he is older and manlier and has more meat on his bones.

"Three months."

The boy nods. "You play?"

Karel shrugs. He has never been much for sports.

"I'll teach you." The boy swings his arm around Karel's shoulder and starts guiding him toward the game. He offers an impish grin that charms. "I'm Eliáš."

Within a week, Karel and Eliáš are inseparable. While the ever-present threat of illness or death is the worst part of Terezín, Eliáš soon emerges as the best. A carefree boy, though he is more young man than boy, Eliáš doesn't let life in Terezín stop him from living. His light draws Karel, especially in a place as dark and clouded as Terezín. Being with Eliáš distracts Karel from their world, the long workdays, the hunger, his father's growing weakness. With Eliáš, life is only about being.

Eliáš' brother, Vilém, who insists on being called Billy, as in Billy the Kid, tags along on the days they can't ditch him. At twelve, Billy tends toward younger games, especially cowboys and Indians, riding broken tree branches as if they were horses. Eliáš calls the game childish but will relent and mount a branch on occasion. Of course, Eliáš always plays the law and Billy always dies in the end.

When alone, Eliáš and Karel explore Terezín. They sneak behind barracks and apartment houses. They peer in the windows of the delousing centers and the holding facilities. They spy on the gendarmes in their offices, who sit around playing cards. They spy on the SS commandant, who mostly reads documents at his desk. On the opposite side of the ghetto, they skulk about the Magdeburg Barracks, where they watch Jakob Edelstein and the Jewish Council of Elders discuss the Talmud or plan lectures.

"They think they'll survive because they're smarter than the rest of us, more important than us," Eliáš smirks. "Before Terezín, they were rabbis and scholars, men of business and wealth. Now they kiss the Nazi ass but will still end up in the pits with the rest of us. Stupid old men."

"You think they'll kill us all?" Karel asks, jarred by Eliáš's certainty.

Eliáš looks at Karel and shrugs. "They'd be stupid not to."

The statement punches at Karel's stomach. Since arriving in Terezín, he has resisted thinking too far ahead. He hasn't speculated on the Nazis' plan for them, despite Havel's warnings. He leans back against the wall, helpless to prevent tears from escaping his eyes.

Reaching out, Eliáš gently touches Karel's cheek before he

glides his thumb up to wipe at Karel's tears. "But not today, so be happy."

Karel smiles, and before he understands what is happening, Eliáš kisses the younger boy's lips. Eliáš laughs nervously, waiting for a reaction.

"Do it again," Karel pleads.

Eliáš does, pressing his lips against Karel's with more certainty, and Karel accepts the kiss, his first. He's unsure at first, only having seen others kiss—his parents, actors in the movies, lovers on the street. But with Eliáš, it feels natural and right and easy.

Not far from the Magdeburg Barracks, Eliáš leads Karel over the top of and then behind the retrenchment in front of the bastion built into the rampart. He shows Karel a small enclosure in the backside of the retrenchment.

"They probably stored ammunition here back when this was just a garrison town," Eliáš speculates to Karel.

They enter the dank, dirty, cold, and unused room, the perfect hideaway. The afternoon light follows them just enough that they are able to see one another.

"Have you done anything before?" Eliáš asks, his lips red, already starting to swell from their kissing.

"No," Karel confesses.

With the invasion of Czechoslovakia and then his work at the factory to help his family survive, Karel hasn't even had a chance to think about anything like girls or boys or anyone until this moment. Maybe he was attracted to some of the younger men at the factory, the ones not long out of school. He envied their brawn. He envied how they carried themselves with such certainty and arrogance. He wondered if their muscles felt as hard as they looked, and maybe his *pyj* reacted to these thoughts, stirred in his pants or in his pajamas, since he most often thought of these men at night in bed. He tried not to think of them when he could not hold off any longer and he needed to touch himself, keeping his movements tight and quiet, as the walls in the Benakov home were thin as paper. He especially did not think of Marek, who worked on the loading docks and sometimes removed his shirt at the end of the day because it was dirty and drenched with his sweat. No, Karel tried to think of girls in the neighborhood rather than Marek. Or he would think of the female movie stars on the cover of the magazines he'd see in the shops in town. Or even friends of Zofia's that would come over to the house. But each time, his mind still found its way to Marek and his broad shoulders and strong chest and even the dirt and the sweat of him, and Karel would not be able to stop himself.

And now Eliáš has kissed him, and it is all he wants in the world.

"Have you done this before?" Karel asks in return.

"Some. Not much."

"Show me?"

And Eliáš grins that impish grin that says he's about to pull Karel into mischief.

47

Not long after the barricades come down and the space opens up, the ghetto surges past capacity again. Every day more Jews are dragged into the camp. Every day more space disappears. The barracks overflow, while the newly claimed buildings in the town attempt to accommodate hundreds more than is feasible. The brief moment of breathing room vanishes.

With the greater influx of prisoners comes a greater scarcity of food. Most days, prisoners receive water and bread for breakfast. On occasion, there will be milk for the children. Soups are the mainstay of meals offered throughout the day; thin cabbage-water broth with the rare piece of potato hiding at the bottom like a prize.

People lose weight in Terezín at an alarming rate. Karel keeps an eye on his family, his father in particular. He ensures they eat their rations and ensures his mother doesn't dole hers out to the children.

"She needs to eat," his mother says as she dishes a bit of potato into Dussie's bowl. "She's still growing."

Karel scowls. When his mother isn't looking, he scoops one of his potatoes into her bowl. It is a silly game of sacrifice.

Of course, there is other food in the camp: meat stews, sweet cakes, chocolates, but only for those with the right ration cards or who still have access to money or other valuable goods. That is the hardest part, watching people have what you can't.

"You have to know the right people," Eliáš informs Karel one evening. "But knowing those kinds of people isn't free."

Every day after work, Karel meets Eliáš in the their hideaway. Arriving first, Karel stands in the cluster of shadows. Before entering, out of safety, Eliáš whispers Karel's name.

"I am here," Karel returns.

They meld into the shadows as they hold on to each other, pressing bodies and lips together. In the first moments, they don't speak. They hold and kiss and touch. Their clothes remain on, for the most part, in case someone might catch them. They pull their shirts up so their chests can touch or tug their pants down enough to rub their penises together. They groan and giggle and moan. The stone and cement walls of the bastion absorb the sounds of them. As the older and more experienced of the two, Eliáš teaches Karel what little he knows, and then they experiment. While the teenagers are driven by their hormones, the majority of their time together is spent sitting in their refuge away from the camp, talking. Eliáš sits against the wall, with Karel nestled between his legs, his back to Eliáš's chest. As much as Karel likes the sex, he lives for Eliáš's embrace, and in those moments he can believe life in Terezín is not so terrible.

With the arrival of more prisoners, the Sudeten Barracks, where Karel and his father have remained, now becomes even more crowded than it was previously. And with the hordes of new men comes a renewed influx of illness. Alexej grows weaker with each day but refuses to go to the infirmary.

"They will put me down like a dog or send me east," he tells his wife and children.

They all know his fears are not unfounded. All in Terezín know the threat of being sent east. No one knows for certain what lies in the east—another camp, yes; worse than Terezín, most likely. Alexej does not want to find out.

"But you need help. You need medicine," Růžena begs.

When Eliáš learns of his condition, he tells Karel he knows a man.

"He will not help for free," Eliáš warns.

Karel nods, as if he understands the price to be paid. "Whatever it takes, if he can get the medicine to help Papa."

The Hohenelbe Barracks in the northeast section of the camp is the hospital.

"They say there are showers in there," Eliáš says. He and Karel watch from the other side of Parkstraße, in the shadows of the girls' barracks. "And a pool! Can you imagine?"

"No." Karel has never seen a pool, so how can he imagine?

They hide near a tree in bloom and watch people come and go with surprising regularity. When a man exits the Hohenelbe Barracks, Eliáš nods.

"There he is."

As the man draws nearer, Eliáš caws out a birdsong that sounds like nothing in nature. The man, tall and thin, stops, then cranes his neck at the sound. His head cocks as his eyes dart in the direction of Eliáš and Karel. Recognizing Eliáš, he approaches. The man is older, in his thirties. His piercing eyes take the measure of Karel.

"Who is this?" the man asks Eliáš without greeting.

"My friend." Eliáš places his hand on Karel's back, edging him forward, as if offering him as a gift. "His father is ill and needs medicine."

After a moment, the man instructs them to follow, but not too closely.

Tall and lanky, the man walks with a long gait. Eliáš and Karel keep up with effort as he merely strolls. Dusk descends as they approach the Hanover Barracks. The man slows his pace, then halts. After a moment of stillness, his head cocked in that bird-like way again as he listens to the surrounding area—the yard, the building, the entirety of the camp, it seems—he motions for them to wait.

In the shadows, Karel stands silently beside Eliáš. Occasionally, the clouds part to reveal the rising moon, its paternal glare harsh and ugly, before another cloud curtains its judgment.

"Is he coming back?" Karel whispers.

Eliáš hushes him.

Soon enough, the man reappears.

"You go wait over there," the man instructs Eliáš, pointing at the end of the building. "Cluck if anyone comes."

Eliáš leaves without a word.

Karel feels the man beside him. A nervous energy emanates from him.

They move deeper into the shadows of the barracks until they are up against the rough stucco of the wall.

"How old are you?" the man asks in a whisper.

"Almost seventeen."

"You look younger," the man remarks. "You should say you are younger."

Karel is wondering why he should say he looks younger when the man touches Karel's shoulder, startling him. The man's fingers grip the muscle and bone, then give way to a caress. The man steps closer, pressing Karel's face to his chest. In surprise, Karel pulls away.

"What is this? Did Eliáš not tell you?" the man asks, irritated by this interruption. "You want something from me, so I get something from you."

Karel is confused.

"If you don't want the medicine . . . ," the man says and starts to walk away.

"No." Karel stops him. "I need the medicine for my father."

With no further discussion, the man steps forward and takes Karel in his arms. It feels less like an embrace and more like he is capturing Karel The man's hips move with a slight pressure against Karel; then he bends to kiss Karel's neck. Karel squelches a gasp. The man's lips are dry and scratchy but warm as they move down Karel's neck and shoulder. By the time the man sinks to his knees, Karel is aroused, even though he does not want to be.

Karel finishes quickly, and the man casually spits the fluid into the grass. He asks for nothing in return. He places a bottle of medicine in Karel's hand.

"One pill in the morning and one pill in the evening," the man says, then walks away.

"Why didn't you tell me?" Karel asks Eliáš, his voice clipped with anger, as they head back to the barracks.

Eliáš shrugs. "I thought you understood. Did you get the medicine?"

"Yes."

"Did it feel good?"

Karel hesitates.

"It's okay," Eliáš assures him. "He's good at it."

"Can he get other things, too?" Karel asks.

Eliáš laughs.

The medicine works, alleviating Alexej's symptoms within days. By the end of the week, Alexej returns to his menial chore of watering the gardens. But he is vital and useful again.

Karel's mother does not ask where he got the medicine. In the ghetto, she knows not to ask too many questions.

But she does ask if he can get more or maybe something different. "Stronger?"

Karel returns to the hospital alone. He does not hide as before or caw like Eliáš did when the man exits. Karel waits in full view until the man sees him. The man halts upon recognizing

Karel, but only a moment goes by before he continues his long-legged stride. As he passes, he tells Karel to follow, "but not too close."

Less nervous than before, now that he understands the situation, Karel takes time to look at the man this time. Besides being thin and lanky, the man is cartoonishly skittish, glancing about constantly. He is not ugly but is far from handsome. If not for the need for the medicine, Karel would not even consider being with him. And Karel understands that the man knows this, as well.

Again, Karel trails the man to the Hanover Barracks, then waits, as instructed. When the man returns, Karel allows himself to enjoy the sensation this time. The man is more experienced than Eliáš with his mouth, with his hands, and most apparent in the way he uses both at the same time on Karel's hard penis. Karel tries to hold off longer than the first time but isn't successful. Again, the man asks nothing of Karel in return.

The man places a bottle of medicine into Karel's hand. "This is stronger than the other. Better. Follow the instructions."

Karel pockets the medicine. The man starts to leave, but Karel stops him. "What is your name?"

"My name?" the man questions, confused for a moment as he lingers on the edge of the moonlight. "I am Kozel."

"I am Karel."

"You should not be so trusting, Karel," Kozel warns before vanishing.

Over the next month, Kozel procures for Karel more medicine, blankets, ration cards, even cigarettes. Each time, Kozel fellates Karel, then vanishes. The fifth time they meet, Kozel lingers and radiates something approaching tenderness. In the moonlight, his translucent skin reveals thick veins along his forearms.

"Yes, Kozel?" Karel asks, curious as to this break in their routine.

Kozel hems, demureness overcoming him as he lowers his eyes.

"There are others," Kozel finally says.

"Others?"

"Men. Who would like to meet you."

Karel doesn't understand.

"They can give you things, too," Kozel says. "Food. Clothing. They can help your family, your father."

"You get me those things, Kozel."

Kozel relaxes against the wall of the barracks. "They can get you more."

"Escape?"

A sardonic laugh cuts through the dark. "If they could, I wouldn't be standing here with you, would I? But they can make your life here better at least."

Kozel bends down and kisses Karel's forehead. His lips are tender in their placement. "You think about it, okay?"

The next day, as he progresses through his day, Karel thinks about these men who want to meet him. From the barracks to the food line to the metal shop, he searches for them, men who resemble Kozel, the way he holds himself, harboring secrets. Karel studies the men, looking for clues, signs of sexual hunger. He watches the men who gather in the square after the workday. In the dining hall he watches men slop their soup on their chins and sneak bread into their coat pockets. And he wonders, What can these men give?

Karel confides in Eliáš.

"He said the same to me," Eliáš says. "But I got what I needed from Kozel, and that was enough."

"Weren't you curious?" Karel asks. They are sitting in their hideaway, on a blanket procured from Kozel. Karel sits between Eliáš's open legs, bare back to bare chest, bare crotch against bare ass, bare legs against bare legs. Eliáš holds Karel to him. He strokes Karel from chest to stomach and back again, his movement slow and lazy.

Eliáš doesn't respond.

"Eliáš, tell me, does it upset you what I've done with Kozel?"

Eliáš kisses Karel's neck. "No. That is just business. Not like what we have."

Karel pushes his back against Eliáš's body and shuts his eyes.

48

"I don't want to meet them, Kozel," Karel states plainly the next time they meet.

"But I promised them," Kozel says, pushing back, a darkness confusing his eyes. He steps closer. "Do you want to make me a liar in front of my friends?"

"No, but . . ."

Stepping back, Kozel lets the moonlight find its way between them again. "That is fine, Karel. I understand. But will your family understand when the medicine runs out?"

"What do you mean? We can still—"

"No." Kozel shakes his head. "If you won't do this for me, then we must not be friends, like I thought. And I help only friends."

"But my father needs the medicine," Karel says.

"I'm sure he does. And I'm sure you don't want him to die because you are being a scared little boy."

Karel gulps and nods.

"Good."

Kozel wastes no time in setting up the first meeting. Two days later Kozel waits for Karel outside the metal shop at the end of the workday. They walk in close proximity to each other rather than together.

"You are to meet Herr Petruska tomorrow evening."

"What am I to do?" Karel asks.

"Anything he tells you to do," Kozel replies, then lurches off.

Herr Petruska is fat and old and smells of boiled potatoes and sweat.

They meet after hours in his office in the Podmokly Barracks, where incoming prisoners are processed.

Karel stands in front of Herr Petruska's desk for inspection.

"You are older than Kozel stated," Herr Petruska says with disdain. When he speaks, white spittle gathers in the corners of his lips.

"I am thirteen," Karel lies, as Kozel instructed.

"You are not. And Kozel will hear from me. But you are beautiful, that is true. Turn."

Karel turns.

"Drop your pants," Herr Petruska barks angry dog snarling at his dinner.

Karel unbuckles his belt and undoes the buttons on his pants. Holding them, he lets them droop around his thighs.

"Drop them, boy! I don't have all night!"

The pants slide to the floor, and the belt buckle makes a startling clunk as it hits the wooden floor. Even though he faces away from Herr Petruska, Karel covers his penis with his hands, feeling more exposed than he does during the delousing process, when he stands naked with a hundred other men. He does not like the feeling. He bends to pull up his pants.

"Don't move!" Herr Petruska shouts, startling Karel. Then Petruska steps forward and clamps his hand on Karel's neck. His thick fingers hold him in place.

"That hurts," Karel pleads.

Herr Petruska shakes him by the scruff of his neck like he is a pestering pup. "Shut up."

Karel holds his whimpers in check. Herr Petruska holds him

at arm's length, his grip firm. "Skinny . . . but who isn't these days?"

Before Karel can protest further, Herr Petruska shoves him forward at the waist. Karel stumbles, but Herr Petruska holds him in place. Karel attempts to orient himself, but a shocking pain shoots through him. Herr Petruska is stabbing him with something—a knife, a stake, something small and hard. It takes Karel a moment to realize it is his cock as he jabs it into Karel's anus. The violence stuns his body and mind, cutting off any impulsive screams. A white light swirls. He edges to the brink of passing out, but Herr Petruska shakes him again, a ragged doll in his bear-paw grip.

"Hold still!" He lurches forward, pushing Karel in front of him, until they are in front of a desk. Herr Petruska bends him over and fucks him, every thrust hard and mean, as if he seeks nothing but vengeance.

After Herr Petruska finishes in a wheezing climax and backs away, Karel stays bent over the desk, waiting for the throbbing pain to pass.

Herr Petruska jolts Karel with a kick to his ass. "Kozel will have your money."

Karel finds the will to pull up his pants, buckle his belt, and hurry out of the office. In the hallway, he pauses to remember the route and reverses his steps until he is outside. The evening air cools his flesh, but his anger still flushes him.

At the hospital, he waits for Kozel.

"Follow, but not too close," Kozel orders as he approaches Karel.

"No."

Kozel halts. He turns back. "No?"

"No," Karel repeats with even greater ferocity.

"Is something the matter, Karel?" Kozel inquires, his voice a soft coo, as if he is speaking to a lost child. Then he smiles. "Ah, yes, Herr Petruska. I should have warned you. Don't worry. The next won't be so . . . shall we say passionate?"

"There won't be a next time, Kozel," Karel says, and his conviction anchors the decree.

Kozel does not respond for a moment. "Then, dear boy, your father will die."

"Then my father will die," Karel agrees.

Stunned, Kozel steps back and looks at Karel, as if meeting someone new.

The decision came from quick but rational thought. His father was dying, anyway; it was only a matter of time. The medicine helps but doesn't heal. It will only help for so much longer. Karel knows that, even if no one else does.

So, his father's death will come sooner because of this decision, and Karel will have to live with that. Such is life. Such is adaptation and survival. Havel was right. Karel understands this now.

49

Within the month, Alexej deteriorates with a swiftness none of them expects. He loses the weight he gained and then some. A permanent cough sets up in his chest. The Benakovs are marked for deportation. Maybe Kozel alerted someone to Alexej's illness. Maybe he pulled strings, though Karel isn't sure Kozel is so high up that he has any strings to pull. Maybe another prisoner turned in Alexej to save someone else. Maybe Alexej was already on a watch list because his health kept him out of the workforce more often than not. Maybe the selection was random. Who knows? Nor does it matter.

His mother does not cry when given the news of their deportation. Resigned, she readies her children for the trip.

Karel spends his final night in Terezín with Eliáš. At first, they do not touch or even speak. Both act bravely for the other, squelching the fear of the moment. Finally, Karel places his hand against Eliáš's chest, and they hold on to each other, more desperate than even the first time they kissed. They spend the night together, neither wanting to part ways, neither having the energy in the middle of the night to risk a return to his barracks. They wake before dawn. With a final kiss, they depart their hideaway and walk side by side through the damp morning. At Eliáš's barracks, they part with no more than a graze of hand AGAINST hand. Karel continues to his own barracks to fetch his father for their trip east.

PART VII

WEST BERLIN, WEST GERMANY 1969

50

Charles cannot travel directly to Czechoslovakia as he had planned. Sitting in a travel agency in New York City, he learns of the downside of the past two decades of political occupation and upheaval in his homeland. He has been oblivious to the world beyond these shores. How American of him, he realizes with a laugh.

"Then how do I get there?" he asks Siobhan, the young travel agent. Siobhan, her red hair plaited away from her round, pretty face, shifts to a cherubic cuteness when she furrows her brow. "Golly, that's a good question, Mr. Ward. I'll have to find out, to be sure."

In the meantime, Charles tidies his life.

He quits his position at Café Marie with little ceremony, resigning by phone to avoid the place should the police be watching. Madame Harriet understands. The police have reached out to her, as they did to all the employees. She gave them no information about Charles.

"I don't believe them," she says emphatically. "You would never have anything to do with something so heinous. We have lawyers, Charles, who could assist."

But, of course, Charles declines the offer. "It is best this way."

Charles stops by Jacques's apartment to explain the resignation. He does not offer Jacques much in the way of facts, in case the police question him again, but he does tell him he was right about the German.

"He is not a good man, Jacques," Charles states, without elaborating.

He already feels like a fool for believing that Berthold had changed merely because he had changed his name, assumed another identity. He didn't need to see that foolishness, that naivete mirrored back to him in Jacques's eyes. Charles has held on to his delusions of Berthold for too long now, and part of him still does, still can't fully merge the man and the murderer into one. But even if Berthold did love him then and does love him now, the ruthlessness undergirding his sense of self-preservation will always supersede any love he might have for anyone else. And it's time Charles understood that to save himself.

"When he comes into the shop, stay clear," Charles adds. "Do not answer his questions or engage beyond our usual service, okay?"

Then Jacques begins to weep. "I need you, Charles. Let me come with you."

With a sweet laugh, Charles gently wipes at Jacques's tears with his thumb. "You do not need me, Jacques."

"I love you, Charles."

"No, you don't—but you are very sweet to think so. You are young and *très beau*, Jacques. There are many men who will love you."

"But not you."

The statement tears at Charles. He looks at Jacques, who is too handsome for his own good and too vulnerable for this world.

"No, I cannot. Not the way you deserve," Charles says.

He kisses Jacques tenderly and apologetically; then the kiss grows deeper and fuller as Charles invests every regret and apology into the act. Frightened by the intensity, Jacques pulls away. Charles offers one last apology with his clouded eyes, then leaves.

Charles returns to the YMCA, where he has been staying since Berthold informed the police about him. He sequesters himself in his tiny room with its narrow bed and bolted-down desk and dresser. The beige of the walls and the light wood of the furniture depress in their blandness, but he reminds himself it is only temporary.

Upon receiving Siobhan's telephone call, he returns to the travel agency.

To make his way to what is now the Czechoslovak Socialist Republic, Charles will need to travel through West Germany and East Germany. The irony is not lost on him.

He will depart New York in less than a week. Twenty years creating this quiet, steady American life, undone in a moment, and he is fleeing once again. He wants to curse Berthold, but he knows he himself is as much to blame.

Before he departs, he hazards a stroll through the city, through his life in New York. He passes by Mrs. Perkins's boardinghouse. He hasn't seen the place in years, not since Mrs. Perkins died some years ago. No longer a boardinghouse, the home has been falling into disrepair and is sad and depressed. He wonders about Miss Miller. Did she ever marry, or does she now haunt some other home in the city? What of Sam? Is he still working the docks? Did Kessler ever rise above the rank of clerk; does he bathe more often? One hopes. Charles marked the rise of Maude Allen in the theatrical world, at least early on. In the beginning, she was cast in quite a few productions, many of which he attended without her knowledge, but then her appearances waned to few and far between. He hasn't seen any notices of her in years, and it appears she is another lost to the passage of time in this city.

He stops in at the New York Public Library. Nothing has

changed beyond Mrs. Ayers retiring at some point. No one knows if she is still alive, so Charles chooses to believe she is.

A week later, a plane carrying Charles Ward lands in West Berlin, in the Federal Republic of Germany.

In his forty-two years, he had never traveled by air. As terrifying as his first flight was, it was offset by the exhilaration that flooded his body at the moment of takeoff. While his grip on his armrest never relaxed, especially during the periodic turbulence that jostled the plane like a toy, the thrill of flying never abated.

Working with a contact in Germany, Siobhan found Charles a short-term apartment in the Hufeisensiedlung complex in the neighborhood of Britz, which is within the American sector of West Berlin. Despite the enormity of the horseshoe-shaped complex, which dominates the area, Britz is a quaint neighborhood and will serve Charles's purposes well enough.

On his second day in West Berlin, Charles walks along the small section of the Berlin Wall a few blocks from his apartment. Tall and imposing, its stone-gray face is cold to the touch. If not for its crown of twisted barbwire, the wall would seem like just another wall in the world. But, of course, the Berlin Wall isn't just another wall. He knows he will need to enter East Berlin and travel through other areas of East Germany to get to Czechoslovakia, and he wonders what he will find on the other side of the Wall.

Thoughts of East Germany under Soviet rule conjure images of a dark, bleak, dystopian world, which might be true in cities such as East Berlin. But despite the political and economy oppression of Soviet rule which deprives its citizens of everyday necessities, East Germany lies under the same sky as West Berlin, the same cold winter sun. In the spring, the grasses will turn green, as they do in the West. Flowers will bloom in the parks and along paths. Leaves will sprout on the trees. East Berliners will stroll the sidewalks of their city. Mothers will dress children for Sunday church service, despite the State's disapproval of religion – just an example of the everyday anarchies that occur under occupation. Men will ogle attractive fräuleins as they skitter past. Life continues, as it does in every town, every country, every nation, occupied or not.

As Charles continues to stroll along the Berlin Wall, he wonders about Bayreuth. He wonders how it rebuilt itself after the bombings he witnessed and then after the war. He wonders how many of the people he knew back then survived, including the regular customers who frequented the café. Most of all, he wonders about Frau Hueber and Elsbeth, who would be in her thirties by now. Is she a mother now, making Frau Hueber a grandmother? He could imagine Frau Hueber teaching her granddaughter how to make strudels and pies and cakes and *Franzbrötchen*, traditional stollen, and *Schneeball* pastries. How wonderful Frau Hueber's desserts must be with true ingredients instead of the ersatz ingredients of the war.

"No," Charles scolds himself aloud, "Bayreuth is not the objective here."

He must stay focused and not dally with daydreams. Next, maybe he'll fancy a quick stop over in Poland to see the old Werden home. And while he's there, he thinks darkly, might as well pop over to the camp and the little farmhouse to complete the stroll down memory lane.

Charles shakes his head to clear the invading absurdities. He turns back toward Britz. The next day he is to meet with Siobhan's contact, and they will start the process of crossing over from West to East Berlin. It is only a matter of time.

51

Much to Charles's surprise, Ernst Mann occupies a proper office in a proper government building in the heart of West Berlin. He assumed Ernst Mann would be another member of that shifty underground network that exists in every city. Those shady characters who work out of deserted cafés or empty office buildings or barren warehouses and supply "official" papers, if you have the money.

But Ernst Mann sits respectably at his desk in the East German embassy, in an affiliate office of the Federal Foreign Office. His engraved wooden nameplate sits on his desk. No secrets here.

"Forgive the mess," Ernst Mann says in stilted English, indicating the stacks of files and folders about his desk.

"*Es ist in ordnung*," Charles says as he shakes Ernst's hand.

"Ah, you speak German?" Ernst relaxes, his heavy brow releasing its knot of concentration.

"Yes, of course, Herr Mann," Charles says and sits at Ernst's behest.

"So many Americans do not. To come to another country

and not even bother to learn how to say hello and thank you . . . disgraceful." Ernst riffles through papers before finding the folder he seeks. "Now, Siobhan informs me you wish to travel to the Czechoslovak Socialist Republic, yes? May I ask the purpose of your visit? It is a visit, yes? You do not plan to stay?"

Charles hesitates. He has not thought beyond his business in Kladno. Of course, he would need a plan from there, not only for visa purposes.

"Mr. Ward?" Ernst Mann prods.

"It is a visit, yes." Charles determines this is good enough for now. If he changes his mind later, he will deal with the consequences.

"Very good," Ernst says and checks the appropriate box on the visa application. "And the purpose of the visit?"

Again, Charles hesitates.

"I need only to know if it is business or personal," Ernst says. "No particulars necessary."

"Personal."

"Very good. Now, may I see your papers?"

With a rueful laugh, Charles produces his passport and driver's license. "It has been a long time since anyone has asked for my papers. I thought those days were behind me."

"Not where you're going," Ernst Mann advises. "You will need to show your papers to almost everyone you encounter, I'm afraid. In East Germany you don't exist if you do not have the papers to prove it. Though, I suppose, that is true of any place, yes? Sometimes I think we live in a society completely constructed of paper."

An hour later, the visa application is complete. The decision will come within nine weeks.

"Sometimes sooner, depending on how many applications they have to process and how quick they feel like processing them. One never knows with the East Germans. But I will call you."

In the ensuing weeks, Charles lives as a West Berliner and, much to his surprise, comes to like the city, despite its history and its wall. West Berlin isn't much different than New York City. As Charles strolls its streets, he finds a metropolis like many others. Modern buildings dwarf older, historic structures that survived the war. Like in New York City, the mix is disconcerting, though comforting in its familiarity.

Unlike New York City, Berlin is not congested. It does not tower over its citizens or overwhelm them. People might hurry, but they do so at a European pace, one that speaks of eventuality versus necessity. So, Charles strolls the busiest of sidewalks in Berlin without any pressure to keep up. Cars and trucks and transit buses speed through the streets alongside electric streetcars. Within the week, Charles determines the energy and the people of West Berlin fit him better than New York ever did.

Of course, the presence of soldiers, with stern postures and narrow eyes, unnerves him; they are reminiscent of the Europe of his youth and a constant reminder that war is still being waged in this land. A Cold War, yes, but this is still a country on the brink, unsure what might tip the situation into chaos again.

Charles takes to frequenting a café on the main thoroughfare. He arrives the same time each afternoon and sits at a table near the window. He orders coffee and a pastry. He might sit and watch the passersby or read *Die Welt* to catch up on the world news. He catches the eye of one of the waiters, a younger man whose eyes seek out Charles repeatedly during his time in the café, who lingers at the table to chat, who finally asks Charles if he'd like to join him for a drink one evening. And while Charles is tempted, as the young man is striking with his dark hair and light green eyes, he declines. He can't allow the distraction, no matter how fleeting.

Among the many historic structures of the city, Charles's favorite is the Kaiser Wilhelm Church, an incongruent yet inspired melding of antiquity and modernity. Not a religious man, long since turned from the idea of gods of any sway, Charles cannot deny the sense of calm and peace and tranquility that overcomes him when he steps inside the church. The renovated church, the modernity of which brings to mind an office building when it is viewed from the outside, is far less sterile on the inside, bathing the devout in the heaven-blue light that shines through the prism of the thousands of stained-glass windows honeycombing the walls. Charles sits in the last pew, away from those who populate the front rows and kneel in silent prayer. He does not pray, yet a sense of serenity flows through him.

He comes to understand it's the church's duality that draws him back time and again. West Berliners live in a constant state of duality. Charles observes its contradictions daily during his morning constitutional. He nods to West Berliners and offers a friendly "*Guten Morgen*," which they return with equal friendliness. He passes tourists who have come to commemorate the Wall in photos, occasionally asking Charles to snap pictures for them. Neighborhood children play on the Wall, which is merely another object in their lives. Teenagers sit atop the Wall in duos and trios and packs, smoking and chatting and holding hands. They steal kisses and sneak sips from concealed bottles of liquor. For most of these youngsters, the Wall has always been. They do not know a Berlin without it.

Adaptation, Charles reminds himself.

52

Ernst Mann calls in seven weeks' time. When they meet, he has Charles Ward's approved visa to enter East Germany and the Czechoslovak Socialist Republic.

"You have a month to conduct your business," Ernst reminds him gently but firmly as he stamps each piece of paper.

He helps Charles secure a car for his trip. He offers insider tips on how to deal with the checkpoint guards of the German Democratic Republic.

"They're different than the SS, Mr. Ward," Ernst Mann says directly. "They may not be quick with their guns, but that doesn't mean they won't arrest you or, at the very least, revoke your visa. I would suggest you not loiter in your business. Those in charge are not very welcoming to outsiders, especially Americans. Their tolerance has its limits."

In his apartment in the Hufeisensiedlung, Charles maps out the most direct route, heeding Ernst's advice not to dawdle. Also, Charles begins crafting a story to justify his reason for being in East Germany.

"You don't have to tell me," Ernst says. "But you need to be able to tell them something with quick confidence, whether it's the truth or not."

This is something Charles Ward can do well.

The next day, at Zimmerstraße and Mauerstraße, the main checkpoint between West and East Berlin, fittingly known as Checkpoint Charlie, Charles sits in the line of cars waiting to cross over. He inches forward until it is his turn at the guard station. He has his papers and story at the ready. He offers the guard a slight, quick smile, nothing too false. The guard does not smile in return.

"Papers."

Charles hands them over. Another guard stands in the doorway of the guardhouse. He holds his rifle at the ready but without conviction, canceling any fear he should elicit. Other soldiers stand near the boom gate, sentries equally as lax as they smoke cigarettes and chat. The guard reviewing his papers glances at Charles and peers into the car. Charles does not move or speak, feeling the long-dormant dread of being at someone else's whim and grace come back to life within him, that uncertainty of not knowing what might tilt the balance in one direction or the other. The guard could be put off by a smile or unwanted eye contact or a bored sigh. In the past, in Kladno, in Terezín, and especially in Bayreuth, Charles adopted an unthreatening air of acquiescence. He's amazed at how his body reverts to this performance as he sits in the glare of the East Berlin guard.

"You are going to Czechoslovakia?" the guard inquires with an air of conversation, but Charles knows the tactic.

He nods. "Jawohl."

The guard waits, but Charles does not continue. "Speak only when spoken to," Havel instructed him years ago in Kladno, and the advice holds true through today. "Give them as little as possible, but don't anger them."

"How will I know if I anger them?"

"When they shoot you."

"You are American," the guard states. "What is your business in the Czechoslovak Socialist Republic?"

"No business," Charles informs him. "I am to see family."

Raised eyebrows question Charles's statement. "Then you are Czech."

"I was born in America, but my family, my parents, and grandparents are from Czechoslovakia. I am going to visit my grandmother, who is ill."

The soldier nods, but his eyes still question Charles's story. Then, with a slight shrug, he hands Charles's papers to the guard in the station house, who stamps the passport with disinterest then hands them back. The guard at Charles's car returns the papers to Charles. *"Willkommen in Ost-Berlin."*

The boom gate rises.

Charles does not relax until the soldiers and the checkpoint have vanished from his rearview mirror. His story is good, he determines, simple, which is always best. He will use it at the other checkpoints.

The drive to Kladno is no more than four hours, given time spent at checkpoints and stopping for petrol. While he does not intend to dawdle, he does not rush, either, keeping his speed at a steady, unprovoking pace. As he drives through the German countryside, the scenery reminds him of that long-ago trip from Oświęcim to Bayreuth. The land is desolate and barren, though there are hints of spring as he drives farther south.

To his surprise, there are fewer checkpoints along his route than he expected. The guards at the Dresden checkpoint are even more lax than the ones in Berlin. An air of "You've made it this far, so why must I check again?" radiates from them. After a perfunctory request for his papers, they wave him through.

South of Dresden, where smaller villages mark the start of the countryside, Charles stops for petrol. The attendant asks him for his papers. After a thorough review, he charges Charles the visitor price, almost double the East Germany price. A short distance down the road, Charles finds a small café. He stops for a pastry and coffee. The waitress is attractive in a small village way. She asks him about America, what it's like being free. Her queries feel genuine, but Charles can't be sure, so keeps his replies neutral.

"It is a nice country," he tells her. "There are many advantages but also many disadvantages, much like here, I would think."

Her exuberance deflates. She offers a terse smile and leaves the check on the table. She charges him the visitor price, as well.

Another hour on the road brings Charles to the Czechoslovak Socialist Republic border and checkpoint. Leaving East Germany, even for another country under Soviet rule, prompts a more grueling inspection. At the checkpoint, after demanding his papers, the guards order Charles to exit his car.

As he stands in front of the guard manning the checkpoint, another guard approaches with a shepherd guard dog, their stroll casual, as if they are out for an afternoon walk. Together they circle Charles's car. The hound sniffs inside and outside the car as the guard performs his own examination.

"Why are you leaving Germany?" the soldier examining his papers inquires. His words are clipped and stern, as if Charles has personally offended him by leaving his beloved country.

"I am on my way to Kladno to visit my family."

The soldier narrows his eyes.

"My grandmother is ill," Charles adds. He infects the lie with as much genuine sincerity as he can muster.

The soldier offers a quick snort, as if this unrequested information amuses him. "You are American."

Charles does not respond.

"Your German is very good." The statement sounds like more of an indictment than a compliment.

"I spent much time in Germany many years ago. I come back as often as I can." Another lie, but one the soldier receives with an agreeable nod.

The guard stamps Charles's passport and sends him off with a wave of his rifle.

Being in Czechoslovakia feels no different than being in East Germany. It should, Charles thinks, emotionally, if not physically, but it doesn't.

While one can go out of one's way to avoid it, the most direct route to Kladno passes through Terezín. Charles knew this when he planned his route, but he did not anticipate the sense of dread that sweeps over him. The camp is now a museum. In the parking lot—was there always parking lot?—he cuts the engine, and the quiet afternoon hovers about him.

"*Vítejte!*" the attendant calls out as he enters the lobby of the visitor center. The girl, not long out of high school, jars Charles from his stupor. She pastes on a smile and adjusts a stack of pamphlets on the table. "Have you been here before, or is this your first time?"

Charles hesitates. In cautious Czech, he tells her, "I've been here before, a long time ago."

Excited, the girl grabs a pamphlet. "I'm sure much has changed. We're always improving the museum. When were you here?"

"When I was a teenager." Charles pauses for the math. "Twenty-seven years ago."

The girl looks confused. "Have we been open that long?"

Charles smiles at her innocence. "No, I was a prisoner here."

The understanding is immediate as a light flickers, then douses within her, and he wishes he hadn't been so blunt.

"I'm sorry." The girl apologizes, as if she were the one who personally imprisoned him. Her sweetness touches him.

Much to his protest, she does not charge him the entrance fee. As the official tour does not start for another hour, he decides to explore on his own. He accepts a map of the grounds, in case his memory fails him.

The preservation and renovation are exacting and impressive. Still, the museum does not feel like the Terezín of his youth: too quiet, too empty, the air too fresh. They have painted the buildings with too much care. They have manicured the lawns and bushes well beyond reality.

Charles wanders the grounds, remembering the places he and Eliáš ventured. He strolls the marketplace where prisoners gathered when they weren't working. He enters buildings, also reconstructed with too much care. Each room displays a vignette of how life, if you could call it that, was during imprisonment. A display of the sleeping quarters allows too much space between the beds. And where are the straw pallets on the floor? In another room, they've re-created the induction process, complete with the delousing room, but it lacks the sense of smell, that soft, powdery scent that belies the burning to come. Another building dramatizes how the children lived and learned and played. Another presents the music hall, constructed after his deportation to Auschwitz.

Charles finds the barracks where he and his father slept. Despite his lack of faith, he finds himself saying a quick prayer. The metal shop where he spent his days manning his machine sits quiet and is entirely too clean. He finds the hospital and the children's barracks and the dining hall. There are other buildings he doesn't remember, also constructed after his deportation: a clothing store, a nightclub, a restaurant. For the children, they designed a playground and a sports area. He can't imagine that any of these luxuries made life more bearable, but maybe they did. It's all fascinating but sterile and distant, or maybe it is he who is sterile and distant now.

Finally, he makes his way to the hideaway in the retrenchment where he and Eliáš secreted themselves away from the world. At some point in the past twenty-something years, the small storage room had been bricked over. He places his palm against the terra cotta colored brick wall. His body remembers the world on the other side of the wall—the smell of dark earth, the comfort of the silence, the feeling of their bodies and their lips, all of which still breathes through him along with desperation and longing and love, his first and possibly his only love.

In the library, where they house the archives, Charles searches the list of prisoners and internees. He finds his family listed among those transported elsewhere. He caresses the page that lists Alexej Benakov, Růžena Benaková, Zofia, Karel, and Dušana. He expects to feel the names under his touch, raised like scars on flesh, but the page is smooth and unblemished. He finds Eliáš's name, along with his mother's and Billy's—all are marked deceased. And for the first time in years, Charles cries. He has always harbored a silent belief that Eliáš made it out and that, somehow, they would find each other again. Such a childish fantasy, but he was a child when the hope took up residence inside him. But now it is dead, along with Eliáš and everything else in this museum.

As he leaves, he thanks the young woman in the visitor center. She flashes another look of guilty apology for his pain.

Back on the road, he is in Kladno within an hour. He is shocked at how close it is to Terezín. So close, they could have walked home.

53

Of course, Kladno has changed in the past thirty years. The global expansion of the Poldi Steel Factory has brought more jobs, more money, and more people to the town. While not a metropolis like West Berlin, Kladno is no longer the sleepy hamlet of the 1930s.

He doesn't recognize the main area of town. There are so many shops and restaurants now, and he has no idea what existed then and what didn't. Of course, the old town hall in the business district still stands, but its grand Neo-Renaissance style appears out of place next to the sleek, trendy, stylized shops that dominate in their collective presence. Unlike West Berlin, Kladno has not figured out how to meld its past with its present.

The small three-room house where he and his family lived still survives. Charles can't imagine how they existed in such a confined space. But they were happy. At least, he remembers, more happy than sad before the occupation.

His tour of the town is short but productive. By the time he's finished, he understands he no longer belongs to Kladno.

There is nothing for him here any longer, if there ever was after their neighbors turned on them and they were deported.

So, he will complete his business and leave.

The next day, at the Kladno Regional Hospital, the receptionist in the main lobby directs him to the administration wing of the hospital. It is so far removed from the patients and doctors and nurses and exam rooms, the antiseptic vapors that permeate the medical wings fade and the air breathes with the stuffiness of business.

"That's some time ago," the records clerk says, responding to Charles's query. "I don't know if we have anything from that period on the premises any longer or whether it's archived."

Charles waits as the clerk investigates. He soon returns.

"Our records go back only ten years. The town hall might have information from before the war."

In the town hall, Charles makes his way to the public records department.

"What kind of records are you looking for?" asks the administrator, an older woman with a gentle smile.

"Birth certificates. From before the war."

The woman nods, unfazed by the request. Pen and paper at hand, she asks, "Parents' names?"

"Alexej and Růžena Benakov."

"Child's name?"

"Karel Benakov."

"And is that you?" the woman asks.

Charles nods. "Yes. I am Karel Benakov."

Still unfazed, for she has no idea how long it has been since he has stated this fact, the woman tears the sheet of paper from the notepad.

"I'll check, but . . . no promises. A lot of records were either destroyed or moved to Prague during the occupation. But every once in a while . . ."

Charles nods and moves to a waiting room chair.

"This will take time," the woman says. "Most likely days. The records are not as . . . organized as they should be, especially the older ones. I can call you."

To offset the dragging anticipation, Charles plans a wider exploration of Kladno to immerse himself in the memories he still retains. He searches for information on Mr. Černý. Charles isn't surprised to learn he passed a few years back, as he was already in his fifties during the war.

"Your father was good to me, to my family, during the war," Charles tells Mr. Černý's daughter, Pavia, who now occupies the family home.

She smiles. Though she is in her sixties now, the sweetness of the smile recalls her youth for a moment. "He was?"

She invites Charles into her home.

"I should not be surprised," Pavia says as she pours the coffee. "Father was a good man. At least he tried to be."

They sit at a small table in the kitchen. Even though Charles used to visit the Černý home as a child, as a schoolmate of Pavia's brother, Bořek, he does not remember her. Nor does she remember him. They reminisce for much of the afternoon, though they have no shared memories beyond Mr. Černý and the Kladno of the past. But still there exists a connection.

Another day, he seeks out Havel's place. He was there only the one time, the day after the Nazis took Havel in the middle of the night. Even though the memory of standing outside Havel's house sits painfully clear in his gut, Charles isn't sure he has the correct home. So much has changed.

He takes a trip to the Poldi Steel Factory, though he doesn't enter. He remains standing at a distance for a few moments. That is all he needs.

Within the week, the administrator from the town hall leaves a message for Charles with the hotel clerk.

"You're a lucky man, Mr. Benakov," the administrator says,

smiling, as she enters the office. "It took some digging. I'll admit we almost gave up, but we found it."

After Charles approaches the counter, she places a piece of paper in front of him. While colored with age, it is otherwise pristine.

"Is this it?" Charles asks as he lifts the paper off the counter as delicately as Mrs. Ayers used to handle the artifacts at the library. He reads the heading at the top of the page. "*Rodný list* for Karel Benakov."

"Do you have sisters?" The administrator presents two more papers. "We found these for the same parents and thought . . ."

The birth certificates for Zofia Benaková and Dušana Benaková. Charles's stomach seizes. He does not try to stop the tears. "They died at Auschwitz with my parents. It is just me now."

The woman's eyes soften. "I'm sorry, Mr. Benakov."

The following day, Charles returns to West Berlin. He senses he will never again need to visit East Germany or Czechoslovakia.

He makes an appointment with Ernst Mann.

"This is who I am," Charles declares as he hands over his birth certificate.

Confused, Ernst examines the document.

"It is a copy, but an official copy," Charles says. "See the stamp? It is acceptable in all legal dealings."

"Yes, it is official," Ernst confirms. "But what do you want me to do with it?"

"Make me him again."

Before Ernst Mann protests, Charles summarizes his life for him. "I was only a boy when it started . . ."

His storytelling rivets the man for the twenty-five minutes that Charles takes to offer his truncated version. Of course, he does not tell Ernst about the death of Raymond Lynch or reveal that Charles Ward is a wanted man in New York. Because that is not why he wants to be rid of the name.

"I am not that man. I have never been him, Ernst. *Bitte*."

Ernst Mann contemplates the request for an unbearably long time. He stares at the birth certificate. He looks up at Charles, still standing in front of his desk, anticipation leaning his body forward, as if he is a flower seeking sunlight. "I would think a passport would be the first order of business, yes?"

And Charles lets go of the agonizing pressure that began to build in his body and his heart thirty years ago. Again, he does not hold back the tears.

"*Danke schön*," is all he can manage.

54

On his day off, Karel Benakov trains to Ostend. He likes the seaside best in the cooler months, when there are fewer, if any, tourists. He likes it even better when it's so cold the locals stay away. The brutal winds that sweep off the North Sea do not deter Karel. He enjoys the desolation, strolling the water's edge, as if he is the only soul on earth. He knows he will end up in Ostend when it is time to retire. For now, he likes living in Brugge and the life he has created there.

Once Ernst Mann brought Karel Benakov back to life via an official West German passport, Karel wasn't sure what to do. Charles might have known, but Karel was at a loss.

"Will you go back to America?" Ernst Mann asked.

"No," Karel insisted. "I am not American."

"The Czechoslovak Socialist Republic?"

Karel shook his head. "There is nothing there for me any longer."

"Then stay in West Berlin," Ernst suggested. "Take some time to figure out where you want to go next."

With no other options at hand, Karel took the advice. He returned to his apartment in the Hufeisensiedlung. He tried to understand what Karel Benakov wanted out of life now that it was his again. He renewed his morning ritual of walking the promenade along the Berlin Wall. He returned to the Kaiser Wilhelm Church, welcoming the serenity, which soothed his thoughts. He sat in cafés and parks. He visited the library and studied the maps of the world, as he had done back in Bayreuth. He attempted to silence any thoughts that rang of Charles Ward, to stifle the instinct to think like him Karel fancied naively that Charles Ward had died that day in Ernst Mann's office, when Ernst had handed Karel his passport. But, of course, Charles Ward hadn't died that day, because Charles Ward had never really lived.

Karel compiled a list of possibilities: London, Paris, Milan, Barcelona, Dublin.

"These are all wonderful cities in their own way," Ernst said as he read the list. "I have been to many of them, but I fear they will lose their charm for you soon enough, Karel."

They were sitting in a biergarten not far from Ernst's office. The map that Karel carried with him everywhere was spread out on the table before them. They drank and surveyed the list and the map.

"I fear you are not a city person," Ernst continued. "I think you need to think smaller. There is no need to hide anymore."

Ernst leaned over the map. His finger traveled the well-worn paper terrain, skimming the roads and highways veining the map. He landed in Belgium and made his way to Brugge.

"Here," Ernst said. "This is where you belong."

Within days of arriving in Brugge, Karel knew he had found his place. He felt at home in Brugge's old-world architecture and its modern elements. He loved the small city's desire to reignite its history rather than discard it or crowd it out with the new.

Once settled in his small flat in the Ezelstraat Quarter, Karel set about finding work. It did not take long. While strolling the streets, he came upon Brot und Mehr, a small German bakery. The aromas upon entering immediately propelled him back to Frau Hueber's konditorei in Bayreuth.

"*Hallo*," said a woman behind the counter as Karel fumbled with his memories.

After stepping up to the bakery cases, Karel examined the strudels and cream puffs and Black Forest and German chocolate cakes. And the stollen breads and baskets of brötchen and . . . "What are these?" Karel puzzled over a tray of small round balls, much like American donuts.

"That is our specialty, *Quarkbällchen*. They are delicious."

She offered Karel a sample. The small ball was light and fluffy, with hints of vanilla.

"I have never had these before. Not even in Germany." Karel purchased a dozen. "I would love to know the recipe."

"You bake?"

Karel nodded. "I worked in a bakery in Germany. Many years ago, but I still make very good *Schneebälle*."

"My favorite! You must make them for me sometime!"

"You wouldn't happen to be hiring, would you?" Karel asked.

"As luck would have it . . ."

A year later, Karel sits on the winter beach at Ostend, watching the violent sea swell and rush and churn and roil. As goes the sea, so goes life, he believes, though for once his life sits calm. If someone, for some odd reason, decided to tell the story of his life from start to finish, they would find a life of chaos, with incredible moments of volatility, a life in a constant state of flux, a flux that abruptly ends in a quiet little village in Belgium, where he lives an equally quiet life as a baker in a local pastry shop.

Most importantly, they would find a man at peace.

After four months in Brugge, Karel took a few days off from

work. At the station, he boarded the train to Ludwigsburg, a town in the West German state of Baden-Württemberg. A lovely little hamlet, Ludwigsburg was well known for the Ludwigsburg Residential Palace, built by Duke Eberhard Ludwig von Württemberg. But Karel did not take the seven-hour train ride to Ludwigsburg to sightsee.

After arriving late in the day, Karel checked into his hotel and had a delicious dinner in a wonderful restaurant nearby. The evening weather invited him to stroll a bit before returning to the hotel, so he did, enjoying the quiet of the evening as the town was shuttered for the night. The next day, he gathered the packet of documents Raymond Lynch had handed over to Charles Ward, copies Berthold never knew existed. Karel knew he would not be alive if Berthold did know of their existence. He headed to the Central Office of the State Justice Administrations for the Investigation of National Socialist Crimes.

At the reception desk, the young woman asked how she could help him.

"I've come to turn in a war criminal," Karel said with surprising calm.

He met with an investigative agent. Behind closed doors, Karel handed the agent the packet. As the agent removed the documents and photos and placed them on the table in front of him, Karel told his story.

"This is Obersturmführer Berthold Werden." Karel pointed at a picture of Berthold in his uniform. "He was one of the men in charge of the Auschwitz camp . . ."

"We know him," the agent said with an edge of excitement in his voice. "Do you know where he is?"

Back in Brugge, Karel watched the news of the arrest. He watched as Berthold was led into the courthouse in New York City, his hands cuffed behind him, for the extradition hearing. Reporters and cameramen crowded the way and shouted questions at the suspected war criminal. But Berthold did not respond, his head kept down and turned away. He looked old, haggard, scared.

Karel looked for Frau Werden, but she was not with her husband. He felt a slight twinge of guilt for her, but only slight, almost imperceptible, and it vanished within a breath.

The investigation to confirm that New York City jeweler Wallace Lynch was indeed Obersturmführer Berthold Werden lasted three months. When the call came from the agent at the Central Office, Karel's soul released a breath it had held for decades.

"What happens next?" Karel asked.

"He will be extradited and tried for his crimes," the agent said. "You will be called to testify."

The information was not a request. Karel hesitated. He would need to sit in a courtroom and face Berthold and tell the story of them.

Which he will do, for he has no alternative if he is ever to be free of his past. Charles Ward would not be able to do this, Karel understands. He was beholden to Berthold for his very life. But no such bonds entangle Karel, so he will do what needs to be done. He will await the call to return to Ludwigsburg.

In the interim, he will continue to live the life he has created for himself in Brugge.

Beyond his work at Brot und Mehr, Karel has met a man. Koen Hollanders has stopped in at the bakery twice a week for years to purchase a loaf of *Zwiebelbrot*. Frau Kraus is well known for her onion bread, which sells out daily. Slightly younger than Karel, Koen is a rather plain-looking, somewhat stout, blond Belgian, not the type of man Karel usually finds attractive. But he is genuine and sweet and has a certain sexual appeal, which drew Karel's attention at their first meeting. They took their time at first, having a drink here and there, then progressing to dinners once or twice a week. They were seeing each other for two months before they had sex, which was more tender than sex with Berthold, reminding Karel of being with Eliáš, exploratory and exciting and new.

Early on, he told his story to Koen, the whole of it, including all the ugliness. He ended with his complicity in the murder of Raymond Lynch, for which he would not be arrested or tried as part of his deal with the Central Office of the State Justice Administrations for the Investigation of National Socialist Crimes, much to the anger of the New York City police commissioner. But the apprehension of a Nazi war criminal responsible for tens of thousands of deaths trumped the arrest of an unwilling accomplice to one murder in America.

"You must know all of my story, Koen," Karel said. "I do not hide anymore."

After some time, Koen nodded. "You did what you had to do. To survive. I'm glad, or you wouldn't be here."

Quite possibly that was the moment Karel fell in love with Koen Hollanders.

In the late afternoon, when the bitter winds of Ostend shift and he can no longer take the full brunt of their assault, Karel trains back to Brugge. That evening, he strolls the perimeter of the canal that wends through the city, as he once strolled along the Berlin Wall, as he once strolled along the barricades in Terezín and the streets and gardens of Bayreuth. Karel touches the cool stones of the canal wall as he passes. From the restaurants and pubs that line the street, voices and music mingle in evening song, which drifts through the salted air and skims along the water. On the canal, a bevy of swans, white feathers capturing the moonlight, glides past as quietly as ghosts returning to their graves.

We Are Only Ghosts

ABOUT THIS GUIDE

The suggested questions are included to enhance your group's reading of Jeffrey L. Richards's *We Are Only Ghosts*!

DISCUSSION QUESTIONS

1. A recurring theme in the book is the idea of identity. In what ways do you think this theme presents/manifests itself throughout the book? In what characters does it present itself?

2. The idea of identity is not the only theme of the novel. What are some others that came through to you?

3. How does the title reflect the contents of book and vice versa? What is the significance of the title?

4. While a work of fiction, the novel is steeped in historical fact. Before reading the book, what was your understanding of the Holocaust? Have your feelings about it changed now that you've read this book?

5. The relationship between Charles and Berthold is a conflict of emotions and motives. What drives each of them both in the past and the present?

6. The narration moves back and forth in time. How did this affect your reading experience? How do you think that experience would be different if the story was told entirely in a linear fashion?

7. Throughout his life, Charles encounters a multitude of people. We get a clearer picture of some but not of others. Which character would you like to have learned more about or delved deeper into their story?

8. The novel is partially set in Eastern Europe during the Holocaust, and the main character is a young Jewish man caught up in the anti-Semitism and genocide of the Nazi

regime. The author is not Jewish. Did you know this prior to reading the novel, and if so, how did that influence your reading experience? If not, does this knowledge alter your thoughts about the novel in hindsight?

9. In the eras in which the novel is set, both in Europe in the 1940s and New York City and Europe in the late 1960s, homosexuality was prosecuted either legally, morally, and/or socially, leading to lives lived in secret and shadow. How does this inform the actions of Charles and Berthold?

10. The events at the little red farmhouse reveal a harrowing truth about Berthold, yet Charles "stays" with him, both then and in the future. Why does he do this? How can one do this? How do you think you would have reacted?

11. During his time in the Werden home, there was no love lost between Frau Werden and Charles, for good reason. Years later, how have Charles's attitude and feelings about her changed? Why have they changed?

Please turn the page for a very special
Q&A with
Jeffrey L. Richards!

Q: You're an American, born and raised in Oklahoma, raised Catholic, I believe, with no discernible connection to World War II or the Holocaust or the plight of the Jewish people. So, why this book? Why you?

A: I've dreaded this question for the longest time because I have wondered myself if I should even write this novel, given my seeming lack of connection to aspects of the subject matter. And I know there might be claims of appropriation and such, as many will look at We Are Only Ghosts as a "Holocaust" novel, and they would be right to some extent. But for me, this has always been a story of a man attempting to reclaim his identity. It's a story of how our identities are shaped by outside forces, subtly and not so subtly. It's a story about a man who decides to take the narrative of his life, of his identity, back into his own hands after years of being at the mercy of others. It just so happens that his story winds through the landscape of the Holocaust and the concentration camps and beyond.

Q: But you could have placed the story in another setting, another time in history, so why the Holocaust?

A: I've always had a fascination with the Holocaust, how it happened, why it happened, how those who survived were changed physically, emotionally, psychologically. It's an extremely harrowing event in history, and I don't think it will ever truly be understood, no matter how many examine it and try to explain it. And even though I am not Jewish, it still haunts me and has for decades. I don't truly know why, though the magnitude of it astounds and fascinates me, as it has so many others who have come before and who will come after me. The sheer volume of participants that it took to perpetrate these horrible acts is truly shocking.

The more personal draw comes in the form of the homosexuals who were imprisoned in the concentration camps along with the Jews. While the majority of the narratives are from the Jewish perspective, which is only right given that they made up the overwhelming majority of the persecuted, other victims have stories that don't get told as often—the Roma (Gypsies), Jehovah's Witnesses, people with disabilities, and even Black people (Afro-Germans, European Blacks, Africans, and African Americans). Being homosexual, I have always gravitated to their stories when I would find them. *The Men with the Pink Triangle* by Heinz Heger; *I, Pierre Seel, Deported Homosexual* by Pierre Seel; *An Underground Life* by Gad Beck; and even *The Berlin Stories* by Christopher Isherwood.

Now, when I first conceived the novel, it was a Holocaust-to-holocaust story: a Jewish gay man who survived the Jewish Holocaust of World War II finds himself decades later in the middle of the AIDS holocaust (and persecuted once again). As happens very often to writers, the story will deviate from the original intent whether you want it to or not. At least that's how it works for me. So, this story morphed into something entirely different than what I set out to write, but ultimately, it was the story I needed to tell. So, to answer your question, yes, I could have oriented the story in another place, another time, another setting, but it wouldn't be *this* story, which is the one I had to tell.

Q: I understand the novel takes place in a time/place that is before your time, but I wonder if there is anything autobiographical that comes through. How do you personally relate to the main character (or characters)?

Well, I'm one of those writers who make no bones about the fact that their experiences infuse their work all the time. If you've read *We Are Only Ghosts* or my first novel, *The Sum-*

mer of Jenny Wade, it will come as no surprise that I am a survivor of sexual abuse, and as any survivor will tell you, the abuse alters you for life in numerous ways, mostly psychologically. I assume I use my writing to work out my demons but also to help other survivors be seen and, hopefully, speak out on their own behalf. I've often said that demons can't live in the light, so we have to get them out of ourselves, out of the dark of our psyches.

Q: Writers are often asked where their ideas for stories come from, so where do the ideas for your stories come from?

Yes, I do get asked this quite often. For me, each story begins with an act or a scenario: the rape of a young girl, a Holocaust survivor contracts AIDS in a modern-day holocaust, an NYC homicide detective on the trail of a reemerged serial killer also deals with his husband's inoperable cancer diagnosis (inciting acts for this novel and other works). I then start to think about the people who have found themselves in these scenarios, these life events. The scenario starts the story, but the characters are the ones that sustain the story, bring life and realism to the story. Not sure that answers the question of where these ideas come from. My mind is always going. Ninety-nine percent of it is your basic internal monologue, which no one needs to hear, but that other 1 percent is that area where these ideas come out and say, "Hey, listen to this." So I do.

Q: Your novel has a gay man as your main character. You're an out gay man, so what are your thoughts on "own voice" works when it comes to minority stories?

"Own voice" is one of those movements that's great in theory and, most often, in practice, as well. We need more LGBTQ+ voices out in the world, speaking from places of knowing and places of truth. Just as we need more African American voices and more Asian American voices and more disabled American voices, and so on. As long as the work is good (well written, well produced, et cetera), we need those voices added to the conversation. Or better yet to start the conversations. But— because there is always a *but*—does that mean others who don't fall into these categories should not write these types of stories or characters? Should I never have an African American character in one of my stories? For that matter, as a cisgender male, should I never have a female character?

If we start limiting who is able to write what kinds of characters and their stories, then we start limiting the points of view that come from myriad voices, or we start eliminating opportunities to find commonality among those from differing identities and groups. I don't think writers should write what they don't know just for the heck of it or to generate buzz, though. There needs to be a reason, a rationale for tackling a subject matter far out of the realm of your experiences. Should I have written a novel from the perspective of a Jewish Holocaust survivor? Some might say, "No, you shouldn't have," but I would argue that I found a commonality with the character of Charles that goes well beyond, and is much deeper than, his being Jewish and a Holocaust survivor, and even beyond his being a gay man. So, I would stand by the statement that I was the right person to tell his story.

Also, if we limit who gets to tell these stories, then we lose amazing work, such as *Call Me By Your Name* by André Aciman, who identifies as a straight, cisgender male. Or one of my favorite LGBTQ+ novels, *As Meat Loves Salt*, about an obsessive gay romance between two men in seventeenth-century England, written by Maria McCann, a cisgender female. And I'm sure there are numerous other examples of writers who stepped out of their allotted lanes to venture into unfamiliar territory and did so brilliantly.